W9-CKL-725
Classic Collection

Sam,
Reading is such
an adventure and
I have always enjoyed
it. this has always been
one of my favorites I hope it
will become one of yours

Love
Mom

The Classic Collection Series

The Classic Collection series' undergirding philosophy is:

- The series should feature books for the entire family, not just one age group.
- The books should lend themselves to being read aloud, thus encouraging families to bring back a time-honored—but, in today's TV-dominated society, almost lost—tradition of the family hour, when the entire family spent time together.
- The books should espouse Judeo-Christian values.
- Generally speaking, the books should be selected from the ranks of those that have stood the test of time: Generations have come and gone, but these books are still loved, still relevant, still speak to the heart.
- The books should as often as possible incorporate early woodcut illustrations or similar art. In other words, the books in this series are intended to be *keepers*, the kind given as heirloom gifts, treasured from generation to generation.
- Each book will include a modest biography of the author, a bibliography of his or her other works, and background material to help the reader understand how a particular book (and author) evolved.
- Finally, if a book is to become real, and fully understood, it must be discussed—hence discussion questions, general and chapter-specific, have been added in an afterword.

As much as possible, we have tried to respect the sanctity of a text. But where a given book is generations, and sometimes centuries, old, editing is almost essential. It is amazing to see how many words still in use today have acquired new meanings and lost old ones. The difficulty for an editor is securing a close enough synonym so that the meaning is unchanged, yet finding a substitute word that would have been in existence when the book was originally published. Substitutions are especially needed where, over the years, words have acquired negative or sexual connotations. In some cases, words have been changed simply because no dictionary short of a million-word unabridged carries them anymore!

It is both an honor and a privilege to have our series welcomed into your home. It is our earnest and prayerful intent that each of the books chosen will significantly enrich your life and that of your family: that it will provide new insights; emotional, intellectual, and spiritual growth; and increased empathy with, and charity toward, others, particularly those viewed as "different."

A Word to Parents

The books in the Classic Collection series have been selected because they are among the finest literary works in history. However, you should be aware that some content might not be suitable for all ages, so we recommend you review the material before sharing it with your family.

This was game indeed!

The Life and Strange, Surprising Adventures of ROBINSON CRUSOE, of York, Mariner, as Related by Himself

by

DANIEL DEFOE

with an Introduction and Afterword by

JOE L. WHEELER, PH.D.

PUBLISHING
Colorado Springs, Colorado

ROBINSON CRUSOE

Library of Congress Cataloging-in-Publication Data
Defoe, Daniel, 1661?–1731.
[Robinson Crusoe]
The life and strange, surprising adventures of Robinson Crusoe, of York, mariner, as related by himself / by Daniel Defoe ; with an introduction and afterword by Joe Wheeler.
p. cm. — (Focus on the Family classic collection ; 3)
Includes bibliographical references.
ISBN 1-56179-557-7
1. Survival after airplane accidents, shipwrecks, etc.—Fiction. 2. Islands—Fiction. I. Title. II. Series.
PR3403.A1 1997
823'.5—dc21 97-3248
CIP

Classic Collection series #3 / Defoe series #1

Published by Focus on the Family Publishing, Colorado Springs, CO 80995

Distributed in the U.S.A. and Canada by Word Books, Dallas, Texas

Illustrations by Walter Paget. Taken from Daniel Defoe, *The Life and Strange, Surprising Adventures of Robinson Crusoe, of York, Mariner, as Related by Himself* (New York: McLoughlin Brothers, 1890). All illustrations from the library of Joe Wheeler.

The author is represented by the literary agency of Alive Communications, 1465 Kelly Johnson Blvd., Suite 320, Colorado Springs, CO 80920.

Editor: Michele A. Kendall
Cover Illustration: Walter Paget
Cover Design: Bradley L. Lind

Printed in the United States of America

97 98 99 00 01 02 03/10 9 8 7 6 5 4 3 2 1

TABLE OF CONTENTS

LIST OF ILLUSTRATIONS

Introduction

THE LONGEVITY OF *ROBINSON CRUSOE*

How or why does one book survive, and another not? This has to be one of life's ultimate rhetorical questions. Very few books outlive the generation they are written for—fewer still the second generation. But to live for more than three centuries, as *Robinson Crusoe* has done—that's a miracle.

Strange as it seems, *Robinson Crusoe*'s resilience astonished even its author, Daniel Defoe. Usually, an author knows instinctively when he has written a great book. Apparently, Defoe did not. Perhaps it was because he didn't really know what he had written—for nothing remotely like *Robinson Crusoe* had ever been published before.

From all indications, Defoe wrote the book, not because he had the proverbial "fire in the gut" (having to write the thing or die), but because he had a fire at his heels: His creditors were after him again. Imagine how much of our greatest literature would never have been created without that eternal struggle to survive—to keep food on one's table and a roof over one's head!

Initially, Defoe was simply trying to capitalize on the current mania for travel books. But he went beyond the genre by personalizing the story with the character of a shipwrecked mariner. Also, Defoe chose to pour a lot of his tormented self and his remarkable life into Robinson Crusoe—especially his growing loneliness.

Defoe could not have written this book earlier in his life. He had to first be battered by the years. Defoe remained on the cutting edge of his time because, for most of his sixty years of life, he gobbled up knowledge. He would rush to buy travel books only hours after they left the press, and he researched his ever-changing world exhaustively and unceasingly. Because of his efforts, we are able to see into the world as it was known at Crusoe's time.

The vast continent of Africa, for example, was still "dark": Not even Livingstone had trekked across it. Also unknown was that frozen world to the north (to be covered in *The Farther Adventures of Robinson Crusoe,* to be published in 1998), that huge land mass that, for all Defoe and his contemporaries knew, stretched from London across Europe to Moscow across Siberia to Alaska across Canada to Nova Scotia. With his books *Robinson Crusoe* (1719), *The Farther Adventures of Robinson Crusoe* (1720), and *Captain Singleton* (1720), Defoe essentially gives us photographs of what was known of our world back then. That is why reading his books is almost like going back through the centuries in a time capsule. His is not reconstructed history but eyewitness history. That's why *Robinson Crusoe* is such a landmark book, and perhaps why it has endured. It is history in the making. Yet, at the same time it is oddly modern. It has dated much less than most eighteenth-century books.

About the Introduction

For decades, one of the few absolutes in my literature classes has been this: *Never read the introduction before reading the book!* Those who ignored my thundering admonition lived to regret their disobedience. Downcast, they would come to me and say, "Dr. Wheeler, I confess that I read the introduction first, and it wrecked the book for me. I couldn't enjoy the story, because all the way through I saw it through someone *else's* eyes. I don't agree with the editor on certain points, but those conclusions are in my head, and now I don't know *what* I think!"

Given that God never created a human clone, no two of us will ever perceive reality in exactly the same way—and no two of us *ever should!* Therefore, no matter how educated, polished, brilliant, insightful, or eloquent the teacher might be, don't ever permit that person to tell you how to think or respond, for that is a violation of the most sacred thing God gives us—our individuality.

My solution to the introduction problem was to split it in two: an introduction, to whet the appetite for, and enrich the reading of, the book; and an afterword, to generate discussion and debate *after* the reader has arrived at his or her own conclusions about the book and is ready to challenge my (the teacher's) perceptions.

About This Edition

It has been a formidable task to update, and make more readable, this three centuries' old icon. I do not think it has ever been done before. Let me explain:

First, the language was generally archaic. What was most confusing was not the words themselves, but their current usage and connotations. Frequently, after reading a section, I would shake my head and think, *What is he saying?* Individually, the words made sense, but the way in which they were grouped was sometimes unclear. I decided to resort to my unabridged dictionary and dig backward in time. Once I discovered what the word meant to Defoe, I could understand what he was saying, and to help the reader I either footnoted the term or phrase (by far the easiest option) or found substitute words that were used during the eighteenth century. In other words, I did not want to use modern words.

Second, the book is filled with sentence-paragraph monstrosities that seem to go on forever (Defoe's trademark, by the way). For the most part, they are brilliantly constructed. So much so, in fact, that I found them hard to restructure without appearing heavy-handed. In most cases, I left the paragraphs as they were, only breaking them up where I found significant topic shifts or a change of speaker.

Third, and even more of a problem, there were no chapter divisions or subheadings to break up the text. Not many of us today relish tackling a book that has absolutely no breaks in it. To remedy this situation, I reread the text carefully to see if, by chance, I could find built-in chapter breaks. Fortunately, Defoe's text has a rhythm to it that made these breaks fairly easy to determine. As for chapter titles, I tried whenever possible to use Defoe's own words (often borrowed from running heads in the original text).

Fourth, I wanted to bring back what has been virtually lost during the last century: marvelous woodcut illustrations. These were true works of art that not only captured wonderfully the essence of the scenes being depicted but also give us faithful depictions of objects, people, cities, landmarks, and so on, at the time.

If I have been successful in doing what I set out to do, you will read a very old text in words that will make sense to you, in paragraphs of humane length, with subheads that will propel the story along, with chapters that will give you places in which to break off, and with illustrations that will enable you to visualize the world you are reading about. In short, you will read an old book that seems contemporary but that still retains the charm and integrity of the original.

Movies

Strangely enough, I have not found any movie versions of *Robinson Crusoe.* Of course, it would be a difficult book to capture in celluloid—especially, aspects such as the cannibalism and ever-present violence and bloodshed of the time. However, if done correctly, it would make a wonderful miniseries.

About the Author

The following sources were used as the backbone of this minibiography of Daniel Defoe: Paula R. Backscheider's monumental *Daniel Defoe: His Life* (Baltimore and London: Johns Hopkins Press, 1989); Brian FitzGerald's eminently readable *Daniel Defoe: A Study in Conflict* (Chicago: Henry Regnery Company, 1955); Peter Earle's *The World of Defoe* (New York: Athenaeum, 1977); Michael Shinagel's Robinson Crusoe: *Norton Critical Edition* (New York: W. W. Norton, 1975); Frank H. Ellis's *Twentieth-Century Interpretation of* Robinson Crusoe (Englewood Cliffs, N.J.: Prentice-Hall, Inc., 1969); and the 1946 edition of *The Encyclopedia Britannica.*

Daniel Defoe was born in London in the year of our Lord 1660. In the eleven years before his birth, a great deal had happened in Britain. On January 30, 1649, the faithless Charles I had been beheaded in front of the Banqueting House in Whitehall; the Puritans had taken control of the government and, under Oliver Cromwell as Lord Protector, effectively abolished feudalism and divine right government. But Cromwell died on September 3, 1658, and his son Richard's feet would prove too small for his father's shoes. Thus it came to pass that Charles II had arrived only weeks before the birth of baby Daniel, the third child born to Alice and James Foe, staunch Puritan Presbyterians.

Charles II's arrival promised a new beginning for England and blessed relief from the bloodshed of the previous eleven years. FitzGerald tells us why: ". . . once more Christmas would be celebrated. No longer would mince-pies be sinful or plum-pudding banned. To visit the theatre would stop being a crime. Sports and pastimes would no longer be frowned on and ruthlessly regulated. And once more the ancient English festival of May Day would be celebrated—there would be music and laughter when villagers and townsmen too danced round the maypole" (FitzGerald, p. 10).

However, no torch of rejoicing burned in the window of the Foe house in Cripplegate. Now that the monarchy had been restored, what would happen to them? The Puritans had been oppressed for many years before they governed supreme under Cromwell. Now they were at the mercy of a new king. Would he respect their rights? It didn't take long to find out.

Charles II and his ministers were determined to pulverize those who refused to conform. The sledgehammer blows were consecutive and devastating: The Corporation Act of 1661 stripped Puritans of their citizenship rights and ruined many financially; the Uniformity Act of 1662 expelled Puritan ministers from the Anglican Church; the Conventicle Act of 1664 banned Puritans from gathering in groups of five or more; and the Five Mile Act of 1665 further restricted the movement of dissenting ministers.

Those who refused to comply with these acts were, in effect, expelled from society: They would be excluded from municipal corporations, barred from civil or military service, forbidden to teach or be taught in the university, and for good measure, subjected to discriminatory fines and laws.

The Foe family life centered around their Nonconformist (or Dissenter) pastor, Dr. Samuel Annesley, a towering figure who would have a great impact on the life of little Daniel. On August 24, the day the Act of Uniformity went into effect, a sober congregation filed into Annesley's church. Annesley stood tall and uncowed behind the pulpit: He was determined to stand true to his convictions. How would his parishioners respond? Were they willing to pay the price?

The Foes were among the 15,000 Nonconformist families and clergymen who did pay the price. All in all, some 60,000 took their stand. Annesley would lead the way, being arrested again and again for his refusal to quit preaching—which he continued to do daily. He preferred to stay in prison rather than pay the fine that would set him free.

It was quite a fall for this eminent man, who was educated at Oxford, was chaplain to the Earl of Warwick, was awarded the honorary doctor of civil law degree at Oxford by recommendation of the Earl of Pembroke, had preached before the House of Commons, had been confirmed in his St. Giles pastorate by King Charles II, and was himself the nephew of the Earl of Anglesey. How could he conscientiously be reordained when his 1644 ordination had taken place in the presence of Warwick, Lord High Admiral of England's navy, been presided over by seven Presbyterian ministers, and been confirmed by the laying-on of hands? To accept reordination would be to render null and void all the marriages, baptisms, and commissions he had performed through the years (Backscheider, pp. 8–9).

Young Daniel would never be able to forget the strength of this man's convictions. Again and again, "the vilest of men" would disrupt his Sunday services; and the minister and his congregation would be fined, each time at a higher rate. The doors of parishioners' homes would be broken down, and children pilloried and then hauled off to Bridewell Prison to do hard labor; boys were publicly scourged. Samuel Wesley, father to Charles and John, remembered how his minister father died from an illness contracted during one of these imprisonments. The worst periods of Dissenter persecution occurred in 1662–1664, 1670, and 1681–1685. So fearful were parents that they had their children copying down the Bible in longhand just in case their Bibles were taken from them. Annesley's own home was broken into, and his household goods and library seized—leaving his family with nothing.

Then, in swift succession, came two terrible natural disasters: The plague of 1665 and the Great Fire of London in February 1666.

During the Middle Ages, one word struck terror in people's hearts: *Plague.* The plague was also called the Black Death, because the skin of its victims often turned blackish in their mortal agonies. The first recorded outbreaks in Europe occurred during the sixth and seventh centuries. Seven hundred years later, it returned with a vengeance, starting in seacoast villages and inexorably spreading inland, killing wherever it went. Not for fifty long years did it recede. In the fourteenth century, it came again. In some areas of Europe, up to 75 percent of the population died. It is estimated that this one occurrence of the epidemic killed 25 million people, one-quarter of the population of Europe. In England, over 75 percent of the population died.

By the sixteenth century, incidences of the plague had decreased drastically. In England, there was hope that it had finally run its course. Not so. Isolated cases were reported late in 1664 before a bitterly cold winter stopped its progress. Then, in the spring of 1665, it sprang up again and slowly marched its deadly way across London. Those who could flee did so—about two-thirds of the population. Of the one-third unable to leave, about half died (close to 100,000 of London's total population of 460,000). The Foes were among those who stayed in the city. Daniel was five years old.

FitzGerald vividly re-creates the experience:

> . . . everyone who possibly could hastened away from the City, and from the window of the upstairs room over the little shop Daniel could see nothing but wagons and carts, with goods, women, servants, and children; and coaches filled with the well-to-do, and horsemen attending them, all hurrying away . . . "a very terrible and melancholy thing to see."
>
> This hurrying away of the people lasted from morning to night and continued for some weeks. . . .Then followed

> terrible days. The death-rate rose with frightening rapidity. The parish of St. Giles, Cripplegate, was thickly populated and the plague raged with particular virulence there. One by one the houses in the neighbourhood of old Foe's shop were closed, some by order of the magistrates, others being voluntarily evacuated. The door of each silent house was marked with a large red cross and the inscription "Lord have mercy upon us!" scrawled across it. Trade and business were brought almost to a standstill. Grass grew among the cobblestones of what were normally busy thoroughfares, and those few persons who ventured along them walked rapidly down the middle of the street to avoid the smells which issued from the infected houses. But few persons did so venture: even at midday the City streets were all but deserted. . . . (FitzGerald, pp. 22–23)

Probably, as the epidemic approached its peak in August, Foe sent his family to the top floor of the house, where he had stockpiled provisions to last a long time. Then, after locking the shop, he joined them. There the Foe family lived for the next few weeks, subsisting on bread, butter, cheese, and beer. They would not have touched any meat for fear of infection. Their only means of communication with the outside world was a watchman standing on the street below.

Occasionally, James Foe ventured outside, only to come back with tales of the horrible scenes. One day, while he was running some errands, a casement window flew open above him and a woman leaned out and shrieked three times before uttering in a tone that chilled his blood: "Oh, death, death, death!" James was the only one on the whole street; no doors or windows opened at the woman's cries—only silence. James continued on his way.

The nights contained their own special horrors: Out of the quiet darkness "would come the ringing of the bell and the ghastly cry of the burial men, 'Bring out your dead! Bring out your dead!' The grinding axles of the dead-carts creaked and groaned under their heavy loads as the wagons made their way down the narrow streets, bound for the great pits which were dug to receive the bodies" (FitzGerald, p. 24).

At fifty-seven years old, Defoe could still vividly recall the horror, the gruesome sights, sounds, and smells, of that summer. In his *Journal of the Plague Year,* he wrote:

> [A] young woman, her mother, and the maid, had been abroad on some occasion . . . ; but, about two hours after they came home, the young lady complained she was not well, in a quarter of an hour more she vomited, and had a violent pain in her head. . . . While the bed was airing, the mother undressed the young woman, and just as she was laid down in the bed, she, looking upon her body with a candle, immediately discovered the fatal tokens on the inside of her thighs. Her mother . . . threw down her candle and shrieked out in such a frightful manner that it was enough to place horror upon the stoutest heart in the world; nor was it one scream, or one cry, but the fright having seized her spirits she fainted first, then recovered, then ran all over the house, up the stairs and down the stairs, like one distracted, . . . and continued screeching, and crying out for several hours, void of all sense, . . . and, as I was told, never came thoroughly to herself again. As to the young maiden she was a dead corpse from that moment. (FitzGerald, p. 25)

After three weeks, the outbreak suddenly ceased. Soon the streets were filled again with people, laughing, shaking hands, calling to each other, praising God. "One by one the houses which had been shut were opened up; the rich emerged from their seclusion in the country; the King and his courtiers returned to Whitehall. Shops started to do business again, the law courts to function, the playhouses to stage performances" (FitzGerald, p. 26). The king and his court were soon engrossed in their empty, decadent lives, and the poor, though acknowledging that God had delivered them, returned to their old amusements. The plague had become a bitter memory.

But scarcely had the last plague-riddled bodies been buried then there came the Great Fire, which engulfed London in flames, destroying the entire old walled City. The fire had begun in a bakery near London Bridge and had spread out from there. Six-year-old Daniel

> saw the great red glow in the sky as the mediaeval and Tudor city, with its rabbit-warren of streets and alleys, disappeared in the flames and smoke. He saw the great commercial houses where the merchants and their households worked and slept grow red-hot before crumbling and crashing to the ground with a mighty roar. He watched with fascinated

> terror the flames as they devoured those abodes of wealth, commerce, and hospitality, licking their way through the gardens behind and the courtyards within, fanned all the time by the easterly breeze, cracking stones with the heat and sending them flying through the air, and causing a boiling stream of molten lead to flow along the gutters. He saw roofs and walls crashing down on every side. . . . He watched the frantic fire-fighters pouring buckets of water into the burning mass. He observed how "the despairing citizens looked on and saw the devastation of their dwellings, with a kind of stupidity." He watched the unending procession of refugees as they passed his Cripplegate doorway. (Backscheider, pp. 4–6)

After five days, the inferno was contained. The Foes' house had been spared, but just barely. Backscheider notes that the conflagration destroyed 90 percent of all living accommodations in the city. With remarkable efficiency, the king and city council set about rebuilding London. Soon a new post office, a customhouse, and several government offices were established. In spite of this achievement, the devastation caused by the fire remained for more than thirty years, causing the people to be taxed again and again to pay for the cost of rebuilding.

Many people, including the Foes, regarded the fire and plague as signs of God's judgment on a sinful England, particularly the wicked and profane court of Charles II. To placate God, Mrs. Foe redoubled her efforts to teach her children the Bible and to instill in them the fear of the Lord, but more important, the fear of hell. "Hell in the first few years of dawning consciousness was a terrible reality to Daniel. It frightened him. It was drummed into him along with the Devil. Only those who lived virtuous and godly lives, renouncing the pomps and vanities of this wicked world and all the sinful lusts of the flesh—only those would be saved, and their business[es] prosper" (FitzGerald, p. 28).

It is hard for us in these enlightened days to conceptualize what it was like to live in a society where death was an ever-present likelihood. First of all, no one, not even doctors, knew what caused diseases to spread. Sanitation was unheard of: People dumped their raw sewage into the streets, there to mingle with the excretions left by horses and other animals passing by. People bathed only once a year, if that, and clothes would often be worn until they virtually fell off. And if there *was* an epidemic of any kind, it would be carried by doctors from one patient to the other, for none of them bothered to wash their hands between patients. The same was true for childbirth, which is why so many women died of complications—and why so many babies died in infancy. Every disease children contracted was likely to be fatal because there was no known way of stopping it, short of letting it run its course. Of every three children born, at best, one would live to adulthood. When one adds to this the terrible drain on men caused by continuous wars—keeping in mind the sad fact that, if they were wounded, the chances were excellent that the wound would be fatal—and the many who died on the dangerous seas, it was small wonder the population tended to either remain static or decrease. Not only did the people not bathe, they mistakenly believed that disease was carried by fresh air; consequently, any germs or viruses shut up in those dark and gloomy houses—with too few windows as it was—were likely to dig in their heels and not leave until every human being in the house was infected.

Surrounded as the people were with ever-present death, it is not at all surprising that they talked and wrote so much about it. Three centuries later, we laugh at them and label them "morbid." Almost certainly, we'd have been morbid, too!

As for Daniel, as if all this were not enough, somewhere between 1668 and 1671, there came a fourth disaster: His mother died. Perhaps one can attribute Defoe's disinterest in beauty, nature, and the arts to this untimely removal of his mother from his life.

Annesley, Morton, and Foe

The most impressionable years of Defoe's life were colored by the brushes of three men: Samuel Annesley, Charles Morton, and James Foe. Dr. Annesley was the hero of Defoe's childhood: His sermons, exhortations, and example became part of the very fiber of young Daniel's being. From childhood on, Annesley studied 20 chapters a day out of his Bible, so he knew it thoroughly. His sermons were distinguished by down-to-earth illustrations, anecdotes, and metaphors, by humor, and by clear prose. According to Backscheider, Annesley once compared one's conscience to a piece of gravel in the shoe, concluding with the simple admonition: "'There's nothing in the world for us to do, but to mind our duty'" (Backscheider, p. 13). Defoe admired Annesley for his devotion to God and his calling, his generosity toward others, and his preaching style.

Out of the pain of their being ostracized by society, the Nonconformists received an unexpected blessing. Now that their children were excluded from attending the university, they would have to find another way for them to be educated. Many of their children, including fourteen-year-old Daniel, went to Morton's Academy in Newington Green. Oxford-educated Charles Morton was as remarkable a man as Dr. Annesley, being both a preacher and an educator. The Great Fire of London had destroyed his income-producing property, and the king had taken away his pulpit, so Morton made his house into a meeting place and opened a one-man academy. It was illegal for a graduate of Oxford to teach anywhere but in Oxford or Cambridge—indeed, all graduates were forced to take an oath that they would not do so; thus people such as Morton who established their own Nonconformist schools were accused of perjury. This Stamford Oath was initiated in 1335 to keep rival universities and colleges from being established, and it was not abolished until 1827, almost half a millennium later. So, in effect, the Nonconformists had their hands tied.

But for now, it was enough that Morton accepted Daniel into his school. Called perhaps the greatest teacher in England, Morton and his academy quickly gained national stature. But, like Annesley, he would pay a heavy price for his success. He was excommunicated by the Church of England and arrested and imprisoned repeatedly. Eventually, Increase Mather lured him to the United States by offering him the presidency of Harvard University.

Students at Morton's Academy could take a three-year law course or a five-year theology course. Defoe took theology. Unlike Oxford and Cambridge, Morton's curriculum was in English rather than in Latin, and it included rhetoric, logic, Latin grammar, arithmetic, geometry, astronomy, and music. After a year of philosophy and logic, students studied Aristotelian philosophy: moral (political, economic, ethical), metaphysical, and natural (physics, biology, botany, and zoology) (Backscheider, pp. 14–15).

Morton's students, and students at sister Nonconformist academies, were conspicuous for their freedom of inquiry; they were permitted to study a wide range of philosophical and theological material, from Lockean to Jesuitical to Epicurean to Episcopalian to Presbyterian to Independent Divines. But Morton went beyond even that, introducing geography, history, and modern languages. And, breaking radically new ground (unlike universities of the day), he used the experimental approach—equipping laboratories for science instruction and, for good measure, incorporating the latest scientific research. Morton and his Nonconformist counterparts legitimized science instruction by noting that it revealed "God as manifested in the world." Morton even wrote a textbook for his students, *Compendium Physicae*, in which he presented the discoveries of William Harvey, Isaac Newton, Robert Hooke, William Gilbert, Pierre Gassendi, and René Descartes. So good was this textbook that Harvard would use it in its classrooms for more than thirty-five years (Backscheider, p. 16).

Morton's curriculum was incredibly rigorous, considerably more difficult than Defoe would have had at Oxford or Cambridge, which were then notorious as places where England's elite sent their sons to have a good time, often returning home dissipated and minus the degree. For the rest of his life, Defoe would bless Morton for teaching him the glories of the English language rather than concentrating only on Latin; for making education practical rather than esoteric; and for teaching him to defend his views rigorously, both in speech and in writing.

Like Annesley, Morton enriched his instruction with fables, parables, allegories, stories, and romances. Defoe never forgot the impact these two men made on him: Rarely would he write much without interspersing entertaining, illustrative stories (Backscheider, pp. 16–17).

The third major influence on Defoe's life was exerted by his father, James Foe, who served as both father and mother for many of Daniel's growing-up years. James helped his son to set lofty goals and so filled him with a love of the Bible and its rhythm that Defoe's prose would always mirror that of Scripture. His father, in spite of multiple reverses of fortune, found ways to secure a solid education for his son and supplied him with mentors who were both intellectually gifted and Spirit-led.

James was a member of the powerful ancient brotherhood of Freemen of the City of London and a member of an ancient livery company. Backscheider notes that "as such, he could practice his trade and vote 'in the City,' the one square mile that had grown behind its Roman wall to become the center of power, wealth, and commerce for the entire nation" (Backscheider, p. 22). A Freeman could vote for common councilmen, but only a liveryman could vote for the higher offices of the city—such as auditors, sheriffs, the Lord Mayor, and members of Parliament. Because liverymen represented the backbone of the nation's economy, they were usually free—for the time—to express themselves; and not surprisingly, they respected ability more than mere birth.

Because of his father's position, Daniel grew up with the ancient rituals of city elections, livery company meetings and dinners, processions on Lord

Mayor's Day, and band drills in Finsbury Field. Few men could have passed the spirit of the city on to their sons better than James did. A master of a livery company had both administrative and ceremonial duties: He was judge of the company courts; he was the final authority on trade rules; he was the intermediary when the monarch requested funding for the nation's wars; and he accompanied the Lord Mayor by barge en route to taking the oath of office. Sadly, when Charles II became king and instituted repressive acts against the Nonconformists, neither James nor Daniel could aspire to become Lord Mayor. Worse yet, the city grew fat on the fines levied on Nonconformist liverymen who were elected to the Lord Mayorship but could not serve without violating their consciences. Nevertheless, both Foes, father and son, would fill high positions in that ancient fraternity.

No higher calling could Daniel imagine than to follow in his father's footsteps. So it was that Daniel too became first an apprentice and then a merchant, specializing in wholesale hosiery—this *instead* of becoming a minister.

Mary Tuffley

When Defoe was twenty-two years old, he decided it was time to look for a wife. Before long he set his sights on Mary Tuffley, the daughter of John Rawlins Tuffley, a well-to-do tradesman with considerable property. We have no picture of Mary, but if she was anything like the three daughters the Defoes would raise, she must have been a beauty in her youth. Mary was sixteen or seventeen when Defoe began his courtship. He managed to win out over his numerous rivals by dedicating a book, *The Historical Collections,* to his "Excellent," "Incomparable," and "Divine" lady, signing himself "The Meanest and Truest of all your Adorers and Servants." Two years later, Daniel and Mary were married. She brought with her a handsome dowry of 3,700 pounds, which her husband quickly spent.

This is a good place to bring up a woman's rights in seventeenth-century England—or, rather, the fact that she hadn't any. Whatever rights, whatever control of property she might have, all ended with marriage. Earle puts her sad condition this way:

> Women were not expected to be individuals; in law they were not supposed to live by themselves. . . . Unless they were widows, they were expected to spend their whole li[ves] in legal and physical subjection to a man, whether he be father, master, or husband. . . . The subjected woman had many duties, but few rights. She was expected to breed and

> rear children, as many as possible. . . . She was expected to work, not just to look after her master's or husband's household. . . . Ideally a woman or girl should never be idle. This was particularly true of the wives, daughters and servants of country folk. When they completed their household duties, if they ever did, they were not supposed to relax in the satisfying glow of a job well done but should immediately address themselves to their spinning wheels or their knitting, to earn a few more pennies for the family budget . . . , but work had another function. Tired women were more likely to be virtuous. For women were expected by society to be models of chastity and virtue, unlike their husbands, whose sins were laughed away as excusable trifles. (Earle, pp. 243–244)

Once married, a woman could own nothing—not even the clothes on her back. In fact, theoretically, a man couldn't even give his wife a present because he'd merely be giving it to himself. Not only did the man have complete control over every asset his wife brought with her into the marriage, but he also had control over the children. She could not even make a contract. If he beat her, and she screamed, no one would lift an eye, for beating was one of his rights. If a woman's husband died, the oldest male heir could evict her from her own house. At best, she might receive one-third of the estate—even if it was all hers to begin with! And if her husband were to wish her out of the way, there was little to stop him from locking her up, either in his own house (à la Rochester in *Jane Eyre)* or in an asylum.

On what basis was she kept in virtual slavery? Generally, because of the following: (1) The Bible declared that, because of her sin in Eden, the price she'd pay would be perpetual subjection to the man. (2) Because she was vain. (3) Because she was deceitful. (4) Because she was passionate rather than rational. (5) Because she was shamelessly wanton in terms of sexual appetite. (6) Because she was inherently stupid and totally incapable of making rational decisions on her own. In intelligence, she was considered halfway between a child and a man (Earle, p. 144). A century or so later, in Victorian England, the only significant change in this view would be that a woman was a cold goddess rather than a wanton seductress (Earle, p. 244). Because overwork and almost continuous pregnancy stripped them of their youth and beauty, women grew old before their time.

Divorce, in that society, wasn't even an option.

And there was marriage itself, based as it was on dowry instead of love. A woman, no matter how lovely, had little chance of a "good" marriage without money. Because these marriages were dynastic or financially based, love was merely an option that might or might not occur. Because of this sad state of affairs, in all but the poorest families, where they were unable to afford dowries, marriage was anything but happy.

Were Daniel and Mary happy? We don't know for sure. Did they marry for love as well as for money? We don't know that either. What we do know is that it was a tough marriage—on both sides. Throughout most of his married life, Defoe had to be on the road; he was in prison off and on as well. In short, he was away from his wife and children about half of the time, if not more. But apparently, in all his straying (he was not faithful to her), Mary remained the core of his life. Backscheider observed, "Defoe's *Collections* suggest that he married a woman he loved and respected. . . . Throughout his life, whenever he was away, she was the 'faithful steward' who would not misuse his stock 'One Penny,' the resourceful woman who could manage ten days without money, and the loving wife and mother. He kept in close touch with her [sometimes up to three letters in a week]" (Backscheider, p. 33).

The Duke of Monmouth

Defoe was twenty-five when Charles II died and James II became king. James was Catholic and most of his subjects were not. Had he been tolerant, humane, and kind, he might well have held the throne. But he was not. Worse yet, he was a firm believer in the divine right of kings—that kings could do no wrong and they were accountable to no one.

The first threat to James's sovereignty came from the Duke of Monmouth, the illegitimate son of Charles II. Monmouth had been a favorite of his father's, a hero in the Dutch war, and beloved by thousands of Englishmen. Dissenters especially felt they had little to lose by flocking to his standard—which Defoe did, leaving his bride of only months to fend for herself. The rebellion proved short-lived. Monmouth's troops were totally untried and poorly armed. Of the 3,000 who fought for the ill-fated duke, about a third died on the field; of the remaining 2,000 who tried to escape, within two weeks 751 had been captured—and more were caught later. Rewards were offered for turning in the rebels (five shillings or the rebel property, whichever was greater). For months, houses all over England continued to be searched. More than 850 rebels were sold into servitude in the colonies. On July 15, 1685, Monmouth was beheaded at Bulwark Gate, London. And those of his hapless followers who remained were whipped, burned, or executed (among the latter were at least four of Defoe's Morton Academy classmates). Not until mid-1686 did James finally issue a pardon for the few rebels who remained. Only twenty-eight besides Defoe were left (Backscheider, pp. 39–40).

The Glorious Revolution

In January 1687, James Foe presented Daniel for membership in the famed Butchers' Company. As a Freeman Liveryman, Defoe rose rapidly in the ranks.

About this time, Defoe began writing pamphlets. The pamphlet filled a unique niche in Defoe's society. It was today's lead story in newspaper, magazine, radio, or television news. In those days, if you wanted to influence public opinion, you wrote a pamphlet (usually only one or two sheets long), then hawked it on street corners and sold it in bookshops. They were throwaways; consequently, few have survived. Defoe would go on to write more opinion-changing pamphlets than any other man of his time—or perhaps ever.

Meanwhile, King James continued in his self-destructive ways—almost as if he were determined to destroy any opportunities he had of surviving as a Catholic monarch in a predominantly Protestant country. Besides persecuting Protestants, he appointed—often quite forcibly—Catholics to a disproportionate number of key positions. He subverted the judicial processes by royal intimidation and viciously attacked the Anglican hierarchy by attempting to substitute Catholicism in its stead. Then, on June 10, 1688, the bells of London rang out the news that the king had a son. That was too much for the people! Seven eminent leaders sent a letter to William of Orange, the king's son-in-law and the premier Protestant leader in Europe, and asked him to come to England with an army. William landed and marched toward London; disaffected lords raised insurrections in the north. James, losing support on all sides, fled to France. After considerable negotiation, it was decided to crown William and his wife, Mary, as joint monarchs—but as empowered by Parliament, not by divine right.

On the first Lord Mayor's Day after the "Glorious Revolution" (so named because it reaffirmed the rights of the people and was accomplished without bloodshed), there was a grand parade honoring the new monarchs. Defoe marched with the other Dissenters welcoming the change in government. The procession attended the king and queen from Whitehall to Guildhall, where a great feast was waiting for them.

Defoe had arrived. Perhaps down the line, if the full rights of Nonconformists were restored, *he* could become Lord Mayor of London. It was a heady feeling to be pointed out as one of the city's rising stars. Whenever he walked into one of the coffeehouses around Guildhall and the Exchange, he was noticed and admitted to the political debate.

Defoe's business continued to expand: into other English towns, into the colonies, into shipping. But then his father-in-law, who had been an astute business adviser to him, died. Never a good financial manager, Defoe's bills began to mount. Defoe—he added the French "De" to imply nobility—was unexcelled at dreaming up concepts, ideas, and plans. But he was terrible at making them work and keeping track of details. In spite of England's war with France, which resulted in a considerable loss of shipping on both sides, Defoe continued to expand in international trade—and to borrow more money to pay for these ventures. He got into the business of civet cats and invested in a diving bell scheme (to recover underwater treasure from sunken ships). In the process, he defrauded several people, including his long-suffering mother-in-law, Joan Tuffley. Defoe had built up this empire in order to support the façade that he was a young man with whom to reckon. In spite of his Puritan upbringing, he found that when backed against the wall financially, he would do things to people, even his wife and family, that would cause him regret and sleepless nights for the rest of his life.

Defoe's creditors finally lost all patience with him, and his grand façade cracked right down the middle. He had taken his wife's fortune—and spent every pound. Worse yet, he was now bankrupt, owing much more than the 17,000 pounds for which he was held accountable. Defoe was so terrified of languishing in debtor's prison for the rest of his life that he went into hiding. At the outskirts of London was an old monastery called Whitefriars. In medieval times, it had been a sanctuary for criminals (sort of a biblical city of refuge) where they were secure from pursuers—but only for a month. Defoe fled to it, most likely lodging among debtors like himself, thieves, highwaymen, prostitutes, and beggars.

From Whitefriars, he fled to various places, finally landing in Bristol. There he hid for several months, surfacing only on Sundays, when he would strut down the streets, "dressed in the height of fashion, with a fine flowing wig, and lace ruffles, and a sword at his side" (FitzGerald, p. 77). A number of times during this period he was arrested, booked, and brought to King's Bend, Fleet Prison, or Newgate Prison, until he, usually with Mary's help, could negotiate his way out.

There were no credit cards in those days; no easy way to recover financially once you were down. And even if you declared bankruptcy, you were still legally liable for all you owed. In those days, bankrupts were locked up and, in theory at least, could be kept there for the rest of their lives, or until all their debts, prison fines, and upkeep were paid off. Of course, being locked up in a prison didn't make the debt easy to repay. The conditions of prisons at that time were anything but pleasant: overcrowded, not enough food, bitterly cold in the winter, foul-smelling, noisy, filled with ruthless criminals and brutal guards, overrunning with lice and rats. They were Dante's Inferno in real life. In Defoe's case, having been a prince of the city, the fall was much greater than for most of the others.

Meanwhile, everything the Defoes owned was garnished by Daniel's creditors. Their five servants were let go, and Mary took the children, including the new baby, and moved in with her mother in Kingsland.

The King and I

The Defoe who emerged from prison in 1692 was a different man from the one who had gone in. He had no illusions about the significance of his imprisonment. He would be tarred by the stigma for the rest of his life: "Bankrupt" would be tacked to the end of his name in much the same way as an academic degree. He'd never be Lord Mayor of London now—or even an alderman, for that matter. He would also never again be the hail-fellow-well-met joiner he had been before he entered prison. The experience pushed him into a lonelier world than he had inhabited before.

But, with all this, it had given him something else: a new empathy with the down-and-outers—*especially* those whose liabilities exceeded their assets: the debtors. Even though debtors were in prison because they had little or no money, the prison keepers demanded garnish money; those who did not or could not pay were stripped, beaten, and tormented. Sometimes prisoners who did have money were tortured to death by guards determined to get it for themselves. The guards would even steal the prisoners' beef allowances and sell their bedding.

Defoe was lucky. With the assistance of his wife and highly placed friends, he was able to come to terms with his many creditors, but he would be in debt for the rest of his life. Piece by piece, job by job, he put together enough cash flow to keep him out of Newgate Prison and able to rejoin society. His biggest asset was his brick and tile factory in Tillbury, where he employed more than 100 workers. The rebuilding of London after the fire would continue for many years, so bricks were needed. That business alone netted Defoe 600 pounds a year. He was able to give his creditors about 1,000–2,000 pounds a year, thus earning back some of their respect. But because he "borrowed repeatedly, pieced loans together, promised profits from expansion, renegotiated agreements, . . . used courts to delay," one gets the impression that he was "a slippery, clever, reprehensible, and perhaps desperate man" (Backscheider, p. 66).

Throughout his life, Defoe used every sliver of time profitably. So, out of the long months in hiding to avoid imprisonment for debt, Defoe produced a work centuries ahead of its time, and one that would have a significant impact on thought-leaders of his age: *Essay on Projects*, published in 1698. This pamphlet included well-thought-out proposals for the improvement of seventeenth-century society: for example, ideas on reforming insurance plans, bankruptcy laws, the education system (including education for women), income tax laws, and labor; on increasing state control of capitalism, banking (he suggested one central Bank of England), taxation (be light on the poor and heavy on the wealthy), pensions, and charity lotteries; on more humane treatment for the developmentally handicapped and mentally ill; and on developing a national highway system (complete with exact measurements, materials used, ditches, side roads, signs, upkeep, policing).

FitzGerald paints a picture of Defoe entering the palace to propose his ideas to the king and his councilors:

> See how all eyes are turned upon him, the stranger, as he comes in with the determined air of a man of distinction. His face is surmounted by a magnificent wig; he wears a richly-laced cravat and a fine loose-flowing coat; and at his side hangs a sword. In his hand he carries a rolled-up bundle of documents. So striking is his appearance that one is hardly aware of the large mole which disfigures his countenance. Certainly he has overcome all his old shyness and sense of inferiority on that account. He scans the courtiers, the ministers, before shaking hands with them. He knows that they too are contemplating him. He must impress them, overawe them, impose his personality upon them. When he talks he raises his voice so that it dominates the others. He wants Lord Halifax to hear what excellent French and Dutch he speaks, and how cleverly he can quote Virgil and Horace. He

> says quite casually, "I have written a great many sheets about the coin, about bringing in plate to the Mint, and about our standards", but all the while he is eyeing those to right and to left to see what effect his words have. He sees that he is the centre of all eyes, that the ministers are eager to hear more. He continues speaking. He says he has only refrained from publishing his views because there are already "so many great heads upon the subject". Lord Halifax smiles. Defoe has gained his end. . . . His self-confidence is stupendous. Call it impudence if you will, there is no denying his courage. There is no enterprise, he lets it be understood, that he cannot undertake. He contrives to talk on every subject like an expert. He has the manners of a diplomat. With consummate ease he unrolls financial schemes and displays a knowledge of figures which Halifax himself, the great financier, may well envy. The subject of State lotteries comes up for discussion. Defoe's advice is sought. He answers confidently the questions put to him. (FitzGerald, pp. 79–80)

Two days after *Essay on Projects* hit the streets, Defoe unleashed *A Poor Man's Plea.* In it he asks why the rich are always trying to reform the poor but do nothing to reform themselves. The pamphlet contains one of his all-time great lines, as relevant today as it was when it was written: "These are all cobweb laws, in which small flies are catched, and the great ones break through." Defoe goes on to point out numerous examples proving that the poor man receives one kind of justice and the rich man another.

Also in 1698, he wrote *An Argument for a Standing Army*, which endeared him to the king, who had been urging Parliament to give him one for a long time. At least partly as a result of the pamphlet, Parliament granted William such an army. What inspired the pamphlet was the latest news: The king of Spain had just died, and the throne was being offered to the Duc d'Anjou, King Louis XIV's grandson. Should France and Spain unite, it would create a monolithic state stretching from Portugal to Italy and, with the Spanish possessions in America, the greatest trading power in the world. To Defoe, economic power was far more important than political power, for in war, "it is not the longest sword, but the longest purse that wins." His arguments woke Parliament to the peril.

Also crucial to Defoe's ability to generate and share ideas was the government position he held from 1695 to 1699 as accountant to the commissioners of glass duty. As his influence and hopes soared, Defoe reveled in the glitter of royal life and the narcotic of power. He developed a friendship with the king, as well as deep relationships with other women, spending little time at home with his faithful wife and growing family.

Quietly but certainly, Defoe built an audience for what he had to say. In 1691, his good friend John Dunton started a journal, initially called the *Athenian Gazette* (later changed to the *Athenian Mercury*), and asked Defoe to help him edit it. Thanks to their joint efforts, it became the first lively and successful nonpolitical journal in English history. Jonathan Swift also contributed to it. Defoe, always interested in growing, hit upon the idea of including things in the journal that women would be interested in. Up till this time, women were excluded from almost everything. So Defoe began a question and answer column, with questions like these: "What is platonic love?" "Is it lawful for a man to beat his wife?" "Is it possible for a tender relationship between persons of the opposite sex to be innocent?" "Why does a horse with a round fundament emit a square excrement?" "Shall Negroes rise at the last day?" That column became the most popular part of the journal.

Meanwhile, King William was not having an easy time of it. Mary had died—and she was heir to the throne, not he. Worse yet, they had no children. In those days, unless there was an heir, the death of a monarch meant bloody wars of succession. William's long war to contain France had been a severe drain on the economy, not to mention the devastating impact on shipping and trade. And, to top it off, he appeared cold, he was an introvert, he spoke English with an accent, and most intolerable of all—he was a Dutchman governing true-born Englishmen!

It was at this auspicious moment that Defoe published his rollicking and satiric *The True-Born Englishman.* Synthesizing it, FitzGerald commented, "True-born Englishman indeed! What is a true-born Englishman? They were the most mongrel race that ever walked upon the face of the earth. There was no such thing as a true-born Englishman—all were the offspring of foreigners"—of Romans, Picts, Celts, Angles, Saxons, Britons, Scots, Norwegians, Danes, and Normans, to name a few (FitzGerald, p. 109). The satire became a best-seller: Eighty thousand were sold on the streets, and by mid-century, it had gone through 50 printings. Not only did it make Defoe a household name, but it also discredited those who insisted on pure royal blood in England's monarchs.

The king, in fact, summoned Defoe to Hampton Court Palace and told him how much the poem had pleased him. The two men had a lot in common: They were both militant Protestants who loved the game of politics; and they were both progressive, seeing further into the future than most people. No matter what the subject, the king found that Defoe had mastered it. So, "at the age of forty-one Defoe found himself the confidential advisor to the King of England" (FitzGerald, pp. 110–13).

These were heady days for Defoe. Now that his time had come, he would triumph over those who had put him down; at last he would make them pay. But it was not to be.

In the autumn of 1701, Defoe was "at the summit of his power, the prince of satirists, and the idol of the London populace" (FitzGerald, p. 116). But then a rapid succession of events occurred that toppled him from his lofty perch: On September 17, 1701, former King James II died in St. Germain, France, and a grieving Louis XIV unwisely announced that James's son was the new king of England. The Whigs and Tories (the two ruling parties at the time) were outraged at this announcement, and Defoe put words to their anger in his tongue-in-cheek *Reasons Against a War with France* (most of the reasons were *for* war). William became a lion and lined up a grand alliance against France, remodeled his ministry, dissolved Parliament (the new Parliament would be solidly behind him), and prepared for war.

Early in February 1702, Defoe galloped to Hampton Court with a plan that could change history and make his fortune: an ingenious military campaign in which England would seize control of Spain's South American colonies, thus dealing a terrible blow to the Franco-Spanish alliance. William prepared to implement them . . . and Defoe would be at the center.

But late in February, the king (already plagued with poor health) was galloping his horse across the palace grounds when the horse stumbled. The king fell and broke his collarbone. Medical help was brought in, but to no avail. The king died on March 8. He was only fifty-two.

The Long Fall

William was succeeded by Anne, daughter of James II but a firm Protestant. Although great things happened during her reign, not much of it was due to her efforts. She loved and respected her husband, Prince George of Denmark; but when it came to producing an heir, Anne was not successful. None of her infants survived.

Anne was a narrow thinker and easily led. During the early part of her reign she was dominated by Sarah Churchill, Duchess of Marlborough; the latter part of her reign, she was led by her prime ministers. She was strong in her convictions, however: She detested Dissenters and Roman Catholics equally and adored the Anglican Church. Anne was a good woman, and she tried to be a good queen. England grew stronger during her reign, benefiting, if not from strong leadership, at least from homely virtues.

Throughout his life, Defoe displayed a talent for making enemies by saying the wrong things at the wrong times. With the publication of the satiric pamphlet *The Shortest Way with the Dissenters,* he proved himself true to form. The circumstances were inopportune for several reasons. First, Defoe had just lost his protector, King William, and the new monarch, Queen Anne, had expressed no sympathy for her predecessor or his views. In fact, everyone knew that she hated Dissenters. Second, as his power with King William had increased, Defoe attracted a great deal of envy. Third, Defoe was still struggling to get out of bankruptcy.

And finally, not long before King William's death, Defoe had written a rather incendiary pamphlet, *An Enquiry Into the Occasional Conformity of Dissenters.* It had to do with Dissenters who felt that holding a position of power in London was worth compromising their beliefs. In order to become Lord Mayor of London, these men were willing to occasionally attend Anglican services. After everything Dissenters had gone through and given up, it angered Defoe that these men would be willing to do some fancy footwork to get the reward. Actually, the years had softened the stance of most Dissenters. Many of them, particularly the second and third generations, no longer wished to be martyrs. At any rate, when Defoe came out with *The Shortest Way,* Anglicans and Dissenters alike were still seething over *An Enquiry Into the Occasional Conformity of Dissenters.*

The problem was that what he had written was too good. It was one of the greatest examples of irony in the English language—it almost certainly inspired Swift's *A Modest Proposal.* The satire appeared to be deadly serious: an anonymous high churchman thundering about an end to pussyfooting tolerance against those dastardly Dissenters. These piddly fines levied on them for not coming to communion—much less the right church!—were accomplishing nothing! What was needed was good old-fashioned leadership, backed up with real courage. Hang these obnoxious Dissenters! Send them to the galleys! Crucify them! As for those spineless Dissenters who would do anything to become Lord Mayor . . . not a chance in the world they'd feel their faith was worth dying for! Have at them as well!

The very audacity of this supposed high churchman stunned London. The enemies of the Dissenters—and there were many—were jubilant: At last, they said, someone had told the truth. A strong hand! That's just what those pesky Nonconformists needed.

As for the Dissenters, they were panic-stricken. After all the time and effort they had put into trying to gain back respectability and full membership rights in the Chamber of Commerce, someone had exposed them. It was too much! If they could just catch the pious old prelate who had written the pamphlet, they would let him know exactly what they thought of him!

When the truth about who had actually written the satire leaked out—that it was none other than that unprincipled stooge Defoe—everyone, from the queen down, went looking for blood.

For the first time in his long and illustrious career, Defoe had alienated both sides equally. Thus there was no one he could go to for help when a month after he unleashed the pamphlet, a warrant for his arrest was issued by the secretary of state, the Earl of Nottingham. An accusation of sedition was far more serious than one of bankruptcy. To be imprisoned was horrible enough—but even that paled beside the likelihood that he would be pilloried as well. This time Defoe was almost paralyzed with terror. He remembered the other pamphleteers who had been accused of similar charges: They had been imprisoned, whipped, and put at hard labor; while in the pillory, they had been pelted with rotten food, street garbage, dung, dirt, and rocks. Sometimes those pilloried were stripped naked and even killed. What would happen to his family? What would happen to his now thriving businesses—especially the bedrock of his fortunes and the means to continue paying back his creditors: the brick and tile factory?

Events moved quickly: A reward of 50 pounds was offered for turning Defoe in; remaining copies of *The Shortest Way* were seized at his printer's, and the pamphlet was declared a "seditious publication" and burned publicly by the hangman (FitzGerald, p. 122).

Defoe fled.

Meanwhile, faithful, long-suffering Mary was needed again. She served as intermediary for Defoe's pleas to the speaker of the house (they didn't yet call the head of the party a "prime minister") and the queen, abjectly begging them for another chance, even volunteering to serve as a soldier overseas at no pay. Mary, now with six children to care for and pregnant with the seventh (four daughters, two sons), bravely forced herself into Nottingham's office with a petition from her husband—only to be humiliated by being offered a bribe to turn her husband in.

Defoe hid for four and a half months before he was caught and taken to Nottingham. He already knew that all his books and papers had been confiscated, so he had nothing with which to defend himself. Nottingham was extremely harsh—almost brutal—in his interrogation. After seizing the writings Defoe had with him when he was arrested, Nottingham placed him under heavy guard and had him taken by coach to dreaded Newgate. Defoe was to be a resident of that hellhole for almost six months. Periodically, Nottingham had the prisoner hauled off to be grilled again.

Defoe's trial opened on July 7 "in a setting a visitor to London described as like the 'Judgment Hall of Pilate.' Visitors paid a shilling a seat and saw 'a vast concourse of people who made such a din that it was often impossible to hear either barristers or judges.' [Defoe] stood at the bar in front of the bench on which the lord mayor or chief magistrate sat with four assessors chosen from the twelve justices of the peace. Defoe did not face friends" (Backscheider, p. 108).

Each of the judges had been the recipient, directly or indirectly, of Defoe's barbed prose, and they were now out for revenge. "The sentence was a savage one. But then, Defoe was a dangerous man—a Puritan intellectual, an enemy of the nobility and clergy, a Whig suspected of levelling—not to say revolutionary—leanings. Away with the fellow! Goal him! Pillory him! Break his spirit—so as to frighten the wits out of any other Puritan intellectuals who may be minded to follow his example!" (FitzGerald, p. 123).

Defoe never had a chance, for the government had gradually been tightening the screws in its attempts to destroy freedom of the press. The court now insisted that *all* criticisms of the monarch, the government, or governing officials was "seditious libel." Juries were advised that the guilt or innocence of the defendant was irrelevant. The only question to be answered was "Is the defendant the author of the papers?" Basically, the trial was a farce.

Defoe was sentenced to pay 134 pounds (fines of 50–100 pounds were standard for heinous offenses), to be pilloried three times (this was almost unheard of—once was enough for a lifetime, if one made it through), and to be left in prison (most pamphleteers were released), and surety was required of all acts for seven years (two was the usual limit). Clearly, the judges had decided to throw the book at Defoe.

The prisoner was taken back to Newgate. Almost certainly, this period was the nadir of Defoe's lifetime. After he recovered some semblance of his normal self, he had his wife, friends, and intermediaries, such as William Penn the son, request that the pillory part of the sentence be softened. Since the seventh century, pillorying had been the means of publicly degrading thieves and tricksters. Later, in Anglo-Saxon times, others were added to the list of pillory victims: for example, those who sold or served spoiled food, loaded their dice, borrowed a child to beg with, lied, or kept dishonest scales. Later yet, the courts added perjurers, homosexuals, and rioters. The purpose was to "stigmatize and dishonor and to mark out an offender as unworthy of trust or respect," to be "shunned and avoided by all credible and honest men," to be made "infamous by law" (Backscheider, p. 116). A pilloried man was marked for life, as much as if he wore a scarlet letter on his chest. He could neither vote nor serve on a jury. On July 21, Defoe was brought before the queen at Windsor Castle on a writ of habeas corpus. Anne was angry at being brought into such a circus, for London was in an uproar. Defoe was grilled again, but to no avail.

Despite the public outcry, he was pilloried—three times. But FitzGerald tells us, it didn't quite have the desired effect:

> The last three days of July found Defoe standing in the pillory, exposed to the sun's heat and the rain—exposed also to the mob. His head, his arms, were locked in the wooden instrument of torture. Below him jostled the great mob of sightseers. What would they do to him, he wondered, as he gazed down upon them from his elevated position on the disgraceful platform. Would they pelt him with rotten eggs and stinking fish, as they were wont to bombard prisoners in his unhappy situation? Indeed, an offender put into the pillory was considered lucky if he escaped with his life from the shower of brickbats and paving-stones which were often hurled at him. But as Defoe stood there those July days a remarkable thing happened. The crowd, the Cockney crowd, far from jeering at him, cheered him. Cheered him and drank his health in tankards of ale and stoups of wine; while the pretty flower-girls garlanded his pillory with flowers. . . . A ring of admirers grouped round the place of punishment handed his pamphlets among the onlookers. They found a ready sale for them. . . . Defoe had triumphed with a vengeance over his opponents. (FitzGerald, pp. 124–25)

Of course it helped that his hot-off-the-press tract *A Hymn to the Pillory* was being hawked everywhere in his vicinity. In it, he used his pen with devastating effect. Not only did he show how unjust his sentence was, but he also turned the tables on his enemies: "Who should be in the pillory? Incompetent military commanders . . . , power-grabbing politicians, money-grubbing financiers, swindling stock-jobbers and brokers, profligate men of fashion, vicious lawyers and magistrates, fanatic Jacobites, drunken priests," and usurious landlords—THEY ought to be standing in the pillory (FitzGerald, p. 125). The people loved it!

Then it was back to Newgate, there to await "Her Majesty's pleasure"—whatever and whenever that might be. FitzGerald points out that even though Defoe was treated better than most of the other prisoners, he "did not shrink with loathing from the companionship of thieves, highwaymen, forgers, coiners, and pirates. He did not disdain the company of the pretty prostitutes" (FitzGerald, p. 127). Defoe not only admired the courage of these people, he also came to love them. And as was his custom, he used his time in prison to good advantage: "He spent many pleasant hours in listening to the tales of his adventurous fellow-prisoners" (FitzGerald, p. 127). His experiences at Newgate and Whitefriars gave him the scenes and the characters he later used in *Moll Flanders, Colonel Jack,* and his other realistic novels.

But with the passing of each dreadful day, and still no word on his future, Defoe began to despair. Was he to be locked up here in this evil-smelling sinkhole for the rest of his life? What about all those monstrous debts he still owed? And the brick factory at Tillbury—who was running it? Without proper supervision, it would go under. *Then* where would he be? What about Mary and the seven children? How would they survive? Defoe realized that this time he had done a superb job of sawing off the limb he had been sitting on. Short of a miracle, he was doomed.

Then he took stock of his assets. What did he possess that the other side might want? That it hadn't taken already, that is. Well, perhaps his writing.

He sent Mary and some friends to negotiate for him. He wrote to Godolphin, the Lord Treasurer, and he wrote to Secretary of State Robert Harley, a rising star in English politics. He also wrote to the house speaker and his personal inquisitor, Nottingham.

Robert Harley was shrewd, and he saw Defoe's request as an opportunity to pick up a lot of talent cheaply. Defoe's gifts were the talk of the age: On the wrong side, he could be a deadly enemy; on the right side, a powerful friend. Harley decided to write Godolphin, insidiously noting that if Defoe "were let off fine-wise, and was willing to serve his Queen, he may do us service, and this may perhaps engage him better than any after rewards, and keep him under the power of an obligation" (FitzGerald, pp. 127–29).

Godolphin agreed with Harley's assessment. Now he'd have to persuade the queen. He pointed out to her that Defoe was "the most popular man in the country at the moment" and that his writings went through printing after printing (FitzGerald, p. 129). At the moment, it just wasn't good press for her and the government. Finally, the queen saw the light. So, after five months in prison, Defoe was released, a free man.

A *free* man? Could he ever be completely free again? True, he would not be in prison, but there are other kinds of prisons besides those composed of iron bars. Up till now Defoe had prided himself on his core of integrity. It's true that he had said, written, and done things he was not proud of, but he had never compromised where his deepest ideals and principles were concerned. Now, for the sake of life, liberty, writing career, and family, he had given in. Where would it lead?

He was drained emotionally and physically. His experience during that harrowing year had aged him. Never again would he be as trusting as he had been, as willing to take risks, as brash, as foolhardy—as *young*. He no longer fully trusted even the Dissenters. He felt as if he had been silenced. More and more, he worked and traveled alone.

Just as Defoe had feared, his year's absence had destroyed his brick business. Without it, how could he keep his family alive and comfortable, as well as continue to pay his debts? At forty-four years of age, Defoe saw writing as his only hope of success. In 1704, he would publish over 400,000 words.

Backscheider points out that the prison experience had a profound impact on his writing, changing its purpose, focus, and tone. Instead of being personal, introspective, intense, and engaged, it became more impersonal, detached, and objectively professional.

Defoe put away forever his dreams of being a merchant prince and king's confidant. His future, he realized, was with a quill and bottle of ink. Yet he still believed that God was in control and had a divine plan for his life.

"He Who Gave Me the Brains Will Give Me the Bread"

Shortly after Defoe's release from Newgate, the third natural disaster of his lifetime occurred: the Great Storm. It proved to be the worst storm England had ever experienced. Defoe had already earned the titles of Father of Pamphleteering and Father of Propaganda. With the piece of investigative reporting he would do on the Great Storm, he would also become known as the Father of Journalism.

Defoe was in London when the storm hit. As a matter of fact, he barely escaped being killed by falling masonry. The streets were swamped with debris, and the barometer was so low, Defoe was certain the children had been playing with it. For two days and nights, the wind howled as buildings collapsed all around his house. When he went down to the coastal cities, which had been hit even harder than London, he saw wreckage of ships everywhere and heard stories of heroic rescue attempts. Out of it all came the book *The Great Storm*. It could be considered one of the earliest (if not the earliest) disaster stories.

Gradually, Defoe became acquainted with his new employer/probation officer, Robert Harley, now speaker of the house and de facto ruler of England. Little did anyone realize that the rule of a weak queen, followed by the rule of several kings who could barely speak English, would lead to the end of royal power and the beginning of parliamentary democracy. At the beginning, Defoe was obsequious with Harley, almost to the point of groveling, but as time went on, his tone changed to that of a colleague, and later yet, a friend.

One of the things Harley wanted Defoe to do was to continue influencing public opinion. To accomplish this, Defoe needed a publication; hence *The Review* was established. The magazine ran for nine years, with issues coming out three times a week. Defoe wrote all the copy himself. Readers loved his question and answer column, "The Scandal Club," a mix of familiar situations, firm morality, common sense, and biting satire. Early circulation was 400–500, each copy being read by ten to fifteen people. Amazingly, even though Defoe lived on the road and had to send his copy by mail, he managed to meet his deadlines.

The next thing Harley wanted of Defoe was to serve as one of his secret agents. If Harley was to govern effectively, he had to know what was happening across the country and what people thought about issues. In the eighteenth century, politicians didn't have the convenience of polls and instantaneous reporting, as they do today. In fact, it was difficult for even government leaders to find out what was happening in the nations they were governing.

Since Defoe loved to travel, his new assignment was an exciting challenge. He visited every corner of England by horseback, developing a support system of individuals who would keep him updated on local developments between his visits. In each place, by getting acquainted with people in pubs and coffeehouses, Defoe discovered who the key thought-leaders were, and which government officials were most admired, which least, and why. Over time, Harley became a far more effective prime minister because of these enlightening reports from Defoe, knowing whom to reward and whom to pass over.

For five years, Defoe traveled around England, spending little time with his wife and children. When he did remain in one place for any length of time, he would write from 8:00 in the morning until noon, and then from 2:00 in the afternoon until 9:00 at night. Normally, it took five to seven hours on horseback to reach the next town, allowing Defoe the evenings to talk politics in clubhouses with dissenting ministers or Harley's other agents. Usually, Defoe would spend only one night in each town. He distributed his own published works wherever he went.

In 1706, Harley sent him on the most significant mission of his life: to live in Scotland until such time as Scotland and England would agree to become one nation. The 372-mile horse ride from London to Edinburgh took ten to fourteen days, with nights spent at inns along the way. Since most of the Scots were not interested in giving up their independence, and were suspicious of all Englishmen right then, Defoe's position was dangerous. If it came out that he was a spy, he would have been lucky to get out of Scotland alive.

Defoe found Edinburgh fascinating. High Street he pronounced clean and pleasant, although he considered the little streets "very steepy and troublesome, and . . . nasty." Because the terrain was rocky, there was little available water, thus severely limiting sanitary facilities: "Each family kept its 'excrements and foul water' in large vessels until 10:00 P.M., when the bells of St. Giles signaled that it was time to dump them into the open street" (Backscheider, p. 211).

When the Scot and English commissioners arrived, everyone got down to business. The debates were long and heated, lasting fourteen to sixteen hours a day. Harley, his associate leaders, and the queen were afraid that if the two kingdoms did not join, Scotland might be swallowed up by France. Defoe did everything he could to help turn the tide toward union. In the streets, the coaches of the commissioners would often be stoned, for the Scots were furious when they discovered that union would mean the end of their independent parliament. But Harley had the votes he needed, so on January 6, 1707, the final vote was taken, and thus was born the United Kingdom.

Harley kept Defoe in Scotland for a while afterward. Backscheider notes that "Defoe's activities and contacts in Scotland were astonishing. His power to penetrate diverse groups ranks him among the greatest spies of all time" (Backscheider, p. 232).

When he finally returned to London, Defoe had been away from home for an entire year. While absent, his father had died; and soon after his return, his daughter Martha took sick and died as well.

Harley resigned in 1708 and was replaced by Godolphin, who promptly sent Defoe back to Scotland. In 1710, Harley was back in office again.

The Harley years taught Defoe a great deal. According to FitzGerald, Harley and Defoe came to depend on each other; gradually, this dependence developed into a friendship. The two men had many characteristics in common: both were shifty and secretive; both were tolerant and kindly; and both had had a Puritan upbringing. There was one difference, however, and this difference cemented the two men's relationship: "Harley was a statesman of power and consequence, but a slovenly and confused writer. Defoe was an undischarged bankrupt—and a writer of genius! . . . Harley, the statesman who spoke poorly and who could not write, employed the journalist of genius to travel round England and report; and, in the *Review*, to preach the cause of national unity to win the war. Defoe performed his task to perfection" (FitzGerald, pp. 135–36).

On the Continent, some of the greatest battles of the age were being fought as the allies gradually trimmed the French empire back to size and, in the process, kept France and Spain from uniting into one monolithic power. Everywhere blood continued to flow.

Meanwhile, Defoe, the secret agent, was traveling around Britain, feeling the pulse of the kingdom. At each town, he would visit the coffeehouses, the fairs, the markets, and the Dissenters' chapels, watching, listening, and sending reports back to Harley. It was dangerous work: Because many suspected that Defoe was not the person he appeared to be, he had several close calls.

Defoe's *Review* continued to gain in popularity. Its articles were widely read and discussed. Literary historians have made much of the *Tattler* and the *Spectator*, but those two magazines lasted only a short time, whereas the *Review* spanned almost a decade. FitzGerald maintains that "there has been nothing quite like the *Review* since. Writing with incomparable brilliancy of method and vivacity of style, Defoe ranged over every conceivable subject—the war, the peace, religious toleration, national unity, trade, industry, and employment. The amount of sheer physical work involved—quite apart from the mental effort—dazzles one; for every word had to be written by hand with a quill pen" (FitzGerald, p. 138).

The Review wasn't the only magazine for which Defoe was writing. He simultaneously submitted poetry, stories, and pamphlets to other publications as well. Off and on—part of the time with Godolphin—Defoe would help Harley with his articles and speeches, until Harley resigned for the last time in 1714, far longer than the court-mandated seven years of servitude with the government. Today we may thank Harley for a good share of the Defoe letters that have survived, for he valued authors like Defoe and Swift and preserved their communications in what has become known as the Harleian Collection.

Shambles

Defoe's fortunes took a turn for the worse again when Queen Anne died unexpectedly on August 1, 1714. Shortly after her successor, George Ludwig, Elector of Hanover and founder of the Hanoverian (or House of Windsor) dynasty, arrived in England, another war on the press began. Since Defoe was considered the champion of the opposition party and the most prominent political writer in the country, he found himself at the center of the conflict. Without the support of Queen Anne or Harley, Defoe was defenseless against his enemies, who quickly moved in to denounce him as an unprincipled mercenary. The charge was unfair because neither Harley nor Godolphin had ever taken that kind of control of Defoe's pen. This time, however, the smear worked.

Defoe's tendency to do foolish things at times of peril held true again. With a witch hunt on, Defoe published a defense of the Harley government at the same time the lords were in the process of impeaching prominent members of his administration and Harley himself had been imprisoned in the Tower of London.

As for George I, he had been one of the most powerful leaders in Europe before he came to England. He was methodical, deliberate, economical, cautious, and definitely not a man to be crossed. As a matter of fact, he had his former wife locked up in a remote German castle—and there she would stay.

So, once again, Defoe was in danger of being imprisoned for "seditious libel." But now he was older, fifty-four, and no longer had the reserves he once had. With the death of Queen Anne, he had felt freed from his shackles. At last he could be his own man again. But clearly the situation had not changed. He could choose prison or accommodation. Again he chose the latter. This time the directive was more devious: He was to worm his way into an extremist opposition publication, Nathaniel Mist's *Weekly Journal* (or *Saturday's Post)* and help to tone it down. Mist was an unusual man who was always being hauled off to prison for the extremist positions he took. Strangely enough, the partnership worked: During Defoe and Mist's long association together, *Saturday's Post* became the most popular journal in the nation, with a weekly circulation of about 10,000 copies. However, years later when Mist found out the real reason Defoe had been hired for the magazine, he tried to kill him with his sword.

A Second Wind

Defoe wrote his best, and most enduring, works in the final years of his life. It was as if God had been preparing him all those years for that moment. Through the years, he had always found a new direction out of the ashes of defeat. Thus he concluded that out of disaster, God always points us to a better way. Defoe began to experiment as he never had before—with new points of view, different kinds of narrators, different kinds of characters and characterizations, different literary forms.

Somewhere between 1714 and 1717, Defoe began thinking about doing something that had never been done before: writing a story in plain English prose so that everyone could understand and enjoy it. It would be a story about life—especially about the loneliness of life. And since Bunyan had set his *Pilgrim's Progress* in England, Defoe would go farther away, perhaps even travel around the world. And instead of a prison of iron bars, his character would be cast on a deserted island in the middle of the ocean. *That* certainly would be a prison! He'd name the protagonist after his childhood friend: Timothy Cruso. Except "Timothy" wasn't quite right. He'd have to come up with a better first name.

Once Defoe unleashed his alter ego, Robinson Crusoe, and put himself in his place, absolutely alone on an island, something began to happen: The story became increasingly real to him. Defoe couldn't have Crusoe do or say anything uncharacteristic, for he saw every reader saying to himself as he read, "Yes! If I were in Crusoe's place, that's exactly what I would have thought/said/done."

Though he himself couldn't travel the world, there were plenty of resources Defoe could use to provide the information he needed. He reread William Daumpier's book *A New Voyage Around the World*, published in 1703, which related the story of a Indian marooned for three years on San Fernando Island. Speaking of San Fernando Island, wasn't that the one that Alexander Selkirk had been left on for four years, until Captain Cook rescued him? That tale was in *A Voyage to the South Sea, and Around the World*, published in 1712. Then there was Captain Woodes Roger's book *A Cruising Voyage Around the World,* also published in 1712. Two other good voyage books were Daniel Beckman's *Voyage to and from the Island of Borneo,* published in 1718; and James Janeway's *Legacy to His Friends,* published in 1674. The latter dealt with God's providence, something most writers ignored. And then there were a number of travel books such as *Hakluyt's Voyages* that would help when Crusoe got off the island and made up for lost time by *really* traveling.

When Defoe delivered the finished manuscript to William Taylor at Sign of the Ship in Paternoster Row, April 25, 1719, he did not do so with pride. He knew *Robinson Crusoe* was good, but this kind of story would be looked down on by so many people. Well, the 100-pound payment would cover quite a few bills.

Sadly for the Defoe family, 100 pounds was all Defoe ever received for the book. It would be others who would make a fortune from it. The first printing in late April was for 1,000 copies; by May 9, a second printing had been done; by June 6, a third printing was ordered. Within a year, *Robinson Crusoe* had been translated into French, German, and Dutch. By the end of the nineteenth century, 181 years later, it had come out in more than 700 different editions—today, that number is well over 1,000. Without question, it is one of the best-selling books of all time.

The second part of the book, *The Farther Adventures of Robinson Crusoe,* was published in August 1719. Many editions include only the first part of the story: Crusoe's life on the island.

The third part, *Serious Reflections During the Life and Surprising Adventures of Robinson Crusoe, with His Vision of the Angelick World,* was first published in 1720. Since it is heavily philosophical and moralistic, it has rarely been included as part of the standard text.

The Fireworks at the End

In the nine-year period beginning with 1719, Defoe unleashed one blockbuster after another. *Robinson Crusoe* was followed by *The Life, Adventures, and Pyracies of the Famous Captain Singleton,* in 1720. This is a powerful book that holds its own with its illustrious predecessor; it covers the parts of the known world *Robinson Crusoe* missed. It must have been heady reading in 1720, for there is excitement on virtually every page. Captain Singleton represents the bridge from the spiritual Robinson Crusoe to the darker characters to come. Most likely, he is based on Will Atkins, the bold troublemaker on Crusoe's island (Backscheider, p. 440).

In Defoe's day, pirates were everywhere. In fact, in some parts of the world, they actually outnumbered legitimate merchants. Defoe knew a number of them personally—and occasionally one would wander home alive. Defoe read every book he could find that described their lives. *Captain Singleton* represents a lifetime of distilling information about pirates. As was true with *Robinson Crusoe*, early editions of the book sported detailed maps. Amazingly, *Captain Singleton* didn't survived. I'm sure there must be copies somewhere, but in all my years of haunting old bookstores, I've never stumbled on one.

Captain Singleton was actually preceded (by one month) by another major book, which today is even scarcer than *Captain Singleton—Memoirs of a Cavalier* (1720). Defoe had been doing research most of his life on one of his personal military heroes, Sweden's Gustavus Adolphus. When he wrote *Memoirs*, he had just reviewed an earlier tour de force, *The History of Wars*, in which he noted a big difference between the egocentric Charles XII and the devout Protestant Gustavus Adolphus, Charles' grandfather. The first part of *Memoirs of a Cavalier* follows the campaigns of Gustavus Adolphus; the second part details the defeat of the Royalists in 1640. The book vividly portrays the misery civil wars leave in their wake. Our protagonist, the Cavalier, eventually is forced to kill those he earlier fought to protect and who would have died for him. Leadership on both sides is "pitifully inept." In retirement, the Cavalier's memories are bitter, burning, and melancholy, as he looks back at all the bloodshed on behalf of Gustavus Adolphus, whose empire no longer exists; on Cromwell's Protectorate, which didn't last a dozen years; and on Charles XII's meaningless death. At the end, Defoe asks this rhetorical question: *For what?* (Backscheider, pp. 444–46). H. G. Wells, in the best-selling history book of the century, *The Outline of History*, made this statement: "The earliest chapters of Defoe's *Memoirs of a Cavalier*, with its vivid description of the massacre and burning of Magdeburg, will give the reader a far better idea of the warfare of this time than any formal history" (FitzGerald, p. 183).

During this period, Defoe began two monumental works that in themselves would have brought fame enough for a lifetime: *Atlas Maritimus*, a huge, oversized geography book, which he began in 1722 but did not publish until 1728; and *A Tour Thro' the Whole Island of Great Britain*, a three-volume work published in 1724, 1725, and 1726.

The *Atlas Maritimus* came out at a time when people everywhere were so interested in geography and maps that it was almost a rage. Royal patents for books were rarely granted, but so much expense went into this work that such a patent was imperative in order to keep it from being pirated. The book was endorsed by three admirals and by the legendary Oxford scientist Edmund Halley (only Isaac Newton was more famous at that time). Some of the greatest names of the time were among the subscribers for the landmark work (one of the publishing events of the age).

England held its breath when the plague again headed north across the Continent. Through almost barbaric containment measures, it was stopped just across the English Channel. But the interest it aroused was too high for an opportunist like Defoe to resist. He went back to his childhood and re-created the terrible plague of 1665; he titled the work *A Journal of the Plague Year*. The book is so powerful that it has remained in print through the centuries and remains a classic even today. Walter Allen, in his best-selling *The English Novel* (New York: E. P. Dutton, 1954), states that *A Journal of the Plague Year* is "perhaps the most convincing re-creation of an historical event ever written" (p. 29).

Also in 1722 came *The Fortunes and Misfortunes of Moll Flanders,* considered by some scholars to be Defoe's greatest book, and by many others, to be one of the most powerful novels ever written. In Defoe's London, there were few career options for a woman. She might be a maid in a tavern, a domestic, or if she was educated, possibly a governess. If she was poor, as most were, without a dowry, she'd have a hard time finding a husband. These young women soon found out that being a servant or working in a tavern was an open invitation to seduction. For a tragically large number of them, the only alternative to starvation was to become a street prostitute.

By 1720, woman criminals were showing up more frequently in court. The war in Europe had ended, and the troops were returning home. The few jobs women had held while the men were away were taken from them; and the depressed economy and 30 percent inflation rate got rid many more jobs. Tens of thousands of women, like Moll Flanders, were sent to the colonies (such as America) in order to help them find new lives: From 1580 to 1650, eighty thousand women were sent to America alone; from 1651 to 1700, ninety thousand more were sent. By 1722, of those convicted at Old Bailey, close to 8 percent were executed; of the remaining 92 percent, 70 percent were shipped out. During the years 1718–1775, Maryland and Virginia alone took 30,000 British women (Backscheider, pp. 492–93).

Many people, including Defoe, wondered if the treatment accorded these women was morally any worse than the custom of selling one's daughter into a loveless marriage by means of a dowry. Defoe got to know these lost souls well when he was in prison, and he developed a great pity for them: To him, they were helpless victims of circumstances beyond their control, valiantly searching for meaning in life. FitzGerald maintains that

> *Moll Flanders* is more subtle, more complex than *Robinson Crusoe*. Moll, the pathetic heroine, so human and lovable, is a much more complicated character than the simple, open-mouthed, manly mariner of York. She is the victim both of heredity and of environment, a magnificently alive common girl, caught in the meshes of her too responsive temperament, her seducer's egoism, and the monster, the lumpish monster, of capitalist society that makes her an outcast. She is both the victim and the product of that society which disowns her. In tracing her fortunes and misfortunes Defoe delves much more deeply into the springs of human behaviour than he does in *Robinson Crusoe*, and the outcome is perhaps the most remarkable example of pure realism in literature. (FitzGerald, p. 188)

The History of Colonel Jack, also published in 1722, is a story of another rogue with a conscience: a pirate of the highways. At this stage of Defoe's career, crime in England was apparently completely out of control, and justice was only an abstract term. Defoe knew how little sense it made to house side by side in Newgate a father unable to pay his debts, a starving woman who killed a bird on a noble's estate, a journalist who offended the wrong people in a pamphlet he wrote, a prostitute who got caught in the act (the aristocrat with her wasn't even booked), a desperate mother who stole a loaf of bread to feed her starving children, an embezzler, a pickpocket, a rapist, and a murderer. There were more than 100 offenses for which one could receive the death penalty.

Like Dickens after him, Defoe was a voice crying in the wilderness: a plea for a more humane way of administering justice. And Colonel Jack was another in a long line of sympathetic character sketches. During this same period (mid-1720s), Defoe interviewed real-life criminals such as Jack Sheppard (1724), Jonathon Wild (1725), and Rob Roy (1723) and wrote character sketches of them as well.

The last of Defoe's great novels was *Roxana* (1724), the grimmest book of all because it lacked hope and optimism. Lady Roxana and her alter ego,

Amy, sink into evil. To punish Roxana, Defoe creates two hellhounds: "Susan, the abandoned child of her body, and Amy, the rejected product of her secret thoughts" (Backscheider, p. 310).

Of these last two books, *Colonel Jack* is rarely seen today, but *Roxana*, that brooding study of evil, has remained in print.

Not Going Gently Into That Good Night

For years, Defoe suffered from bladder stones. Finally, in 1725, he agreed, in despair, to have them removed. The operation was horrible, like being torn apart on the rack. First of all, the instruments they used were frightening. Second, given the nature of the operation, Defoe had to be strapped to the table with his wrists tied to his ankles; once he was secured, three strong orderlies held him in position to keep his bent legs apart. Third, they used no anesthesia. Fourth, since the doctors didn't clean their instruments between patients, operations, besides being excruciatingly painful, often resulted in months of continued pain as infection spread, many times leading to putrefaction and death. Defoe thought it would have been better to be hanged and be done with it.

Defoe had no fear of death. To him, death was merely "a passing out of life." In 1727, he noted that he was "soon to come before" the great Judge of his life and intentions. All his life Defoe had daily talked with God as with a friend; and he faithfully attended church every Sunday. He was confident that God, in spite of Defoe's many mistakes, would understand and forgive him, knowing that he had tried to do what was right.

On April 24, 1731, while hiding from a creditor, Defoe was felled by a stroke. He was buried in Bunham Fields with at least 100,000 other Dissenters, such as John Bunyan, George Fox, Isaac Watts, and the Cromwell family.

So ended the life of Daniel Defoe, the Father of Journalism, the Father of Propaganda, the Father of the Novel. In his lifetime, with only a quill and an ink bottle by his side, he had written as much, perhaps, as anyone who has ever lived.

One last letter brings Defoe's life full circle. It was written to his son-in-law Henry Baker, who was married to Defoe's youngest and favorite daughter, Sophie:

> I am near my journey's end, and am hastening to the place where the weary are at rest, and where the wicked cease to trouble; be it that the passage is rough, and the day stormy,

by what way soever He please to bring me to the end of it, I desire to finish life with this temper of soul in all cases: *Te Deum Laudamus*. . . . It adds to my grief that I must never see the pledge of your mutual love, my little grandson. Give him my blessing, and may he be to you both your joy in youth, and your comfort in age, and never add a sigh to your sorrow. But alas! that is not to be expected. Kiss my Sophy once more for me; and if I must see her no more, tell her [that her] father loved her above all his comforts, to his last breath. (FitzGerald, pp. 238–39)

Joseph Leininger Wheeler, Ph.D.
The Grey House
Conifer, Colorado

Works by or Attributed to Daniel Defoe

NOTE: Unless otherwise indicated, place of publication is London. Dates are as printed on the title pages and may be Old Style. This bibliography is taken from Paula R. Backscheider's *Daniel Defoe: His Life* (Baltimore and London: Johns Hopkins University Press, 1989). Reprinted by permission of the publisher.

An Account of the Conduct of Robert Earl of Oxford. 1715.

An Account of the Great and Generous Actions of James Butler. [1715].

An Account of the Late Horrid Conspiracy to Depose Their Present Majesties K. William and Q. Mary, to Bring in the French and the Late King James, and Ruine the City of London. 1691.

An Account of the Proceedings Against the Rebels. 1716.

The Advantages of the Present Settlement, and the Great Danger of a Relapse. 1689.

The Advantages of Peace and Commerce; with Some Remarks on the East-India Trade. 1729.

Advertisement from Daniel De Foe, to Mr. Clark. [Edinburgh, 1710].

Advice to the People of Great Britain, with Respect to Two Important Points of

Their Future Conduct: I. What They Ought to Expect from the King; II. How They Ought to Behave by Him. 1714.

"The Age of Wonders." 1710.

The Anatomy of Exchange-Alley. 1719.

And What If the Pretender Should Come? Or Some Considerations of the Advantages and Real Consequences of the Pretender's Possessing the Crown of Great Britain. 1713.

The Annals of King George, Year the Second. 1717.

The Annals of King George, Year the Third. 1718.

An Answer to a Paper Concerning Mr. De Foe, Against His History of the Union. Edinburgh, 1708.

An Answer to a Question That No Body Thinks of, Viz. But What If the Queen Should Die? 1713.

An Answer to the Late K. James's Last Declaration. 1693.

An Apology for the Army. 1715.

The Apparent Danger of an Invasion. 1701.

An Appeal to Honour and Justice. 1715. In *The Shortest Way with the Dissenters and Other Pamphlets.* Shakespeare Head edition. Oxford: Blackwell, 1974.

Applebee's Original Weekly Journal.

An Argument Shewing That a Standing Army, with Consent of Parliament, Is Not Inconsistent with a Free Government. 1698.

Arguments About the Alteration of Triennial Elections of Parliament. 1716.

Armageddon: Or, the Necessity of Carrying on the War. [1711].

Atlantis Major. 1711.

Atlas Maritimus & Commercialis. 1728.

Augustus Triumphans. 1728.

The Ballad: Or, Some Scurrilous Reflections in Verse . . . with the Memorial, Alias Legion Reply'd to Paragraph by Paragraph. [1701].

The Ballance of Europe: Or, An Enquiry Into the Respective Dangers of Giving the Spanish Monarchy to the Emperour as Well as to King Phillip. 1711.

The Ban[bur]y Apes: Or, The Monkeys Chattering to the Magpye. [1710].

A Brief Explanation of a Late Pamphlet, Entitled The Shortest Way with the Dissenters. [1703].

A Brief Historical Account of the Lives of the Six Notorious Street-Robbers, Executed at Kingston. 1726. In vol. 16 of *Romances and Narratives by Daniel Defoe*, edited by George A. Aitken. London: Dent, 1905.

A Brief History of the Poor Palatine Refugees, Lately Arrived in England. 1709.

A Brief Reply to the History of Standing Armies in England. 1698.

A Brief State of the Question, Between the Printed and Painted Callicoes and the Woollen and Silk Manufacture. 1719.

A Brief Survey of the Legal Liberties of the Dissenters. 1714.

Caledonia. Edinburgh, 1706.

The Candidate: Being a Detection of Bribery and Corruption as It Is Just Now in Practice All Over Great Britain. 1715.

Captain Singleton. 1720. Shakespeare Head edition. Oxford: Blackwell, 1974.

The Case of Dissenters as Affected by the Late Bill Proposed in Parliament for Preventing Occasional Conformity. 1703.

The Case of Mr. Law, Truly Stated, in Answer to a Pamphlet, Entituled A Letter to Mr. Law. 1721.

The Character of the Late Dr. Samuel Annesley. 1697.

Chicken Feed Capons. 1731.

Colonel Jack. 1723. Shakespeare Head edition. Oxford: Blackwell, 1974.

A Collection of Miscellany Letters. 4 vols. 1722, 1727.

A Collection of the Writings of the Author of The True-Born Englishman. 1703.

Commentator. 1 Jan.–16 Sept. 1720.

The Compleat English Gentleman. Edited by Karl D. Bülbring. London: David Nutt, 1890.

The Complete English Tradesman. 1726.

A Condoling Letter to the Tattler: On Account of the Misfortunes of Isaac Bickerstaff, Esq. [1710].

The Conduct of Christians Made the Sport of Infidels. 1717.

The Conduct of Parties in England, More Especially of Those Whigs Who Now Appear Against the New Ministry and a Treaty for Peace. 1712.

The Conduct of Robert Walpole, Esq. 1717.

Conjugal Lewdness. 1727. Edited by Maximillian E. Novak. Gainesville, Fla.: Scholars' Facsimiles & Reprints, 1967.

Considerations in Relation to Trade Considered. [Edinburgh], 1706.

Considerations on the Present State of Affairs in Great Britain. 1718.

Considerations Upon the Eighth and Ninth Articles of the Treaty of Commerce and Navigation. 1713.

The Consolidator. 1705. Edited by Malcolm J. Bosse. New York: Garland, 1972.

A Continuation of Letters Written by a Turkish Spy at Paris. 1718.

Daily Post. 3 Oct. 1719–c. 27 Apr. 1725.

The Danger and Consequences of Disobliging the Clergy. 1717.

The Danger of Court Differences. 1717.

The Danger of the Protestant Religion Consider'd. 1701.

Daniel Defoe's Hymn for the Thanksgiving. 1706.

The Defection Farther Considered. 1718.

A Defence of the Allies. 1712.

A Dialogue Between a Dissenter and the Observator. 1703.

Director. 5 Oct. 1720–16 Jan. 1721.

The Dissenter[s] Misrepresented and Represented. [1704].

The Dissenters Answer to the High-Church Challenge. 1704. In *A Second Volume of the Writings of the Author of The True-Born Englishman.* 1705.

The Dissenters in England Vindicated. [Edinburgh, 1707].

[*Dormer's News Letter.* June 1716–Aug. 1718?]

The Double Welcome: A Poem to the Duke of Marlboro. 1705.

Due Preparations for the Plague as Well for Soul as Body. 1722.

The Dyet of Poland: A Satyr. 1705.

The Dyet of Poland: A Satyr. Consider'd Paragraph by Paragraph. 1705.

An Effectual Scheme for the Immediate Preventing of Street Robberies. 1731.

An Elegy on the Author of The True-Born Englishman. 1704.

An Encomium Upon the Parliament. 1699.

The Englishman's Choice, and True Interest. 1694.

An Enquiry Into Occasional Conformity, Shewing That the Dissenters Are in No Way Concerned in It. 1702.

An Enquiry Into the Danger and Consequences of a War with the Dutch. 1712.

An Enquiry Into the Disposal of the Equivalent. Edinburgh, 1706.

An Enquiry Into the Occasional Conformity of Dissenters, in Cases of Preferment. 1697.

An Enquiry Into the Occasional Conformity of Dissenters Shewing That the Dissenters Are No Way Concern'd in It. 1702. In *A True Collection of the Writings of the Author of The True-Born Englishman.* 1703.

An Enquiry Into the Real Interest of Princes. 1712.

An Essay at a Plain Exposition of That Difficult Phrase A Good Peace. 1711.

An Essay at Removing National Prejudices Against a Union with Scotland, to Be Continued During the Treaty Here. Part I. 1706.

An Essay at Removing National Prejudices Against a Union with Scotland, to Be Continued During the Treaty Here. Part II. 1706.

An Essay, at Removing National Prejudices Against a Union with Scotland, Part III. [Edinburgh], 1706.

An Essay on the History and Reality of Apparitions. 1727.

An Essay on the History of Parties, and Persecution in Britain: Beginning with a Brief Account of the Test-Act and an Historical Enquiry Into the Reasons, the Original and the Consequences of the Occasional Conformity of Dissenters. 1711.

An Essay on the Late Storm. 1704.

An Essay on the Regulation of the Press. 1704. Edited by J. R. Moore. Luttrell Society Reprints, no. 7. Oxford: Blackwell, 1948.

An Essay on the South-Sea Trade. 1711.

An Essay on the Treaty of Commerce with France. 1713.

An Essay Upon Projects. 1697. Menston, Eng.: Scholar, 1969.

An Essay Upon Publick Credit. 1710.

Every-body's Business, Is No-body's Business. 1725.

The Experiment: Or, The Shortest Way with the Dissenters Exemplified. 1705.

An Expostulatory Letter, to the B[ishop] of B[angor]. [1717].

Faction in Power: Or, The Mischiefs and Dangers of a High-Church Magistracy. 1717.

Fair Payment No Spunge. 1717.

The Family Instructor, in Three Parts, with a Recommendatory Letter by the Reverend Mr. S. Wright. Newcastle, 1715.

The Family Instructor, in Three Parts . . . The Second Edition. Corrected by the Author. 1715.

The Family Instructor, in Two Parts. I. Relating to Family Breaches, and Their Obstructing Religious Duties. II. To the Great Mistake of Mixing the Passions in the Managing and Correcting of Children. . . . Vol. II. 1718.

The Farther Adventures of Robinson Crusoe. 1719. Shakespeare Head edition. Oxford: Blackwell, 1974.

The Fears of the Pretender Turn'd Into the Fears of Debauchery. 1715.

The Felonious Treaty. 1711.

A Fifth Essay, at Removing National Prejudices. [Edinburgh], 1607 (for 1707).

The Fortunate Mistress: Or, A History of the Life and Vast Variety of Fortunes of Mademoiselle de Beleau, Afterwards Call'd the Countess de Wintelsheim, in Germany. Being the Person Known by the Name of the Lady Roxana. [1724]. Shakespeare Head edition. Oxford: Blackwell, 1974.

The Fortunes and Misfortunes of the Famous Moll Flanders, &c. 1721. Shakespeare Head edition. Oxford: Blackwell, 1974.

The Four Years Voyages of Capt. George Roberts. 1726.

The Fourth Essay, at Removing National Prejudices. [Edinburgh], 1706.

The Free-holders Plea Against Stock-Jobbing Elections of Parliament Men. 1701.

A Friendly Epistle by Way of Reproof from One of the People Called Quakers. 1715.

A Further Search Into the Conduct of the Allies. 1712.

A General History of Discoveries and Improvements. Oct. 1725–Jan. 1726; 1727.

A General History of the Pyrates. 1724. Edited by Manuel Schonhorn. Columbia: University of South Carolina Press, 1972.

The Great Law of Subordination Consider'd. 1724.

Hannibal at the Gates. 1712.

Hanover or Rome. 1715.

His Majesty's Obligations to the Whigs Plainly Proved. 1715.

An Historical Account of the Bitter Sufferings, and Melancholly Circumstances of the Episcopal Church in Scotland, Under the Barbarous Usage and Bloody Persecution of the Presbyterian Church Government. Edinburgh, 1707.

An Historical Account of the Voyages and Adventures of Sir Walter Raleigh. 1719.

"Historical Collections: Or, Memoirs of Passages Collected from Several Authors." William Andrews Clark Library, UCLA. Manuscript. 1682.

A History of the Clemency of Our English Monarchs. 1717.

The History of the Kentish Petition. 1701.

The History of the Remarkable Life of John Sheppard. [1724].

The History of the Union of Great Britain. Edinburgh, 1709.

The History of the Wars, of His Late Majesty Charles XII. King of Sweden. 1720.

The History of the Wars, of His Present Majesty Charles XII. King of Sweden. 1715.

The Honour and Prerogative of the Queen's Majesty Vindicated and Defended Against the Unexampled Insolence of the Author of the Guardian, in a Letter from a Country Whig to Mr. Steele. 1713.

An Humble Proposal to the People of England, for the Encrease of Their Trade, and Encouragement of Their Manufactures. 1729.

A Hymn to Peace. 1706.

A Hymn to the Pillory. 1703. In *The Shortest Way with the Dissenters and Other Pamphlets.* Shakespeare Head edition. Oxford: Blackwell, 1974.

A Hymn to Victory. 1704.

The Immorality of the Priesthood. 1715.

An Impartial Enquiry Into the Conduct of the Right Honourable Charles Lord Viscount T[ownshend]. 1717.

An Impartial History of the Life and Actions of Peter Alexowitz, the Present Czar of Muscovy. 1723.

Instructions from Rome, in Favour of the Pretender. [1710].

A Journal of the Earl of Marr's Proceedings. [1716].

A Journal of the Plague Year. 1722. Shakespeare Head edition. Oxford: Blackwell, 1974.

A Journeye to the World in the Moon. [1705].

Jure Divino: A Satyr in Twelve Books. 1706.

The Just Complaint of the Poor Weavers. 1719.

The Justice and Necessity of Restraining the Clergy. 1715.

A Justification of the Dutch. 1712.

The King of Pirates. 1712. Vol. 8 of *The Works of Daniel Defoe,* edited by G. H. Maynadier. Boston: Brainard, 1904.

The Layman's Sermon Upon the Late Storm. 1704.

The Layman's Vindication of the Church of England. 1716.

Legion's Humble Address to the Lords. [1704].

Legion's Memorial. [1701].

Legion's New Paper. 1702.

A Letter from a Dissenter in the City to a Dissenter in the Country, Advising Him to a Quiet and Peaceable Behaviour in This Present Conjuncture. 1710.

A Letter from a Member of the House of Commons. 1713.

A Letter from Mr. Reason. [Edinburgh, 1706].

A Letter from One Clergyman to Another. 1716.

A Letter from Some Protestant Dissenting Laymen. 1718.

A Letter from the Man in the Moon. [1705].

A Letter to a Dissenter from His Friend at the Hague, Concerning the Penal Laws and the Test. [1688].

A Letter to a Merry Young Gentleman. 1715.

A Letter to Mr. How. 1701.

A Letter to Mr. Steele. 1714.

A Letter to the Author of the Flying-Post. 1718.

A Letter to the Dissenters. 1713, 1714.

A Letter to the Dissenters. 1719.

The Letters of Daniel Defoe. Edited by George H. Healey. 1955. Oxford: Clarendon Press, 1969.

The Life and Strange, Surprising Adventures of Robinson Crusoe. 1719.

The Life of Jonathan Wild. 1725.

The Livery Man's Reasons, Why He Did Not Give His Vote for a Certain Gentleman Either to Be Lord Mayor, or Parliament Man for the City of London. 1701.

Manufacturer. 13 Oct. 1719–17 Feb. 1720. Introduced by Robert N. Gosselink. Delmar, N.Y.: Scholars' Facsimiles & Reprints, 1978.

The Master Mercury. Introduced by Frank Ellis and Henry Snyder. ARS no. 184. Los Angeles: Clark Library, 1977.

"Meditaçons." Huntington Library. Manuscript. 1681.

The Meditations of Daniel Defoe Now First Published. Edited by George Harris Healey. Cummington, Mass.: Cummington, 1946.

Memoirs of a Cavalier. [1720]. Shakespeare Head edition. Oxford: Blackwell, 1974.

The Memoirs of an English Officer. 1728. In *Memoirs of an English Officer and Two Other Short Novels.* Introduced by J. T. Boulton. London: Gollancz, 1970.

Memoirs of Count Tariff, &c. 1713.

Memoirs of John, Duke of Melfort. 1714.

The Memoirs of Majr. Alexander Ramkins. 1719. In *Memoirs of an English Officer and Two Other Short Novels.* Introduced by J. T. Boulton. London: Gollancz, 1970.

Memoirs of Publick Transactions in the Life and Ministry of His Grace the D. of Shrewsbury. 1718.

Memoirs of Some Transactions During the Late Ministry of Robert, E. of Oxford. 1717.

Memoirs of the Church of Scotland. 1717.

Memoirs of the Conduct of Her Late Majesty and Her Last Ministry. 1715.

Memoirs of the Life and Eminent Conduct of That Learned and Reverend Divine, Daniel Williams, D.D. 1718.

A Memorial to the Nobility of Scotland, Who Are to Assemble in Order to Choose the Sitting Peers for the Parliament of Great Britain. Edinburgh, 1708.

Mercator: Or, Commerce Retrieved. 26 May 1713–20 July 1714.

Mercurius Brittanicus. Jan. 1718–March 1719.

Mercurius Politicus. May 1716–Oct. 1720.

Minutes of the Negotiations of Monsr. Mesnager. 1717.

The Mock-Mourners: A Satyr. 1702.

A Modest Vindication of the Present Ministry. 1707.

More Reformation: A Satyr Upon Himself, by the Author of The True-Born Englishman. 1703.

More Short Ways with the Dissenters. 1704.

A Narrative of All the Robberies, Escapes, &c of John Sheppard. 1724. In Vol. 16 of *Romances and Narratives by Daniel Defoe,* edited by George A. Aitken. London: Dent, 1905.

A New Discovery of an Old Intreague. 1691.

A New Family Instructor. 1727.

A New Map of the Laborious and Painful Travels of Our Blessed High Church Apostle. 1710.

A New Test of the Church of England's Honesty. 1704.

A New Test of the Church of England's Loyalty. 1702.

A New Test of the Sence of the Nation. 1710.

No Queen, or No General. 1712.

Novels and Selected Writings. 2d ed. Shakespeare Head edition. Oxford: Blackwell, 1974.

Observations on the Fifth Article of the Treaty of Union. [Edinburgh, 1706].

Of Royall Education: A Fragmentary Treatise. Edited by Karl D. Bülbring. London: Nutt, 1985.

On the Fight at Ramellies. Review 3 (1706): 242–44.

The Original Power of the Collective Body of the People of England. 1702.

Original Weekly Journal (later called *Applebee's Original Weekly Journal*). 25 June 1720–14 May 1726 (and occasionally thereafter).

The Pacifactor: A Poem. 1700.

Parochial Tyranny. [1727].

Passion and Prejudice. Edinburgh, 1707.

Peace, or Poverty. 1712.

Peace Without Union. 1703.

The Pernicious Consequences of the Clergy's Intermeddling with Affairs of State. [1714?].

"The Petition of Dorothy Distaff." *Mercurius Politicus,* Dec. 1719.

A Plan of the English Commerce. 1728, 1730. Shakespeare Head edition. Oxford: Blackwell, 1974.

The Political History of the Devil. 1726.

The Poor Man's Plea. 1698.

Preface to *De Laune's Plea for the Non-Conformists.* 1706.

Preface to *De Laune's Plea for the Non-Conformists.* In *Dr. Sacheverell's Recantation.* 1709.

The Present Negotiations of Peace Vindicated. 1712.

The Present State of Jacobitism Considered. 1701.

The Present State of the Parties in Great Britain. 1712.

The Protestant Jubilee. 1714.

The Protestant Monastery. 1727.

The Quarrel of the School-Boys at Athens. 1717.

Queries Upon the Bill Against Occasional Conformity. [1704].

The Question Fairly Stated, Whether Now Is Not the Time to Do Justice to the

Friends of the Government as Well as to Its Enemies? 1717.

Reasons Against a War with France. 1701.

Reasons Against Fighting: Being an Enquiry Into This Great Debate, Whether It Is Safe for Her Majesty, or Her Ministry, to Venture an Engagement with the French. 1712.

Reasons Against the Succession of the House of Hanover. 1713.

Reasons for a Peace: Or, The War at an End. 1711.

Reasons for Im[peaching] the L[or]d H[igh] T[reasure]r. [1714].

Reasons Why a Party Among Us, and Also Among the Confederates, Are Obstinately Bent Against a Treaty of Peace with the French at This Time. 1711.

Reasons Why This Nation Ought to Put a Speedy End to This Expensive War. 1711.

Reflections Upon the Late Great Revolution. 1689.

Reformation of Manners. 1702.

Religious Courtship. 1722.

Remarks on the Bill to Prevent Frauds Committed by Bankrupts. 1706.

Remarks on the Speeches of William Paul Clerk, and John Hall. 1716.

The Remedy Worse Than the Disease. 1714.

A Reply to a Pamphlet Entituled, the L[or]d H[aversham]'s Vindication. 1706.

A Reply to a Traiterous Libel Entituled English Advice to the Freeholders of Great Britain. 1715.

A Reply to the Remarks Upon the Lord Bishop of Bangor's Treatment of the Clergy and Convocation. 1717.

The Representation Examined: Being Remarks on the State of Religion in England. 1711.

The Reproof to Mr. Clark, and a Brief Vindication of Mr. De Foe. [Edinburgh, 1710].

A Re-Representation: Or, A Modest Search After the Great PLUNDERERS of the NATION. 1711.

Resignacion. 1708. In Frank Ellis, "Defoe's 'Resignacion' and the Limitations of Mathematical Plainness." 1985.

Review. 9 vols. 19 Feb. 1704–11 June 1713. Edited by A. W. Secord. 22 vols. New York: Columbia University Press, 1938.

The Royal Progress: Or, A Historical View of the Journeys or Progresses, Which Several Great Princes Have Made to Visit Their Dominions. 1724.

Royal Religion: Being Some Enquiry After the Piety of Princes. 1704.

The Scot's Narrative Examin'd. 1709.

The Scots Nation and Union Vindicated; from the Reflections Cast on Them, in an Infamous Libel, Entitl'd the Publick Spirit of the Whigs. 1714.

A Scots Poem: Or, A New-Years Gift, from a Native of the Universe, to His Fellow-Animals in Albania. Edinburgh, 1707.

A Seasonable Warning and Caution Against the Insinuations of Papists and Jacobites. 1712.

A Second and More Strange Voyage to the World in the Moon. [1705].

Second Thoughts Are Best: Or, A Further Improvement of a Late Scheme to Prevent Street Robberies. 1729.

A Second Volume of the Writings of the Author of The True-Born Englishman. 1705.

The Secret History of the October Club. 1711.

The Secret History of the October Club. . . . Part II. 1711.

The Secret History of State Intrigues. 1715.

The Secret History of the Scepter. 1715.

The Secret History of the Secret History of the White Staff. 1715.

The Secret History of the White Staff. . . . [Pt. I.] 1714.

The Secret History of the White Staff. . . . Pt. II. 1714.

The Secret History of the White Staff. . . . Pt. III. 1715.

Secret Memoirs of a Treasonable Conference at S[omerset] House. 1717.

Secret Memoirs of the New Treaty of Alliance with France. 1716.

A Serious Inquiry Into This Grand Question, Whether a Law to Prevent the Occasional Conformity of Dissenters Would Not Be Inconsistent with the Act of Toleration. 1704.

Serious Reflections During the Life and Surprising Adventures of Robinson Crusoe, with His Vision of the Angelick World. 1720. Vol. 3 of *The Works of Daniel Defoe,* edited by G. H. Maynadier. New York: Crowell, 1903.

A Short Letter to the Glasgow-men. [Edinburgh, 1706].

A Short Narrative of the Life and Actions of His Grace John, D. of Marlborough. 1711.

A Short View of the Present State of the Protestant Religion. Edinburgh, 1707.

The Shortest Way to Peace and Union. 1703.

The Shortest Way with the Dissenters: Or, Proposals for the Establishment of the Church. 1702. In *The Shortest Way with the Dissenters.* Shakespeare Head edition. Oxford: Blackwell, 1974.

The Sincerity of the Dissenters Vindicated. 1703.

The Six Distinguishing Characters of a Parliament-Man. 1700.

Some Considerations on a Law for Triennial Parliaments. 1716.

Some Considerations on the Reasonableness and Necessity of Encreasing and Encouraging the Seamen. 1728.

Some Considerations Upon Street-Walkers. [1726].

Some Methods to Supply the Defects of the Late Peace. [1715].

Some Persons Vindicated Against the Author of the Defection. 1718.

Some Reasons Offered by the Late Ministry in Defence of Their Administration. 1715.

Some Reflections on a Pamphlet Lately Publish'd Entitl'd An Argument Shewing That a Standing Army Is Inconsistent with a Free Government. 1697.

Some Remarks on the First Chapter in Dr. Davenant's Essays. 1703.

Some Thoughts of an Honest Tory in the Country. 1716.

Some Thoughts Upon the Subject of Commerce with France. 1713.

The Spanish Descent. 1702.

[*A Speech of a Stone Chimney-Piece*]. [1711].

A Speech Without Doors. 1710.

The Storm: Or, A Collection of the Most Remarkable Casualties and Disasters Which Happen'd in the Late Dreadful Tempest, Both by Sea and Land. 1704.

Street-Robberies Consider'd. [1728].

A Strict Enquiry Into the Circumstances of a Late Duel. 1713.

Strike While the Iron's Hot: Or, Now Is the Time to Be Happy. 1715.

The Succession of Spain, Considered. 1711.

The Succession to the Crown of England, Considered. 1701.

A Supplement to the Faults on Both Sides. 1710.

A System of Magick. 1727.

"To the Athenian Society." In *The History of the Athenian Society,* by Charles Gildon. [1692].

To the Honourable, the C——s of England Assembled in P——t. 1704.

A Tour thro' the Whole Island of Great Britain. 1724–27. Introduction by G.D.H. Cole. 2 vols. New York: Kelley, 1968.

The Trade of Britain Stated. [Edinburgh, 1707].

The Trade of Scotland with France, Consider'd. 1713.

The Trade to India Critically and Calmly Consider'd. 1720.

Treason Detected, in an Answer to That Traiterous and Malicious Libel, Entitled English Advice to the Freeholders of England. 1715.

A True Account of the Proceedings at Perth. 1716.

The True and Genuine Account of the Life and Actions of the Late Jonathan Wild. 1725. In vol. 16 of *Romances and Narratives by Daniel Defoe,* edited by George A. Aitken. London: Dent, 1905.

The True-Born Englishman. 1700.

The True-Born Englishman. Rev. ed. 1716.

A True Collection of the Writings of the Author of The True-Born Englishman. 1703.

A True Relation of the Apparition of One Mrs. Veal. 1706.

A True State of the Contracts Relating to the Third Money-Subscription Taken by the South-Sea Company. 1721.

A True State of the Difference Between Sir George Rook, Knt., and William Colepeper, Esq. 1704.

"Truth and Honesty." *London Post.* 1705.

Two Great Questions Considered. [Edinburgh], 1707.

Union and No Union. 1713.

Universal Spectator and Weekly Journal. 12 Oct. 1728.

Unparallel'd Cruelty. 1726.

The Validity of the Renunciations of Former Powers. 1712.

A View of the Scots Rebellion. 1715.

The Villainy of Stock-Jobbers Detected. 1701.

A Vindication of Dr. Snape. [1717].

A Vindication of the Honour and Justice of Parliament. [1721].

A Vindication of the Press. 1718.

The Vision: A Poem. [Edinburgh, 1706].

The Weakest Go to the Wall. 1714.

Weekly-Journal: or Saturday's Evening Post. (*Mist's Weekly-Journal*). c. Feb. 1717–24 Oct. 1724.

What If the Swedes Should Come? 1717.

White-Hall Evening Post. 18 Sept. 1718–c. 14 Oct. 1720.

Wise as Serpents. 1712.

A Word to the Reader

Robinson Crusoe is a troubling book because it is an honest one. In it, Daniel Defoe faithfully re-creates the violence and injustices of the seventeenth and eighteenth centuries. It was a time when the plague swept repeatedly through nations, leaving millions of corpses behind; it was a time when men, women, and children could be forced from their homes and sold into slavery; it was a time when thousands of women died in childbirth, when only one in three children survived to adulthood, when the majority of men lived, and died, on battlefields. It was a time when people faced the realities of life daily.

Sadly, many people today, particularly among the media, perceive Christians as being unwilling or unable to accept these realities. They believe that we deliberately close ourselves off from the world's ugliness, thinking that if we don't know it's there, it won't affect us. But if Christians really believed this, we would not read our Bibles. After all, the Scriptures cover a particularly bloody period in human history, and biblical writers didn't sugarcoat or shy away from discussing topics such as wars, slavery, idolatry, cannibalism, adultery, pride, incest, and treachery. They realized that God gave us minds capable of dealing with life in a fallen world, because God knows that is how we will be able to grow in compassion and wisdom. Our consciences are not V-chips that block evil from our too-impressionable souls; rather, they are divine prisms through which we are to discern good from bad, truth from lies.

It is no coincidence that many great Christians were worldly in the sense of being well educated and well read—for example, Moses, Daniel, Paul, Augustine, Luther, Bonhoeffer, C. S. Lewis. They knew what life could offer—the good and the bad—so when they chose to serve God and His ways, their decisions were well informed: They understood exactly what they were doing. These saints of the church would recognize that if one would truly understand a classic work of literature, it is essential to first understand the world in which the author wrote it, for no human being writes in a vacuum: We are all products of our age.

With that in mind, the educated Christian will wish to read *Robinson*

Crusoe side by side with history books dealing with the seventeenth and eighteenth centuries. Slavery? Americans practiced it for a quarter of a millennium, and in some ways, we're still feeling the repercussions of it. Cannibalism? We need to go no further back than the Donner party to find its American counterpart.

We live in a fallen world, and if we are to have a positive impact on it, we must first understand how it works. Books such as *Robinson Crusoe* provide powerful vehicles for helping us do just that.

JLW

Chapter 1

My Father's Advice and My Obstinacy

I was born in the year 1632, in the city of York, of a good family, though not of that country, my father being a foreigner, of Bremen, who settled first at Hull. He got a good estate by merchandise and, leaving off his trade, lived afterward at York; in which place he had married my mother, whose relations were named Robinson, a very good family in that country and from whom I was called Robinson Kreutznaer; but, by the usual corruption of words in England, we are now called—nay, we call ourselves and write our name—Crusoe; and so my companions always called me.

I had two elder brothers, one of whom was lieutenant colonel to an English regiment of infantry in Flanders, formerly commanded by the famous Colonel Lockhart, and who was killed at the battle near Dunkirk against the Spaniards. What became of my second brother I never knew, any more than my father or mother would know what became of me.

My Father's Advice

Being the third son of the family and not bred to any trade, my head began to be filled very early with rambling thoughts. My father, who was very aged, had given me a competent share of learning, as far as house education and a country free school generally go, and designed me for the law. But

I would be satisfied with nothing but going to sea; and my inclination to this led me so strongly against the will—nay, the commands—of my father, and against all the entreaties and persuasions of my mother and other friends, that there seemed to be something fatal in that strong inclination of nature, tending directly to the life of misery that was to befall me.

My father, a wise and grave man, gave me serious and excellent counsel against what he foresaw was my design. He called me one morning into his bedroom, where he was confined by the gout, and expostulated very warmly with me upon this subject. He asked me what reasons, more than a mere wandering inclination, I had for leaving my father's house and my native country, where I might be well introduced, and had a prospect of raising my fortune by application and industry, to a life of ease and pleasure. He told me it was men of desperate fortunes on one hand, or of aspiring, superior fortunes on the other, who went abroad upon adventures, to rise by enterprise and make themselves famous in undertakings of a nature out of the ordinary; that these things were all either too far above me or too far below me; that mine was the middle state, or what might be called the upper station of low life, which he had found by long experience was the best state in the world, the most suited to human happiness, not exposed to the miseries and hardships, the labor and sufferings, of those who worked with their hands, and not embarrassed with the pride, luxury, ambition, and envy of the upper part of mankind. He told me I might judge of the happiness of this state by this one thing: namely, that this was the state of life which all other people envied; that kings have frequently lamented the miserable consequences of being born to great things and wished they had been placed in the middle of two extremes, between the lowly and the great; that the wise man gave his testimony to this, as the just standard of true happiness, when he prayed to have neither poverty nor riches.

He bade me observe it and said I should always find that the calamities of life were shared among the upper and lower parts of mankind, but that the middle station had the fewest disasters and was not exposed to so many vicissitudes as the higher or lower parts of mankind. Nay, they were not subjected to so many derangements and uneasiness, either of body or mind, as those were who, by vicious living, luxury, and extravagances on one hand, or by hard labor, want of necessaries, and inferior or insufficient diet on the other hand, bring disorders upon themselves by the natural consequences of their way of living. Also, that the middle station of life was calculated for all kinds of virtues and all kinds of enjoyments; that peace and plenty were the handmaids of a middle fortune; that temperance, moderation, quietness, health, society, all agreeable diversions, and all desirable pleasures were the blessings attending the middle station of life. That this way men went silently and smoothly through the world and comfortably out of it, not embarrassed with the labors of the hands or of the head, not sold to a life of slavery for daily bread, nor harassed with perplexed circumstances, which rob the soul of peace and the body of rest; nor inflamed with the passion of envy, or the secret burning lust of ambition for great things; but, in easy circumstances, sliding gently through the world and wisely tasting the sweets of living without the bitter; feeling that they are happy and learning by every day's experience to know it more sensibly.

After this he pressed me earnestly, and in the most affectionate manner, not to play the fool, nor to throw myself headlong into miseries that nature, and the station of life I was born in, seemed to have provided against; that I was under no necessity of seeking my bread; that he would do well for me and endeavor to enter me fairly into the station of life that he had just been recommending to me; that if I was not very easy and happy in the world, it must be my mere fate or fault that must hinder it and that he should have nothing to answer for, having thus discharged his duty in warning me against measures that he knew would be to my hurt. In a word, that as he would do very kind things for me, if I would just stay and settle at home as he directed, so he would not have so much hand in my misfortunes as to give me any encouragement to go away. And in concluding, he told me I had my elder brother for an example, to whom he had used the same earnest persuasions to keep him from going into the Low Country wars, but could not prevail, his young desires prompting him to run off to the army, where he was killed. And though he said he would not cease to pray for me, yet he would venture to say to me that if I *did* take this foolish step, God would not bless me, and I should have leisure hereafter to reflect upon having disregarded his counsel, when there might be none to assist in my recovery.

I observed in this last part of his discourse, which was truly prophetic—though I suppose my father did not know it to be so himself—the tears running plentifully down his face, especially when he spoke of my brother who was killed; and that when he spoke of my having leisure to repent and none to assist me, he was so moved that he broke off the discourse and told me his heart was so full he could say no more to me.

I was sincerely affected with this discourse—as indeed who could be otherwise?—and I resolved not to think of going abroad anymore, but to settle at home according to my father's wishes. But, alas, a few days wore it all off; and, in short, to prevent any of my father's further urgent requests, a few weeks afterward I resolved to run away from him. However, I did not act quite so hastily as the first heat of my resolution prompted me to, but I spoke to my mother at a time when I thought her a little more pleasant than usual, and told her that my thoughts were so entirely bent upon seeing the world that I should never settle to anything with resolution enough to go through with it, and my father had better give me his consent rather than force me to go without it. That I was now eighteen years old, which was too late to be apprenticed to a trade, or offered as clerk to an attorney; that I was sure, if I did, I should never serve out my time, but I should certainly run away from my master before my time was out and go to sea. That if she would just ask my father to let me go on *one* voyage abroad, if I came home again and hadn't liked it, I would leave no more, and I would promise, by working with double diligence, to recover the time I had lost.

This put my mother into a great quandary. She told me she knew it would be of no avail to speak to my father upon any such subject; that he knew too well what was in my best interests to give his consent to such a thing—and that she wondered how I could think of doing it after the talk I had had with my father, especially with the kind and tender counsel she knew my father had expressed to me; and that, in short, if I was determined to ruin myself, there was no help for me; but one thing was for sure: I should never have their consent to it. As for her part, she would never participate in my destruction, and I should never be able to say that my mother was willing when my father was not.

Though my mother refused to propose it to my father, yet I heard afterward that she reported all the discourse to him, and that my father, after showing great concern, said to her with a sigh: "That boy might be happy if he would stay at home; but if he goes abroad, he will be the most miserable wretch that ever was born—I can give no consent to it."

It was not till almost a year after this that I broke loose, though, in the meantime, I continued obstinately deaf to all proposals of settling down to business and frequently argued with my father and mother about their being so positively determined against what they knew my inclinations prompted me to. But being one day at Hull, where I went casually and without any purpose of running away at that time—I say "being there," because one of my companions was going by sea to London in his father's ship, and he prompted me to go with him, with the common allurement of a seafaring man that it should cost me nothing for my passage—I consulted neither Father nor Mother anymore, nor so much as sent them word of it. But leaving them to hear of it as they might, without asking God's blessing or my father's, without any consideration of circumstances or consequences, and in an unlucky hour, God knows, on the first of September 1651 I went on board a ship bound for London. Never any young adventurer's misfortunes, I believe, began sooner or continued longer than mine. The ship was no sooner got out of the Humber than the wind began to blow and the sea to rise in a most frightful manner; and, as I had never been at sea before, I was most inexpressibly sick in body and terrified in mind. I began now to seriously reflect upon what I had done and how justly I was overtaken by the judgment of Heaven for wickedly leaving my father's house and abandoning my duty. All the good counsels of my parents, my father's tears, and my mother's entreaties came now fresh into mind; and my conscience, which was not yet come to the pitch of hardness to which it has come since, reproached me for my contempt of advice and the breach of duty to my God and my father.

All this while, the storm increased and the waves grew very high, though nothing like what I have seen many times since; no, nor even what I saw a few days afterward; but it was enough to affect me then, being but a young sailor and never having known anything like it. I expected each wave to swallow us up, and every time the ship dropped down, as I thought it did, in the trough or hollow of the sea, I expected we should never rise more. In this agony of mind, I made many vows and resolutions: that if it would please God to spare my life in this one voyage, if ever I once got my foot upon dry land again, I would go directly home to my father and never set foot on ship again as long as I lived; that I would take his advice and never get myself into such miseries as these anymore. Now I saw plainly the wisdom of his observations about the middle station of life, how easy, how comfortably, he had lived all his days, never having been exposed to tempests at sea or troubles on shore. In short, I resolved that I would, like a true repenting prodigal, go home to my father.

After the Storm

These wise and sober thoughts continued as long as the storm lasted, and indeed some time after; but the next day, the wind was abated, the sea became calmer, and I began to be a little inured to it. However, I was very serious all that day, also still being a little seasick; but toward night, the weather cleared up, the wind died down, and a charming fine evening followed. The sun went down perfectly clear and rose so the next morning; and having little or no wind and a smooth sea, the sun shining upon it, the sight was, I thought, the most delightful that I had ever seen.

I had slept well in the night and was now no more seasick, but very cheerful, looking with wonder upon the sea that was so rough and terrible the day before and could be so calm and so pleasant in so little a time after. And now, lest my good resolutions should continue, my companion who had enticed me away came to me.

"Well, Bob," said he, clapping me upon the shoulder, "how are you doing? I'll warrant you were frightened, weren't you, last night, when it blew but a capful of wind?"

"A capful d'you call it?" said I. "'Twas a terrible storm."

"A storm, you fool you!" replied he. "Do you call that a storm? Why, it was nothing at all. Give us but a good ship and sea room, and we think nothing of such a squall of wind as that; but you're only a freshwater sailor, Bob. Come, let us make a bowl of punch, and we'll forget all that. D'ye see what charming weather 'tis now?"

To make short this sad part of my story, we went the way of all sailors. The punch was made, and I was made half drunk with it; and in that one night's wickedness, I drowned all my repentance, all my reflections upon my past conduct, all my resolutions for the future. In a word, as the sea was returned to its smoothness of surface and settled calmness by the abatement of that storm, so the urgent demands of my thoughts being over, my fears and apprehensions of being swallowed up by the sea being forgotten, and the current of my former desires returned, I entirely forgot the vows and promises that I made in my distress. I found, indeed, some intervals of reflection; and the serious thoughts did, as it were, endeavor to return again sometimes; but I shook them off and roused myself from them as it were from a fever, and applying myself to drinking and company, I soon mastered the return of those fits—for so I called them—and had, in five or six days, got as complete a victory over my conscience as any young fellow that resolved not to be troubled with it could desire. But I was yet to have another trial, for Providence, as in such cases it generally does, resolved to leave me entirely without excuse. For if I would not take *this* for a deliverance, the next was to be such a one as the worst and most hardened wretch among us would confess both the danger and the mercy.

The Storm in Yarmouth Roads

The sixth day of our being at sea, we came into Yarmouth Roads. The wind having been contrary and the weather calm, we had made but little way since the storm. Here we were obliged to come to an anchor, and here we lay, the wind continuing contrary, namely, at southwest, for seven or eight days, during which time a great many ships from Newcastle came into the same Roads, as the common harbor where the ships might wait for a wind for the river.

We had not, however, ridden here so long that we shouldn't have drifted up the river with the tide, but the wind blew too fresh; and, after we had lain four or five days, it blew very hard. However, the Roads being reckoned as good as harbor, the anchorage good, and our ground tackle very strong, our men were unconcerned and not in the least apprehensive of danger, but spent the time in rest and mirth, after the manner of the sea. But the eighth day, in the morning, the wind increased, and we had all hands at work to strike our topmasts and make everything snug and close, so that the ship might ride as easy as possible. By noon the waves towered high indeed, and our ship rode with the bow under water, shipped several seas, and we thought once or twice our anchor had come loose; upon which our master ordered out the sheet anchor, so that we rode with two anchors ahead and the cables veered out to their utmost length.

By this time, it blew a terrible storm indeed; and now I began to see terror and amazement even in the faces of the seamen. The master, though vigilant in the business of preserving the ship, as he went in and out of his cabin by me, I could hear him softly say to himself several times, "Lord, be merciful to us! We shall be all lost! We shall be all undone!" and the like. During these first actions, I was insensible, lying still in my cabin, which was in the steerage, and could not sort out my feelings. I could scarcely resume the first penitence, which I had so apparently trampled upon and hardened myself against. I had thought the threat of death had passed, and that this would be nothing to worry about, as was the first; but when the master himself came by me, as I said just now, and said we should all be lost, I was dreadfully frightened. I got up out of my cabin and looked out. Such a dreadful sight I had never seen: The sea ran mountains high and broke upon us every three or four minutes. When I could look about, I could see nothing but distress around us. Two ships that rode near us, we found, had cut their masts by the board, being deep-laden; and our men cried out that a ship which rode about a mile ahead of us was foundering. Two more ships, being driven from their anchors, were run out of the Roads to sea, completely helpless, with not a mast standing. The light ships fared the best, not laboring so much in the sea; but two or three of them drove and came close by us, running away with only their sprit-sails out before the wind.

Toward evening, the mate and boatswain begged the master of our ship to let them cut away the foremast, which he was very unwilling to do; but when the boatswain protested to him that if he did not, the ship would founder, he consented. When they had cut away the foremast, the mainmast stood so loose and shook the ship so much that they were obliged to cut that away also and make a clear deck.

And one must judge what a condition I must be in at all this, who was but a young sailor and who had never been so terrified before. But if I can express at this distance the thoughts I had at that time, I was in tenfold more horror of mind upon account of my former convictions, and having wickedly rejected my resolutions, than I was at death itself; and these, added to the terror of the storm, put me into such a condition that I can by no words describe it.

But the worst was yet to come. The storm continued with such fury that the seamen themselves acknowledged they had never seen a worse one. We had a good ship, but she was deep-laden and wallowed in the sea, so that the seamen every now and then cried out that she would founder. It was my advantage, in one respect, that I did not know what they meant by *founder*, till I inquired. However, the storm was so violent that I saw what is not often seen: the master, the boatswain, and some others more knowledgeable than the rest, at their prayers and expecting every moment that the ship would go to the bottom.

In the middle of the night, adding even more to our distress, one of the men who had gone down to inspect cried out that we had sprung a leak; another said there was four feet of water in the hold! Then all hands were called to the pump. At that word, my heart, as I thought, died within me; and I fell backward upon the side of my bed, where I had been sitting, into the cabin. However, the men roused me and told me that I, who had been unable to do anything before, was as able to pump as another; at which I recovered, went to the pump, and worked very heartily. While this was going on, the master, seeing some light coal barges that, not able to ride out the storm, were obliged to slip and run away to the sea, and were not far from us, ordered a gun fired as a signal of distress. I, not knowing what that meant, thought the ship had broken or some dreadful thing had happened. In a word, I was so surprised that I fell down in a swoon. As this was a time when everybody had his own life to think of, nobody noticed me or what had become of me; but another man quickly stepped up to the pump and, thrusting me aside with his foot, let me lie, thinking I had been dead—it was a great while before I came to myself.

We worked on, but the water increasing in the hold, it was apparent that the ship would founder. The storm began to abate a little, yet, as it was not possible the ship could stay afloat long enough to get us into a port, the master continued firing guns for help; and a light ship, which had ridden it out just ahead of us, ventured a boat out to help us. It was with the utmost

danger that the boat came near us; but it was impossible for us to either get on board or for the boat to safely remain near the ship's side. At last, with the men rowing very heartily and risking their lives to save ours, our men cast them a rope over the stern with a buoy to it and then veered it out a great length, which they, after much labor and hazard, took hold of, and we hauled them close under our stern, and then all of us got into their boat. It served no purpose for them or us, after we were in the boat, to even think of reaching their own ship; so all agreed to let her drift and only to pull her in toward shore as much as we could. Our master promised them that if the boat were smashed in upon reaching the shore, he would make it good to their master—so partly rowing and partly driving, our boat went away to the northward, sloping toward the shore almost as far as Winterton Ness.

We were not much more than a quarter of an hour out from our ship when we saw her sink, and then I understood for the first time what was meant by a ship *foundering* in the sea. I must acknowledge I didn't even want to look when the seamen told me she was sinking; for from the moment that they shoved me into the boat—for I didn't really know what I was doing—my heart was, as it were, dead within me: partly with fright, partly with horror of mind, and partly from dread of what was yet before me.

While we were in this condition, the men yet laboring at the oar to bring the boat near the shore, we could see (when, our boat mounting the waves, we were able to see the shore) a great many people running along the strand to assist us when we should come near; but we made slow progress toward the shore; nor were we able to reach the shore till, being past the lighthouse at Winterton, the shore fell off to the westward, toward Cromer, and so the land cut off a little the violence of the wind. Here we got in and, though not without much difficulty, got all safe on shore and walked afterward on foot to Yarmouth, where, as unfortunate men, we were treated with great kindness, both by the magistrates of the town, who assigned us good quarters, and by individual merchants and owners of ships; we also had money given us sufficient to carry us either to London or back to Hull, as we thought fit.

My Obstinacy

Had I now had the sense to have gone back to Hull and gone home, I would have been happy; and my father, an emblem of our blessed Savior's parable, would have even killed the fatted calf for me. For hearing that the ship I went away in broke apart in Yarmouth Roads, it was a great while before he had any assurances that I had not drowned.

But my unlucky fate pushed me on now with an obstinacy that nothing could resist; and though I had several loud demands from my reason and my better judgment to go home, yet I was powerless to do it. I know not what to call this, nor will I urge that it is a secret overruling decree that hurries us on to be the instruments of our own destruction, even though it be before us, and that we rush upon it with our eyes open. Certainly, nothing but some unavoidable misery decreed for me, and which it was impossible for me to escape, could have pushed me forward against the calm reasonings and persuasions of my most inward thoughts, and especially against two such visible obstructions as I had met with in my first attempt.

My comrade, who had helped to harden me before, and who was the master's son, was now less determined than I. The first time he spoke to me after we were at Yarmouth, which was not till two or three days had passed, for we were sent to separate quarters—I say, the first time he saw me, it appeared his tone was altered; and looking very melancholy and shaking his head, he asked me how I was doing—and telling his father who I was and how I had come on this voyage only for a trial before traveling farther abroad, his father turned to me with a very grave and concerned tone.

"Young man," said he, "you ought never to go to sea anymore. You ought to take this for a plain and visible token that you are not to be a seafaring man."

"Why, sir," said I, "will you go to sea no more?"

"That is another case," said he. "It is my calling and therefore my duty; but as you made this voyage for a trial, you see what a taste Heaven has given you of what you are to expect if you persist. Perhaps this has all befallen us on your account, like Jonah in the ship of Tarshish. Pray tell," he continued, "what are you, and on what account did you go to sea?"

Upon that, I told him some of my story; at the end of which, he burst out into a strange kind of passion.

"What have I *done*," said he, "that such an unhappy wretch should come into my ship? I would not set my foot in the same ship with you again for a thousand pounds!"

This indeed was, as I said, clear evidence of his feelings, which were yet depressed by the sense of his loss; but further than that he had no authority to go. However, he afterward talked very gravely to me, urging me to go back to my father and not tempt Providence to my ruin; telling me I might see a visible hand of Heaven against me.

"And, young man," said he, "depend upon it, if you do not go back, wherever you go, you will meet with nothing but disasters and disappointments, till your father's words are fulfilled upon you."

We parted soon after, for I made him little answer, and I saw him no more; which way he went I know not. As for me, having some money in my pocket, I traveled to London by land; and there, as well as on the road, had many struggles with myself in terms of what course of life I should take, and whether I should go home or go to sea.

As to going home, shame opposed my better judgment; and it immediately occurred to me that I would be laughed at among the neighbors and should be ashamed to see, not my father and mother only, but everybody else as well. From this source, I have often since observed how incongruous and irrational the common response of mankind is, especially of youth, to that reason which ought to guide them in such cases, namely, that they are not ashamed to sin and yet are ashamed to repent; not ashamed of the action for which they ought justly to be esteemed fools, but are ashamed of the returning that only can make them be esteemed as wise men.

In this state of life, however, I remained some time, uncertain what measures to take and what course of life to lead. An irresistible reluctance continued to keep me from going home; and as I stayed awhile, the remembrance of the distress I had been in wore off; and as that abated, the little inclination I had to return wore off, till at last I quite laid aside any thoughts of it and started looking around for a voyage.

Chapter 2

Escape from the Moors

That evil influence which carried me first away from my father's house, which instilled within me the wild and undigested notion of making my fortune, and which so forcibly impressed those conceits upon me as to make me deaf to all good advice and to the entreaties and even the commands of my father—I say, the same influence, whatever it was, presented the most unfortunate of all enterprises to my view. Thus I went on board a vessel bound to the coast of Africa; or, as our sailors vulgarly call it, a "voyage to Guinea."[1]

It was my great misfortune that in all these adventures, I did not ship myself as a sailor; when, though I might indeed have worked a little harder than ordinary, yet at the same time I should have learned the duty and office of a foremast man and, in time, might have qualified myself for a mate or lieutenant, if not for a master. But as it was always my fate to choose for the worst, so I did here. For having money in my pocket and good clothes upon my back, I would always go on board in the dress of a gentleman; and so I neither had any business in the ship nor learned to do any.

It was my lot first of all to fall into pretty good company in London, which does not always happen to such loose and misguided young fellows as I then was, the devil generally not omitting to lay some snare for them very early; but it was not so with me. I first got acquainted with the master of a ship who had been on the coast of Guinea and who, having had very good success there, was resolved to go again. This captain taking a fancy to my conversation, which was not at all disagreeable at that time, hearing me say I had a mind to see the world, told me that if I would go the voyage with him, I should be at no

1. *Guinea,* a district of that part of the west coast of Africa where the land runs nearly due east and west. The six countries into which it is divided are known to sailors under the names of Sierra Leone, Grain Coast, Ivory Coast, Gold Coast, Slave Coast, and Benin.

expense; I should be his messmate and his companion. And if I could carry anything with me, I should have all the advantage of it that the trade would admit; and perhaps I might meet with some success.

I embraced the offer; and entering into a strict agreement with this captain, who was an honest, plain-dealing man, I went on the voyage with him and carried a small stake with me, which, by the disinterested honesty of my friend the captain, I increased very considerably; for I carried about forty pounds' worth of such toys and trifles as the captain directed me to buy. This forty pounds I had mustered together by the assistance of some of my relations whom I corresponded with, and who, I believe, got my father, or at least my mother, to contribute that much to my first adventure.

This was the only voyage that I would consider successful in all my adventures; and that I owe to the integrity and honesty of my friend the captain. Under him, I also got a competent knowledge of the mathematics and the rules of navigation and learned how to keep an account of the ship's course, take an observation, and, in short, to understand some things that were needful to be understood by a sailor. For, as he took delight in instructing me, I took delight in learning; and, in a word, this voyage made me both a sailor and a merchant, for I brought home five pounds nine ounces of gold-dust for my adventure, which yielded me, in London, at my return, almost three hundred pounds. This filled me with those aspiring thoughts that have since so completed my ruin.

Yet even in this voyage, I had my misfortunes, too; particularly, that I was continually sick, being thrown into a violent delirium by the excessive heat of the climate; our principal trading being upon the coast, from the latitude of fifteen degrees north, even to the equator itself.

I was now set up for a Guinea trader; and my friend, to my great misfortune, dying soon after his arrival, I resolved to go again. So I embarked in the same vessel with one who was his mate in the former voyage and had now got the command of the ship. This was the unhappiest voyage that ever man made; for though I did not carry quite one hundred pounds of my newly gained wealth—that I had two hundred pounds left, which I had entrusted to my friend's widow, who was very just to me—yet I fell into terrible misfortunes in this voyage. The first was this: Our ship making her course toward the Canary Islands, or rather between those islands and the African shore, was surprised in the gray of the morning by a Moorish rover of Sallee, who gave chase to us with all the sail she could make. We crowded also as much canvas as our yards would spread, or our masts carry, to have got clear; but

finding the pirate gained on us and would certainly catch up within a few hours, we prepared to fight, our ship having twelve guns, and the rogue eighteen. About three in the afternoon, the pirate came up with us, and bringing-to, by mistake, just across from our quarter, instead of across from our stern as he intended, we brought eight of our guns to bear on that side and poured in a broadside upon him, which made him sheer off again, after returning our fire and pouring in also his small shot from the nearly two hundred men whom he had on board. However, we had not a man touched, all our men keeping close. The pirate prepared to attack us again, and we to defend ourselves; but laying us on board the next time upon our other quarter, he launched sixty men upon our decks, who immediately fell to cutting and hacking the sails and rigging. We plied them with small shot, half-pikes, powder chests, and such, clearing our deck of them twice. However, to cut short this melancholy part of our story, our ship being disabled, three of our men killed and eight wounded, we were obliged to yield and were all carried prisoners into Sallee, a port belonging to the Moors.

Prisoner at Sallee

The usage I had there was not so dreadful as at first I anticipated; nor was I carried up the country to the emperor's court, as the rest of our men were, but was kept by the captain of the rover as his proper prize and made his slave, being young and nimble and fit for his business. At this surprising change of my circumstances from a merchant to a miserable slave, I was perfectly overwhelmed; and now I looked back upon my father's prophetic discourse to me: that I should be miserable and have none to relieve me; which I thought was now so effectually brought to pass that it could not be worse—for now the hand of Heaven had overtaken me, and I was undone without redemption. But, alas, this was but a taste of the misery I was to go through, as will appear in the sequel of this story.

As my new patron, or master, had taken me home to his house, I was in hopes that he would take me with him when he went to sea again, believing that it would some time or another be his fate to be taken by a Spanish or Portuguese man-of-war, and that then I should be set at liberty. But this hope of mine was soon taken away; for when he went to sea, he left me on shore to look after his little garden and do the common drudgery of slaves about his house; and when he came home again from his cruise, he ordered me to lie in the cabin to look after the ship.

Here I meditated nothing but my escape and what method I might take to effect it. But I found no course of action that looked promising, for I had nobody to communicate with who would embark with me—no fellow slave, no Englishman, Irishman, or Scotsman there with me. So for two years, though I often arrived at escape plans in my mind, yet I never had the least encouraging prospect of putting them into practice.

After about two years, an odd circumstance occurred that put the old determination to escape back into my head again. My patron lying at home longer than usual without fitting out his ship, which, as I heard, was for lack of money, he used to constantly—once or twice a week, sometimes oftener, if the weather was fair—to take the ship's pinnace[2] and go out fishing. As he always took me and a young Moor with him to row the boat, we made him very merry, and I proved very dexterous in catching fish; so much so, in fact, that sometimes he would send me with a Moor, one of his kinsmen, and the youth, the Moresco, as they called him, to catch a dish of fish for him.

It happened one time that, going fishing with him in a calm morning, a fog rose so thick that, though we were not half a league from the shore, we lost sight of it; and rowing we knew not whither or which way, we labored all day and all the next night. When the morning came, we found we had pulled out to sea instead of pulling in for the shore, and that we were at least two leagues from the land. However, we got back in again, though with a

2. *Pinnace,* tender, a light sailing ship.

great deal of labor and some danger, for the wind began to blow pretty fresh in the morning; and by that time, we were ravenously hungry.

But our patron, warned by this disaster, resolved to take more care of himself in the future; and having lying by him the longboat of our English ship that he had taken, he resolved he would not go fishing anymore without a compass and some provision. So he ordered the carpenter of the ship, who also was an English slave, to build a little stateroom, or cabin, in the middle of the longboat, like that of a barge, with a place to stand behind it to steer and haul home the mainsheet, and room before for a hand or two to stand and work the sails. She sailed with what we call a shoulder-of-mutton sail; and the boom jibbed over the top of the cabin, which lay very snug and low and had in it room for him to lie, with a slave or two, and a table to eat on, with some small lockers to put in some bottles of such liquor as he thought fit to drink and, particularly, his bread, rice, and coffee.

We went frequently out fishing with this boat; and as I was most dexterous in catching fish for him, he never went without me. It happened that he had planned to go out in this boat, either for pleasure or for fishing, with two or three Moors of some distinction in that place and for whom he had provided extraordinarily. He had therefore sent on board the boat overnight a larger store of provisions than usual and had ordered me to get ready three fusils[3] with powder and shot, which were on board his ship, for they planned to do some fowling as well as fishing.

I got all things ready as he had directed and waited the next morning with the boat washed clean, her ancient[4] and pendants[5] out, and everything to

3. *Fusil,* a French word, meaning a light musket or firelock.

4. *Ancient,* the old word, derived from the French *enseigne,* for a flag or the man who carries it.

5. *Pendant,* a pennant.

accommodate his guests. When by and by my patron came on board alone, he told me his guests had postponed going because of some business that fell through, and he ordered me, with the man and boy, as usual, to go out with the boat and catch them some fish; for his friends were to later sup at his house. He commanded me, too, that as soon as I had caught some fish, I should bring them home to his house, all of which I prepared to do.

My Escape

At this moment, however, my former dreams of deliverance darted into my thoughts, now that I found I was likely to have a little ship at my command. My master being gone, I prepared to furnish myself, not for fishing business, but for a voyage; though I knew not, neither did I so much as consider, where I would steer; for just to get away from that place was my only goal.

My first contrivance was to speak to this Moor in order to get something for our subsistence on board, for I told him we must not presume to eat of our patron's bread. He said that was true; so he brought a large basket of rusk, or biscuit of their kind, and three jars with fresh water, into the boat. I knew where my patron's case of bottles stood. It was evident, by the way they were designed, that they were taken out of some English prize, and I conveyed them into the boat while the Moor was on shore, as if they had been there before for our master. I conveyed also a great lump of beeswax into the boat, which weighed about half a hundredweight, with a parcel of twine or thread, a hatchet, a saw, and a hammer, all of which were of great use to us afterward, especially the wax to make candles. Another trick I played on him, he innocently accepted. His name was Ismael, which they call Muley, or Moely; so I called to him.

"Moely," said I, "our patron's guns are all on board the boat. Can you not get a little powder and shot? It may be we may kill some alcamies (a fowl like our curlews) for ourselves, for I know he keeps the gunner's stores in the ship."

"Yes," said he, "I'll bring some."

Accordingly, he brought a great leather pouch, which held about a pound and a half of powder, or rather more; and another with shot that had five or six pounds, with some bullets, and put it all into the boat. At the same time, I had found some powder of my master's in the great cabin, with which I filled one of the large bottles in the case, which was almost empty, pouring what was in it into another. Thus furnished with everything needful, we sailed out of the port to fish.

The castle, which is at the entrance of the port, knew who we were and took no notice of us. We were not a mile out of the port before we hauled in our sail and sat us down to fish. The wind blew from the north-northeast, which was contrary to my desire; for had it blown southerly, I had been sure to have made the coast of Spain and at least reached the bay of Cadiz. But my resolutions were, blow which way it would, I would be gone from that horrid place and leave the rest to fate.

After we had fished some time and caught nothing—for when I had fish on my hook I would not pull them up, that he might not see them—I said to the Moor, "This will not do. Our master will not be thus served. We must get farther out."

He, unsuspicious, agreed and, being in the head of the boat, set the sails; and, as I had the helm, I ran the boat out nearly a league farther and then brought her to as if I would fish. When, giving the boy the helm, I stepped forward to where the Moor was, and making as if I stooped for something behind him, I took him by surprise with my arm around his waist and tossed him clear overboard into the sea. He rose immediately, for he swam like a cork, and called to me, begging to be taken in, telling me he would go all over the world with me. He swam so strong after the boat that he would have reached me very quickly, there being but little wind; upon which I stepped into the cabin, and fetching one of the fowling-pieces, I aimed it at him and told him I had done him no hurt and if he would be quiet, I would do him none.

"But," said I, "you swim well enough to reach the shore, and the sea is calm. Make the best of your way to shore, and I will do you no harm. But if you come near the boat, I'll shoot you through the head, for I am resolved to have my liberty."

So he turned himself about and swam for the shore, and I have no doubt that he reached it with ease, for he was an excellent swimmer.

With Xury in the Boat

I could have been content to have taken this Moor with me and have drowned the boy, but it would not have been safe to trust him. When he was gone, I turned to the boy, whom they called Xury, and said to him, "Xury, if you will be faithful to me, I'll make you a great man. But if you will not stroke your face to be true to me (that is, swear by Mahomet and his father's beard), I must throw you into the sea, too."

The boy smiled in my face and spoke so innocently that I could not mistrust him; he swore to be faithful to me and go all over the world with me.

While I was in the view of the Moor that was swimming, I stood directly

"If you come near the boat, I'll shoot you!"

out to sea, with the boat rather stretching to windward, that they might think me going toward the Straits'[6] mouth (as indeed anyone that had been in their wits must have been supposed to do). For who would have supposed we were sailing on to the southward, to the truly barbarian coast, where whole nations of negroes were sure to surround us with their canoes and destroy us; where we could never once go on shore but we should be devoured by savage beasts, or instead merciless savages of human kind?

But as soon as it grew dusk in the evening, I changed my course and steered directly south and by east, bending my course a little toward the east that I might keep in view of the shore. Having a fair, fresh gale of wind and a smooth, quiet sea, I made such sail that I believed by the next day at three o'clock in the afternoon, when I first made the land, I could not be less than one hundred and fifty miles south of Sallee—quite beyond the emperor of Morocco's dominions, or indeed of any other king thereabouts, for we saw no people.

Yet such was the fright I had taken at the Moors, and the dreadful apprehensions I had of falling into their hands, that I would not stop, or go on shore, or come to an anchor, the wind continuing fair, till I had sailed in that manner five days. Then, the wind shifting to the southward, I concluded that if any vessels were in chase of me, they also would now give up. So I ventured toward the coast and came to an anchor in the mouth of a little river, I knew not what nor where; neither what latitude, what country, what nation, or what river. I neither saw nor desired to see any people; the principal thing I wanted was fresh water. We came into this creek in the evening, resolving to swim to shore as soon as it was dark and explore the country. But as soon as it was quite dark, we heard such dreadful noises of the barking, roaring, and howling of wild creatures, of we knew not what kinds, that the poor boy was ready to die with fear and begged me not to go on shore till day.

"Well, Xury," said I, "then I won't; but it may be we may see men by day who will be as bad to us as those lions."

"Then we give them the shoot-guns," said Xury, laughing, "make them run wey."

Such English Xury spoke by conversing among us slaves. However, I was glad to see the boy so cheerful, and I gave him a dram (out of our patron's case of bottles). . . . After all, Xury's advice was good, and I took it. We dropped our little anchor and lay still all night: I say still, for we slept none; for in two or three hours, we saw vast creatures (we knew not what to call them) of many sorts come down to the seashore and run into the water, wallowing and wash-

---

6. *Straits*, the Straits of Gibraltar.

ing themselves for the pleasure of cooling themselves. They made such hideous howlings and yellings that I never indeed heard the like.

Xury was dreadfully frightened, and indeed so was I; but we were both more frightened yet when we heard one mighty creature come swimming toward our boat. We could not see him, but we could tell by his blowing that he was a monstrous, huge, and furious beast. Xury said it was a lion, and it might be so for all I know; but poor Xury cried to me to weigh the anchor and row away. "No," said I. "Xury, we can slip our cable, with the buoy to it, and go to sea; they cannot follow us far."

I had no sooner said so but I perceived the creature, whatever it was, within two oars' length, which somewhat surprised me. However, I immediately stepped to the cabin door and, taking up my gun, fired at him; upon which he immediately turned about and swam toward the shore again.

But it is impossible to describe the horrid noises and hideous cries and howlings that were raised, as well upon the edge of the shore as higher within the country, upon the noise or report of a gun, a thing I have some reason to believe those creatures had never heard before. This convinced me that there was no going on shore for us in the night upon that coast. How to venture on shore in the day was another question, too. For to have fallen into the hands of any of the savages had been as bad as to have fallen into the paws of lions and tigers; at least we were equally apprehensive of the danger of it.

We Venture on Shore

Be that as it may, we were obliged to go on shore somewhere or other for water, for we had not a pint left in the boat—when or where to get it was the point. Xury said that if I would let him go on shore with one of the jars, he would find out if there was any water and bring some to me. I asked him why he should; why shouldn't I go, and he stay in the boat?

The boy answered with so much affection that it made me love him ever after: "If wild mans come, they eat me, you go wey."

"Well, Xury," said I, "we will both go, and if the wild mans come, we will kill them, they shall eat neither of us."

So I gave Xury a piece of rusk bread to eat and a dram out of our patron's case of bottles that I mentioned before; and we hauled the boat in as near the shore as we thought was proper and waded on shore, carrying nothing but our arms and two jars for water.

I did not care to go out of sight of the boat, fearing the coming of canoes with savages down the river. But the boy, seeing a low place about a mile up the country, rambled to it, and by and by, I saw him come running toward me. I

thought he was pursued by some savage or frightened by some wild beast, and thus ran forward toward him to help him. But when I came nearer to him, I saw something hanging over his shoulders, which was a creature that he had shot, like a hare, but different in color, and with longer legs. However, we were very glad of it, and it was very good meat. But the great joy that poor Xury came with was to tell me he had found good water and seen no wild mans.

But we found afterward that we need not have taken such pains for water, for a little higher up the creek where we were, we found the water fresh when the tide was out, which flows but a little way up. We filled our jars and feasted on the hare he had killed, then prepared to go on our way, having seen no footprints of any human creature in that part of the country.

As I had taken one voyage to this coast before, I knew very well that the islands of the Canaries, and the Cape de Verd Islands also, lay not far off from the coast. But as I had no instruments to take an observation to know what latitude we were in, and did not exactly know, or at least not remember, what latitude they were in, I knew not where to look for them, or when to stand off to sea toward them. Otherwise, I might now easily have found some of these islands. But my hope was that if I stood along this coast till I came to that part where the English traded, I should find some of their vessels upon their usual route of trade, and they would rescue and take us in.

By the best of my calculations, that place where I now was must be that country which, lying between the emperor of Morocco's dominions and the negroes', lies waste and uninhabited, except by wild beasts; the negroes having abandoned it and gone farther south, for fear of the Moors; and the Moors not thinking it worth inhabiting, by reason of its barrenness. Indeed, both forsook it because of the prodigious numbers of tigers, lions, leopards, and other furious creatures that harbor there; so that the Moors use it for their hunting only, where they go like an army, two or three thousand men at a time. Indeed, for nearly a hundred miles together upon this coast, we saw nothing but uninhabited wasteland by day and heard nothing but howlings and roarings of wild beasts by night.

Once or twice in the daytime, I thought I saw the Pico of Teneriffe, being the high top of the mountain Teneriffe in the Canaries. I had a great mind to venture out, in hopes of reaching there, but having failed twice, I was forced in again by contrary winds, the sea also going too high for my little vessel. I resolved to pursue my first design and keep along the shore.

Several times I was obliged to land for fresh water, after we had left this place. Once in particular, being early in the morning, we came to an anchor under a little point of land, which was pretty high. The tide beginning to flow, we lay still to go farther in. Xury, whose eyes were sharper than it seems mine were, called softly to me and told me that we had best go farther off the shore.

"For look," said he. "Yonder lies a dreadful monster on the side of that hillock, fast asleep."

I looked where he pointed and saw a dreadful monster indeed, for it was a terrible great lion that lay on the side of the shore, under the shade of a piece of the hill that hung as it were a little over him.

"Xury," said I, "you shall go on shore and kill him."

Xury looked frightened and said, "Me kill! He eat me at one mouth"—one mouthful, he meant.

However, I said no more to the boy, but bade him be still. I took our biggest gun, which was almost musket-bore, loaded it with a good charge of powder and two slugs, and laid it down; then I loaded another gun with two bullets; and the third (for we had three pieces) I loaded with five smaller bullets. I took good enough aim with the first piece to have shot him in the head; but he lay so, with his leg raised a little above his nose, that the slugs hit his leg about the knee and broke the bone. He started up, growling at first; but finding his leg broken, he fell down again. Then he got up upon three legs and gave the most hideous roar I have ever heard. I was a little surprised that I had not hit him in the head; however, I took up the second piece immediately, and though he began to move off, I fired again and shot him in the head and had the pleasure to see him drop. Making but little noise, he lay struggling for life. Then Xury took heart and would have me let him go on shore.

"Well, go," said I.

So the boy jumped into the water and, taking the little gun in one hand, swam to shore with the other hand. Coming close to the creature, he put the muzzle of the piece to his ear and shot him in the head again, which dispatched him.

This was game indeed to us, but this was no food; and I was very sorry to lose three charges of powder and shot on a creature that was good for nothing to us. However, Xury said he would have some of him; so he came on board and asked me to give him the hatchet.

"For what, Xury?" said I.

"Me cut off his head," said he.

However, Xury could not cut off his head, but he cut off a foot and brought it with him, and it was a monstrous great one.

I bethought myself, however, that perhaps the skin might, one way or other, be of some value to us; and I resolved to take off his skin if I could. So Xury and I went to work with him; but Xury was much the better workman at it, for I knew not how to do it. Indeed, it took us both the whole day, but at last we got the hide off him, and spreading it on top of our cabin, the sun effectually dried it in two days' time, and it afterward served me to lie upon.

Traffic with the Negroes

After this stop, we sailed southward continuously for ten or twelve days, living very sparingly on our provisions, which began to diminish very much. We went no oftener onto the shore than we were obliged to for fresh water. My design in this was to make the River Gambia or Senegal; that is to say, anywhere about the Cape de Verd, where I was in hopes of meeting with some European ship. If I did not, I knew not what course I had to take, but to seek for the islands, or perish there among the negroes. I knew that all the ships from Europe, which sailed either to the coast of Guinea or to Brazil, or to the East Indies, made this cape, or those islands. In a word, I risked everything on this single point: either that I must meet with some ship—or must perish.

When I had pursued this resolution about ten days longer, as I have said, I began to see that the land was inhabited. In two or three places, as we sailed by, we saw people stand upon the shore to look at us; we could also perceive they were quite black and stark naked. I was once inclined to have gone on shore to them; but Xury was my better counselor and said to me, "No go, no go." However, I hauled in nearer the shore that I might talk to them, and I found they ran along the shore by me a good way. I observed they had no weapons in their hands, except one, who had a long slender stick, which Xury said was a lance, and that they could throw them a great way with good aim. So I kept at a distance, but talked with them by signs as well as I could, and particularly made signs for something to eat. They beckoned to me to stop my boat, and they would fetch me some meat. Upon this, I lowered the top of my sail and lay by, and two of them ran up into the country. In less than half an hour, they came back and brought with them two pieces of dry flesh and some corn, such as is the produce of their country. But we neither knew what the one or the other was. However, we were willing to accept it, but how to come at it was our next dispute, for I would not venture on shore to them, and they were as much afraid of us. But they took a safe way for us all, for they brought it to the shore and laid it down and went and stood a great way off till we fetched it on board. Then they came close to us again.

We made signs of thanks to them, for we had nothing to make them amends with; but an opportunity offered that very instant to oblige them wonderfully. While we were lying on the shore, two mighty creatures came, one pursuing the other (as we took it) with great fury from the mountains toward the sea; whether it was the male pursuing the female, or whether they were in sport or in rage, we could not tell, any more than we could tell whether it was usual or strange. I believe it was the latter, because, in the first place, those ravenous creatures seldom appear but in the night; and, in the second place, we found the people terribly frightened, especially the women. The man who had the lance or dart did not fly from them, but the rest did. However, as the two creatures ran directly into the water, they did not offer to fall upon any of the negroes, but plunged themselves into the sea and swam about, as if they had come for their diversion. At last one of them began to come nearer our boat than at first I expected; but I lay ready for it, for I had loaded my gun with all possible expedition and bade Xury load both the others. As soon as it came fairly within my reach, I fired and shot it directly in the head. Immediately, it sank down into the water, but rose instantly and plunged up and down, as if it was struggling for life, and so indeed it was. It immediately made to the shore; but between the wound, which was its mortal hurt, and the strangling of the water, it died just before it reached the shore.

It is impossible to express the astonishment of these poor creatures at the noise and fire of my gun. Some of them were ready even to die for fear and fell down as dead with the very terror. But when they saw the creature dead and sunk into the water, and that I made signs to them to come to the shore, they took heart and came to the shore and began to search for the creature. I found it by its blood staining the water; and by the help of a rope, which I slung around it and gave the negroes to haul, they dragged it on shore and found that it was a most curious leopard, spotted and fine to an admirable degree. The negroes held up their hands with admiration, wondering what it was I killed it with.

The other creature, frightened with the flash of fire and the noise of the gun, swam to the shore and ran up directly to the mountains from whence they came; nor could I at that distance know what it was. I found quickly that the negroes were for eating the flesh of this creature, so I was willing to have them take it as a favor from me; for which, when I made signs to them that they might take it, they were very thankful. Immediately, they fell to work on it, and though they had no knife, yet, with a sharpened piece of wood, they took off its skin as readily, and much more skillfully, than we would have done with a knife. They offered me some of the flesh, which I declined, making signs as if I would give it them; but I indicated I would like the skin, which they gave me very freely. They also brought me a great deal more of their provision, which, though I did not understand what it was, yet I accepted. Then I made signs to them for some water and held out one of my jars to them, turning its bottom upward to show that it was empty and that I wanted to have it filled. They called immediately to some of their friends, and there came two women who brought a great vessel made of earth and burnt, as I suppose, in the sun. This they set down for me, as before, and I sent Xury on shore with my jars and filled them all three. The women were as stark naked as the men.

I was now furnished with roots and corn, such as it was, and water. Leaving my friendly negroes, I moved on for about eleven days more, without offering to go near the shore, till I saw the land run out a great length into the sea, at about the distance of four or five leagues before me. The sea being very calm, I kept well away from the shore in order to make this point. At length, doubling the point at about two leagues from the land, I plainly saw land on the other side, to seaward. Then I concluded, as it was most certain indeed, that this was the Cape de Verd and those the islands called, from thence, Cape de Verd Islands. However, they were at a great distance, and I could not well tell what I had best do; for if I should be taken with a fresh gale of wind, I might reach neither one nor the other.

Picked Up by a Portuguese Ship

In this dilemma, as I was debating, I stepped into the cabin and sat me down, Xury having the helm.

Suddenly, the boy cried out, "Master, Master, a ship with a sail!"

The foolish boy was frightened out of his wits, thinking it must needs be some of his master's ships sent to pursue us, when I knew we were gotten far enough out of their reach. I jumped out of the cabin and immediately saw, not only the ship, but that it was a Portuguese ship; and, as I thought, it was bound to the coast of Guinea for negroes. But when I observed the course she steered, I was soon convinced they were bound some other way and did not design to go any nearer the shore. Thereupon I moved out to the sea as much as I could, resolving to speak with them if possible.

With all the sail I could make, I found I should not be able to get to them in time, but that they would be gone by before I could make any signal to them. However, after I had crowded the sail to the utmost and began to despair, they, it seems, saw me by the help of their perspective glasses,[7] and that ours was some European boat, which they supposed must belong to some ship that was lost. So they shortened sail to let me come up. I was encouraged with this, and as I had my patron's ancient on board, I made a waft of it to them for a signal of distress and fired a gun, both of which they saw; for they told me they saw the smoke, though they did not hear the gun. Upon these signals, they very kindly brought to and lay by for me; and in about three hours' time, I came up with them.

They asked me what I was, in Portuguese, in Spanish, and in French, but I understood none of them. At last a Scotch sailor, who was on board, called to me; and I answered him and told him I was an Englishman who had made my escape out of slavery from the Moors at Sallee. They then bade me come on board and very kindly took me in, and all my goods.

---

7. *Perspective glasses,* telescopes.

It was an inexpressible joy to me, which anyone will believe, that I was thus delivered from such a miserable and almost hopeless condition as I was in. I immediately offered all I had to the captain of the ship, as a return for my deliverance; but he generously told me he would take nothing from me, but that all I had should be delivered safely to me when I came to the Brazils.

"For," said he, "I have saved your life on no other terms than as I would be glad to be saved myself; and it may, one time or other, be my lot to be taken up in the same condition.

"Besides," said he, "when I carry you to the Brazils, so great a way from your own country, if I should take from you what you have, you will be starved there, and then I only take away the life that I have given. No, no," said he, "*Seignior Inglese* [Mr. Englishman], I will carry you there in charity, and these things will help you to buy your subsistence there and your passage home again."

As he was charitable in this proposal, so he was just in the performance of it, for he ordered the seamen that none should dare to touch anything I had. Then he took everything into his own possession and gave me back an exact inventory of them that I might have them later, even to my three earthen jars.

As to my boat, it was a very good one, and that he saw. He told me he would like to buy it for the ship's use and asked me what I would take for it. I told him he had been so generous to me in everything that I could not state a price for the boat, but left it entirely to him. Upon which, he told me he would give me a note of his hand to pay me eighty pieces of eight[8] for it at Brazil; and when he came there, if anyone offered to give more, he would make up the difference. He offered me also sixty pieces of eight more for my boy Xury, which I was loath to take; not that I was unwilling to let the captain have him, but I was very reluctant to sell the poor boy's liberty, who had assisted me so faithfully in procuring my own. However, when I let him know my reason, he owned it to be just and offered me this compromise: that he would take the boy with an obligation to set him free in ten years if he turned Christian. Upon hearing this, and Xury saying he was willing to go with him, I let the captain have him.

We had a very good voyage to the Brazils, and I arrived in the Bay de Todos los Santos, or All Saints Bay, about twenty-two days later. And now I was once more delivered from the most miserable of all conditions of life; and what to do next with myself I was to consider.

8. *Pieces of eight,* Spanish silver dollars (marked with the figure "eight").

Chapter 3

SHIPWRECK

The generous treatment the captain gave me, I shall never forget. He would take nothing of me for my passage, gave me twenty ducats[1] for the leopard's skin and forty for the lion's skin, which I had in my boat, and caused everything I had in the ship to be punctually delivered to me. What I was willing to sell, he bought of me, such as the case of bottles, two of my guns, and a piece of the lump of beeswax, for I had made candles of the rest. In a word, I made about two hundred and twenty pieces of eight of all my cargo; and with this stock, I went on shore in the Brazils.

I had not been there long, but being recommended to the house of a good, honest man, like himself, who had an *ingenio*, as they call it (that is, a plantation and a sugar house), I lived with him some time and acquainted myself, by that means, with the manner of their planting and making of sugar. I saw how well the planters lived and how they got rich suddenly, and I resolved that, if I could get a license to settle there, I would turn planter among them. I determined, in the meantime, to find out some way to get my money, which I had left in London, remitted to me. To this purpose, getting a kind of letter of naturalization, I purchased as much land that was unplanted as my money would cover and formed a plan for my plantation and settlement: such a one as might be suitable to the stock that I proposed to myself to receive from England.

I had a neighbor, a Portuguese, of Lisbon, but born of English parents, whose name was Wells, and he was in much the same circumstances as I was. I call him neighbor because his plantation lay next to mine, and we got along very well together. My stock was low, just as his was; thus we planted for food rather than anything else, for about two years. However, we began to increase, and our land began to come into order; so that the third year we

---

1. *Ducat,* Spanish gold coin.

planted some tobacco, and each of us made ready a large piece of ground for planting canes in the year to come. But we both wanted help and now I realized, more than ever before, that I had done wrong in parting with my boy Xury.

But, alas, for me to do wrong that never did right was no great wonder. I had no remedy but to go on: I had got into employment quite unsuited to my gifts and directly contrary to the life I delighted in, and for which I forsook my father's house and rejected all his good advice; nay, I was coming into the very middle station, or upper degree of low life, which my father advised me to seek before and which, if I resolved to go on with it, I might as well have stayed at home and never exhausted myself so far from home, as I have done. I used often to say to myself, "I could have done this as well in England, among my friends, as have gone five thousand miles off to do it among strangers and savages, in a wilderness and at such a distance as never to hear from any part of the world that has the least knowledge of me."

In this manner I used to look upon my condition with the utmost regret. I had nobody to converse with but now and then this neighbor; no work to be done but by the labor of my hands; and I used to say, "I live just like a man cast away upon some desolate island that has nobody there but himself." But how just it has been; and how all men should reflect that when they compare their present conditions with others that are worse, Heaven may oblige them to make the exchange and be convinced of their former felicity by their experience—I say again, how just it has been that the truly solitary life I reflected on, on an island of mere desolation, should be my lot, who had so often unjustly compared it with the life that I then led, in which, had I continued, I had in all probability become exceedingly prosperous and rich.

I was, in some degree, settled in my measures for carrying on the plantation before my kind friend, the captain of the ship that took me up at sea, went back; for the ship remained there, in providing her lading and preparing for her voyage, nearly three months. When telling him what little stock I had left behind me in London, he gave me this friendly and sincere advice.

"*Seignior Inglese,*" said he (for so he always called me), "if you will give me letters and a procuration here in form to me, with orders to the person who has your money in London to send your effects to Lisbon, to such persons as I shall direct and in such goods as are proper for this country, I will bring you the produce of them, God willing, at my return. But since human affairs are all subject to changes and disasters, I would have you give orders but for one hundred pounds sterling, which, you say, is half your stock. And let the hazard be run for the first; so that, if it come safe, you may order the rest the same way; and if it miscarry, you may have the other half to have recourse to for your supply."

This was such sound advice, and he had been so kind, that I could not but be convinced it was the best course I could take. So I accordingly prepared letters to the gentlewoman with whom I had left my money and a procuration to the Portuguese captain, as he desired.

I wrote the English captain's widow a full account of all my adventures, my slavery, escape, and how I had met with the Portuguese captain at sea, the humanity of his behavior, and what condition I was now in, with all other necessary directions for my supply. When this honest captain came to Lisbon, he found means, by some of the English merchants there, to send over not the order only, but a full account of my story, to a merchant in London, who explained it in such detail to her that she not only delivered the money, but out of her own pocket sent the Portuguese captain a very handsome present for his humanity and charity to me.

The merchant in London investing this hundred pounds in English goods, such as the captain had written for, sent them directly to him at Lisbon, and he brought them all safe to me in the Brazils; among which, without my direction (for I was too young in my business to think of them), he had taken care to have all sorts of tools, ironwork, and utensils necessary for my plantation and which were of great use to me.

When this cargo arrived, I thought my fortune made, for I was overcome by joy at it. And my good steward, the captain, had laid out the five pounds, which my friend had sent him for a present for himself, to purchase and bring me over a servant, under bond for six years' service, and would not accept of any consideration, except a little tobacco, that I would have him accept, being of my own produce.

Neither was this all: For my goods being all English manufacture, such as cloth, stuffs,[2] baize, and things particularly valuable and desirable in the country, I found means to sell them at a very great profit, so that I had received more than four times the value of my first cargo and was now infinitely better off than my poor neighbor—I mean in the advancement of my plantation. For the first thing I did, I bought me a negro slave and a European servant also—I mean another besides that which the captain brought me from Lisbon.

---

2. *Stuffs,* English woven material—but could also mean a line of miscellaneous things.

My Plantation in the Brazils

But as abused prosperity is oftentimes made the very means of our greatest adversity, so it was with me. I went on the next year with great success in my plantation. I raised fifty great rolls of tobacco on my own ground, more than I had disposed of for necessaries among my neighbors; and these fifty rolls, being each of above a hundredweight, were well cured and laid by against the return of the fleet from Lisbon. And now increasing in business and wealth, my head began to be full of projects and undertakings beyond my reach, such as are indeed often the ruin of the best heads in business. Had I continued in the station I was now in, I had room for all the happy things to have yet befallen me, for which my father so earnestly recommended a quiet, retired life, and which he had so sensibly described the middle station of life to be full of. But other things attracted me, and I was still to be the willful agent of all my own miseries; and particularly, to increase my guilt, and double the reflections upon myself, which in my future sorrows I should have leisure to make, all these miscarriages were procured by my apparent obstinate adhering to my foolish inclination to wander abroad. I pursued that inclination, in contradiction to the clearest views of doing myself good in a fair and plain pursuit of those prospects and those measures of life that nature and Providence concurred to present me with and made my duty.

As I had once done before in breaking away from my parents, so I could not be content now, but I must leave the happy life I had (being a rich and thriving man upon my new plantation), only to pursue a rash and immoderate desire to rise faster than the nature of the thing admitted. Thus I cast myself down again into the deepest gulf of human misery that ever man fell into, or perhaps could be consistent with life and a state of health in the world.

To come then by just degrees to the particulars of this part of my story: You may suppose that having now lived almost four years in the Brazils, and beginning to thrive and prosper very well upon my plantation, I had not only learned the language, but had contracted acquaintance and friendship among my fellow planters, as well as among merchants of St. Salvadore, which was our port; and that, in my discourse among them, I had frequently given them an account of my two voyages to the coast of Guinea, the manner of trading with the negroes there, and how easy it was to purchase upon the coast for trifles—such as beads, toys, knives, scissors, hatchets, bits of glass, and the like—not only gold-dust, Guinea grain,[3] elephants' teeth, etc., but negroes, for the service of the Brazils, in great numbers.

They always listened very attentively to my discourse on these subjects, but especially to that part which related to the buying of negroes; which was a trade, at that time, not only not rarely entered into, but, as far as it was, had been carried on by the *Assiento*,[4] or permission, of the kings of Spain and Portugal, and thus few negroes were brought, and those were excessively expensive.

It happened, being in company one day with some merchants and planters of my acquaintance and talking of those things very earnestly, three of them came to me the next morning and told me they had been thinking a great deal about what I had discussed with them the previous night, and they had come to make a secret proposal to me. After first enjoining me to secrecy, they told me that they had a mind to fit out a ship to go to Guinea; that all plantations were in desperate need for servants; that as it was a trade that could not be

3. *Guinea grain*, a spice (from an African plant).

4. *Assiento*, a very lucrative contract to supply slaves to the Spanish and Portuguese colonies.

profitably conducted, because they could not publicly sell the negroes when they came home, they desired to make but one voyage, to bring the negroes on shore privately and divide them among their own plantations. In a word, the question was: Would I oversee their supercargo in the ship, managing the trading part upon reaching the coast of Guinea? They offered me, in return, an equal share of the negroes, without providing any part of the stock.

This was a fair proposal, it must be confessed, had it been made to anyone that had not had a settlement and plantation of his own to look after, which was in a fair way of becoming very successful and with a good stock upon it. But for me, who was thus entered and established and had nothing to do but go on as I had begun, for three or four years more, and to have sent for the other hundred pounds from England; and who in that time, and with that little addition, could scarce have failed of being worth three or four thousand pounds sterling, and that increasing, too—for me to think of such a voyage was the most preposterous thing that ever man in such circumstances could be guilty of.

But I, that was born to be my own destroyer, could no more resist the offer than I could restrain my first rambling designs, when my father's good counsel was lost upon me. In a word, I told them I would go with all my heart, if they would undertake to look after my plantation in my absence and would dispose of it as I should direct, if I miscarried. This they all engaged to do and entered into writings and covenants to do so. I made a formal will, disposing of my plantation and effects in case of my death, making the captain of the ship that had saved my life, as before, my universal heir, but obliging him to dispose of my effects as I had directed in my will: one-half of the produce being to himself, and the other to be shipped to England.

In short, I took all possible caution to preserve my effects and to keep up my plantation. Had I used half as much prudence to have looked into my own interests, and have made a judgment of what I ought to have done and not to have done, I would certainly have never gone away from so prosperous an undertaking, leaving all the probable increases in my businesses, to go upon a voyage to sea, attended with all its common hazards, to say nothing of the reasons I had to expect particular misfortunes to myself.

But I hurried on and obeyed blindly the dictates of my fancy rather than my reason. Accordingly, the ship being fitted out, the cargo finished, and all things done as by agreement by my partners in the voyage, I went on board in an evil hour again, the 1st of September 1659, being the same day eight years before that I went from my father and mother at Hull, in order to act the rebel to their authority and the fool to my own interests.

Our ship was about one hundred and twenty tons burden, carried six guns, and eleven men, besides the master, his boy, and myself. We had on board no large cargo of goods, except of such toys as were fit for our trade with the negroes, such as beads, bits of glass, shells, and odd trifles, especially little looking glasses, knives, scissors, hatchets, and the like.

A Violent Hurricane

The same day I went on board, we set sail, standing away to the northward upon our own coast, intending to set course for the African coast, when they came into about ten or twelve degrees of northern latitude, which, it seems, was the manner of their course in those days. We had very good weather, only excessively hot, all the way up our own coast till we came to the height of Cape St. Augustino; from there, keeping farther off at sea, we lost sight of land and steered as if we were bound for the isle of Fernando de Noronha, holding our course northeast by north and leaving those isles on the east. In this course, we passed the equator in about twelve days' time and were, by our last observation, in seven degrees twenty-two minutes northern latitude, when a violent tornado, or hurricane, took us way off course. It began from the southeast, came about to the northwest, and then settled into the northeast. From this direction, it blew in such a terrible manner that for twelve days together we could do nothing but drive and, scudding away before it, let it carry us wherever fate and the fury of the winds directed. During these twelve days, I need not say that I expected every day to be swallowed up; nor did any in the ship expect to save their lives.

In this distress, we had, besides the terror of the storm, other tragedies: One of our men died of the tropical fever, and a man and a boy washed overboard. About the twelfth day, the weather abating a little, the master made an observation as well as he could and found that he was in about eleven degrees of north latitude, but that he was twenty-two degrees of longitude difference west from Cape St. Augustino; so that he found he was close upon the coast of Guiana,[5] or the northern part of Brazil, beyond the river Amazones,[6] toward that of the river Oroonoko, commonly called the Great River. Now he began to consult with me what course he should take; for the ship was leaky and very much disabled, and he was all for going directly back to the coast of Brazil.

I was positively against that; and looking over the charts of the seacoast of America with him, we concluded there was no inhabited country for us to have recourse to till we came within the circle of the Caribbee[7] Islands. We therefore resolved to stand away for Barbadoes, which, by keeping off at sea,

---

5. *Guiana*, the Guianas.

6. *Amazones*, the Amazon River.

7. *Caribbee*, Caribbean.

to avoid the in-draft of the Bay or Gulf of Mexico, we might easily accomplish, as we hoped, in about fifteen days' sail, since we could not possibly make our voyage to the coast of Africa without some assistance both to our ship and to ourselves.

Shipwrecked

With this design, we changed our course and steered away northwest by west, in order to reach some of our English islands, where I hoped for relief; but our voyage was otherwise destined. For, being in the latitude of twelve degrees eighteen minutes, a second storm came upon us, which carried us away with the same impetuosity westward and drove us so out of the way of all human commerce that had all our lives been saved as to the sea, we were still in more danger of being devoured by savages than in hopes of ever returning to our own country.

In this distress, the wind still blowing very hard, one of our men early one morning cried out, “Land!” and we had no sooner run out of the cabin to look out, in hopes of seeing where in the world we were, when the ship struck upon a sandbar. In a moment, her motion being so stopped, the sea broke over her in such a manner that we expected we should all have perished immediately, and we were even driven into our close quarters, to shelter us from the very foam and spray of the sea.

It is not easy for anyone who has not been in the like condition to describe or conceive the consternation of men in such circumstances. We knew nothing of where we were, or upon what land it was we were driven; whether an island or the mainland, whether inhabited or not inhabited. As the rage of the wind was still great, though rather less than at first, we could not so much as hope to have the ship hold together many minutes without breaking into pieces, unless the winds, by a kind of miracle, should turn immediately about. In a word, we sat looking one upon another and expecting death every moment, and every man acting accordingly, as preparing for another world; for there was little or nothing more for us to do in this. That which was our present comfort, and all the comfort we had, was that, contrary to our expectation, the ship did not break yet and that the master reported that the wind had begun to abate.

Now, though we thought that the wind did a little abate, yet the ship having thus struck upon the sand, and sticking too fast for us to expect her to get off, we were in a dreadful condition indeed and had nothing to do but to think of saving our lives as well as we could. We had a boat at our stern just before the storm, but she was first staved by dashing against the ship's rudder, and in the next place, she broke away and either sank or was driven off to sea; so there was no hope from her. We had another boat on board, but how to get her off into the sea was a doubtful thing; however, there was no room to debate, for we expected the ship to break into pieces every minute, and some told us she was actually broken already.

In this distress, the mate of our vessel lay hold of the boat, and with the help of the rest of the men, they got her flung over the ship's side. Getting all into her, we let go and committed ourselves, being eleven in number, to God's mercy and the wild sea. For though the storm was abated considerably, yet the sea went dreadfully high upon the shore and might be well called *den wild zee*, as the Dutch call the sea in a storm.

And now our case was very dismal indeed; for we all saw plainly that the waves rose so high that the boat could not escape and that we should be

inevitably drowned. As to making sail, we had none, nor, if we had, could we have done anything with it. So we worked at the oar toward the land, though with heavy hearts, like men going to execution; for we all knew that when the boat came near the shore, she would be dashed into a thousand pieces by the breaking waves. However, we committed our souls to God in the most earnest manner; and the wind driving us toward the shore, we hastened our destruction with our own hands, pulling as well as we could toward land.

What the shore was, whether rock or sand, whether steep or shoal, we knew not; the only hope that could rationally give us the least shadow of expectation was that we might perhaps happen into some bay or gulf, or the mouth of some river, where by great chance we might have run our boat in, or got under the lee of the land and perhaps made smooth water. But nothing of this sort appeared; rather, as we made nearer and nearer the shore, the land looked more frightful than the sea.

After we had rowed, or rather driven, about a league and a half, as we reckoned it, a raging wave, mountainlike, came rolling astern of us and plainly bade us expect the coup de grâce. In a word, it took us with such a fury that it overset the boat at once; and separating us as well from the boat as from one another, it gave us not time hardly to say, "O God!" for we were all swallowed up in a moment.

Nothing can describe the confusion of thought that I felt when I sank into the water; for though I swam very well, yet I could not deliver myself from the waves so as to draw breath, till that wave having driven me, or rather carried me, a vast way on toward the shore, and having spent itself, went back and left me upon the land almost dry, but half-dead with the water I took in. I had enough presence of mind, as well as breath left, however, that seeing myself nearer the mainland than I expected, I got up on my feet and endeavored to move on toward the land as fast as I could, before another wave should return and take me up again. But I soon found it impossible to avoid it; for I saw the sea coming after me as high as a great hill and as furious as an enemy, which I had no means or strength to contend with. My business was to hold my breath and raise myself upon the water, if I could. So I swam to preserve my breathing and piloted myself toward the shore if possible—my greatest determination now being that the wave, as it would carry me a great way toward the shore when it came on, should not carry me back again with it when it rolled back toward the sea.

The wave that came upon me again buried me at once twenty or thirty feet deep in its own body, and I could feel myself carried with a mighty force and swiftness toward the shore a very great way; but I held my breath and forced myself to swim forward with all my might. I was ready to burst with holding my breath when I felt myself rising up. To my immediate relief, I found my head and hands shooting out above the surface of the water. Though it was not two seconds of time that I could keep myself so, yet it relieved me greatly and gave me breath and new courage. I was covered again with water a good while, but not so long but I held out; and finding the water had spent itself and began to return, I struck forward against the return of the waves and felt ground again with my feet. I stood still a few moments to recover breath and to wait till the waters went from me; then I took to my heels and ran with what strength I had farther toward the shore. But neither would this deliver me from the fury of the sea, which came pouring in after me again; and twice more I was lifted up by the waves and carried forward as before, the shore being very flat.

The last time of these two had well-nigh been fatal to me, for the sea having hurried me along, as before, landed me, or rather dashed me, against a piece of a rock, and that with such force as it left me senseless, and indeed helpless, in terms of my own deliverance. For the blow, taking my side and chest, beat the breath as it were quite out of my body. Had it returned again immediately, I must inevitably have been strangled in the water; but I recovered a little before the return of the next wave, and seeing I should be covered again with the water, I resolved to hold fast to a piece of rock and so to hold my breath, if possible, till the wave receded. Now, as the waves were not so high as at first, being nearer land, I held to the rock till the wave abated and then fetched another run, which brought me so near the shore that the next wave, though it went over me, did not so swallow me up as to carry me away. The next run I took I got to the mainland, where, to my great comfort, I clambered up the cliffs of the shore and sat me down upon the grass, free from danger and quite out of the reach of the water.

Chapter 4

THE CALM BETWEEN STORMS

I was now landed safely on shore, and I began to look up and thank God that my life was saved, in a case wherein just minutes before . . . there was scarcely any room to hope. I believe it is impossible to adequately express what the ecstasies and transports of the soul are when it is so saved—as I may say, out of the very grave—and I do not wonder now at that custom, when a malefactor, who has the halter about his neck, is tied up and is just going to be dropped off the platform and has a reprieve brought to him—I say, I do not wonder that they bring a surgeon with it, to drain blood that very moment they tell him of it, that the surprise may not drive the animal spirits from the heart and overwhelm him. "For sudden joys, like griefs, confound at first."

I walked about on the shore, lifting up my hands and my whole being, as I may say, wrapped up in a contemplation of my deliverance; making a thousand gestures and motions, which I cannot describe; reflecting upon all my comrades that were drowned and that there had not been one soul saved but myself. For, as for them, I never saw them afterward, or any sign of them,

except three of their hats, one cap, and two shoes that did not match.

I cast my eyes to the stranded vessel, where, the breach and froth of the sea being so turbulent, I could hardly see it, it lay so far off; and I considered: *Lord, how was it possible I could get to shore?*

After I had solaced my mind with the comfortable part of my condition, I began to look round me, to see what kind of place I was in and what was next to be done. I soon found my solace ebb away—in a word, I had experienced a dreadful deliverance. For I was wet, had no clothes to change to, nor anything either to eat or drink, to comfort me; neither did I see any prospect before me but that of perishing with hunger or being devoured by wild beasts—and that which was particularly afflicting to me was that I had no weapon, either to hunt and kill any creature for my sustenance, or to defend myself against any other creature that might desire to kill me for theirs. In a word, I had nothing about me but a knife, a tobacco pipe, and a little tobacco in a box. This was all my provision; and this threw me into terrible agonies of mind that for a while I ran about like a madman. Night coming upon me, I began, with a heavy heart, to consider what would be my lot if there were any ravenous beasts in that country, seeing that at night they always come abroad for their prey.

The only remedy that came to me, at that time, was to get up into a thick bushy tree, like a fir, but thorny, that grew near me, and where I resolved to sit all night and consider the next day what death I should die, for as yet I saw no prospect of life. I walked about a furlong from the shore to see if I could find any fresh water to drink, which I did to my great joy; and having drunk and put a little tobacco in my mouth to prevent hunger, I went to the tree and, getting up into it, endeavored to place myself so that if I should sleep, I

might not fall. And having cut me a short stick, like a truncheon, for my defense, I took up my lodging. Being excessively fatigued, I fell fast asleep and slept as comfortably as, I believe, few could have done in my condition and found myself more refreshed with it than I think I ever was on such an occasion.

When I waked, it was broad day, the weather clear, and the storm abated, so that the sea did not rage and swell as before. But that which surprised me most was that the ship had been lifted off in the night from the sand where she lay, by the swelling of the tide, and was now driven up almost as far as the rock that I at first mentioned, where I had been so bruised by the wave dashing me against it. This being within about a mile from the shore where I was, and the ship seeming to stand upright still, I wished myself on board that at least I might save some necessary things for my use.

When I came down from my refuge in the tree, I looked about me again, and the first thing I found was the boat, which lay, as the wind and sea had tossed her up, upon the land about two miles up the beach. I walked as far as I could upon the shore to have got to her, but found a neck, or inlet, of water between me and the boat that was about half a mile broad; so I came back for the present, being more intent upon getting at the ship, where I hoped to find something for my present subsistence.

A Visit to the Wreck

A little after noon, I found the sea very calm and the tide ebbed so far out that I could come within a quarter of a mile of the ship. And here I found a fresh renewing of my grief, for I now realized that if we had just stayed on board, we had been all safe; that is to say, we had all got safe on shore, and I would not have been left miserable, so entirely destitute of all comfort and company, as I now was. This brought tears to my eyes again; but as there was little relief in that, I resolved, if possible, to get to the ship. So I pulled off my clothes, for the weather was extremely hot, and entered the water. But when I came to the ship, my difficulty was still greater, for how was I to get on board? For, as she lay aground and high out of the water, there was nothing within my reach to lay hold of. I swam round her twice, and the second time I espied a small piece of rope, which I wondered I hadn't seen at first, hanging down by the fore-chains just low enough so that, with great difficulty, I got hold of it and, by the help of that rope, got up into the forecastle of the ship. Here I found that the ship was bulged and had a great deal of water in her hold; but that she lay so on the side of a bank of hard sand, or rather earth, that her stern lay lifted up upon the bank and her head low, almost to the water. By this means, all her quarter was free, and all that was in that part was dry; for you may be sure my first work was to search and see what was spoiled and what was loose. First, I found that all the ship's provisions were dry and untouched by the water, and being very well disposed to eat, I went to the bread room and filled my pockets with biscuit and ate it as I went about other things, for I had no time to lose. I also found some rum in the great cabin, of which I took a large dram and which I had, indeed, need enough of to fortify me for what was before me. Now I lacked nothing but a boat to furnish myself with many things that I foresaw would be very necessary to me.

It was in vain to sit still and wish for what was not to be had; and this extremity roused my ingenuity. We had several spare yard poles, two or three large spars of wood, and a spare topmast or two in the ship: I resolved to fall

I espied a small piece of rope.

to work with these, and I flung as many of them overboard as I could manage for their weight, tying every one with a rope, so that they might not drift away. When this was done, I went down the ship's side, and pulling them to me, I tied four of them together at both ends, as well as I could, in the form of a raft, and laying two or three short pieces of plank upon them crossways, I found I could walk upon it very well, but that it was not able to bear any great weight, the pieces being too light. So I went to work, and with the carpenter's saw, I cut a spare topmast into three lengths and added them to my raft, with a great deal of labor and pains. But the hope of furnishing myself with necessaries gave me the strength to accomplish more than could have been possible otherwise.

Loading the Raft

My raft was now strong enough to bear any reasonable weight. My next question was, what should I load onto it, and how was I to preserve what I laid upon it from being destroyed by the surf of the sea? But I was not long considering this. I first laid all the planks or boards upon it that I could get, and having considered well what I most wanted, I first got three of the seamen's chests, which I had broken open and emptied, and lowered them down upon my raft. The first of these I filled with provisions—namely, bread, rice, three Dutch cheeses, five pieces of dried goat's flesh (which we lived much upon), and a little remainder of European corn, which had been laid by for some fowls that we brought to sea with us, but the fowls had been killed. There had been some barley and wheat together; but, to my great disappointment, I found afterward that the rats had eaten or spoiled it all. As for liquors, I found several cases of bottles belonging to our skipper, in which were some cordial waters; and, in all, about five or six gallons of arrack.[1] These I stowed by themselves, there being no need to put them into the chest, nor any room for them. While I was doing this, I found the tide began to flow, though very calmly; and I had the mortification of seeing my coat, shirt, and waistcoat, which I had left on shore upon the sand, swim away. As for my breeches, which were only linen, and open-kneed, I swam on board in them and my stockings. However, this got me to rummaging for clothes, of which I found enough, but took no more than I wanted for present use, for I had other things that I needed more, such as tools to work with on shore. It was only after long searching that I found the carpenter's chest, which was indeed a very useful prize to me and much more valuable than a ship laden with gold would have been at that time. I got it down to my raft,

1. *Arrack,* East Indian liquor.

just as it was, without losing time to look into it, for I knew in general what it contained.

My next search was for some ammunition and arms. There were two very good fowling-pieces in the great cabin, and two pistols. These I secured first, with some powder horns, a small bag of shot, and two old rusty swords. I knew there were three barrels of powder in the ship, but knew not where our gunner had stowed them; but with much search I found them. Two of them were dry and good; the third had taken water. Those two I got to my raft, with the weapons. And now I thought myself pretty well freighted and began to wonder how I should get to shore with them, having neither sail, oar, nor rudder; and the least capful of wind would have overset all my navigation.

I had three encouragements: first, a smooth, calm sea; secondly, the tide rising and moving toward shore; thirdly, what little wind there was blew me toward the land. And thus, having found two or three broken oars, belonging to the boat, and besides the tools that were in the chest—two saws, an ax, and a hammer—with this cargo, I put to sea. For a mile, or thereabouts, my raft went very well. Only, I found that it drove a little distant from the place where I had landed before, by which I perceived that there was some indraught of the water. Consequently, I hoped to find some creek or river there, which I might make use of as a port to get to land with my cargo.

As I imagined, so it was. There appeared before me a little opening of the land. I found a strong current of the tide moving into it; so I guided my raft as well as I could, to keep in the middle of the stream.

But here I almost suffered a second shipwreck, which, if I had, I think verily it would have broken my heart; for, knowing nothing of the coast, I let my raft run aground at one end of it upon a shoal; and not being aground at the other end, it would have taken but little and all my cargo would have slipped off toward the end that was afloat and so have fallen into the water. I did my utmost, by setting my back against the chests, to keep them in their places, but could not thrust off the raft with all my strength. Neither dared I stir from the posture I was in, but holding up the chests with all my might, I stood in that manner nearly half an hour, in which time the rising of the water brought me a little more upon a level. A little after, the water still rising, my raft floated again, and I thrust it off with the oar I had into the channel, and then driving up higher, I at length found myself in the mouth of a little river, with land on both sides and a strong current or tide running up. I looked on both sides for a proper place to get to shore, for I was not willing to be driven too high up the river, hoping in time to see some ship at sea. Therefore I resolved to place myself as near the coast as I could.

At length I spied a little cove on the right shore of the creek, to which, with great pain and difficulty, I guided my raft and at last got so near that reaching ground with my oar, I could thrust it directly in. But here I had like to have dipped all my cargo into the sea again; for that shore lying pretty steep—that is to say, sloping—there was no place to land but where one end of my float, if it ran on shore, would lie so high, and the other sink lower, as before, that it would endanger my cargo again. All that I could do was to wait till the tide was at the highest, keeping the raft with my oar like an anchor, to hold the side of it fast to the shore, near a flat piece of ground, which I expected the water would flow over; and so it did. As soon as I found water enough, for my raft drew about a foot of water, I thrust it upon that flat piece of ground and there fastened or moored it, by sticking my two broken oars into the ground—one on one side, near one end, and one on the other side, near the other end. Thus I lay till the water ebbed away and left my raft and all my cargo safe on shore.

My next work was to view the country and seek a proper place for my habitation and to stow my goods, to secure them from whatever might happen. Where I was, I yet knew not; whether on the continent or an island; whether inhabited or not inhabited; whether in danger of wild beasts or not. There was a hill not above a mile from me, which rose up very steep and high, and which seemed to overtop some other hills that lay as in a ridge from it, northward. I took out one of the fowling-pieces, one of the pistols, and a horn of powder, and thus armed, I traveled for discovery up to the top of that hill, where, after I had with great labor and difficulty got to the top, I saw my fate, to my great despondency—namely, that I was on an island surrounded on all sides by the sea: no land to be seen except some rocks, which lay a great way off, and two small islands, less than that, which lay about three leagues to the west.

I found also that the island I was in was barren, and, as I saw good reason to believe, uninhabited, except by wild beasts, of which, however, I saw none. Yet I saw an abundance of fowls, but knew not their kinds; neither, when I killed them, could I tell what was fit for food and what not. At my coming back, I shot at a great bird that I saw perched upon a tree on the side of a great wood. I believe it was the first gun that had been fired there since the creation of the world. I had no sooner fired but from all parts of the wood there arose an innumerable number of fowls of many sorts, making a confused screaming and crying, every one according to its usual note, but not one of them of any kind that I knew. As for the creature I killed, I took it to be a kind of hawk, its color and beak resembling it; but it had no talons or claws more than common. Its flesh was carrion and fit for nothing.

Contented with this discovery, I came back to my raft and fell to work to bring my cargo to shore, which took me the rest of the day. What to do with myself at night I knew not, nor indeed where to rest, for I was afraid to lie down on the ground, not knowing but some wild beast might devour me; though, as I afterward found, there was really no need for such a fear.

However, as well as I could, I barricaded myself round with the chests and boards that I had brought on shore and made a kind of hut for that night's lodging. As for food, I did not yet know how to supply myself, except that I had seen two or three creatures, like hares, run out of the wood where I shot the fowl.

A Second Cargo

I now began to consider that I might yet get a great many things out of the ship that would be useful to me, particularly some of the rigging and sails and such other things as might come to land. So I resolved to make another voyage to board the vessel, if possible. And as I knew that the first storm that blew must necessarily break her all in pieces, I resolved to put off doing other things until I got everything out of the ship that I could get. Then I called a council—that is to say, in my thoughts—whether I should take back the raft, but this appeared impracticable. So I resolved to go as before, when the tide was low; and I did so, only that I stripped before I left my hut, having nothing on but a checkered shirt, a pair of linen drawers, and a pair of pumps on my feet.

I got on board the ship as before and prepared a second raft; and, having learned from my first experience, I neither made this so unwieldy, nor loaded it so hard, but yet I brought away several things very useful to me; as, first, in the carpenter's stores, I found two or three bags full of nails and spikes, a great screw jack, a dozen or two hatchets, and, above all, that most useful thing called a grindstone. All these I secured, together with several things belonging to the gunner, particularly two or three iron crowbars and two barrels of musket bullets, seven muskets, another fowling-piece, some small quantity of powder more, a large bag full of small shot, and a great roll of sheet lead; but this last was so heavy, I could not hoist it up to get it over the ship's side.

Besides these things, I took all the men's clothes that I could find and a spare fore-topsail, a hammock, and some bedding. With this I loaded my second raft and brought them all safe on shore, to my very great comfort.

I was under some apprehension, during my absence from the land, that my provisions might be devoured on shore; but when I came back I found no sign of any visitor; only there sat a creature like a wild cat upon one of the chests, which, when I came toward it, ran away a little distance and then stood still. It sat very composed and unconcerned and looked full in my face, as if it had a mind to be acquainted with me. I presented my gun to it, but, as it did not understand it, it was perfectly unconcerned at it; nor did it offer to move away. I tossed her a bit of biscuit, though, by the way, I was not very free of it, for my store was not great; however, I spared the creature a bit, I say, and it went to it, smelled it, ate it, and looked (as if pleased) for more. But I thanked it and could spare no more; so it marched off.

Having got my second cargo on shore—though I was obliged to open the barrels of powder and bring them by parcels, for they were too heavy, being large casks—I went to work to make me a little tent, with the sail and some poles which I cut for that purpose. Into this tent, I brought everything that I knew would spoil either with rain or sun; and I piled all the empty chests and casks up in a circle round the tent to fortify it from any sudden attack, either from man or beast.

When I had done this, I blocked up the door of the tent with some boards within and an empty chest set up on end without. Spreading one of the beds upon the ground, laying my two pistols just at my head and my gun at length by me, I went to bed for the first time and slept very quietly all night. I was very weary, for the night before I had slept little and had labored very hard all day, as well to fetch those things from the ship as to get them to shore.

I had the biggest magazine of all kinds now that ever was laid up, I believe, for one man; but still I was not satisfied, for while the ship remained upright in that posture, I thought I ought to get everything out of her that I could. So every day, at low water, I went on board and brought away something or other. The third time I went, I brought away as much of the rigging as I could, and also all the small ropes and rope twine I could get, with a piece of spare canvas, which was to mend the sails upon occasion, and the barrel of wet gunpowder. In a word, I brought away all the sails, first and last; only I tended to cut them into pieces and bring as much at a time as I could, for they were no more useful to me for sails, but as mere canvas only.

But that which comforted me more still was that, last of all, after I had made five or six such voyages as these and thought I had nothing more to expect from the ship that was worth my meddling with—but after all this, I found a great hogshead of bread; three large runlets[2] of rum, or spirits; a box of fine sugar; and a barrel of fine flour. This was surprising to me, because I had given up expecting any more provisions except what was spoiled by the water. I soon emptied the hogshead of the bread and wrapped it up, parcel by parcel, in pieces of the sails that I cut out; and, in a word, I got all this safe on shore also, though it took several trips.

The next day I made another voyage, and now, having plundered the ship of what was portable and fit to hand out, I began with the cable. Cutting the great cable into pieces such as I could move, I got two cables and a hawser on shore, with all the ironwork I could get; and having cut down the spritsail yard, the mizzen yard, and everything I could to make a large raft, I loaded it with all those heavy goods and came away. But my good luck began to leave me, for this raft was so unwieldy and so overladen that after I entered the little cove, where I had landed the rest of my goods, not being able to guide it so handily as I did the other, it overset and threw me and all my cargo into the water. As for myself, it was no great harm, for I was near the shore; but as to my cargo, a great part of it was lost, especially the iron, which

2. *Runlet* (rundlet), eighteen gallons.

I expected would have been of great use to me. However, when the tide was out, I got most of the pieces of cable ashore, and some of the iron, though with infinite labor; for I was fain to dip for it into the water, a work that fatigued me very much. After this, I went every day on board and brought away what I could get.

I had now been thirteen days on shore and had been eleven times on board the ship, in which time I had brought away all that one pair of hands could well be supposed capable of bringing; though I verily believe, had the calm weather held, I should have brought away the whole ship, piece by piece. But preparing the twelfth time to go on board, I found the wind began to rise. However, at low water I went on board, and though I thought I had rummaged the cabin so effectually that nothing more could be found, yet I discovered a locker with drawers in it, in one of which I found two or three razors and one pair of large scissors, with some ten or a dozen good knives and forks; in another I found about thirty-six pounds value in money—some European coin, some Brazilian, some pieces of eight, some gold, and some silver.

I smiled to myself at the sight of this money. "O drug!" said I aloud. "What art thou good for? Thou art not worth anything to me—no, not the taking off the ground. One of those knives is worth all this heap. I have no manner of use for thee; e'en remain where thou art and go to the bottom, as a creature whose life is not worth saving."

However, upon second thought, I took it away; and wrapping all in a piece of canvas, I began to think of making another raft; but while I was preparing this, I found the sky overcast. The wind began to rise, and in a quarter of an hour, it blew a fresh gale from the shore. It presently occurred to me that it was in vain to pretend to make a raft with the wind offshore, and that it was my business to be gone before the tide of flood began; otherwise, I might not be able to reach the shore at all. Accordingly, I let myself down into the water and swam across the channel that lay between the ship and the sands, and even that with difficulty enough, partly from the weight of the things I had about me and partly from the roughness of the water. For the wind rose very hastily, and before it was quite high water, it blew a storm.

The Last of the Ship

But I made it back home to my little tent, where I lay, with all my wealth about me, feeling very secure. It blew very hard all that night, and in the morning, when I looked out, behold, no more ship was to be seen. I was a little surprised, but recovered myself with this satisfactory reflection: I had lost no time, nor abated any diligence, to get everything out of her that could be useful to me. Indeed, there was little left in her that I was able to bring away, if I had had more time.

I now gave over any more thoughts of the ship, or of anything out of her, except what might drive on shore from her wreck; as, indeed, divers pieces of her afterward did; but those things were of small use to me.

Chapter 5

First Year on the Island

My thoughts were now wholly employed about securing myself against either savages, if any should appear, or wild beasts, if any were on the island. I had many thoughts of the method of how to do this, and what kind of dwelling to make—whether I should make me a cave in the earth, or a tent upon the earth. In short, I resolved upon both; the manner and description of which it may not be improper to give an account of.

I soon found the place I was in was not fit for my settlement, particularly because it was upon a low moorish ground near the sea, and I believed it would not be wholesome, more particularly because there was no fresh water near it. So I resolved to find a more healthy and more convenient spot of ground.

I consulted several things in my situation that I found would be proper for me: first, health and fresh water, I just now mentioned; secondly, shelter from the heat of the sun; thirdly, security from ravenous creatures, whether man or beast; fourthly, a view to the sea, that if God sent any ship in sight, I might not lose any advantage for my deliverance, of which I was not willing to banish my expectation yet.

In search of a place proper for this, I found a little plain on the side of a rising hill, whose front toward this little plain was steep as a house side, so that nothing could come down upon me from above. On the side of a rock, there was a hollow place, worn a little way in, like the entrance or door of a cave; but there was not really any cave, or way into the rock, at all.

On the flat of the green, just below this hollow place, I resolved to pitch my tent. This plain was not above a hundred yards broad and about twice as long, and it lay like a green before my door; at the end of it, it descended irregularly every way down into the low ground by the seaside. It was on the north-northwest side of the hill; so that it was sheltered from the heat of the day, till it came to the west and by south sun or thereabouts, which, in those countries, is near the setting.

Before I set up my tent, I drew a half-circle before the hollow place, which took in about ten yards in its semi-diameter from the rock, and twenty yards in its diameter from its beginning and ending.

In this half-circle, I pitched two rows of strong stakes, driving them into the ground till they stood very firm like piles, the biggest end being out of the ground about five feet and a half and sharpened on the top. The two rows did not stand above six inches from one another.

Then I took the pieces of cable that I had cut in the ship and laid them in rows, upon one another, within the circle, between these two rows of stakes, up to the top, placing other stakes in the inside, leaning against them, about two feet and a half high, like a spur to a post. This fence was so strong that neither man nor beast could get into it or over it. This cost me a great deal of time and labor, especially to cut the piles in the woods, bring them to the place, and drive them into the earth.

The entrance into this place I made to be, not by a door, but by a short ladder to go over the top; which ladder, when I was in, I lifted over after me; and so I was completely fenced in and fortified, as I thought, from all the world and consequently slept secure in the night, which otherwise I could not have done. Though, as it appeared afterward, there was no need of all this caution from the enemies that I apprehended danger from.

Into this fence, or fortress, with infinite labor, I carried all my riches—all my provisions, ammunition, and stores, of which you have the account above. I made me a large tent also, to preserve me from the rains that in one part of the year are very violent there. I made it double—namely, one smaller tent within, and one larger tent above it; and I covered the uppermost part of it with a large tarpaulin that I had saved among the sails.

And now I lay no more for a while in the bed that I had brought on shore, but in a hammock, which was indeed a very good one and belonged to the mate of the ship.

Into this tent, I brought all my provisions and everything that would spoil by the wet; and having thus enclosed all my goods, I made up the entrance, which till now I had left open, and so passed and repassed, as I said, by a short ladder.

When I had done this, I began to work my way into the rock, and bringing all the earth and stones that I dug out through my tent, I laid them up within my fence, in the nature of a terrace, so that it raised the ground within about a foot and a half. Thus I made me a cave, just behind my tent, which served me like a cellar to my house.

It cost me much labor and many days before all these things were brought to perfection; and therefore I must go back to some other things that took up some of my thoughts. At the same time it occurred, after I had laid my scheme for setting up the tent and making the cave, that a storm of rain falling from a thick, dark cloud, a sudden flash of lightning happened, and after that, a great clap of thunder, as is naturally the effect of it. I was not so much surprised with the lightning as I was with the thought that darted into my mind as swift as the lightning itself: *Oh, my powder!* My very heart sank within me when I thought that, at one blast, all my powder might be destroyed; on which not my defense only, but the providing me food, as I thought, entirely depended. I was not nearly so anxious about my own danger; though, had the powder taken fire, I would have never known who had hurt me.

Such impression did this make upon me that after the storm was over, I laid aside all my work, my building and fortifying, and applied myself to make bags and boxes to separate my powder and to keep it in little parcels, in hopes that, whatever might come, it might not all take fire at once; and to keep it so apart that it should not be possible to make one part fire another. I finished this work in about a fortnight; and I think my powder, which in all was about one hundred and forty pounds in weight, was divided into no less than a hundred parcels. As to the barrel that had been wet, I did not apprehend any danger from that; so I placed it in my new cave, which, in my fancy, I called my kitchen; and the rest I hid up and down in holes among the rocks, so that no wet might come to it, marking very carefully where I laid it.

In the interval of time while this was happening, I went out at least once every day with my gun, as much just to divert myself as to see if I could kill anything fit for food and, as near as I could, to acquaint myself with what the island produced. The first time I went out, I discovered that there were goats on the island, which was a great satisfaction to me. But then it was attended with this misfortune to me, namely, that they were so shy, so subtle, and so swift of foot that it was the most difficult thing in the world to come at them. I was not discouraged at this, however, not doubting but I might now and then shoot one, as it soon happened. For after I had found some of their haunts, I lay in wait in this manner for them: I observed that if they saw me in the valleys, though they were upon the rocks, they would run away, as

in a terrible fright; but if they were feeding in the valleys and I was upon the rocks, they took no notice of me. From this I concluded that, by the position of their optics, their sight was so directed downward that they did not readily see objects that were above them; so afterward I took this method—I always climbed the rocks first, to get above them, and thus frequently got close enough to get in a good shot.

The first shot I made among these creatures, I killed a she-goat, which had a little kid by her, which she gave suck to, which grieved me heartily; for, when the old one fell, the kid stood stock-still by her, till I came and took her up. Not only so, but when I carried the old one with me upon my shoulders, the kid followed me quite to my enclosure; upon which I laid down the dam, took the kid in my arms, and carried it over my pale, in hopes to have bred it up tame. But it would not eat; so I was forced to kill it and eat it myself. These two supplied me with flesh for a great while, for I ate sparingly and saved my provisions, my bread especially, as much as I possibly could.

Having now fixed my habitation, I found it absolutely necessary to provide a place to make a fire in, and fuel to burn. What I did for that, as also how I enlarged my cave and what conveniences I made, I shall give a full account of in its place; but I must now give some little account of myself and of my thoughts about living, which, it may well be supposed, were not a few.

Comforting Reflections

I had a dismal prospect of my condition, for as I was not cast away upon that island without being driven, as is said, by a violent storm quite out of the course of our intended voyage and a great way, namely, some hundreds of leagues, out of the ordinary course of the trade of mankind, I had great reason to consider it as a determination of Heaven that in this desolate place and in this desolate manner, I should end my life. The tears would run plentifully down my face when I made these reflections; and sometimes I would argue with myself about why Providence should thus completely ruin its creatures and render them so absolutely miserable, so without help, so abandoned, and so entirely depressed that it could hardly be rational to be thankful for such a life.

But something always happened soon after to check these thoughts and to reprove me. One day while walking with my gun in my hand by the seaside, I was full of thoughts having to do with my present condition, when reason, as it were, argued from a different direction: *Well, you are in a desolate condition, it is true; but, pray remember, where are the rest of your crew? Did not eleven of you get into the boat? Where are the ten? Why were not they saved, and you lost? Why are you singled out? Is it better to be here or* there*?* (and then I pointed to the sea). All evils are to be considered with the good that is in them and with what worse attended them.

Then it occurred to me again how well I was furnished for my subsistence, and what would have been my case if it had not happened (which was a hundred thousand to one) that the ship floated from the place where she first struck and was driven so near to the shore that I had time to get all these things out of her? What would have been my case if I had been forced to live in the condition in which I at first came on shore, without necessaries of life or any means to supply and procure them?

"Particularly," said I aloud (though to myself), "what should I have done without a gun, without ammunition, without any tools to make anything, or to work with? Without clothes, bedding, a tent, or any manner of coverings?"

Now I had all these to a sufficient quantity and was in a fair way to provide myself in such a manner as to live without my gun when my ammunition was spent. So I had a tolerable view of subsisting without any want as long as I lived, for I considered from the beginning how I would provide for the accidents that might happen and for the time that was to come, not only after my ammunition should be spent, but even after my health and strength should decay.

I confess I had not then entertained any notion of my ammunition being destroyed at one blast—I mean my powder being blown up by lightning;

and this made the thoughts of it surprising to me, when it lightened and thundered, as I observed just now.

And now, being about to relate a melancholy story of silent life, such, perhaps, as was never heard of in the world before, I shall take it from its beginning and continue it in the order that it happened. It was, by my account, the 30th of September when, in the manner just described, I first set foot upon this horrid island, when the sun being to us in its autumnal equinox, was almost just over my head. For I reckoned myself, by observation, to be in the latitude of nine degrees twenty-two minutes north of the equator.

After I had been there about ten or twelve days, it came to me that I should lose my reckoning of time for lack of books, pen, and ink, and should even lose track of the Sabbath-day in all the working days. To prevent this, I carved an inscription with my knife upon a large post, in capital letters; and making it into a great cross, I set it up on the shore where I first landed, namely, "I came on shore here on the 30th day of September 1659."

Upon the sides of this square post, I cut every day a notch with my knife, and every seventh notch was as long again as the rest, and every first day of the month as long again as that long one; and thus I kept my calendar, or weekly, monthly, and yearly reckoning of time.

In the next place, we are to observe that among the many things that I brought from the ship in the several voyages that, as above mentioned, I made to it, I got several things of less value, but not at all less useful to me, which I omitted setting down before: in particular, pens, ink, and paper; several parcels in the captain's, mate's, gunner's, and carpenter's keeping; three or four compasses, some mathematical instruments, dials, perspectives, charts, and books of navigation; all of which I stored together, whether I might want them or not. Also, I found three very good Bibles, which came to me in my cargo from England and which I had packed up among my things; some Portuguese books also; and, among them, two or three Catholic prayer books and several other books; all of which I carefully secured. And I must not forget that we had in the ship a dog and two cats, of whose eminent history I must have occasion to say something later on, for I carried both the cats with me; and, as for the dog, he jumped out of the ship on his own and swam to shore with me the day after I went on shore with my first cargo. He was a trusty servant to me many years; I lacked nothing that he could fetch me, nor any company that he could make up to me. I only lacked having him talk to me, but that he could not do. As I observed before, I found pens, ink, and paper, and I conserved them as carefully as I could; and I shall show that while my

ink lasted I kept a very exact record, but after that was gone I could not, for I could not make any ink by any means that I could devise.

And this reminded me that I still lacked many things, notwithstanding all that I had amassed together; and of these, ink was one; also, a spade, pickax, and shovel to dig or remove the earth; needles, pins, and thread—as for linen, I soon learned to get along without that.

This lack of tools made all the work I did go slowly. Thus it took nearly a whole year before I had entirely finished my little pale, or surrounded habitation. The piles or stakes, which were as heavy as I could lift, were a long time in cutting and preparing in the woods, and a longer time yet, by far, in bringing home. I spent sometimes two days in cutting and bringing home one of those posts, and a third day in driving it into the ground; for which purpose, at first, I used a heavy piece of wood, but at last bethought myself of one of the iron crowbars; which, however, though I found it, yet made driving those posts or piles very laborious and tedious work. But why should I have been concerned at the tediousness of anything I had to do, seeing I had time enough to do it in? Nor had I any other employment, if that had been over, at least that I could foresee, except ranging the island to seek food, which I did, more or less, every day.

The Evil—The Good

I now began to consider seriously my condition and the circumstances I was reduced to; and I drew up the state of my affairs in writing, not so much to leave them to any that were to come after me—for I was likely to have but few heirs—as to rescue my thoughts from daily poring upon them and afflicting my mind. And as my reason now began to master my despondency, I began to comfort myself as well as I could, and to set the good against the evil, that I might have something to distinguish my case from worse. I stated it very impartially, like debtor and creditor, the comfort I enjoyed against the miseries I suffered, thus:

EVIL	GOOD
I am cast upon a horrible, desolate island; void of all hope of recovery.	But I am alive—and not drowned, as all my ship's company was.
I am singled out and separated, as it were, from all the world, to be miserable.	But I am singled out, too, from all the ship's crew, to be spared from death; and He that miraculously saved me from death can deliver me from this condition.
I am divided from mankind, a solitary; one banished from human society.	But I am not starved or perishing on a barren place affording no sustenance.
I have no clothes to cover me.	But I am in a hot climate, where if I had clothes, I could hardly wear them.
I am without any defense or means to resist any violence of man or beast.	But I am cast on an island where I see no wild beasts to hurt me, as I saw on the coast of Africa; and what if I had been shipwrecked there?
I have no one to speak to or relieve me.	But God wonderfully sent the ship in near enough to the shore that I have got out so many necessary things as will either supply my wants or enable me to supply myself, as long as I live.

On the whole, here was an undoubted testimony that there was scarcely any condition in the world so miserable but there was something positive to be thankful for in it. And let this stand as a principle, from the experience of the most miserable of all conditions in this world—that we may always find in it something to comfort ourselves with, and to weigh in, in the description of good and evil, on the credit side of the account.

Having now brought my mind a little to relish my condition, and ceasing to look continually out to sea to see if I could spy a ship—I say, giving up these things, I began to apply myself to smooth my way of living and to make things as easy for me as I could.

I have already described my habitation, which was a tent under the side of a rock, surrounded with a strong pale of posts and cables; but I might now rather call it a wall, for I raised a kind of wall up against it of turfs, about two feet thick, on the outside; and after some time (I think it was a year and a half), I raised rafters from it, leaning to the rock, and thatched or covered it with boughs of trees and such things as I could get to keep out the rain, which I found at some times of the year very violent.

I have already observed how I brought all my goods into this pale and into the cave that I had made behind me. But I must observe, too, that at first this was a confused heap of goods, which, as they lay in no order, so they took up all my place. I had no room to turn myself in, so I set about to enlarge my cave and worked farther into the earth; for it was a loose, sandy rock that yielded easily to the labor I bestowed on it. So when I found I was pretty safe as to beasts of prey, I worked sideways, to the right hand, into the rock and then turning to the right again, dug clear through and made me a door to come out through, on the outside of my pale or fortification.

This gave me not only egress and regress, as it was a back way to my tent and to my storehouse, but also gave me room to stow my goods.

And now I began to apply myself to make such necessary things as I found I most wanted: particularly, a chair and a table. For without these, I was not able to enjoy the few comforts I had in the world: I could not write, or eat, or do several things with so much pleasure without a table.

So I went to work; and here I must needs observe that as reason is the substance and basis of mathematics, so by stating and squaring everything by reason, and by making the most rational judgment of things, every man may be, in time, master of every mechanical art. I had never handled a tool in my life; and yet, in time, by labor, application, and contrivance, I found, at last, that I lacked nothing but I could have made it, especially if I had had tools.

However, I made an abundance of things even without tools, and some with no more tools than an adze and a hatchet, which, perhaps, were never made that way before, and that with infinite labor. For example, if I wanted a board, I had no other way but to cut down a tree, set it on an edge before me, and hew it flat on either side with my ax, till I had brought it to be as thin as a plank, and then dub it smooth with my adze. It is true, by this method I could make but one board out of a whole tree; but this I had no remedy for but patience, anymore than I had for the prodigious amount of time and labor that it took me to make a plank or board. But my time or labor was not worth much, and so it was as well employed one way as another.

However, I made me a table and a chair, as I observed earlier; and this I did out of the short pieces of boards that I brought on my raft from the ship. But when I had wrought out some boards as above, I made large shelves of the breadth of a foot and a half, one over another, all along one side of my cave, to lay all my tools, nails, and ironwork on—in a word, to separate everything at large into their places that I might easily find them. Also, I knocked pieces into the wall of the rock to hang my guns and all things that would hang up, so that had anyone else seen my cave, it looked like a general magazine of all necessary things; and I had everything so ready at my hand that it was a great pleasure for me to see all my goods in such order and especially to find my stock of all necessaries so great.

I Begin My Journal

And now it was when I began to keep a journal of every day's employment; for, indeed, at first I was in too much of a hurry, and not only in a hurry as to labor, but in too much turbulence of mind; and my journal would have been full of many dull things. For example, I must have said thus:

"*September the 30th*—After I had got to shore and had escaped drowning, instead of being thankful to God for my deliverance, having first vomited, with the great quantity of saltwater that was gotten into my stomach, and recovering myself a little, I ran about the shore, wringing my hands and beating my head and face, exclaiming at my misery and crying out I was undone, undone, till, tired and faint, I was forced to lie down on the ground to repose, but dared not sleep, for fear of being devoured."

Some days after this, after I had been on board the ship and had got all I could out of her, I could not resist climbing to the top of a little mountain and looking out to sea, in hopes of seeing a ship. I fancied I espied at a vast distance a sail, pleased myself with the hopes of it, and then, after looking steadily till I was almost blind, I lost sight of it and sat down and wept like a child, thus increasing my misery by my folly.

But having gotten over these things in some measure, and having settled my household stuff and habitation, made me a table and a chair, and everything as handsome about me as I could make it, I began, I say, to keep my journal—of which I shall here give you the copy (though in it will be told all these particulars over again), as long as it lasted. For at last, having no more ink, I was forced to cease writing.

Chapter 6

BEGINNING THE DIARY

September 30, 1659—I, poor, miserable Robinson Crusoe, being shipwrecked, during a dreadful storm, in the offing, came on shore on this dismal, unfortunate island, which I call "The Island of Despair," all the rest of the ship's company being drowned and myself almost dead.

All the rest of the day I spent in afflicting myself at the dismal circumstances I was brought to: namely, I had neither food, house, clothes, weapon, nor place to fly to; and, in despair of any relief, saw nothing but death before me—either that I should be devoured by wild beasts, murdered by savages, or starved to death for want of food. At the approach of night, I climbed into a tree, for fear of wild creatures; but I slept soundly, though it rained all night.

October 1—In the morning I saw, to my great surprise, that the ship had floated with the high tide and was driven on shore again, much nearer the island; which, as it was some comfort, on one hand (for seeing her still upright and not broken into pieces, I hoped, if the wind abated, I might get on board and get some food and necessaries out of her for my relief), so, on the other hand, it renewed my grief at the loss of my comrades, who, I now realized, if we had all stayed on board, might have saved the ship, or, at least, that they would not have all been drowned, as they were; and that, had the men been saved, we might perhaps have built us a boat out of the ruins of the ship to have carried us to some other part of the world. I spent a great part of this day in tormenting myself with these things; but at length, seeing the ship almost dry, I walked out as far as I could and then swam to it. This day also it continued raining, though with no wind at all.

From the 1st of October to the 24th—All these days entirely spent in many voyages to get all I could out of the ship, which I brought on shore, every flood tide, upon rafts. Much rain also, in these days, though with some intervals of fair weather; but it seems this was the rainy season.

Oct. 24—I overturned my raft and all the goods I had got upon it; but being in shoal water, and the things being chiefly heavy, I recovered many of them when the tide was out.

Oct. 25—It rained all night and all day, with some gusts of wind; during which time the ship broke into pieces, the wind blowing a little harder than before, and was no more to be seen, except the wreck of her, and that only at low water. I spent this day in covering and securing the goods that I saved, so that the rain might not spoil them.

Oct. 26—I walked along the shore almost all day, searching a place where I could construct my habitation, determined to secure myself from any attack in the night, either from wild beasts or men. Toward night I chose a good place, under a rock, and marked out a semicircle for my encampment, which I resolved to strengthen with a work, wall, or fortification, made of double piles, lined within by cables and without with turf.

From the 26th to the 30th—I worked very hard in carrying all my goods to my new habitation, though some part of the time it rained exceedingly hard.

The 31st—In the morning, I went out into the island with my gun, to seek some food and discover the country. I killed a she-goat, and her kid followed me home, which I afterward killed also, because it would not feed.

November 1—I set up my tent under a rock and lay there for the first night—making it as large as I could, with stakes driven in to swing my hammock upon.

Nov. 2—I set up all my chests and boards and the pieces of timber that made my rafts, and with them, formed a fence round me, a little within the place I had marked out for my fortification.

Nov. 3—I went out with my gun and killed two fowls like ducks, which were very good food. In the afternoon, I went to work to make me a table.

Nov. 4—This morning I began to organize my work schedule: of going out with my gun, time of sleep, and time of diversion—namely, every morning I walked out with my gun for two or three hours, if it did not rain; then I employed myself to work till about eleven o'clock; then I ate what I had to live on. From twelve to two, I lay down to sleep, the weather being excessively hot; and then, in the evening, I worked again. The working part of this day and the next were wholly employed in making this table, for I was yet but a very poor workman, though time and necessity made me a complete natural carpenter soon after, as I believe would be true of anyone else.

Nov. 5—This day I went abroad with my gun and my dog and killed a wild cat. Its skin was pretty soft, but its flesh was good for nothing. Every creature I killed, I took off the skins and preserved them. Coming back by the seashore, I saw many sorts of sea fowls, which I did not recognize; but I was surprised, and almost frightened, by two or three seals, which, while I was gazing at them, not yet knowing what they were, slipped into the sea and escaped me for that time.

Nov. 6—After my morning walk, I went to work on my table again and finished it, though not to my liking; nor was it long before I learned to mend it.

Nov. 7—Now it began to be settled fair weather. The 7th, 8th, 9th, 10th, and part of the 12th (for the 11th was Sunday according to my reckoning), I spent making me a chair and, with much ado, brought it to a tolerable shape, but never to please me; and even in the making I pulled it to pieces several times.

Note—I soon neglected keeping Sundays; for, failing to carve my mark for them on my post, I forgot which day was which.

Nov. 13—This day it rained, which refreshed me exceedingly and cooled the earth; but it was accompanied with terrible thunder and lightning, which frightened me dreadfully for fear of my powder being fired. As soon as it was over, I resolved to separate my stock of powder into as many little parcels as possible, so that it might not be in danger.

Nov. 14, 15, 16—These three days I spent in making little square chests, or boxes, that might hold about a pound, or two pounds at most, of powder; and so, putting the powder in, I stowed it in places as secure and remote from one another as possible. On one of these three days, I killed a large bird that was good to eat, but I knew not what to call it.

Nov. 17—This day I began to dig behind my tent into the rock to make room for my other needs.

Note—Three things I wanted exceedingly for this work: namely, a pickax, a shovel, a wheelbarrow, and a basket; so I desisted from my work and began to consider how to supply that want and make me some tools. As for the pickax, I made use of the iron crowbars, which were adequate enough, though heavy; but the next thing was a shovel or spade; this was so absolutely necessary that indeed I could do nothing effectively without it; but what kind of one to make I knew not.

Nov. 18—In searching the woods, I found a tree of that wood, or like it, which in the Brazils they call the iron-tree[1] for its exceeding hardness; of this, with great labor and almost spoiling my ax, I cut a piece and brought it home, with difficulty enough, for it was exceedingly heavy. The excessive hardness of the wood, and having no other way, kept me a long time work-

1. *Iron-tree,* "Lignum vitae," an extremely hard wood with a density approaching that of iron. It quickly dulls saw blades.

ing on it, for I gradually shaped it, little by little, into the form of a shovel or spade; the handle exactly shaped like ours in England, only that the board part having no iron shod upon it at bottom, it would not last me so long. However, it served well enough for the uses that I had occasion to put it to; but never was a shovel, I believe, made after that fashion, or so long in the making.

I was still deficient, for I lacked a basket or a wheelbarrow. A basket I could not make by any means, having no such things as twigs that would bend to make wickerware—at least, none yet found. As to the wheelbarrow, I fancied I could make all but the wheel—making that seemed an impossibility. Besides, I had no possible way to make iron gudgeons for the spindle or axis of the wheel to run in, so I gave it up. So, for carrying away the earth that I dug out of the cave, I made me a thing like a hod, which the laborers carry mortar in when they serve the bricklayers. This was not as difficult to me as was the making of the shovel; and yet this and the shovel, and the attempt that I made in vain to make a wheelbarrow, took me no less than four days, always excepting my morning's walk with my gun, which I seldom failed. I very seldom failed, also, of bringing home something fit to eat.

My Diary Continued

Nov. 23—My other work having stood still because of my making these tools, when they were finished I went on, and working every day, as my strength and time allowed, I spent eighteen days entirely in widening and deepening my cave, so that it might hold my goods commodiously.

Note—During all this time, I worked to make this room, or cave, spacious enough to accommodate me as a warehouse or magazine, a kitchen, a dining room, and a cellar. As for a lodging, I remained in the tent; except that sometimes, in the wet season of the year, it rained so hard that I could not keep myself dry, which caused me afterward to cover all my place within my pale with long poles, in the form of rafters, leaning against the rock, and load them with flags[2] and large leaves of trees, like a thatch.

December 10—I began now to think my cave or vault finished, when suddenly (it seems I had made it too large) a great quantity of earth fell down from the top and one side; so much that, in short, it frightened me, and not without reason, too; for if I had been under it, I would never have needed a grave digger. Upon this disaster, I had a great deal of work to do over again, for I had the loose earth to carry out; and, what was of more importance, I had the ceiling to prop up, so that I might be sure no more would come down.

2. *Flag,* plant with swordlike leaves.

Dec. 11—This day I went to work on it accordingly and got two shores or posts pitched upright to the top, with two pieces of board across over each post. This I finished the next day, and setting more posts up with boards, in about a week or more, I had the roof secured. The posts, standing in rows, served me for partitions to divide up my house.

Dec. 17—From this day to the 20th I placed shelves and hammered in nails on the posts to hang everything up that could be hung up. Now I began to see some order within doors.

Dec. 20—Now I carried everything into the cave and began to furnish my house and set up some pieces of board like a dresser, to place my victuals upon; but boards began to be very scarce with me. Also, I made me another table.

Dec. 24—Much rain all night and all day; no stirring out.

Dec. 25—Rain all day.

Dec. 26—No rain, and the earth much cooler than before, and pleasanter.

Dec. 27—Killed a young goat and lamed another so that I caught it and led it home on a rope. When I got it home, I bound up and splinted its leg, which was broken.

N.B.[3]—I took such care of it that it lived, and the leg grew well and as strong as ever. But by nursing it so long, it grew tame and fed upon the little grass at my door and would not go away. This was the first time that I entertained a thought of breeding some tame creatures, so that I might have food when my powder and shot were all spent.

Dec. 28, 29, 30, 31—Great heat and no breeze, so that there was no stirring abroad, except in the evening, for food. This time I spent in putting all my things in order within doors.

January 1—Very hot still, but I went abroad early and late with my gun and lay still in the middle of the day. This evening, going farther into the valleys that lay toward the center of the island, I found there were plenty of goats, though exceedingly shy and hard to come at. However, I resolved to try, with my dog, to hunt them down.

Jan. 2—Accordingly, the next day I went out with my dog and set him upon the goats. But I was mistaken, for they all faced about upon the dog, and he knew his danger too well, for he would not come near them.

Jan. 3—I began my fence, or wall; which, being still afraid of my being attacked by somebody, I resolved to make very thick and strong.

N.B.—This wall being described before, I purposely omit what was said in the journal; it is sufficient to observe that it took no less time than from the

3. *N.B.*, take notice, note well.

3rd of January to the 14th of April working, finishing, and perfecting this wall, though it was no more than about twenty-four yards in length, being a half-circle, from one place in the rock to another place, about eight yards from it, the door of the cave being in the center behind it.

All this time, I worked very hard, the rains hindering me many days, nay, sometimes weeks together; but I knew I should never be perfectly secure till this wall was finished. It is scarcely credible what inexpressible labor everything was done with, especially the bringing piles out of the woods and driving them into the ground, for I made them much bigger than I needed to have done.

When this wall was finished, and the outside double-fenced, with a turf wall raised up close to it, I convinced myself that if any people were to come on shore there, they would not perceive anything like a habitation; and it was very well I did so, as may be observed hereafter, on a very significant occasion.

During this time, I made rounds in the woods for game every day, when the rain permitted me, and made frequent discoveries in these walks of something or other to my advantage. Particularly, I found a kind of wild pigeons that build, not as wood pigeons in a tree, but rather as house pigeons, in the holes of the rocks. Taking some young ones, I endeavored to breed them up tame, and did so; but when they grew older, they all flew away, which perhaps was at first because I failed to feed them, for I had nothing to give them. However, I frequently found their nests and got their young ones, which were very good meat.

Household Affairs

And now, in managing my household affairs, I found myself lacking in many things, which I thought at first it was impossible for me to make; as, indeed, for some of them it was. For instance, I could never make a hooped cask. I had a small runlet or two, as I observed before; but I could never actually make one of them, though I spent many weeks trying; I could neither put in the heads, nor join the staves so true to one another as to make them hold water; so I gave up on that.

In the next place, I was at a great loss for candles; so that as soon as it was dark, which was generally by seven o'clock, I was obliged to go to bed. I remembered the lump of beeswax with which I made candles in my African adventure; but I had none of that now. The only remedy I had was that when I had killed a goat I saved the tallow, and with a little dish made of clay, which I baked in the sun, to which I added a wick of some oakum, I made me a lamp; and this gave me light, though not a clear steady light like a candle. In the middle of all my labors it happened that, rummaging through my things, I found a little bag that, as I hinted before, had been filled with corn for the feeding of poultry—not for this voyage, but before, as I suppose, when the ship came from Lisbon. What little remainder of

corn had been in the bag was all devoured by the rats, and I saw nothing in the bag but husks and dust; and being willing to keep the bag for some other use (I think it was to put powder in, when I divided it for fear of the lightning, or some such use), I shook the husks of corn out of it on one side of my fortification, under the rock.

It was a little before the great rains just now mentioned that I threw this stuff away, taking no notice of anything and not so much as remembering that I had thrown anything there, when, about a month after, or thereabouts, I saw some few stalks of something green shooting out of the ground, which I fancied might be some plant I had not seen; but I was surprised and perfectly astonished when, after a little longer time, I saw about ten or twelve ears come out which were perfectly green barley, of the same kind as our European—nay, as our English barley.

Chapter 7

EARTHQUAKE, STORM, AND GOD

It is impossible to express the astonishment and confusion of my thoughts on this occasion. I had hitherto acted upon no religious foundation at all; indeed, I had very few notions of religion in my head, nor had considered anything that had befallen me to be the result of anything other than mere chance, or, as we lightly say, "what pleases God," without so much as inquiring into the end of Providence in these things, or His order in governing events in the world. But after I saw barley grow there in a climate that I knew was not proper for corn, and especially when I knew not how it came there, it startled me strangely, and I began to wonder if God had miraculously caused this corn to grow without any help of seed sown, and that it was so directed purely for my sustenance in that wild, miserable place.

This touched my heart a little and brought tears from my eyes, and I began to bless myself that such a miracle of nature should happen upon my account; and this was the more strange to me because I saw near it, all along by the side of the rock, some other straggling stalks, which proved to be stalks of rice, and which I recognized, because I had seen it grow in Africa when I was ashore there.

I not only thought these the pure productions of Providence for my support, but not doubting but that there was more in the place, I went all over that part of the island where I had been before, peering in every corner and under every rock, in order to find more of it, but I could not find any. At last it occurred to me that I had shaken the bag of chicken food out in that place; and the wonder began to cease; and I must confess, my religious thankfulness to God's providence began to abate too, upon discovering that all this was nothing but what was natural; though I ought to have been as thankful for so strange and unforeseen providence as if it had been miraculous; for it *was* really the work of Providence to me: that should order or appoint that ten or twelve seeds of corn should remain unspoiled, when the rats had destroyed all the rest, as if it had been dropped from Heaven; also that I should throw it out into that particular place, where, it being in the shade of a high rock, it sprang up immediately; whereas, if I had thrown it anywhere else at that time, it had been burnt up and destroyed.

I carefully saved the ears of this corn, you may be sure, in their season, which was about the end of June; and laying up every kernel, I resolved to sow them all again, hoping in time to have some quantity, sufficient to supply me with bread. But it was not till the fourth year that I would allow myself the least bit of this corn to eat, and even then but sparingly, as I shall say afterward, in its order; for I lost all that I sowed the first season, by not observing the proper time; for I sowed it just before the dry season, so that it never came up at all, at least, not as it should have done: more of that, later.

Besides this barley, there were, as mentioned, twenty or thirty stalks of rice, which I preserved with the same care, and whose use was of the same kind, or to the same purpose, namely, to make me bread, or rather food; for I found ways to cook it up without baking, though I did that also after some time.

But to return to my journal:

I worked excessively hard these three or four months, to get my wall done; and on the 14th of April, I closed it up, contriving to go into it, not by a door, but over a wall, by a ladder, that there might be no human sign on the outside of my habitation.

April 16—I finished the ladder; so I climbed the ladder to the top, then pulled it up after me and let it down on the inside. This was a complete enclosure to me; for within I had room enough, and nothing could come at me from without, unless it could first mount my wall.

Earthquake and Storm

The very next day after this wall was finished, I almost had all my labor overthrown at once and myself killed as well. The case was thus: As I was busy on the inside of it, behind my tent, just in the entrance into my cave, I was terribly frightened with a most dreadfully surprising thing indeed. For, suddenly, I found the earth came tumbling down from the roof of my cave and from the edge of the hill over my head, and two of the posts I had set up in the cave cracked in a frightful manner. I was heartily scared, but thought nothing of what really was the cause, only thinking that the top of my cave was falling in, as some of it had done before. For fear I should be buried in it, I ran forward to my ladder, and not thinking myself safe there either, I got over my wall for fear of the pieces of the hill, which I expected might roll down upon me. I had no sooner stepped down upon the firm ground than I plainly saw it was a terrible earthquake; for the ground I stood on shook three times in about eight minutes, with three such shocks as would have overturned the strongest building that could be supposed to have stood upon the earth; and a great piece of the top of the rock that stood about half a mile from me, next to the sea, fell down with such a terrible noise as I never heard in all my life. I perceived also the very sea was put into violent motion by it; and I believe the shocks were stronger under the water than on the island.

I was so amazed with the thing itself, having never felt the like, or discoursed with anyone that had, that I was like one dead or stupefied; and the motion of the earth made my stomach sick like one that was tossed at sea; but the noise of the falling of the rock awakened me as it were, and rousing me from the stupefied condition I was in, filled me with horror, and I thought of nothing then but the hill falling upon my tent and all my household goods and burying all at once; and this sank my very soul within me a second time.

After the third shock was over, and I felt no more for some time, I began to take courage; and yet I had not heart enough to climb over my wall again, for fear of being buried alive, but still sat upon the ground, greatly cast down and disconsolate, not knowing what to do. All this while, I had not the least serious religious thought; nothing but the common "Lord have mercy upon me!" and when it was over, that went away, too.

While I sat thus, I found the air overcast, and it grew cloudy, as if it would rain. Soon after that, the wind arose by little and little, so that in less than half an hour it blew a most dreadful hurricane of wind: The sea was suddenly covered with foam and froth; the shore was covered with the breach of the water; the trees were torn up by the roots; and a terrible storm it was. This continued about three hours and then began to abate; and then in two hours more it was calm and began to rain very hard. All this while I sat upon the ground very much terrified and dejected; when suddenly it came to me that these winds and rain being the consequences of the earthquake, the earthquake itself was now spent and over, and I might venture into my cave again. With this thought, my spirits began to revive; and the rain also helping to persuade me, I went in and sat down in my tent; but the rain was so violent that my tent was ready to be beaten down with it; and I was forced to go into my cave, though very much afraid and uneasy, for fear it should fall on my head.

This violent rain forced me into some additional work, namely, to cut a hole through my new fortifications, like a sink, to let the water go out, which would otherwise have drowned my cave.

After I had been in my cave some time and felt no more earthquake shocks, I began to be more composed. And now to give me courage, which indeed was very low, I went to my little store and took a small sup of rum; which, however, I did then and always very sparingly, knowing I could have no more when that was gone. It continued raining all that night and a great part of the next day, so that I could not stir abroad; but my mind being more at rest, I began to think of what I had best do. I concluded that if the island was subject to these earthquakes, there would be no living for me in a cave, but I must consider building me some little hut in an open place that I might surround with a wall, as I had done here, and so make myself secure from wild beasts or men; for I concluded if I stayed where I was, I should certainly, one time or other, be buried alive.

With these thoughts, I resolved to move my tent from the place where it now stood, which was just under the hanging precipice of the hill, and which, if it should be shaken again, would certainly fall upon my tent; and I spent the next two days, being the 19th and 20th of April, in debating where and how to remove my habitation. The fear of being swallowed up alive was such that I never slept in quiet; and yet the apprehensions of lying abroad without any fence were almost equal to it; but still, when I looked about and saw how everything was put in order, how pleasantly concealed I was, and how safe from danger, it made me reluctant to move. In the meantime, it occurred to me that it would require a vast deal of time for me to do this, and that I must be contented to run the venture where I was, till I had found another camp for myself and had secured it so as to move to it. So with this resolution I composed myself for a time and resolved that I would go to work with all speed to build me a wall with piles and cables, etc., in a circle, as before, and set my tent up in it, when it was finished; but that I would venture to stay where I was till it was finished and fit to move to it. This was the 21st.

April 22—The next morning I began to consider the means for putting this resolve into execution; but I was at a great loss about my tools. I had three large axes and an abundance of hatchets (for we carried the hatchets for traffic with the Indians); but with much chopping and cutting knotty, hard wood, they were all full of notches and dull; and though I had a grindstone, I could not turn it and grind my tools, too. This cost me as much thought as a statesman would have bestowed upon a grand issue of politics, or a judge upon the life and death of a man. At length I contrived a wheel with a string to turn it with my foot that I might have both my hands free.

Note—I had not seen any such thing in England, or at least not to notice how it was done, though since, I have observed it was very common there; besides that, my grindstone was very large and heavy. This machine cost me a full week's work to bring it to perfection.

April 28, 29—These two whole days I took up in grinding my tools, my machine for turning my grindstone performing very well.

April 30—Having perceived my bread had been low a great while, I now took a survey of it and reduced myself to one biscuit-cake a day, which made my heart very heavy.

May 1—In the morning, looking toward the seaside, the tide being low, I saw something lie on the shore bigger than ordinary, and it looked like a cask. When I came to it, I found a small barrel and two or three pieces of the wreck of the ship, which were driven on shore by the late hurricane; and looking toward the wreck itself, I thought it seemed to lie higher out of the water than it used to. I examined the barrel that was driven on shore and soon found it was a barrel of gunpowder; but it had taken water, and the powder was caked as hard as a stone. However, I rolled it farther on shore for the present and went on upon the sands, as near as I could to the wreck of the ship, to look for more.

A Visit to the Wreck

When I came down to the ship, I found it strangely removed. The forecastle, which before lay buried in sand, was heaved up at least six feet, and the stern, which was broken into pieces and parted from the rest by the force of the sea soon after I had ceased rummaging in her, was tossed, as it were, up and cast on one side; and the sand was thrown so high on that side next to the stern that, whereas there was a great expanse of water before so that I could not come within a quarter of a mile of the wreck without swimming, I could now walk almost up to her when the tide was out. I was surprised with this at first, but soon concluded it must have been done by the earthquake; and as by this violence the ship was more broken open than formerly, so many things came daily on shore, which the sea had loosened, and which the winds and water rolled by degrees to the land.

This wholly diverted my thoughts from the design of removing my habitation, and I busied myself mightily, that day especially, in searching whether I could find a way into the ship; but I found nothing was to be expected of that kind, as all the inside of the ship was choked up with sand. However, as I had learned not to despair of anything, I resolved to pull everything to pieces that I could of the ship, concluding that everything I could get from her would be of some use or other to me.

May 3—I began with my saw and cut a piece of a beam through, which I thought held some of the upper part or quarterdeck together, and when I had cut it through, I cleared away the sand as well as I could from the side that lay highest; but the tide coming in, I was obliged to cease for that time.

May 4—I went fishing, but caught not one fish that I dared eat of, till I was weary of my sport; when, just about to quit, I caught a young dolphin. I had made me a long line of some rope-yarn, but I had no hooks; yet I frequently caught fish enough, as much as I cared to eat; all which I dried in the sun and ate dry.

May 5—Worked on the wreck; cut another beam asunder and brought three great fir planks off from the decks, which I tied together and floated to shore when high tide came in.

May 6—Worked on the wreck; got several iron bolts out of her, and other pieces of ironwork; worked very hard and came home very much tired, and had thoughts of giving it up.

May 7—Went to the wreck again, but not planning to work; found the weight of the wreck had broken itself down, the beams being cut; that several pieces of the ship seemed to lie loose, and the inside of the hold lay so open

that I could see into it; but it was almost full of water and sand.

May 8—Went to the wreck and carried an iron crowbar to wrench up the deck, which lay now quite clear of the water or sand. I wrenched open two planks and brought them on shore also with the tide. I left the iron crowbar in the wreck for the next day.

May 9—Went to the wreck and, with the crowbar, made way into the body of the wreck. I felt several casks and loosened them with the crowbar, but could not break them up. I felt also a roll of English lead, but could not stir it, as it was too heavy to move.

May 10, 11, 12, 13, 14—Went every day to the wreck and got a great deal of pieces of timber, and boards, or planks, and two or three hundredweight of iron.

May 15—I carried two hatchets, to see if I could not cut a piece off the roll of lead, by placing the edge of one hatchet and driving it with the other; but as it lay about a foot and a half in the water, I could not make any blow to drive the hatchet.

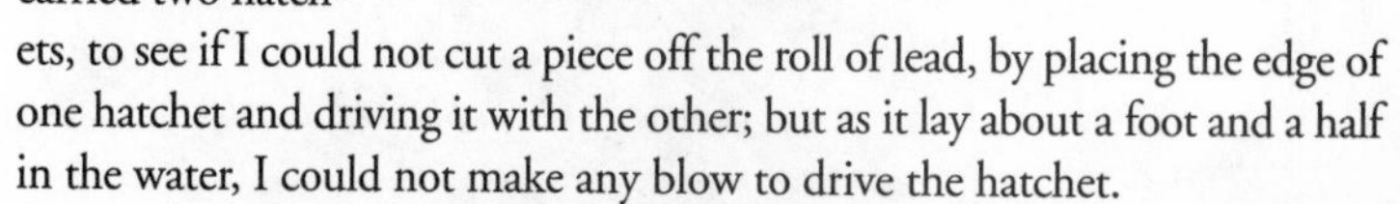

May 16—It had blown hard in the night, and the wreck appeared more

broken by the force of the water; but I stayed so long in the woods, to get pigeons for food, that the tide prevented me from going to the wreck that day.

May 17—I saw some pieces of the wreck blown on shore, at a great distance, nearly two miles off from me, but resolved to see what they were, and found they were pieces of the head, but too heavy for me to bring away.

May 24—Every day, to this day, I worked on the wreck; and with hard labor I loosened some things so much with the crowbar that the next flowing tide floated several casks out, and two of the seamen's chests; but the wind blowing from the shore, nothing came to land that day but pieces of timber and a hogshead, which had some Brazilian pork in it; but the saltwater and the sand had spoiled it. I continued this work every day to the 15th of June, except for the time necessary to get food, which I always appointed, during this part of my employment, to be when the tide was up, that I might be ready when it was ebbed out; and by this time I had gotten timber, and

plank, and ironwork enough to have built a good boat, if I had known how; and also I got, at several times, and in several pieces, nearly one hundredweight of the sheet lead.

June 16—Going down to the seaside, I found a large tortoise, or turtle.

Note—This was the first I had seen, which, it seems, was only my misfortune, not any defect of the place or the scarcity; for had I happened to be on the other side of the island, I might have had hundreds of them every day, as I found afterward, but perhaps had paid dearly enough for them.

June 17—I spent the day cooking the turtle. I found in her threescore eggs; and her flesh was to me, at that time, the most savory and pleasant that ever I tasted in my life, having had no flesh, but of goats and fowls, since I landed in this horrible place.

Violent Ague

June 18—Rained all the day, and I stayed within. I thought, at this time, the rain felt cold, and I was somewhat chilly, which I knew was not usual in that latitude.

June 19—Very ill and shivering, as if the weather had been cold.

June 20—No rest all night; violent pains in my head, and feverish.

June 21—Very ill; frightened almost to death with the apprehensions of my sad condition—to be sick, and no help. Prayed to God for the first time since the storm off Hull, but scarcely knew what I said or why, my thoughts being all confused.

June 22—A little better, but under dreadful apprehensions of sickness.

June 23—Very bad again; cold and shivering, and then a violent headache.

June 24—Much better.

June 25—An ague, very violent. The fever held me seven hours; cold fever, and hot with faint sweats after it.

June 26—Better; and having no victuals to eat, took my gun, but found myself very weak; however, I killed a she-goat and with much difficulty got it home, broiled some of it, and ate. I would fain have stewed it and made some broth, but had no pot to put it in.

June 27—The ague again so violent that I lay abed all day and neither ate nor drank. I was ready to perish for thirst; but so weak I had no strength to stand up, or to get myself any water to drink. Prayed to God again, but was light-headed; and when I was not, I knew not what to say; only I lay and cried, *Lord, look upon me! Lord, pity me! Lord, have mercy upon me!* I suppose I did nothing else for two or three hours; till the fever wearing off, I fell asleep and did not awake till far in the night. When I awoke, I found myself much refreshed, but weak and exceedingly thirsty; however, as I had no water in my whole habitation, I was forced to lie there till morning and went to sleep again. In this second sleep, I had this terrible dream. In it I was sitting on the ground, on the outside of my wall, where I sat when the storm blew after the earthquake, and I saw a man descend from a great black cloud, in a bright flame of fire, and light upon the ground. He was all over as bright as a flame, so that I could scarcely bear to look toward him; his countenance was most inexpressibly dreadful, impossible for words to describe. When he stepped upon the ground with his feet, I thought the earth trembled, just as it had done before in the earthquake; and all the air looked, to my apprehension, as if it had been filled with flashes of fire. He was no sooner landed upon the earth but he moved toward me, with a long spear or weapon in his hand to kill me; and when he came to a rising ground, at some distance, he spoke to me—or I heard a voice so terrible that it is impossible to express the terror of it. All that I can say I understood was this: *Seeing that all these things have not brought thee to repentance, now thou shalt die;* at which words, I thought he lifted up the spear that was in his hand to kill me.

Thoughts in Sickness

No one who shall ever read this account will expect that I should be able to describe the horrors of my soul at this terrible vision. It seemed to me then to be a dream within a dream. Nor is it any more possible to describe the impression that remained upon my mind when I awakened and found it was but a dream.

I had, alas, no divine knowledge. What I had received by the good instruction of my father was then worn out by an uninterrupted series, for eight years, of seafaring wickedness and a constant conversation with none but such as were, like myself, wicked and profane to the last degree. I do not remember that I had, in all that time, one thought that so much as tended either to looking upward toward God, or inward toward a reflection upon my own ways; but a certain stupidity of soul, without desire of good or conscience of evil, had entirely overwhelmed me; and I was all that the most hardened, unthinking, wicked creature among our common sailors can be supposed to be—not having the least sense, either of the fear of God in dangers, or of thankfulness to God in deliverances.

In the relating what is already past of my story, this will be the more easily believed when I shall add that through all the variety of miseries that had to this day befallen me, I never had so much as one thought of its being the hand of God, or that it was a just punishment for my former sins—my rebellious behavior against my father—or my present sins, which were great, or so much as a punishment for the general course of my wicked life. When I was on the desperate expedition on the desert shores of Africa, I never had so much as one thought of what would become of me, or one wish to God to direct me where I should go, or to keep me from the danger that apparently surrounded me, as well from voracious creatures as cruel savages; but I was merely thoughtless of God or a Providence. I acted like a mere brute, from the principles of nature, and by the dictates of common sense only, and indeed hardly that. When I was delivered and taken up at sea by the Portuguese captain, well used, and dealt justly and honorably with, as well as charitably, I had not the least thankfulness in my thoughts. When, again, I was shipwrecked, ruined, and in danger of drowning on this island, I was far from remorse, or looking on it as a judgment. I only said to myself often that I was an unfortunate dog and born to be always miserable.

It is true, when I first got on shore here and found all my ship's crew drowned and myself spared, I was surprised with a kind of ecstasy and some transports of soul, which, had the grace of God assisted, might have come up to true thankfulness. But it ended where it began, in a mere common flight of joy, or, as I may say, being glad I was alive, without the least reflection upon the distinguishing goodness of the Hand that had preserved me and had singled me out to be preserved when all the rest were destroyed, or an inquiry why Providence had been thus merciful to me. Even just the same common sort of joy, which seamen generally have after they have got safe ashore from a shipwreck, all of which they drown in the next bowl of punch and forget almost as soon as it is over; and all the rest of my life was like it. Even when I was afterward, on due consideration, made sensible of my condition, how I was cast on this dreadful place, out of the reach of humankind, out of all hope of relief, or prospect of redemption, as soon as I saw a probability of living, and that I should not starve and perish for hunger, all the sense of my affliction wore off; and I began to be very easy, applied myself to the works proper for my preservation and supply, and was far enough from considering my condition to be judgment from Heaven or as the hand of God against me. Well, these were thoughts that very seldom entered into my head.

I Reflect on My Ingratitude

The growing up of the corn, as is hinted in my diary, had, at first, some little influence upon me and began to affect me with seriousness, as long as I thought it had something miraculous in it; but as soon as ever the miracle part of it was removed, all the impressions that resulted from it wore off also, as I have noted already. Even the earthquake—though nothing could be more terrible in its nature, or more immediately directing one to the in-visible Power that alone directs such things—yet no sooner was the first fright over but the impression it had made went away also. I had no more sense of God or His judgments—much less of the present affliction of my circumstances being from His hand—than if I had been in the most prosperous condition of life. But now, when I became sick and in the long hours of pain had time to think about the miseries of death; when my spirits began to sink under the burden of a strong fever, and my nature was exhausted by the violence of it; conscience, which had slept so long, began to awake, and I began to reproach myself with my past life, in which I had so evidently, by uncommon wickedness, so provoked the justice of God as to lay me under uncommon strokes and to deal with me in so vindictive a manner. These reflections oppressed me from the second or third day of my illness and in the violence, as well of the fever as of the dreadful reproaches of my conscience, extorted some words from me like praying to God, though I cannot say they were either a prayer attended with desires or with hopes: It was rather the voice of mere fright and distress. My thoughts were confused, the convictions deep, and the horror of dying in such a miserable condition raised such apprehension in my head with the mere thought of it that in these cries of my soul, I knew not what my tongue might express. But it was rather exclamations such as "Lord, what a miserable creature I am! If I should be sick, I shall certainly die for want of help, and what will become of me?" Then the tears ran down from my eyes, and I could say no more for a good while.

In this interval, the good advice of my father came to my mind, and presently his prediction, which I mentioned at the beginning of this story, namely, that if I did take this foolish step, God would not bless me, and I would have leisure hereafter to reflect upon having neglected his counsel, when there might be none to assist me in my recovery.

"Now," said I aloud, "my dear father's words are come to pass: God's justice has overtaken me, and I have none to help or hear me. I rejected the voice of Providence, which had mercifully put me in a position or station of life wherein I might have been happy and easy; but I would neither see it myself, nor learn to know the blessing of it from my parents. I left them to mourn over my folly; and now I am left to mourn under the consequences of it. I refused their help and assistance, who would have lifted me into the world and would have made everything easy for me; and now I have difficulties to struggle with too great for even nature itself to support, and no assistance, no help, no comfort, no advice." Then I cried out, "Lord, be my help, for I am in great distress."

This was the first prayer, if I might call it so, that I had prayed for many years. But I return to my diary:

June 28—Having been somewhat refreshed with the sleep I had had, and

the fever being entirely gone, I got up; and though the fright and terror of my dream was very great, yet I considered that the ague would return again the next day, and now was my time to get something to refresh and support myself when I should be ill. The first thing I did, I filled a large square case-bottle with water and set it upon my table, in reach of my bed; and to take off the likely chill or anguish, I put about a quarter of a pint of rum into it and mixed them together. Then I got me a piece of goat's flesh and broiled it on the coals, but could eat very little. I walked about, but was very weak and withal very sad and heavyhearted in the sense of my miserable condition, dreading the return of my disease the next day. At night, I made my supper of three of the turtle's eggs, which I roasted in the ashes and ate, as we call it, in the shell, and this was the first bit of meat I had ever asked God's blessing for, even, as I could remember, in my whole life.

After I had eaten, I tried to walk, but found myself so weak that I could hardly carry the gun, for I never went out without that; so I went out but a little way and sat down upon the ground, looking out upon the sea, which was just before me and very calm and smooth. As I sat there, some thoughts such as these occurred to me: *What is the earth and sea, of which I have seen so much? Where is it produced? And what am I, and all the other creatures, wild and tame, human and brute? From what source are we? Surely we are all made by some secret Power, who formed the earth and sea, the air and sky. And who is that?* Then it followed most naturally—*It is God that has made it all. Well, but then,* it came on strongly, *if God has made all these things, He guides and governs them all, and all things that concern them; for the Being that could make all things must certainly have power to guide and direct them. If so, nothing can happen, in the great circuit of His works, either without His knowledge or His appointment.*

And if nothing happens without His knowledge, He knows that I am here and am in this dreadful condition; and if nothing happens without His appointment, He has appointed all this to befall me.

Nothing occurred in my thoughts to contradict any of these conclusions, and therefore it rested upon me with the greater force that it must needs be that God had appointed all this to befall me; that I was brought to this miserable circumstance by His direction, He having the sole power, not of me only, but of everything that happened in the world. Immediately it foliowed—*Why has God done this to me? What have I done to be thus used?*

My conscience presently checked me in that inquiry, as if I had blasphemed and methought it spoke to me like a voice, *Wretch, dost* thou *ask what thou hast done? Look back upon a dreadful, misspent life and ask thyself what thou hast* not *done? Ask, why is it that thou wert not long ago destroyed? Why wert thou not drowned in Yarmouth Roads? Killed in the fight when the ship was taken by the Sallee man-of-war? Devoured by the wild beasts off the coast of Africa? Or drowned here, when all the crew perished but thyself? Dost* thou *ask, "What have I done?"*

I was struck dumb with these reflections, as one astonished, and had not a word to say—no, not to even answer myself—but rose up pensive and sad, walked back to my retreat, and went up over my wall, as if I had been going to bed; but my thoughts were sadly disturbed, and I had no inclination to sleep; so I sat down in my chair and lighted my lamp, for it began to be dark. Now, as the apprehensions of the return of my fever terrified me very much, it occurred to me that the Brazilians take no medicine but their tobacco for almost all fevers, and I had a piece of a roll of tobacco in one of the chests, which was quite cured, and some also that was green and not quite cured.

Gradual Recovery

I went, directed by Heaven, no doubt; for in this chest I found a cure both for soul and body. I opened the chest and found what I looked for, namely, the tobacco; and as the few books I had saved lay there, too, I took out one of the Bibles that I mentioned before, and which to this time I had not found leisure, or so much as inclination, to look into. I say I took it out and brought both that and the tobacco with me to the table. What use to make of the tobacco I knew not, as to my disease, or whether it was good for it or not; but I tried several experiments with it, as if I was resolved it should heal one way or another. I first took a piece of leaf and chewed it in my mouth, which indeed, at first, almost stupefied my brain, the tobacco being green and strong, and that I had not been used to it. Then I took some and steeped it an hour or two in some rum and resolved to take a dose of it when I lay down; and, lastly, I burnt some upon a pan of coals and held my nose close over the smoke of it as long as I could bear it, as well for the heat as for the healing of it, and I held it almost to suffocation.

In the interval of this operation, I took up the Bible and began to read; but my head was too much disturbed with the tobacco to bear reading, at least at that time; only having opened the book casually, the first words I noticed were these: *Call upon Me in the day of trouble, and I will deliver thee, and thou shalt glorify Me.* These words were very apt to my case and made some impression upon my thoughts at the time of reading them, though not so much as they did afterward; for, as for being *delivered,* the word had no meaning, as I may say, to me. The thing was so remote, so impossible in my apprehension of things, that I began to say, as the children of Israel did when they were promised flesh to eat, "Can God spread a table in the wilderness?"; so I began to say, "Can God Himself deliver me from this place?" And as it was not for many years that any hope for deliverance seemed likely, this prevailed very often upon my thoughts; however, the words made a great impression upon me, and I mused upon them very often.

It grew now late, and the tobacco had, as I said, made me so drowsy that I was inclined to sleep. So I left my lamp burning in the cave, lest I should want anything in the night, and went to bed. But before I lay down, I did what I never had done in all my life: I knelt down and prayed to God to fulfill the promise to me that if I called upon Him in the day of trouble, He would deliver me. After my broken and imperfect prayer was over, I drank the rum in which I had steeped the tobacco, which was so strong and rank of the tobacco that indeed I could scarcely get it down. Immediately upon this I went to bed; and I found presently it flew up into my head violently; but I fell into a sound sleep and waked no more till, by the sun, it must necessarily be nearly three o'clock in the afternoon of the next day. Nay, to this hour I am partly of the opinion that I slept all the next day and night and till almost three the day after; for otherwise I know not how I should lose a day out of my reckoning in the days of the week, as it appeared some years after I had done; for if I had lost it by crossing and recrossing the date line, I should have lost more than one day; but in my account it was lost, and I never knew which way. Be that, however, one way or another, when I awakened I found myself exceedingly refreshed and my spirits lively and cheerful; when I got up I was stronger than I was the day before, and my stomach better, for I was hungry; and, in short, I had no fever the next day, but continued much altered for the better. This was the 29th.

The 30th was my well day, of course, and I went abroad with my gun, but did not care to travel too far. I killed a sea fowl or two, something like a brand[1] goose, and brought them home, but was not very inclined to eat them; so I ate some more of the turtle's eggs, which were very good. That evening I renewed the medicine, which I had supposed did me good the day before, that is, the tobacco steeped in rum; only I did not take so much as before, nor did I chew any of the leaf or hold my head over the smoke. However, I was not so well the next day, which was the 1st of July, as I hoped I should have been; for I had a little bit of a cold fever, but it was not much.

---

1. *Brand,* Brant or Brent.

July 2—I renewed the medicine all the three ways, and dosed myself with it as at first, and doubled the quantity that I drank.

July 3—The fever did not return, though I did not recover my full strength for some weeks after. While I was thus gathering strength, my thoughts ran exceedingly upon this scripture, "I will deliver thee"; and the impossibility of my deliverance lay much upon my mind, discouraging me from ever expecting it. But as I was depressing myself with such thoughts, it occurred to me that I brooded so much upon my deliverance from the main affliction that I disregarded the deliverance I had already received, and I was, as it were, made to ask myself such questions as these, namely: "Have I not been delivered, and wonderfully too, from sickness? From the most distressed condition that could possibly be and that was so frightful to me? And what notice had I taken of it? Had I done my part? God had delivered me, but I had not glorified Him; that is to say, if I had not given recognition and been thankful for that as a deliverance, how could I expect greater deliverance?" This touched my heart very much; and immediately I knelt down and gave God thanks aloud for my recovery from my sickness.

July 4—In the morning, I took the Bible; and beginning with the New Testament, I began seriously to read it and imposed upon myself to read awhile every morning and every night, not tying myself to the number of chapters, but as long as my thoughts should engage me. It was not long after I set myself seriously to this task that I found my heart more deeply and sincerely affected with the wickedness of my past life. The impression of my dream revived; and the words, "All these things have not brought thee to repentance," ran seriously in my thoughts. I was earnestly begging God to give me repentance, when it happened providentially the very day that, reading the Scripture, I came to these words: "He is exalted a Prince and a Savior, to give repentance and to give remission." I threw down the book; and with my heart as well as my hands lifted up to heaven, in a kind of ecstasy of joy, I cried aloud, "Jesus, Thou Son of David! Jesus, Thou exalted Prince and Savior, give me repentance!" This was the first time I could say, in the true sense of the words, that I prayed in all my life; for now I prayed with a sense of my condition and with a true scriptural view of hope, founded on the encouragement of the Word of God; and from this time on, I can say, I began to have hope that God would hear me.

Now I began to construe the words mentioned above, "Call on Me, and I will deliver thee," in a different sense from what I had ever done before; for then I had no notion of anything being called *deliverance* but my being delivered from the captivity I was in; for though I was indeed at large in the place, yet the island was certainly a prison to me, and that in the worst sense of the word. But now I learned to take it in another way: Now I looked back upon my past life with such horror, and my sins appeared so dreadful, that my soul sought nothing of God but deliverance from the load of guilt that bore down all my comfort. As for my solitary life, it was nothing; I did not so much as pray to be delivered from it, or think of it; it was all of no consideration, in comparison to this. And I add this part here, to whoever shall read it, that whenever they come to a true sense of things, they will find deliverance from sin a much greater blessing than deliverance from affliction.

But, leaving this part, I return to my journal:

My condition began now to be, though not less miserable as to my way of living, yet much easier to my mind; and my thoughts being directed, by a constant reading of the Scripture and praying to God, to things of a higher nature, I had a great deal of comfort within, which, till now, I knew nothing of. Also, as my health and strength returned, I bestirred myself to furnish myself with everything that I lacked and made my way of living as regular as I could.

From the 4th of July to the 14th, I was chiefly employed in walking about with my gun in my hand, a little at a time, as a man who was gathering up his strength after a bout of sickness; for it is hardly to be imagined how low I was and to what weakness I was reduced. The application of tobacco that I made use of was perfectly new, and perhaps what had never cured an ague before; neither can I recommend it to anyone to practice, by this experiment; and though it did carry off the fever, yet it rather contributed to weaken me; for I had frequent convulsions in my nerves and limbs for some time. I learned from it also this, in particular, that being abroad in the rain was the most pernicious thing to my health that could possibly be, especially in those rains that came attended with storms and hurricanes of wind; for as the rains that came in a dry season were almost always accompanied by such storms, so I found those rains were much more dangerous than the rains that fell in September and October.

Chapter 8

The Other Side of the Island

I had now been in this unhappy island above ten months; all possibility of deliverance from this condition seemed to be entirely taken from me; and I firmly believed that no human shape had ever set foot upon that place. Having now fully secured my habitation, or so I thought, I had a great desire to make a more perfect discovery of the island and to see what else I might find, which yet I knew nothing of.

The Fertile Side of the Island

It was the 15th day of July that I began to take a more particular survey of the island itself. I went up the creek first, where, as I mentioned before, I brought my rafts on shore. I found, after I came about two miles up, that the tide did not flow any higher; and that it was no more than a little brook of running water, and very fresh and good; but this being the dry season, there was hardly any water in some parts of it; at least, not enough to run in any stream, at least as far as I could see. On the banks of this brook, I found many pleasant savannahs or meadows, plain, smooth, and covered with grass; and on the rising parts of them, next to the higher grounds, where the water, as it might be supposed, never overflowed, I found a great deal of tobacco, green, and growing to a great and very strong stalk; there were divers other plants, which I had no knowledge of and might, perhaps, have virtues of their own, but which I had no way of finding out. I searched for the cassava root, which all the Indians in that climate make their bread of, but I could find none. I saw large plants of aloes, but did not understand what to do with them. I saw several sugarcanes, but wild and, for want of cultivation, imperfect. I contented myself with these discoveries for the time and came back, wondering what course I might take to discover the virtue and goodness of any of the fruits or plants that I should discover; but I could arrive at

no conclusion. For, in short, I had been so unobserving while I was in the Brazils that I knew little of the plants of the field, at least, very little that might serve me to any purpose now in my distress.

The next day, the 16th, I went up the same way again; and after going somewhat farther than I had gone the day before, I found the brook and the savannahs to cease, and the country became more woody than before. In this part I found different fruits, and particularly I found melons upon the ground, in great abundance, and grapes upon the trees—the vines had spread indeed over the trees, and the clusters of grapes were just now in their prime, very ripe and rich. This was a surprising discovery, and I was exceedingly glad of it; but I was warned by my experience to eat sparingly of them, remembering that, when I was ashore in Barbary, the eating of grapes killed several of our Englishmen, who were slaves there, by throwing them into dysentery and fevers. But I found an excellent use for these grapes, and that was, to cure or dry them in the sun and keep them as dried grapes or raisins are kept, which I thought would be, as indeed they were, wholesome and as agreeable to eat, when no grapes might be had.

Fresh Discoveries

I spent all that evening there and went not back to my habitation, which, by the way, was the first night, as I might say, I had stayed away from home. In the night I found it necessary to climb up into a tree, where I slept well. The next morning I proceeded upon my expedition of discovery, traveling nearly four miles, as I might judge by the length of the valley, keeping still due north, with a ridge of hills on the south and north of me. At the end of this march I came to an opening, where the country seemed to descend to the west; and a little spring of fresh water, which issued out of the side of the hill by me, ran the other way, that is, due east; and the country appeared so fresh, so green, so flourishing, everything being in a constant verdure, or flourish of spring, that it looked like a planted garden.

I descended a little on the side of that delicious valley, surveying it with a secret kind of pleasure, though mixed with other afflicting thoughts, to think that this was all my own; that I was king and lord of all this country, without question, and had a right of possession; and, if I could convey it, I might have it in inheritance as completely as any lord of a manor in England. I saw here abundance of cocoa trees, orange and lemon, and citron trees; but all wild, and few bearing any fruit, at least not then. However, the green limes that I gathered were not only pleasant to eat, but very wholesome; and I mixed their juice afterward with water, which made it very cool and refreshing. I found now I had food enough to gather and carry home; and I resolved to lay up a store of grapes as well as limes and lemons, to furnish myself for the wet season, which I knew was approaching. In order to do this, I gathered a great heap of grapes in one place, a lesser heap in another place, and a great parcel of limes and lemons in another place; and taking a few of each with me, I traveled homeward, and resolved to come again, and bring a bag or sack, or what I could make to carry the rest home. Accordingly, having spent three days in this journey, I came home (so I must now call my tent and my cave); but before I got there, the grapes were spoiled; the richness of the fruit, and the weight of the juice, having broken them and bruised them, they were good for little or nothing; as for the limes, they were good, but I could bring but a few.

The next day, being the 19th, I went back, having made me two small bags to bring home my harvest; but I was surprised when, coming to my heaps of grapes, for they were so rich and fine when I gathered them, I found them all spread abroad, trodden to pieces, and dragged about, some here, some there, and most eaten and devoured. By this I concluded there were

I descended a little on the side of that delicious valley.

some wild creatures thereabouts, which had done this; but what they were I knew not. However, as I found there was no laying them up in heaps and no carrying them away in a sack—that one way they would be destroyed, and the other way they would be crushed with their own weight—I took another course: I gathered a large quantity of the grapes and hung them upon the outermost branches of the trees that they might cure and dry in the sun; and as for the limes and lemons, I carried as many back as my strength permitted.

When I came home from this journey, I contemplated with great pleasure the fruitfulness of that valley and the pleasantness of the situation, the security from storm on that side of the water, and the wood; and concluded that I had pitched upon a place to fix my abode that was by far the worst part of the country. Upon the whole, I began to consider removing my habitation and to look out for a place equally safe as where now I was situated, if possible, in that pleasant, fruitful part of the island.

This thought ran long in my head, and for some time I was almost convinced, the pleasantness of the place tempting me; but when I came to a more serious view of it, I considered that I was now by the seaside, where it was at least possible that something might happen to my advantage; and that the same ill fate that brought me hither might bring some other unhappy wretches to the same place; and though it was scarcely probable that any such thing should ever happen, yet to enclose myself among the hills and woods in the center of the island was to confirm my bondage and to render an escape not only improbable but impossible; and that therefore I ought not by any means to move. However, I was so enamored with this place that I spent much of my time there for the whole remaining part of July; and though, upon second thought, I had resolved not to move, yet I built me a little bower and surrounded it at a distance with a strong fence, being a double hedge, as high as I could reach, well staked, and filled between with brushwood. Here I lay very secure, sometimes two or three nights together, always going over it with a ladder as before; so that I now fancied I had my country house and my seacoast house—and this work took me up to the beginning of August.

I had but newly finished my fence, and was beginning to enjoy my labor, when the rains came and made me stick close to my first habitation; for though I had made me a tent like the other, with a piece of a sail, and spread it very well, yet I had not the shelter of a hill to keep me from storms, nor a cave behind me to retreat into when the rains were extraordinarily heavy.

About the beginning of August, as I said, I had finished my bower and began to enjoy myself. The 3rd of August, I found the grapes I had hung up were perfectly dried and indeed were excellent good raisins of the sun; so I began to take them down from the trees, and it was very fortunate that I did so, for the rains that followed would have spoiled them, and I would have lost the best part of my winter food (for I had above two hundred large bunches of them). No sooner had I taken them all down and carried most of them home to my cave, but it began to rain; and from hence, which was the 14th of August, it rained more or less every day till the middle of October, and sometimes so violently that I could not stir out of my cave for several days.

In this season, I was much surprised with the increase of my family. I had been concerned for the loss of one of my cats, who ran away from me, or, as I thought, had been dead, and I heard no more tidings of her till, to my astonishment, she came home about the end of August with three kittens. This was the more strange to me because, though I had killed a wild cat, as I called it, with my gun, yet I thought it was a quite different kind from our European cats; but the young cats were the same kind of house-breed as the old one; and both my cats being females, I thought it very strange. But from these three cats I afterward came to be so pestered with cats that I was forced to kill them like vermin, or wild beasts, and to drive them from my house as much as possible.

From the 14th of August to the 26th, there was incessant rain, so that I could not stir, and I was now very careful not to get too wet. In this confinement, I began to be straitened for food: but venturing out twice, I one day killed a goat; and the next day, which was the 26th, found a very large tortoise, which was a treat to me, and my food was regulated thus: I ate a bunch of raisins for my breakfast; a piece of the goat's flesh, or of the turtle, for my dinner, broiled (for, to my great misfortune, I had no vessel to boil or stew anything); and two or three of the turtle's eggs for supper.

During this confinement in my cover by the rain, I worked daily two or three hours at enlarging my cave, and by degrees worked it on toward one side, till I came to the outside of the hill and made a door or way out, which came beyond my fence or wall; and so I came in and out this way. But I was not perfectly at ease at lying so open; for, as I had managed myself before, I was in a perfect enclosure; whereas now, I thought, I lay exposed, and yet I could not perceive that there was any living thing to fear; the biggest creature that I had yet seen upon the island being a goat.

The Anniversary of My Shipwreck

Sept. 30—I was now come to the unhappy anniversary of my landing. I added up the notches on my post and found I had been on shore three hundred and sixty-five days. I kept this day as a solemn fast, setting it apart for religious exercise, prostrating myself on the ground with the most serious humiliation, confessing my sins to God, acknowledging His righteous judgment upon me, and praying to Him to have mercy on me through Jesus Christ; and having not tasted the least refreshment for twelve hours, even till the going down of the sun, I then ate a biscuit-cake and a bunch of grapes and went to bed, finishing the day as I began it. I had all this time observed no Sabbath-day, for as at first I had no sense of religion upon my mind, I had, after some time, omitted to distinguish the weeks by making a longer notch than ordinary for the Sabbath-day, and so did not really know what any of the days were; but now, having cast up the days as above, I found I had been there a year; so I divided it into weeks and set apart every seventh day for a Sabbath; though I found at the end of my account I had lost a day or two in my reckoning. A little after this, my ink began to fail me, and so I contented myself to use it more sparingly and to write down only the most remarkable events of my life, without continuing a daily memorandum of other things.

The rainy season and the dry season began to now appear regular to me, and I learned to divide them so as to provide for them accordingly; but I bought all my experience before I had it, and this I am going to relate was one of the most discouraging experiments that I made of all.

I have mentioned that I had saved the few ears of barley and rice that had so surprisingly sprung up, I thought, of themselves. I believed there were about thirty stalks of rice and about twenty of barley; and now I thought it a proper time to sow it, after the rains, the sun being in its southern position, going from me. Accordingly, I dug up a piece of ground as well as I could with my wooden spade, and dividing it into two parts, I sowed my grain; but as I was sowing, it casually occurred to me that I would not sow it all at first, because I did not know when was the proper time for it, so I sowed about two-thirds of the seed, leaving about a handful of each. It was a great comfort to me afterward that I did so, for not one corn of what I sowed this time came to anything; for the dry months following, the earth having had no rain after the seed was sown, it had no moisture to assist its growth and never came up at all till the wet season had come again, and then it grew as if it had been newly sown.

Finding my first seed did not grow, which I easily imagined was because of

the drought, I sought for a moister piece of ground to make another trial in, and I dug up a piece of ground near my new bower and sowed the rest of my seed in February, a little before the vernal equinox; and this, having the rainy months of March and April to water it, sprang up very pleasantly and yielded a very good crop; but having only part of the seed remaining, and not daring to sow all that I had reaped, I had but a small quantity left, my whole crop not amounting to above half a peck of each kind. But by this experiment I was made master of my business and knew exactly when the proper season was to sow, and that I might expect two seedtimes and two harvests every year.

While this corn was growing, I made a little discovery, which was of use to me afterward. As soon as the rains were over and the weather began to settle, which was about the month of November, I made a visit up the country to my bower, where, though I had not been there for some months, I found all things just as I left them. The circle or double hedge that I had made was not only firm and unbroken, but the stakes that I had cut off of some trees that grew thereabouts were all shot out and grown with long branches, as much as a willow tree usually shoots the first year after lopping its head. I could not tell what tree to call it that the stakes were cut from. I was surprised, and yet very well pleased, to see the young trees grow; and I pruned them and led them up to grow as much alike as I could; and it is scarcely credible how beautiful a picture they grew into, in three years; so that though the hedge made a circle of about twenty-five yards in diameter, yet the trees, for such I might call them now, soon covered it, and it was a complete shade, sufficient to lodge under all the dry season. This made me resolve to cut some more stakes and make me a hedge like this in a semicircle around my wall (I mean that of my first dwelling), which I did; and placing the trees or stakes in a double row, at about eight yards distant from my first fence, they grew presently and were at first a fine cover to my habitation and, afterward, served for a defense also, as I shall observe later.

I found now that the seasons of the year might generally be divided, not into summer and winter, as in Europe, but into the rainy seasons and the dry seasons, which were generally thus:

The half of February, the whole of March, and the half of April—rainy, the sun being then on or near the equinox.

The other half of April, the whole of May, June, and July, and the half of August—dry, the sun being then to the north of the equinox.

The half of August, the whole of September, and the half of October—rainy, the sun then returning.

The half of October, the whole of November, December, and January, and the half of February—dry, the sun being then to the south of the equinox.

Basket-Making

The rainy seasons sometimes held on longer or shorter as the winds happened to blow. After I had found, by experience, the ill consequences of being abroad in the rain, I took care to furnish myself with provisions beforehand that I might not be obliged to go out, and I sat within doors as much as possible during the wet months. In this time I found much employment, and very suitable also to the time of year, for I found it lent itself to the making of many things that I had no way to furnish myself with but by hard labor and constant application. In particular, I tried many ways to make myself a basket, but all the twigs I could get for the purpose proved so brittle that they were worthless. It proved of excellent advantage to me now that when I was a boy I used to take great delight in standing at a basket-maker's, in the town where my father lived, to see them make their wickerware; and being, as boys usually are, very eager to help and a great observer of the methods they used in making them, and sometimes lending a hand, I had by this means so full knowledge of the methods of it, all I lacked were the materials. When it came to me that the twigs of that tree from which I cut my stakes that grew might possibly be as tough as the sallows, willows, and osiers in England, I resolved to try. Accordingly, the next day I went to my country house, as I called it, and cutting some of the smaller twigs, I found them to my purpose as much as I could desire; whereupon I came the next time prepared with a hatchet to cut down a quantity, which I soon found, for there was a great plenty of them. These I set up to dry within my circle of hedges, and when they were fit for use, I carried them to my cave; and here, during the next season, I employed myself in making, as best I could, a great many baskets, both to carry earth or to carry or lay up anything, as I had occasion. Though I did not finish them very handsomely, yet I made them sufficiently serviceable for my purpose; and thus, afterward, I took care never to be without them. As my wickerware decayed, I made more, especially strong, deep baskets to place my corn in, instead of sacks, when I should come to have any quantity of it.

Having mastered this difficulty, and taken a world of time to do it, I bestirred myself to see, if possible, how to supply two wants. I had no vessel to hold anything that was liquid, except two runlets, which were almost full of rum, and some glass bottles—some of the common size, and others that were case-bottles, square, for the holding of water, spirits, etc. I had not so much as a pot to boil anything in, except a great kettle, which I saved out of the ship, and which was too big for such uses as I desired it for—namely, to make broth and stew a bit of meat by itself. The second thing I fain would have had was a tobacco pipe,[1] but it was impossible for me to make one; however, I found a contrivance for that, too, at last. I employed myself in planting my second row of stakes or piles, and in this wicker-working, all the summer, or dry season; when another business took up more time than it could be imagined I could spare.

I mentioned before that I had a great mind to see the whole island, and that I had traveled up the brook and so on, to where I built my bower and where I had an opening quite to the sea on the other side of the island. I now

1. Apparently, something happened to the pipe he had earlier.

resolved to travel clear across to the seashore on that side; so, taking my gun, a hatchet, and my dog, and a larger quantity of powder and shot than usual, with two biscuit-cakes and a great bunch of raisins in my pouch for my store, I began my journey. When I had passed the vale where my bower stood, as above, I came within view of the sea to the west, and it being a very clear day, I could clearly discern land—whether an island or a continent I could not tell; but it lay very high, extending from the west to the west-southwest, at a very great distance; by my guess, it could not be less than fifteen or twenty leagues off.

I could not tell what part of the world this might be, other than that I knew it must be part of America, and, as I concluded by all my observations, it must be near the Spanish dominions and perhaps was all inhabited by savages, where, if I should have landed, I had been in a worse condition than I was now; and therefore I acquiesced in the dispositions of Providence, which I began now to own and to believe ordered everything for the best; so I quieted my mind with this and left off tormenting myself with fruitless wishes of being there.

Besides, after some pause upon this situation, I considered that if this land was the Spanish coast, I should certainly, sooner or later, see some vessel pass or repass one way or another; but if not, then it was the savage coast between the Spanish country and the Brazils, which was indeed infested by the worst of savages; for they are cannibals and fail not to murder and devour all the humans who fall into their hands.

With these considerations, I walked very leisurely on. I found that side of the island where I now was much pleasanter than mine—the open or savannah fields sweet, adorned with flowers and grass, and full of very fine woods. I saw an abundance of parrots and fain would I have caught one, if possible, to have kept it to be tame and taught it to speak to me. I did, after taking some pains, catch a young parrot, for I knocked it down with a stick, and having recovered it, I brought it home; but it was some years before I could make him speak; however, at last, I taught him to call me by my name very familiarly. But the accident that followed, though it be a trifle, will be very diverting to hear about.

A Table in the Wilderness

I was exceedingly intrigued by this journey. I found in the low grounds hares (as I thought them to be) and foxes; but they differed greatly from all the other kinds I had met with, nor could I bring myself to eat them, though

I killed several. But I had no need to be venturous, for I had no want of food, and of that which was very good, too, especially these three sorts: goats, pigeons, and turtle, or tortoise, which, added to my grapes, Leadenhall Market could not have furnished a table better than I, in proportion to the company; and though my case was deplorable enough, yet I had great cause for thankfulness that I was not driven to any extremities for food, but had plenty, even to dainties.

I never traveled in this journey more than two miles outright in a day, or thereabouts; but I took so many turns and returns to see what discoveries I could make, that I came weary enough to the place where I resolved to sit down for all night; and then I either reposed myself in a tree, or surrounded myself with a row of stakes set upright in the ground, either from one tree to another, or so no wild creature could come at me without waking me.

As soon as I came to the seashore, I was surprised to see that I had taken up my lot on the worst side of the island, for here, indeed, the shore was covered with innumerable turtles, whereas, on the other side I had found but three in a year and a half. Here was also an infinite number of fowls of many kinds, some of which I had not seen before, and many of them very good meat, but such as I knew not the names of, except those called penguins.

I could have shot as many as I pleased, but was very sparing of my powder and shot, and therefore had preferred to kill a she-goat, if I could, which I could better feed on; and though there were many goats here, more than on the other side of the island, yet it was with much more difficulty that I could come near them, the country being flat and even, and they saw me much sooner than when I was on the hills.

I confess this side of the country was much pleasanter than mine; but yet I had not the least inclination to move here, for as I was fixed in my habitation it became natural to me, and I seemed all the while I was here to be as it were upon a journey and far from home. However, I traveled along the shore of the sea toward the east, I suppose about twelve miles, and then setting up a great pole upon the shore for a mark, I concluded I would go home again, and that the next journey I took should be on the other side of the island east from my dwelling, and so round till I came to my post again, of which more later.

I took another way to come back than that I went, thinking I could easily keep all the island so much in my view that I could not miss finding my first dwelling by viewing the country; but I found myself mistaken, for, having come about two or three miles, I found myself descending into a very large valley, but so surrounded with hills, and those hills covered with woods, that I could not see which was my way by any direction other than that of the sun, nor even then unless I knew very well the position of the sun at that time of the day. It happened, to my further misfortune, that the weather proved hazy for three or four days while I was in this valley, and not being able to see the sun, I wandered about very uncomfortably, and at last was obliged to return to the seaside, look for my post, and come back the same way I went; and then, by easy journeys, I turned homeward, the weather being exceedingly hot, and my guns, ammunition, hatchet, and other things, very heavy.

In this journey my dog surprised a young kid and seized upon it, and I, running in to take hold of it, caught it and saved it alive from the dog. I had a great mind to bring it home if I could, for I had often been wondering whether it might not be possible to get a kid or two and so raise a breed of tame goats, which might supply me when my powder and shot should be spent. I made a collar for this little creature, and with some twine, which I made of some rope-yarn, which I always carried about me, I led him along, though with some difficulty, till I came to my bower, and there I enclosed him and left him; for I was very impatient to get home, from whence I had been absent above a month.

I cannot express what a satisfaction it was to me to come into my old hutch and lie down in my hammock-bed. This little wandering journey, without settled place of abode, had been so unpleasant to me that my own house, as I called it to myself, was a perfect settlement to me, compared with that; and it rendered everything about me so comfortable that I resolved I would never go a great way from it again, while it should be my lot to stay on the island.

I reposed myself here a week, to rest and regale myself after my long journey; during which, most of the time was taken up in the weighty affair of making a cage for my Poll, who began now to be a mere[2] domestic and to be mighty well acquainted with me. Then I began to think of the poor kid that I had penned in within my little circle and resolved to go and fetch it

2. *Mere*, essential.

home, or give it some food; accordingly I went and found it where I left it, for indeed it could not get out, but was almost starved for want of food. I then cut boughs of trees, and branches of such shrubs as I could find, and threw them over, and having fed it, I tied it as I did before, to lead it away; but it was so tame from being hungry that I had no need to have tied it, for it followed me like a dog; and as I continually fed it, the creature became so loving, so gentle, and so fond that it became from that time one of my domestics also and would never leave me afterward.

Chapter 9

Farming and Inventing Operations

The rainy season of the autumnal equinox was now come, and I kept the 30th of September in the same solemn manner as before, being the anniversary of my landing on the island, having now been there for two years and no more prospect of being delivered than the first day I came there. I spent the whole day in humble and thankful acknowledgments of the many wonderful mercies that my solitary condition was attended with, and without which it might have been infinitely more miserable. I gave humble and hearty thanks that God had been pleased to disclose to me that it was possible I might be more happy in this solitary condition than I should have been in the liberty of society and in all the pleasures of the world: that He could fully make up to me the deficiencies of my solitary state, and the want of human society, by His presence and the communication of His grace to my soul; supporting, comforting, and encouraging me to depend upon His providence here and hope for His eternal presence hereafter.

It was now that I became aware of how much more happy the life I now led was, with all its miserable circumstances, than the wicked, cursed, abominable life I led all the earlier part of my days; and now having changed both my sorrows and my joys, my very desires altered, my affections and my delights were perfectly new from what they were at first coming, or, indeed, for the two years past.

Before, as I walked about, either on my hunting or for viewing the country, the anguish of my soul at my condition would break out suddenly, and my very heart would die within me, to think of the woods, the mountains, the deserts I was in, and how I was a prisoner, locked up with the eternal bars and bolts of the ocean, in an uninhabited wilderness, without redemption. In the midst of perfect composure, these thoughts would break out upon me like a storm and make me wring my hands and weep like a child; sometimes it would happen in the middle of my work, and I would immediately sit down and sigh, and look upon the ground for an hour or two together. This was still worse to me, for if I could burst out into tears, or vent myself by words, it would go away, and the grief having exhausted itself would abate.

But now I began to exercise myself with new thoughts. I daily read the Word of God and applied all the comforts of it to my present state. One morning, being very sad, I opened the Bible upon these words: "I will never leave thee, nor forsake thee." Immediately it occurred that these words were to me; why else should they be directed in such a manner, just at the moment when I was mourning over my condition, as one forsaken of God and man?

"Well, then," said I, "if God does not forsake me, of what ill consequence can it be, or what matters it, though the world should all forsake me, seeing, on the other hand, if I had all the world and should lose the favor and blessing of God, there would be no comparison in the loss?"

From this moment, I began to conclude in my mind that it was possible for me to be more happy in this forsaken, solitary condition than it was probable I should ever have been in any other particular state in the world; and with this thought I was going to give thanks to God for bringing me to this place. I know not what it was, but something shocked my mind at that thought, and I dared not speak the words. "How canst thou become such a hypocrite," said I, even audibly, "to pretend to be thankful for a condition which, however thou mayest endeavor to be contented with, thou wouldst rather pray heartily to be delivered from?" So I stopped there; but though I could not say I thanked God for being there, yet I sincerely gave thanks to God for opening my eyes, by whatever afflicting providences, to see the former condition of my life and to mourn for my wickedness and repent. I never opened the Bible, or shut it, but my very soul within me blessed God for directing my friend in England, without any order of mine, to pack it up among my goods and for assisting me afterward to save it out of the wreck of the ship.

Thus, and in this disposition of mind, I began my third year; and though I have not given the reader the trouble of so particular an account of my works this year as the first, yet in general it may be observed that I was very seldom idle, but having regularly divided my time according to several daily employments that were before me, such as, first, my duty to God and the reading of the Scriptures, which I constantly set apart some time for, thrice every day; secondly, the going abroad with my gun for food, which generally took up three hours in every morning, when it did not rain; thirdly, the ordering, curing, preserving, and cooking what I had killed or caught for my supply: these took up a great part of the day. Also, it is to be considered that in the middle of the day, when the sun was in the zenith, the violence of the heat was too great to stir out; so that about four hours in the evening was all the time I could be supposed to work in, with this exception, that sometimes I changed my hours of hunting and working and went to work in the morning and abroad with my gun in the afternoon.

To this short time allowed for labor may be added the exceeding laboriousness of my work—the many hours that, for want of tools, want of help, and want of skill, everything I did took up much of my time. For example, I was full two-and-forty days in making a board for a long shelf, which I wanted in my cave; whereas two sawyers, with their tools and a saw-pit, would have cut six of them out of the same tree in half a day.

My case was this: It was to be a large tree that was to be cut down, because my board was to be a broad one. This tree I was three days cutting down, and two more cutting off the boughs and reducing it to a log, or piece of timber. With inexpressible hacking and hewing, I reduced both the sides of it into chips till it began to be light enough to move; then I turned it and made one side of it smooth and flat as a board from end to end; then turning that side downward, I cut the other side till I brought the plank to be about three inches thick and smooth on both sides. Anyone may judge the labor of my hands in such a piece of work; but labor and patience carried me through that and many other things; I only observe this in particular, to show the reason why so much of my time passed with so little work to show for it, that what might be a little to be done with help and tools, was a vast labor and required a prodigious time to do alone and by hand. But notwithstanding this, with patience and labor, I accomplished many things, and indeed everything that my circumstances made necessary for me to do, as will appear by what follows.

Marauders

I was now in the months of November and December, expecting my crop of barley and rice. The ground I had manured or dug up for them was not great; for, as I observed, my seed of each was not above the quantity of half a peck, as I had

lost one whole crop by sowing in the dry season; but now my crop promised very well, when suddenly I found I was in danger of losing it all again by enemies of several sorts, which it was scarcely possible to keep from it; as, first, the goats and wild creatures that I called hares, which, tasting the sweetness of the blade, lay in it night and day, as soon as it came up and ate it so close that it could get no time to shoot up into stalk.

This I saw no remedy for but by making an enclosure about it with a hedge, which I did with a great deal of toil, and the more because it required a great deal of speed, the creatures daily spoiling my corn. However, as my arable land was but small, suited to my crop, I got it totally fenced in about three weeks' time; and shooting some of the creatures in the daytime, I set my dog to guard it in the night, tying him up to a stake at the gate, where he would stand and bark all night long; so in a little time the enemies forsook the place, and the corn grew very strong and well and began to ripen apace.

But as the beasts ruined me before, while my corn was in the blade, so the birds were as likely to ruin me now, when it was in the ear; for going along by the place to see how it throve, I saw my little crop surrounded with fowls, of I know not how many kinds, that stood, as it were, watching till I should be gone. I immediately let fly among them, for I always had my gun with me. I had no sooner shot but there rose up a little cloud of fowls, which I had not seen at all, from among the corn itself.

This disturbed me greatly, for I foresaw that in a few days they would devour all my hopes; that I should be starved and never be able to raise a crop at all; and what to do I could not tell. However, I resolved not to lose my corn, if possible, though I should watch it day and night. In the first place, I went among it, to see what damage was already done, and found they had spoiled a good deal of it; but that as it was yet too green for them, the loss was not so great but the remainder was likely to be a good crop, if it could be saved.

I stayed by it to load my gun, and then coming away, I could easily see the thieves roosting upon all the trees about me, as if they only waited till I was gone away, and the event proved to be so; for as I walked off, as if I was gone, I was no sooner out of their sight than they dropped down one by one into the corn again. I was so provoked that I did not have patience to stay till more came on, knowing that every corn that they ate now was, as it might be said, a peckload to me in consequence; but coming up to the hedge, I fired again and killed three of them. This was what I wished for; so I took them up and served them as we serve notorious thieves in England, namely, hanged them in chains, for a terror to others. It is impossible to imagine that this should have had such an effect as it had, for the fowls would not only not come at the corn, but, in short, they forsook all that part of the island, and I would never see a bird near the place as long as my scarecrows hung there. This I was very glad of, you may be sure, and about the latter end of December, which was my second harvest of the year, I reaped my corn.

Farming Operations

I was sadly put to it for a scythe or sickle to cut it down, and all I could do was to make one, as well as I could, out of one of the broadswords, or cutlasses, that I saved among the arms out of the ship. However, as my crop was but small, I had no great difficulty in cutting it down; in short, I reaped it in my way, for I cut nothing off but the ears and carried it away in a great basket that I had made, and so rubbed it out with my hands; and at the end of all my harvesting, I found that out of my half-peck of seed I had nearly two bushels of rice and above two bushels and a half of barley; that is to say, by my guess, for I had no measure at that time.

However, this was a great encouragement to me, and I foresaw that in time it would please God to supply me with bread. And yet here I was perplexed again, for I neither knew how to grind or make meal of my corn, or indeed how to clean it and part it; nor, if made into meal, how to make bread of it; and if how to make it, yet I knew not how to bake it. These things being added to my desire of having a good quantity for store and to secure a constant supply, I resolved not to taste any of this crop, but to preserve it all for seed against the next season; and, in the meantime, to employ all my study and hours of working to accomplish this great work of providing myself with corn and bread.

It might be truly said that now I worked for my bread. It is a little wonderful, and what I believe few people have thought much upon, that is, the strange multitude of little things necessary in the providing, producing, curing, dressing, making, and finishing this one article of bread.

I, who was reduced to a mere state of nature, found this to my daily discouragement and was made more and more sensible of it every hour, even after I had got the first handful of seed corn, which, as I have said, came up unexpectedly and indeed was a surprise.

First, I had no plow to turn up the earth; no spade or shovel to dig it. Well, this I conquered by making me a wooden spade, as I observed before, but this did my work in a wooden manner; and though it cost me a great many days to make it, yet for want of iron it not only wore out the sooner, but made my work the harder and made it be performed much worse. However, this I bore, too, and was content to work it out with patience and bear with the badness of the performance. When the corn was sown, I had no harrow, but was forced to go over it myself and drag a great heavy bough of a tree over it, to scratch it, as it may be called, rather than rake or harrow it. When it was growing, or grown, I have observed already how many things I wanted to fence it, secure it, mow or reap it, cure and carry it home, thrash and part it from the chaff, and save it. Then I wanted a mill to grind it, sieves to dress it, yeast and salt to make it into bread, and an oven to bake it in; and all these things I did without, as shall be observed; and yet the corn was an inestimable comfort and advantage to me, too. But this, as I said, made everything laborious and tedious to me; but that there was no help for; neither was my time so much loss to me, because, as I had divided it, a certain part of it was every day appointed to these works; and as I had resolved to use none of the corn for bread till I had a greater quantity by me, I had the next six months to apply myself wholly, by labor and invention, to furnish myself with utensils proper for the performing of all the operations necessary for making the corn, when I had it, fit for my use.

I Make Some Earthenware

But first I was to prepare more land, for I had now seed enough to sow more than an acre of ground. Before I did this, I had a week's work at least to make me a spade, which, when it was done, was but a sorry one indeed, and very heavy, and required double labor to work with it. However, I went through that and sowed my seed in two large flat pieces of ground, as near my house as I could find them. I fenced them in with a good hedge, the stakes of which were all cut of that wood which I had set before, which I knew would grow; so that in one year's time I knew I should have a quick or living hedge that would need but little repair. This work was not so little as to take me less than three months, because a great part of that time was in the wet season, when I could not go abroad. Within-doors—that is, when it rained and I could not go out—I found employment in the following occupations, always observing that all the while I was at work I diverted myself with talking to my parrot, teaching him to speak; and I quickly taught him to know his own name and at last to speak it out pretty loud—"Poll," which was the first word I ever heard spoken on the island by any mouth but my own. This, therefore, was not my work, but an assistant to my work; for now, as I said, I had a great employment upon my hands, as follows—namely, I had long studied, by some means or other, to make myself some earthen vessels, which, indeed, I wanted sorely, but knew not where to come at them. However, considering the heat of the climate, I did not doubt but if I could search out some clay, I might botch up some such pot as might, being dried by the sun, be hard enough and strong enough to bear handling and to hold

anything that was dry and required to be kept so; and as this was necessary in preparing corn, meal, etc., which was the thing I was working on, I resolved to make some as large as I could and fit only to stand like jars to hold what should be put into them.

It would make the reader pity me, or rather laugh at me, to tell how many awkward ways I took to raise this paste; what odd, misshapen, ugly things I made; how many of them fell in, and how many fell out—the clay not being stiff enough to bear its own weight; how many cracked by the over-violent heat of the sun, being set out too hastily; and how many fell to pieces with only removing, as well before as after they were dried; and, in a word, how, after having labored hard to find the clay—to dig it, to temper it, to bring it home and work it—I could not make above two large earthen ugly things (I cannot call them jars) in about two months' labor.

However, as the sun baked these two very dry and hard, I lifted them very gently up and set them down again in two great wicker baskets, which I had made on purpose for them, that they might not break; and as between the pot and the basket there was a little room to spare, I stuffed it full of the rice and barley straw; and these two pots being to stand always dry, I thought would hold my dry corn, and perhaps the meal, when the corn was bruised.

Though I miscarried so much in my design for large pots, yet I made several smaller things with better success, such as little round pots, flat dishes, pitchers, and pipkins, and anything my hand turned to, and the heat of the sun baked them strangely hard.

But all this would not answer my end, which was to get an earthen pot to hold what was liquid and bear the fire, which none of these could do. It happened after some time, making a pretty large fire for cooking my meat, when I went to put it out after I had done with it, I found a broken piece of one of my earthenware vessels in the fire, burnt as hard as a stone and red as a tile. I was agreeably surprised to see it and said to myself that certainly they might be made to burn whole if they would burn broken.

This set me to study how to order my fire so as to make it burn me some pots. I had no notion of a kiln such as the potters burn in, or of glazing them with lead, though I had some lead to do it with; but I placed three large pipkins and two or three pots in a pile, one upon another, and placed my firewood around them, with a great heap of embers under them. I plied the fire with fresh fuel around the outside and upon the top till I saw the pots in the inside red-hot quite through and observed that they did not crack at all. When I saw them clear red, I let them stand in that heat about five or six hours, till I found one of them, though it did not crack, did melt or run; for the sand that was mixed with the clay melted by the violence of the heat and would have run into glass if I had gone on; so I slacked my fire gradually till the pots began to abate of the red color, and watching them all night, that I might not let the fire cool too fast, in the morning I had three very good (I will not say handsome) pipkins and two other earthen pots as hard burnt as could be desired, and one of them perfectly glazed with the running of the sand.

After this experiment, I need not say that I wanted no sort of earthenware for my use; but I must needs say, as to the shapes of them, they were very indifferent, as anyone may suppose, when I had no way of making them but as the children make dirt pies, or as a woman would make pies that never learned to raise paste.

No joy at a thing of so mean a nature was ever equal to mine when I found I had made an earthen pot that would bear the fire, and I had hardly patience to stay till they were cold before I set one on the fire again, with some water in it, to boil me some meat, which it did admirably well; and with a piece of a kid I made some very good broth, though I lacked oatmeal and several other requisite ingredients to make it as good as I would have wished it.

My next concern was to get me a stone mortar to stamp or beat some corn in; for as to the mill, there was no thought of arriving to that perfection of art with one pair of hands. To supply this want, I was at a great loss, for, of all the trades in the world, I was most perfectly unqualified for being a stonecutter, neither had I any tools to go about it with. I spent many a day finding a great stone big enough to cut hollow and make fit for a mortar and could find none at all, except what was in the solid rock, and which I had no way to dig or cut out; nor, indeed, were the rocks in the island of hardness sufficient, but were all of a sandy, crumbling stone, which would neither bear the weight of a heavy pestle, nor would break the corn without filling it with sand. So, after a great deal of time lost in searching for a stone, I gave it up and resolved to look out for a great block of hard wood, which I found, indeed, much easier; and getting one as big as I had strength to contour, I rounded it and formed it on the outside with my ax and hatchet and then, with the help of fire and infinite labor, made a hollow place in it, as the Indians in Brazil make their canoes. After this I made a great heavy pestle, or beater, of the wood called ironwood; and this I prepared and laid by against when I had my next crop of corn, which I proposed to myself to grind, or rather pound my corn into meal to make my bread.

My next difficulty was to make a sieve, or sierce, to dress my meal and to part it from the bran and husk; without which I did not see it possible I could have any bread. This was a most difficult thing, difficult just to think about, for to be sure I had nothing like the necessary things to make it with—I mean fine, thin canvas, or stuff to sierce the meal through. And here I was at a full stop for many months, nor did I really know what to do. Linen I had none left but what was mere rags. I had goats' hair, but neither knew I how to weave or spin it; and had I known how, there were no tools to work it with. All the remedy that I found for this was that at last I remembered I had, among the seamen's clothes that were saved out of the ship, some neckcloths of calico or muslin; and with some pieces of these I made three small sieves, but proper enough for the work; and thus I made shift for some years. How I did afterward I shall show later.

The baking part was the next thing to be considered, and how I should make bread when I came to have corn; for, first, I had no yeast. As to that part, as there was no supplying the lack, so I did not concern myself much about it. But for an oven I was indeed in great need. At length I found out an experiment for that also, which was this: I made some earthen vessels very broad, but not deep—that is to say, about two feet in diameter and not above nine inches deep; these I burned in the fire as I had done the others, and laid them by; and when I wanted to bake, I made a great fire upon the hearth, which I had paved with some square tiles, of my own making and burning also. But I ought not to call them square, for they were not.

When the firewood was burned pretty much into embers, or live coals, I drew them forward upon this hearth, so as to cover it all over, and there I let them lie till the hearth was very hot; then, sweeping away all the embers, I set down my loaf or loaves, and whelming down the earthen pot upon them, drew the embers all round the outside of the pot to keep in and add to the heat; and thus, as well as in the best oven in the world, I baked my barley loaves and became, in little time, a good pastry cook in the bargain; for I made myself several cakes and puddings of the rice. But I made no pies, neither had I anything to put into them, supposing I had, except the flesh either of fowls or goats.

It need not be wondered at if all these things took me the most part of the third year of my abode here; for it is to be observed that, in the intervals of these things, I had my new harvest and husbandry to manage; for I reaped my corn in its season, carried it home as well as I could, and laid it up by the ear in my large baskets till I had time to rub it out, for I had no floor to thrash it on, or instrument to thrash it with.

And now, indeed, my stock of corn increasing, I really wanted to build my barns bigger. I wanted a place to lay it up in, for the increase of the corn now yielded me so much that I had of the barley about twenty bushels, and of the rice as much, or more; insomuch that I now resolved to begin to use it freely, for my bread had been gone quite a great while; also I resolved to see what quantity would be sufficient to supply me for a whole year and to sow but once a year.

Upon the whole, I found that the forty bushels of barley and rice were much more than I could consume in a year; so I resolved to sow just the same quantity every year that I sowed the last, in hopes that such a quantity would fully provide me with bread, etc.

Chapter 10

A Canoe to Escape In

All the while these things were happening, you may be sure my thoughts ran many times upon the prospect of the land that I had seen from the other side of the island; and I was not without secret wishes that I was on shore there, fancying that, seeing the mainland and an inhabited country, I might find some way or other to convey myself farther and perhaps at last find some means of escape.

But all this while I made no allowance for the dangers of such a condition, and how I might fall into the hands of savages, and perhaps such as I might have reason to think far worse than the lions and tigers of Africa; that if I once came into their power, I should run a hazard more than a thousand to one of being killed, and perhaps of being eaten; for I had heard that the people of the Caribbean coasts were cannibals, or man-eaters, and I knew by the latitude that I could not be far off from that shore; that suppose they were not cannibals, yet they might kill me, as many Europeans who had fallen into their hands had been served, even when they had been ten or twenty together—how much worse it would be for me, who was but one and could make little or no defense. All these things, I say, that I ought to have considered well, and I did cast up in my thoughts afterward, yet took up none of my apprehensions at first, and my head ran mightily upon the thought of getting over to that shore.

Now, I wished for my boy Xury, and the longboat with the shoulder-of-mutton sail, with which I sailed above a thousand miles on the coast of Africa; but this was in vain. Then I thought I would go and look at our ship's boat, which, as I have said, was blown up upon the shore a great way in the storm when we were first cast away. She lay almost where she did at first, but not quite, and was turned, by the force of the waves and the winds, almost bottom upward against the high ridge of beachy, rough sand, but no water about her as before. If I had had hands to have refitted her and to have launched her into the water, the boat would have done well enough, and I might have gone back into the Brazils with her easily enough; but I might have easily foreseen that I could no more turn her and set her upright upon her bottom than I could remove the island. However, I went to the wood and cut levers and rollers and brought them to the boat; resolved to try what I could do, suggesting to myself that if I could but turn her down, I might easily repair the damage she had received, and she would be a very good boat, and I might go to sea in her very easily.

I spared no pains, indeed, in this piece of fruitless toil, and spent, I think, three or four weeks about it. At last, finding it impossible to heave it up with my little strength, I fell to digging away the sand, to undermine it, and so to make it fall down, setting pieces of wood to thrust and guide it right in the fall.

But when I had done this, I was unable to stir it up again, or to get under it, much less to move it forward toward the water, so I was forced to give it up; and yet, though I gave up any hopes of the boat, my desire to venture over to the mainland increased, rather than decreased, as the means for it seemed more and more impossible.

I Make a Canoe

This at length set me upon thinking whether it was not possible to make myself a canoe, or *periagua*, such as the natives of those climates make, even without tools, or, as I might say, without hands—that is, of the trunk of a great tree. This I not only thought possible but easy, and I pleased myself extremely with my thoughts of making it and with my having much more convenience[1] for it than any of the negroes or Indians; but not at all considering the particular inconveniences that I lay under more than the Indians did—namely, want of hands to move it into the water when it was made, a difficulty much harder for me to surmount than all the consequences of want of tools could be to them. For what was it to me that when I had chosen a vast tree in the wood, I might with great trouble cut it down; if after I might be able with my tools to hew and dub the outside into the proper shape of a boat and burn or cut out the inside to make it hollow, so as to make a boat of it—if, after all this, I must leave it just there where I found it, and was not able to launch it into the water?

One would have thought I could not have had the least reflection upon what it would take to make such a boat, but I should have immediately

1. *Convenience,* state of being advantageous.

thought how I should get it into the sea; but my thoughts were so intent upon my voyage over the sea in it that I never once considered how I should get it off the land; and it was really, in its own nature, more easy for me to guide it over forty-five miles of sea than about forty-five fathoms of land, where it lay, to set it afloat in the water.

I went to work upon this boat the most like a fool that ever man did, who had any of his senses awake. I pleased myself with the design without determining whether I was ever able to undertake it; not but that the difficulty of launching my boat came often into my head; but I put a stop to my inquiries into it by this foolish answer that I gave myself: *Let me first make it; I warrant I shall find some way or other to get it along when it is done.*

This was a most preposterous method; but the eagerness of my fancy prevailed, and to work I went and felled a cedar tree. I question much whether Solomon ever had such a one for building the Temple at Jerusalem; it was five feet ten inches in diameter at the lower part near the stump, and four feet eleven inches in diameter at the end of twenty-two feet; after which it lessened for a while and then parted into branches. It was not without infinite labor that I felled this tree. I was twenty days hacking and hewing at it at the bottom; I was fourteen more getting the branches and limbs and the vast spreading head of it cut off, which I hacked and hewed through with my ax and hatchet and inexpressible labor; after this it cost me a month to shape it and dub it to the right proportion, and to something like the bottom of a boat, that it might float upright as it ought to do. It cost me nearly three months more to clear the inside and work it out so as to make an exact boat of it; this I did, indeed, without fire, by mere mallet and chisel, and by the dint of hard labor, till I had brought it to be a very handsome *periagua* and big enough to have carried six-and-twenty men, and consequently big enough to have carried me and all my cargo.

When I had gone through this work, I was extremely delighted with it. The boat was really much bigger than ever I saw a *periagua* that was made of one tree in my life. Many a weary stroke it had cost, you may be sure—for there remained nothing but to get it into the water; and had I gotten it into the water, I made no question but I should have begun the maddest voyage, and the most unlikely to be performed, that ever was undertaken.

But all my devices to get it into the water failed me, though they cost infinite labor, too. It lay about one hundred yards from the water, and not more; but the first inconvenience was, it was uphill toward the creek. Well, to take away this discouragement, I resolved to dig into the surface of the earth, and so make a declivity. This I began, and it cost me a prodigious deal of pains (but who will grudge pains who have their deliverance in view?); but when this was worked through, and this difficulty managed, it was still no better, for I could no more stir the canoe than I could the other boat. Then I measured the distance of ground and resolved to cut a dock or canal, to bring the water up to the canoe, seeing I could not bring the canoe down to the water. Well, I began this work; and when I began to enter into it and calculate how deep it was to be dug, how broad, how the stuff was to be thrown out, I found that, by the number of hands I had—being none but my own—it must have been ten or twelve years before I could have gone through with it; for the shore lay so high that at the upper end it must have been at least twenty feet deep; so at length, though with great reluctance, I gave this attempt over also.

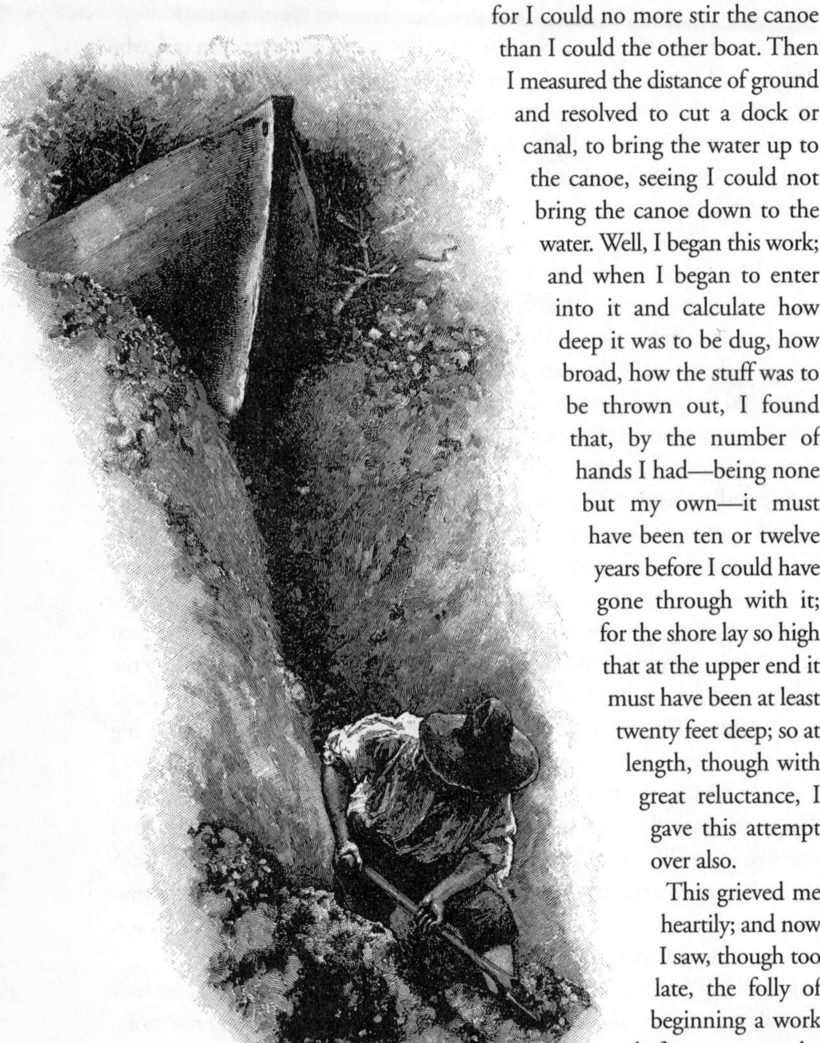

This grieved me heartily; and now I saw, though too late, the folly of beginning a work before we count the cost and before we judge rightly of our own strength to go through with it.

In the middle of this work, I finished my fourth year in this place and kept my anniversary with the same devotion and with as much comfort as ever before; for, by a constant study and serious application of the Word of God, and by the assistance of His grace, I gained a different knowledge from what I had before. I entertained different notions of things. I looked now upon the world as a thing remote, which I had nothing to do with, no expectations from, and, indeed, no desires about; in a word, I had nothing indeed to do with it, nor was ever likely to have. So I thought it looked, as we may perhaps look upon it hereafter, that is, as a place I had lived in, but was come out of it; and well might I say, as Father Abraham to the Rich Man: "Between me and thee is a great gulf fixed."

In the first place, I was removed from all the wickedness of the world here; I had neither the lust of the flesh, the lust of the eye, nor the pride of life. I had nothing to covet, for I had all I was now capable of enjoying; I was lord of the whole manor; or, if I pleased, I might call myself king or emperor over the whole country that I had possession of. There were no rivals; I had no competitor, none to dispute sovereignty or command with me. I might have raised shiploads of corn, but I had no use for it; so I let as little grow as I thought enough for my needs. I had tortoises, or turtles, enough, but now and then one was as much as I could put to any use. I had timber enough to have built a fleet of ships; and I had grapes enough to have made wine, or to have cured into raisins, to have loaded that fleet when it had been built.

But all I could make use of was all that was valuable; I had enough to eat and to supply my wants, and what was all the rest to me? If I killed more flesh than I could eat, the dog must eat it, or the vermin; if I sowed more corn than I could eat, it must be spoiled; the trees that I cut down were lying to rot on the ground; I could make no more use of them than for fuel, and that I had no occasion for but to dress my food.

In a word, the nature and experience of things dictated to me, upon just reflection, that all the good things of this world are no further good to us than they are for our use; and that, whatever we may heap up indeed to give others, we enjoy as much as we can use and no more. The most covetous, griping miser in the world would have been cured of the vice of covetousness, if he had been in my case; for I possessed infinitely more than I knew what to do with. I had no room for desire, except it was of things that I had not, and they were but trifles, though, indeed, of great use to me. I had, as

I hinted before, a parcel of money, as good as silver, about thirty-six pounds sterling. Alas, there the nasty, sorry, useless stuff lay! I had no manner of business for it; and I often thought with myself that I would have given a handful of it for a gross of tobacco pipes; or for a hand mill to grind my corn; nay, I would have given it all for sixpenny-worth of turnip and carrot seed out of England, or for a handful of peas and beans and a bottle of ink. As it was, I had not the least advantage by it or benefit from it; but there it lay in a drawer and grew moldy with the damp of the cave in the wet seasons; and if I had had the drawer full of diamonds, it had been the same case, they had been of no manner of value to me, because of no use.

Thankfulness

I had now brought my state of life to be much easier in itself than it was at first, and much easier to my mind, as well as to my body. I frequently sat down to meat with thankfulness and admired the hand of God's providence, which had thus spread my table in the wilderness. I learned to look more upon the bright side of my condition and less upon the dark side, and to consider what I enjoyed rather than what I wanted; and this gave me sometimes such secret comforts that I cannot express them, and which I take notice of here, to put those discontented people in mind of it, who cannot enjoy comfortably what God has given them, because they see and covet something that He has not given them. All our discontents about what we want appear to me to spring from the lack of thankfulness for what we have.

Another reflection was of great use to me, and doubtless would be so to anyone that should fall into such distress as mine was; and this was to compare my present condition with what I at first expected it would be; nay, with what it would certainly have been, if the good providence of God had not wonderfully ordered the ship to be cast up nearer to the shore, where I not only could come at her, but could bring what I got out of her to the shore for my relief and comfort; without which, I had lacked for tools to work, weapons for defense, and gunpowder and shot for getting my food.

Resigned to My Fate

I spent whole hours, I may say whole days, in imagining to myself, in the most lively colors, how I must have acted if I had got nothing out of the ship. How I could not have so much as got any food, except fish and turtles; and that, as it was long before I found any of them, I must have perished first; that I should have lived, if I had not perished, like a mere savage; that if I had killed a goat or a fowl, by any contrivance, I had no way to flay or open it, or part the flesh from the skin and the bowels, or to cut it up; but must gnaw it with my teeth and pull it with my claws, like a beast.

These reflections made me very sensible of the goodness of Providence to me, and very thankful for my present condition, with all its hardships and misfortunes; and this part also I cannot but recommend to the reflection of those who are apt, in their misery, to say, "Is any affliction like mine?" Let them consider how much worse the cases of some people are, and their case might have been, if Providence had thought fit.

I had another reflection, which assisted me also to comfort my mind with hopes; and this was comparing my present situation with what I had deserved and had therefore reason to expect from the hand of Providence. I had lived a dreadful life, perfectly destitute of the knowledge and fear of God. I had been well instructed by Father and Mother; neither had they been wanting to me in their early endeavors to infuse a religious awe of God into my mind, a sense of my duty, and what the nature and end of my being required of me. But, alas, falling early into the seafaring life, which, of all lives, is the most destitute of the fear of God, though His terrors are always before them—I say, falling early into the seafaring life, and into seafaring company, all that little sense of religion that I had entertained was laughed out of me by my messmates; by a hardened despising of dangers and the views of death, which grew habitual to me; by my long absence from all manner of opportunities to converse with anything but what was like myself, or to hear anything of what was good or tended toward it.

So void was I of everything that was good, or of the least sense of what I was or was to be, that, in the greatest deliverances I enjoyed—such as my escape from Sallee, my being taken up by the Portuguese master of the ship, my being planted so well in the Brazils, my receiving the cargo from England, and the like—I never once had the words, "Thank God!" so much as on my mind or in my mouth; nor in the greatest distress had I so much as thought to pray to Him, or so much as said, "Lord, have mercy upon me!"; no, not even to mention the name of God, unless it was to swear by and blaspheme it.

I had terrible reflections upon my mind for many months, as I have already observed, on the account of my wicked and hardened past life; and when I looked about me and considered what particular providences had attended me since my coming into this place and how God had dealt bountifully with me—had not only punished me less than my iniquity had deserved, but had so plentifully provided for me—this gave me great hopes that my repentance was accepted and that God had yet mercies in store for me.

With these reflections, I worked my mind up, not only to resignation to the will of God in the present disposition of my circumstances, but even to a sincere thankfulness for my condition; and that I, who was yet a living man, ought not to complain, seeing I had not yet received the due punishment of my sins. That I enjoyed so many mercies that I had no reason to have expected in that place. That I ought nevermore to complain about my condition, but to rejoice and to give daily thanks for that daily bread, which nothing but a crowd of wonders could have brought. That I ought to consider I had been fed even by a miracle, even as great as that of feeding Elijah by ravens—nay, by a long series of miracles. And that I could hardly have named a place in the uninhabited part of the world where I could have been cast more to my advantage; a place where, as I had no society, which was my affliction on one hand, so I found no ravenous beasts, no furious wolves or tigers, to threaten my life; no venomous creatures or poisonous, which I might have fed on to my hurt; no savages to murder and devour me. In a word, as my life was a life of sorrow one way, so it was a life of mercy in another; and I lacked nothing to make it a life of comfort but to be able to make my sense of God's goodness to me, and care over me in this condition, be my daily consolation; and after I made a just improvement of these things, I went away and was no more sad. I had now been here so long that many things that I brought on shore for my help were either quite gone or very much weakened and nearly spent.

My ink, as I observed, had been gone some time, all but a very little, which I eked out with water, a little at a time, till it was so pale, it scarcely left any appearance of black upon the paper. As long as it lasted, I made use of it to write down the days of the month on which any remarkable thing happened to me; and first, by casting up times past, I remembered that there was a strange concurrence of days in the various providences that befell me, and which, if I had been superstitiously inclined to observe days as fatal or fortunate, I might have had reason to have looked upon with a great deal of curiosity.

First, I had observed that the same day that I broke away from my father and my friends and ran away to Hull, in order to go to sea, the same day afterward I was taken by the Sallee man-of-war and made a slave; the same day of the year that I escaped out of the wreck of that ship in Yarmouth Roads, that same day of the year afterward I made my escape from Sallee in a boat; the same day of the year I was born on—that is, the 30th of September—the same day I had my life so miraculously saved twenty-six years after, when I was cast on shore in this island; so that my wicked life and solitary life began both on the same day.

The next thing to my ink being used up was that of my bread—I mean the biscuit that I brought out of the ship. This I had husbanded to the last degree, allowing myself but one cake of bread a day for more than a year; and yet I was quite without bread for a year before I got any corn of my own; and great reason I had to be thankful that I had any at all, the getting it being, as has been already observed, next to miraculous.

My clothes, too, began to decay mightily; as to linen, I had had none a good while, except some checkered shirts that I found in the chests of the other seamen, and which I carefully preserved; because many times I could bear no other clothes on but a shirt; and it was a very great help to me that I had, among all the men's clothes of the ship, almost three dozen shirts. There were also several thick watch coats of the seamen's that were left behind, but they were too hot to wear; and though it is true that the weather was so violently hot that there was no need of clothes, yet I could not go quite naked—no, though I had been inclined to it, which I was not; nor could I abide the thoughts of it, though I was all alone. One reason why I could not go naked was, I could not bear the heat of the sun so well when quite naked as with some clothes on; nay, the very heat frequently blistered my skin; whereas, with a shirt on, the air itself made some motion and, whistling under the shirt, was twofold cooler than without it. No more could I ever bring myself to go out in the heat of the sun without a cap or a hat; the heat of the sun, beating with such violence as it does in that latitude, would give me a headache presently, by darting so directly on my head, without a hat or cap on, so that I could not bear it; whereas, if I put on my hat, it would presently go away.

My Suit of Clothes

Taking this into consideration, I began to consider putting the few rags I had, which I called clothes, into some order. I had worn out all the waistcoats I had, and my business was now to try if I could not make jackets out of the great watch coats that I had by me and with such other materials as I had; so I set to work tailoring, or rather indeed, botching, for I made most piteous work of it. However, I made shift to make two or three waistcoats, which I hoped would serve me a great while; as for breeches or drawers, I made but a very sorry shift indeed till afterward.

I have mentioned that I saved the skins of all the creatures that I killed—I mean four-footed ones—and I had them hung up, stretched out with sticks in the sun, by which means some of them were so dry and hard that they were fit for little; but others, it seems, were very useful. The first thing I made of these was a great cap for my head, with the hair on the outside, to keep off the rain; and this I performed so well that after, I made me a suit of clothes wholly of those skins—that is to say, a waistcoat and breeches open at the knees, and both loose; for they were rather failing to keep me cool than failing to keep me warm. I must not omit to acknowledge that they were wretchedly made; for if I was a bad carpenter, I was a worse tailor. However, they were such as I made a very good shift with, and when I was abroad, if it happened to rain, the hair of the waistcoat and cap being outermost, I was kept very dry.

After this, I spent a great deal of time and pains to make an umbrella. I was indeed in great want of one and had a great desire to make one. I had seen them made in the Brazils, where they are very useful in the great heat there, and I felt the heat every jot as great here, and greater too, being nearer the equator; besides, as I was obliged to be much outside, it was a most useful thing to me, as well for the rain as for the heat. I took a world of pains at it and was a great while before I could make anything likely to hold; nay, after I thought I had figured out the way, I spoiled two or three before I made one good enough. But at last I made one that answered indifferently well; the main difficulty, I found, was to make it fold. I could make it spread, but if it did not fold too, and draw in, it would not be portable for me any way but just over my head, which would not do. However, at last, as I said, I made one that worked. I covered it with skins, the hair upward, so that it cast off the rain like a penthouse and kept off the sun so effectively that I could walk out in the hottest of the weather with greater advantage than I could before in the coolest; and when I had no need of it, I could close it and carry it under my arm.

Thus I lived mighty comfortably, my mind being entirely composed by my resignation to the will of God and throwing myself wholly upon the disposal of His providence. This made my life better than sociable, for when I began to regret the lack of conversation, I would ask myself whether this conversing mutually with my own thoughts, and (as I hope I may say) with even my Maker, by conversations and petitions, was not better than the utmost enjoyment of human society in the world?

I cannot say that, after this, for five years, any extraordinary thing happened to me, but I lived on in the same course, in the same posture and place, just as before. The chief thing that took my time, besides my yearly labor of planting my barley and rice and curing my raisins—of both which I always kept up just enough to have sufficient stock of the year's provisions beforehand—I say, besides this yearly labor and my daily labor of going out with my gun, I had one labor, to make me a canoe, which at last I finished; so that, by digging a canal to it of six feet wide and four feet deep, I brought it into the creek, almost half a mile. As for the first, which was so vastly big, as I made it without considering beforehand, as I ought to have done, how I should be able to launch it, so, never being able to bring it into the water, or bring the water to it, I was obliged to let it lie where it was, as a memorandum to teach me to be wiser the next time. Indeed, the next time, though I could not get a tree proper for it and was in a place where I could not get the water to it at any less distance than, as I have said, of nearly half a mile, yet, as I saw it was practicable at last, I never gave it up; and though I was nearly two years at it, yet I never grudged my labor, in hopes of having a boat to go off to sea at last.

However, though my little *periagua* was finished, yet the size of it was not at all answerable to the design that I had in view when I made the first—I mean of venturing over to the terra firma, where it was above forty miles across. Accordingly, the smallness of my boat assisted to put an end to that design, and now I thought no more of it. As I had a boat, my next design was to make a tour round the island; for as I had been on the other side in one place, crossing, as I have already described it, over the land, so the discoveries I made in that journey made me very eager to see other parts of the coast; and now that I had a boat, I thought of nothing but sailing round the island.

I Venture Out in My Boat

For this purpose, and that I might do everything with discretion and consideration, I fitted up a little mast in my boat and made a sail to it out of some of the pieces of the ship's sails that lay in store, and of which I had a great store left. Having fitted my mast and sail and tried the boat, I found she would sail very well; then I made little lockers, or boxes, at each end of my boat, to put provisions, necessaries, ammunition, etc., into, to be kept dry, either from rain or the spray of the sea; and a little, long, hollow place I cut in the inside of the boat, where I could lay my gun, making a flap to hang down over it, to keep it dry.

I fixed my umbrella also in a notch at the stern, like a mast, to stand over my head and keep the heat of the sun off of me, like an awning. And thus I every now and then took a little voyage upon the sea; but never went far out, nor far from the little creek. At last, being eager to view the circum-ference of my little kingdom, I resolved upon my tour; and accordingly I victualed my ship for the voyage, putting in two dozen loaves (cakes I should rather call them) of barley bread, an earthen pot full of parched rice (a food I ate a great deal of), a little bottle of rum, half a goat and powder with shot for killing more, and two large watch coats (of those that, as I mentioned before, I had saved out of the seamen's chests). These I took, one to lie upon and the other to cover me in the night.

It was the 6th of November, in the sixth year of my reign, or my captivity, whichever you please, that I set out on this voyage, and I found it much longer than I expected; for though the island itself was not very large, yet when I came to the east side of it, I found a great ledge of rocks that lay out about two leagues into the sea—some above water, some under it; and beyond that a shoal of sand, lying dry half a league more, so that I was obliged to go a great way out to sea to get around that point.

When I first discovered them, I was going to give up my enterprise and come back again, not knowing how far it might oblige me to go out to sea and, above all, doubting how I should get back again; so I came to an anchor; for I had made a kind of an anchor with a piece of a broken grappling that I got out of the ship.

Having secured my boat, I took my gun and went on shore, climbing up a hill that seemed to overlook that point, where I saw the full extent of it and resolved to venture on.

In my viewing the sea from the hill where I stood, I perceived a strong and, indeed, a most furious current that ran to the east and even came close to the point; and I took the more notice of it because I saw there might be some danger that when I came into it, I might be carried out to sea by the strength of it and not be able to make the island again. And, indeed, had I not got first upon this hill, I believe it would have been so, for there was the same current on the other side of the island, only that it set off at a farther distance, and I saw there was a strong eddy under the shore; so I had nothing to do but to get out of the first current, and I should presently be in an eddy.

I lay here, however, two days, because the wind, blowing pretty fresh at east-southeast, and that being just contrary to the current, made a great breach of the sea upon the point; so that it was not safe for me to keep too close to the shore for the breach, nor to go too far off, because of the stream.

The third day, in the morning, the wind having abated overnight, the sea was calm, and I ventured. But I am a warning-piece to all rash and ignorant pilots, for no sooner was I come to the point, when I was not even my boat's length from the shore, but I found myself in a great depth of water and a current like the sluice of a mill. It carried my boat along with it with such violence that all I could do could not keep her so much as on the edge of it; but I found it hurried me farther and farther out from the eddy, which was on my left hand. There was no wind stirring to help me, and all that I could do with my paddles signified nothing. And now I began to give myself over for lost, for as the current was on both sides of the island, I knew in a few leagues' distance they must join again, and then I was irrevocably gone; nor did I see any possibility of avoiding it; so that I had no prospect before me but of perishing, not by the sea, for that was calm enough, but of starving from hunger. I had, indeed, found a tortoise on the shore, as big almost as I could lift, and had tossed it into the boat; and I had a great jar of fresh water—that is to say, one of my earthen pots; but what was all this to being driven into the vast ocean, where, to be sure, there was no shore, no mainland or island, for a thousand leagues at least?

And now I saw how easy it was for the providence of God to make the most miserable condition that mankind could be in worse. Now I looked back upon my desolate, solitary island as the most pleasant place in the world, and all the happiness my heart could wish for was to be there again. I stretched out my hands to it with eager wishes. "O happy desert!" said I. "I shall never see thee more. O miserable creature! Where am I going?" And then I reproached myself with my unthankful temper and how I had repined at my solitary condition; and now what would I give to be on shore there again? Thus, we never see the true state of our condition till it is illustrated to us by its contraries, nor know how to value what we enjoy, but by the lack of it. It is scarcely possible to imagine the consternation I was now in, being driven from my beloved island (for so it appeared to me now to be) into the wide ocean, almost two leagues, and in the utmost despair of ever recovering it again. However, I worked hard till, indeed, my strength was almost exhausted, and kept my boat as much to the northward—that is, toward the side of the current that the eddy lay on—as possibly I could, when about noon, as the sun passed the meridian, I thought I felt a little breeze of wind in my face, springing up from the south-southeast. This cheered my heart a little, and especially when, in about half an hour more, it blew a pretty small, gentle gale. By this time I had got at a frightful distance from the island; and had the least cloudy or hazy weather intervened, I had been undone another way, too; for I had no compass on board and should never have known how to have steered toward the island, if I had but once lost sight of it. But the weather continuing clear, I applied myself to get up my mast again and spread my sail, standing away to the north as much as possible, to get out of the current.

My Happy Deliverance

Just as I had set up my mast and sail and the boat began to stretch away, I saw even by the clearness of the water some alteration of the current was near; for where the current was so strong, the water was foul; but perceiving the water clear, I found the current abate; and presently I found to the east, at about half a mile, a breach of the sea upon some rocks. These rocks, I found, caused the current to part again, and as the main stress of it ran away more southerly, leaving the rocks to the northeast, so the other returned by the repulse of the rock and made a strong eddy, which ran back again to the northwest, with a very sharp stream.

They who know what it is to have a reprieve brought to them upon the scaffold, or to be rescued from thieves just going to murder them, or who have been in such extremities, may guess what my present surprise of joy was and how gladly I put my boat into the stream of this eddy; and the wind also freshening, how gladly I spread my sail to it, running cheerfully before the wind and with a strong tide or eddy underfoot.

This eddy carried me about a league in my way back again, directly toward the island, but about two leagues more toward the northward than the current lay that carried me away at first; so that when I came near the island, I found myself open to the northern shore of it—that is to say, the other end of the island, opposite to that which I went out from.

When I had made something more than a league of way by help of this current or eddy, I found it was spent and saved me no further. However, I

found that being between two great currents—namely, that on the south side, which had hurried me away, and that on the north, which lay about two leagues on the other side—I say, between these two, in the wake of the island, I found the water at least still and running nowhere; and having still a breeze of wind fair for me, I kept on steering directly for the island, though not moving as quickly as I did before.

About four o'clock in the evening, being then within about a league of the island, I found that the point of the rocks that occasioned this disaster by stretching out, as described before, to the southward and casting off the current more southerly had, of course, made another eddy to the north; and this I found very strong, but not directly setting the way my course lay, which was due west, but almost full north. However, having a fresh gale, I stretched across this eddy, slanting northwest, and in about an hour came within about a mile of the shore, where, it being smooth water, I soon got to land.

When I was on shore, I fell on my knees and gave God thanks for my deliverance, resolving to lay aside all thoughts of my deliverance by my boat; and refreshing myself with such things as I had, I brought my boat close to the shore, in a little cove that I had spied under some trees, and laid me down to sleep, being quite spent with the labor and fatigue of the voyage.

I was now at a great loss which way to get home with my boat! I had run so much hazard, and knew too much of the case, to think of attempting it by the way I went out; and what might be at the other side (I mean the west side) I knew not, nor had I any mind to run any more ventures. So I resolved on the next morning to make my way westward along the shore and to see if there was no creek where I might lay up my frigate in safety, so as to have her again, if I wanted her. In about three miles or thereabouts, coasting the shore, I came to a very good inlet, or bay, about a mile across, which narrowed till it came to a very little rivulet or brook, where I found a very convenient harbor for my boat and where she lay as if she had been in a little dock made on purpose for her. Here I put in, and having stowed my boat very safe, I went on shore to look about me and see where I was.

I soon found I had but little passed the place where I had been before, when I had traveled on foot to that shore; so, taking nothing out of my boat but my gun and umbrella, for it was exceedingly hot, I began my march. The way was comfortable enough after such a voyage as I had been upon, and I reached my old bower in the evening, where I found everything standing as I left it; for I always kept it in good order, being, as I said before, my country house.

I got over the fence and laid me down in the shade to rest my limbs, for I was very weary, and fell asleep. But judge you, if you can, that read my story, what a surprise I must have been in when I was awakened out of my sleep by a voice calling me by my name several times: "Robin, Robin, Robin Crusoe! Poor Robin Crusoe! Where are you, Robin Crusoe? Where are you? Where have you been?"

I was so dead asleep at first, being fatigued with rowing, or paddling, as it is called, the first part of the day and walking the latter part that I did not awaken thoroughly, and dozing between sleeping and waking, I thought I dreamed that somebody spoke to me; but as the voice continued to repeat, "Robin Crusoe! Robin Crusoe!" at last I began to awake more perfectly and was at first dreadfully frightened, and started up in the utmost consternation. But no sooner were my eyes open but I saw my Poll sitting on the top of the hedge, and immediately I knew that it was he that spoke to me; for in just such bemoaning language I used to talk to him and teach him; and he had learned it so perfectly that he would sit upon my finger, lay his bill close to my face, and cry, "Poor Robin Crusoe! Where are you? Where have you been? How came you here?" and such things as I had taught him.

However, even though I knew it was the parrot, and that indeed it could be nobody else, it was a good while before I could compose myself. First, I was amazed how the creature got thither; and then, how he should just keep about the place and nowhere else; but as I was well satisfied it could be nobody but honest Poll, I got over it; and holding out my hand and calling him by his name, "Poll," the sociable creature came to me and sat upon my thumb, as he used to do, and continued talking to me, "Poor Robin Crusoe!" and "How came you here?" and "Where have you been?" just as if he had been overjoyed to see me again; and so I carried him home along with me.

Chapter 11
Pots, Wickerware, and Goats

I had now had enough of rambling to sea for some time and had enough to do for many days to just sit still and reflect upon the danger I had been in. I would have been very glad to have had my boat again on my side of the island; but I knew not how it was practicable to get it around. As to the east side of the island, which I had gone around, I knew well enough there was no venturing that way; my very heart would shrink, and my very blood run chill, but to think of it; and as to the other side of the island, I did not know how it might be there. But supposing the current ran with the same force against the shore at the east as it passed by it on the other, I might run the same risk of being driven down the stream and carried by the island as I had been before of being carried away from it. So with these thoughts I contented myself to be without any boat, though it had been the product of so many months' labor to make it, and of so many more to get it into the sea.

In this condition, I remained nearly a year and lived a very sedate, retired life, as you may well suppose; and my thoughts being very much composed as to my condition, and fully comforted in resigning myself to the dispositions of Providence, I thought I lived really very happily in all things, except that of society.

I improved myself in this time in all the mechanical exercises that my necessities demanded; and I believe I should, upon occasion, have made a very good carpenter, especially considering how few tools I had.

My Pots and Wickerware

Besides this, I arrived at an unexpected perfection in my earthenware and contrived well enough to make them with a wheel, which I found infinitely easier and better, because I made things round and shaped, which before were disgusting things indeed to look on. But I think I was never more vain of my own performance, or more joyful for anything I found out, than for my being able to make a tobacco pipe; and though it was a very ugly, clumsy thing when it was done, and only burnt red, like other earthenware, yet as it was hard and firm and would draw the smoke, I was exceedingly comforted with it, for I had been always used to smoke; and there were pipes in the ship, but I forgot them at first, not thinking that there was tobacco in the island; and afterward, when I searched the ship again, I could not find any pipes.

In my wickerware also I improved much and made an abundance of necessary baskets, as well as my ingenuity showed me; though not very handsome, yet they were such as were very handy and convenient for laying things up in or fetching things home. For example, if I killed a goat abroad, I could hang it up in a tree, flay it, dress it, cut it in pieces, and bring it home in a basket; and the like with a turtle: I could cut it up, take out the eggs, and a piece or two of the flesh, which was enough for me, and bring them home in a basket, leaving the rest behind me. Also, large deep baskets were my receivers for my corn, which I always rubbed out as soon as it was dry, and cured, and kept it in great baskets, instead of a granary.

I began now to perceive my powder abated considerably; and as this was a lack that it was impossible for me to supply, I began seriously to consider what I must do when I should have no more powder; that is to say, how I should kill my goats. I had, as I observed in the third year of my being here, kept a young kid and bred her up tame; I was in hopes of getting a he-kid; but I could not by any means bring it to pass, till my kid grew to be an old goat; and as I could never find in my heart to kill her, she died at last of mere age.

But being now in the eleventh year of my residence, and, as I have said, my ammunition growing low, I set myself to study some art to trap and snare the goats, to see whether I could not catch some of them alive; and particularly I wanted a she-goat great with young. To this purpose, I made snares to hamper them; and I believe they were more than once taken in them; but my tackle was not good, for I had no wire, and I always found them broken and my bait devoured. At length, I resolved to try a pitfall; so I dug several large pits in the earth, in places where I had observed the goats used to feed, and over these pits I placed hurdles, of my own making too, with a great weight upon them; and several times I put ears of barley and dry rice, without setting the trap; and I could easily perceive that the goats had gone in and eaten up the corn, for I could see the marks of their feet. At length, I set three traps in one night, and going the next morning, I found them all standing, and yet the bait eaten and gone: This was very discouraging. However, I altered my traps; and, not to trouble you with particulars, going one morning to see my traps, I found in one of them a large old he-goat; and in one of the others, three kids, a male and two females.

As to the old one, I knew not what to do with him. He was so fierce, I dared not go into the pit to him; that is to say, to go about to bring him away alive, which was what I wanted. I could have killed him, but that was not my business, nor would it answer my end; so I merely let him out, and he ran away, as if he had been frightened out of his wits. I had forgot then what I learned afterward, that hunger will tame a lion. If I had let him stay there three or four days without food, and then have carried him some water to drink, and then a little corn, he would have been as tame as one of the kids; for they are mighty sagacious, tractable creatures, where they are well used.

However, for the present I let him go, knowing no better at that time; then I went to the three kids, and, taking them one by one, I tied them with rope together and with some difficulty brought them all home.

It was a good while before they would feed; but throwing them some sweet corn, it tempted them, and they began to be tame. And now I found that if I expected to supply myself with goats' flesh, when I had no powder or shot left, breeding some up tame was my only way, when, perhaps, I might have them about my house like a flock of sheep. But, then, it occurred to me that I must keep the tame from the wild, or else they would always run wild when they grew up; and the only way for this was to have some enclosed piece of ground, well fenced either with hedge or pale, to keep them up so effectually that those within might not break out, or those without break in.

This was a great undertaking for one pair of hands; yet, as I saw there was an absolute necessity for doing it, my first piece of work was to find out a proper piece of ground—that is, where there was likely to be herbage for them to eat, water for them to drink, and cover to keep them from the sun.

My Paddock for the Goats

Those who understand such enclosures will think I had very little ingenuity, when I pitched upon a place very proper for all these, being a plain, open piece of meadowland, or savannah (as our people call it in the western colonies), which had two or three little rills of fresh water in it, and at one end was very woody; I say, they will smile at my prediction, when I shall tell them I began by enclosing this piece of ground in such a manner that my hedge or pale must have been at least two miles around. Nor was the madness of it so great as to the compass, for if it was ten miles about, I was like to have time enough to do it in; but I did not consider that my goats would be as wild in so much space as they would if they had had the whole island, and I should have so much room to chase them in that I should never catch them.

My hedge was begun and carried on, I believe, about fifty yards, when this thought occurred to me; so I presently stopped short, and, for the first beginning, I resolved to enclose a piece of about one hundred and fifty yards in length and one hundred yards in breadth, as it would maintain as many as I should have in any reasonable time; so, as my flock increased, I could add more ground to my enclosure.

This was acting with some prudence, and I went to work with courage. I was about three months hedging in the first piece; and, till I had done it, I tethered the three kids in the best part of it and used to feed them as near me as possible, to make them tamer; and very often I would go and carry them some ears of barley, or a handful of rice, and feed them out of my hand; so that, after my enclosure was finished, and I let them loose, they would follow me up and down, bleating after me for a handful of corn.

This answered my end, and in about a year and a half I had a flock of about twelve goats, kids and all; and in two years more I had three-and-forty, besides several that I took and killed for my food; and after that, I enclosed five several pieces of ground to feed them in, with little pens to drive them into, to take them as I wanted them, and gates out of one piece of ground into another.

But this was not all; for now I not only had goats' flesh to feed on when I pleased, but milk, too—a thing that, indeed, in my beginning I did not so much as think of, and which, when it came into my thoughts, was really an agreeable surprise; for now I set up my dairy and had sometimes a gallon or two of milk in a day. And as nature, which gives supplies of food to every creature, dictates naturally how to make use of it, so I, that never milked a cow, much less a goat, or saw butter or cheese made, very readily and handily, though after a great many essays and miscarriages, made me both butter and cheese at last and never lacked it afterward. How mercifully can our Creator treat His creatures even in those conditions in which they seem to be overwhelmed in destruction! How can He sweeten the bitterest providences and give us cause to praise Him for dungeons and prisons! What a table was here spread for me in a wilderness where I saw nothing at first but to perish for hunger!

It would have made a stoic smile to have seen me and my little family sit down to dinner. There was my majesty, the prince and lord of the whole island. I had the lives of all my subjects at absolute command; I could hang, draw, give life and liberty and take it away, and no rebels among all my subjects. Then to see how like a king I dined, too, all alone, attended by my servants! Poll, as if he had been my favorite, was the only person permitted to talk to me; my dog, who was now grown very old and crazy and had found no species to multiply his kind upon, sat always at my right hand; and two cats, one on one side of the table and one on the other, expecting now and then a bit from my hand, as a mark of special favor.

But these were not the two cats that I brought on shore at first, for they were both of them dead and had been interred near my habitation by my own hand; but one of them having multiplied by I know not what kind of creature, these were two that I preserved tame; whereas the rest ran wild in the woods and became, indeed, troublesome to me at last, for they would often come into my house and plunder me, too, till at last I was obliged to shoot them and did kill a great many; at length they left me. With this attendance and in this plentiful manner I lived; neither could I be said to want anything but society; and of that, in some time after this, I was likely to have too much.

I was something impatient, as I have observed, to have the use of my boat, though very reluctant to run any more hazard; and, therefore, sometimes I sat contriving ways to get her around the island, and at other times I sat myself down, contented enough without her. But I had a strange uneasiness in my mind about going down to the point of the island where, as I have said, in my last ramble, I went up the hill to see how the shore lay, and how the current set, that I might see what I had to do. This inclination increased upon me every day, and at length I resolved to travel there by land; and, following the edge of the shore, I did so. Had anyone in England met such a man as I was, it must either have frightened them or raised a great deal of laughter; and as I frequently stood still to look at myself, I could not but smile at the notion of my traveling through Yorkshire with such an equipage and in such a dress. Be pleased to take a sketch of my figure, as follows:

My New Clothes

I had a great, high, shapeless cap made of goatskin, with a flap hanging down behind, as well to keep the sun from me as to keep the rain from running into my neck, nothing being so hurtful in these climates as the rain upon the flesh under the clothes.

I had a short jacket of goatskin, the skirts coming down to about the middle of the thighs, and a pair of open-kneed breeches of the same; the breeches were made of the skin of an old he-goat, whose hair hung down such a length on either side that, like pantaloons, it reached to the middle of my legs. Stockings and shoes I had none, but I had made me a pair of something—I scarce knew what to call them—like buskins,[1] to flap over my legs and lace on either side like spatterdashes,[2] but of a most barbarous shape, as, indeed, were all the rest of my clothes.

I had on a broad belt of goatskin, which I drew together with two thongs of the same, instead of buckles; and in a kind of a frog[3] on either side of this, instead of a sword and dagger, hung a little saw and a hatchet, one on one side, one on the other. I had another belt not so broad and fastened in the same manner, which hung over my shoulder; and at the end of it, under my left arm, hung two pouches, both made of goatskin, too, in one of which hung my powder, in the other my shot. At my back I carried my basket, on my shoulder my gun, and over my head a great clumsy, ugly goatskin

1. *Buskins,* half-boots.

2. *Spatterdashes,* leggings or "spats."

3. *Frog,* belt loops for a scabbard.

umbrella, but which, after all, was the most necessary thing I had about me next to my gun. As for my face, the color of it was really not so mulattolike as one might expect from a man not at all careful of it and living within nine or ten degrees of the equator. My beard I had once suffered to grow till it was about a quarter of a yard long; but as I had both scissors and razors sufficient, I had cut it pretty short, except what grew on my upper lip, which I had trimmed into a large pair of Mahometan whiskers, such as I had seen worn by some Turks at Sallee; for the Moors did not wear such, though the Turks did. Of these mustachios, or whiskers, I will not say they were long enough to hang my hat upon them, but they were of a length and shape monstrous enough and such as in England would have passed for frightful.

But all this is by the by; for, as to my figure, I had so few to observe me that it was of no manner of consequence, so I say no more to that part. In this kind of dress I went on my new journey and was out five or six days. I traveled first along the seashore, directly to the place where I first brought my boat to an anchor, to get up upon the rocks; and having no boat now to take care of, I went over the land a nearer way to the same height that I was upon before, when, looking forward to the point of the rock that lay out, and which I was obliged to clear with my boat, as I said above, I was surprised to see the sea all smooth and quiet—no rippling, no motion, no current any more there than in other places. I was at a strange loss to understand this and resolved to spend some time in observing it, to see if nothing from the sets of the tide had occasioned it; but I was presently convinced how it was—namely, that the tide of ebb setting from the west, and joining with the current of waters from some great river on the shore, must be the occasion of this current; and that according as the wind blew more forcibly from the west or from the north, this current came near or went farther from the shore. For, waiting thereabouts till evening, I went up to the rock again, and then the tide of ebb being made, I plainly saw the current again as before, only that it ran farther off, being nearly half a league from the shore, whereas in my case it set close upon the shore and hurried me in my canoe along with it, which at another time it would not have done.

This observation convinced me that I had nothing to do but to observe the ebbing and the flowing of the tide, and I might very easily bring my boat about the island again; but when I began to think about putting it in practice, I was in such terror at the remembrance of the danger I had been in that I could not think of it again with any patience. On the contrary, I took up another resolution, which was more safe, though more laborious—and this was that I would build, or rather make me, another *periagua* and so have one for one side of the island and one for the other.

You are to understand that now I had, as I may call it, two plantations on the island; one of my little fortification or tent, with the wall about it, under the rock, with the cave behind me, which by this time I had enlarged into several apartments, or caves, one within another. One of these, which was the driest and largest and had a door out beyond my wall or fortification—that is to say, beyond where my wall joined to the rock—was all filled up with the large earthen pots, of which I have given an account, and with fourteen or fifteen great baskets, which would hold five or six bushels each, where I laid up my stores of provisions, especially my corn, some in the ear, cut off short from the straw, and the other rubbed out with my hand.

As for my wall, made, as before, with long stakes or piles, those piles grew all like trees and were by

this time grown so big, and spread so very much, that there was not the least appearance, to anyone's view, of any habitation behind them.

Near this dwelling of mine, but a little farther within the land and upon lower ground, lay my two pieces of corn land, which I kept duly cultivated and sowed, and which duly yielded me their harvest in its season; and whenever I had occasion for more corn, I had more land adjoining as fit as that.

My Countryseat

Besides this, I had my countryseat, and I had now a tolerable plantation there also; for first, I had my little bower, as I called it, which I kept in repair—that is to say, I kept the hedge that circled it in constantly fitted up to its usual height, the ladder standing always in the inside. I kept the trees, which at first were no more than my stakes, but were now grown very firm and tall, always so cut that they might spread and grow thick and wild and make the more agreeable shade, which they did effectively to my mind. In the middle of this I had my tent always standing, being a piece of a sail spread over poles set up for that purpose, and which never wanted any repair or renewing; and under this I had made me a squab, or couch, with the skins of the creatures I had killed and with other soft things, and a blanket laid on them, such as belonged to our sea bedding, which I had saved, and a great watch coat to cover me; and here, whenever I had occasion to be absent from my chief seat, I took up my country habitation.

Adjoining this I had my enclosures for my cattle—that is to say, my goats; and as I had taken inconceivable pains to fence and enclose this ground, I was so anxious to see it kept unbroken, lest the goats should break through, that I never left off till, with infinite labor, I had stuck the outside of the hedge so full of small stakes, and so near to one another, that it was rather a pale than a hedge, and there was scarce room to put a hand through between them. Afterward, when those stakes grew, as they all did in the next rainy season, they made the enclosure strong like a wall—indeed, stronger than any wall.

This will testify for me that I was not idle, and that I spared no pains to bring to pass whatever appeared necessary for my comfortable support; for I considered that keeping up a breed of tame creatures thus at my hand would be a living magazine of flesh, milk, butter, and cheese for me as long as I lived in the place, if it were to be forty years; and that keeping them in my reach depended entirely upon my perfecting my enclosures to such a degree that I might be sure of keeping them together, which, by this method, indeed, I so effectively secured that when these little stakes began to grow, I had planted them so very thick, I was forced to pull some of them up again.

In this place also I had my grapes growing, which I principally depended on for my winter store of raisins, and which I never failed to preserve very carefully as the best and most agreeable dainty of my whole diet; and, indeed, they were not only agreeable, but curative, wholesome, nourishing, and refreshing to the last degree.

As this was also about halfway between my other habitation and the place where I had laid up my boat, I generally stayed and lay here on my way there, for I used frequently to visit my boat; and I kept all things about, or belonging to her, in very good order. Sometimes I went out in her to divert myself, but on no more hazardous voyages would I go, scarcely ever more than a stone's cast or two from the shore, I was so apprehensive of being hurried out into the unknown again by the currents or winds, or any other accident. But now I came to a new scene of my life.

Chapter 12

Footprint in the Sand

It happened one day, about noon, going toward my boat, I was exceedingly surprised with the print of a man's naked foot on the shore, which was very plain to be seen on the sand. I stood like one thunderstruck, or as if I had seen an apparition. I listened, I looked around me, but I could hear nothing nor see anything; I went up to a rising ground, to look farther; I went up the shore and down the shore, but it was all one: I could see no other impression but that one. I went to it again to see if there were any more, and to observe if it might not be my imagination; but there was no room for that, for there was exactly the print of a foot—toes, heel, and every part of a foot. How it came there I knew not, nor could in the least imagine. But after innumerable fluttering thoughts, like a man perfectly confused and out of myself, I came home to my fortification, not feeling, as we say, the ground I went on, but terrified to the last degree, looking behind me at every two or three steps, mistaking every bush and tree and fancying every stump at a distance to be a man. Nor is it possible to describe how many various shapes my affrighted imagination represented things to me in; how many wild ideas were formed every moment in my fancy, and what strange unaccountable whimsies came into my thoughts by the way.

When I came to my castle (for so I think I called it ever after this), I fled into it like one pursued. Whether I went over by the ladder, as first contrived, or went in at the hole in the rock, which I called a door, I cannot remember; for never a frightened hare fled to cover, or fox to earth, with more terror of mind than I to this retreat.

I had no sleep that night; the further I was from the occasion of my fright, the greater my apprehensions were, which is something contrary to the nature of such things, and especially to the usual practice of all creatures in fear; but I was so confused with my own frightful ideas of the thing, that I

I stood like one thunderstruck.

formed nothing but dismal imaginations to myself, even though I was now a great way off from it. Sometimes I fancied it must be the devil; and reason joined in with me upon this supposition: For how should any other thing in human shape come into the place? Where was the vessel that brought them? What marks were there of any other footsteps? And how was it possible a man should come there? But then to think that Satan should take human shape upon him in such a place, where there could be no manner of occasion for it, but to leave the print of his foot behind him, and that even for no purpose too, for he could not be sure I should see it—this was bewildering in another way. I considered that the devil might have found out an abundance of other ways to have terrified me than this of the single print of a foot; that as I lived quite on the other side of the island, he would never have been so simple as to leave a mark in a place where it was ten thousand to one whether I should ever see it or not, and in the sand, too, which the first surge of the sea, upon a high wind, would have obliterated entirely. All this seemed inconsistent with the thing itself and with all the notions we usually entertain of the subtlety of the devil.

Abundance of such things as these assisted to argue me out of all apprehensions of its being the devil; and I presently concluded then that it must be some more dangerous creature; that is, that it must be some of the savages of the mainland over across from me, who had wandered out to sea in their canoes and, either driven by the currents or by contrary winds, had made the island and had been on shore, but were gone away again to sea; being as reluctant, perhaps, to have stayed in this desolate island as I would have been to have had them.

While these reflections were rolling through my mind, I was very thankful in my thoughts that I had not been thereabouts at that time, nor had they seen my boat, by which they would have concluded that some inhabitants had been in the place and perhaps have searched further for me. Then terrible thoughts racked my imagination about their having found my boat, and that there were people here; and that, if so, I should certainly have them come again in greater numbers and devour me; that if it should happen that they should not find me, yet they would find my enclosure, destroy all my corn, and carry away all my flock of tame goats, and I should perish at last for mere hunger.

Thus my fear banished all my religious hope. All that former confidence in God, which was founded upon such wonderful experience as I had had of His goodness, now vanished; as if He that had fed me by miracle hitherto, could not preserve by His power the provisions that He had made for me by His goodness. I reproached myself with my laziness that would not sow any more corn one year than would just serve me till the next season, as if no accident could intervene to prevent my enjoying the crop that was upon the ground; and this I thought so just a reproof that I resolved for the future to have two or three years' corn beforehand, so that, whatever might come, I might not perish for want of bread.

How strange a checkerwork of Providence is the life of man! And by what secret differing springs are the affections hurried about, as differing circumstances present! Today we love what tomorrow we hate; today we seek what tomorrow we shun; today we desire what tomorrow we fear, nay, even tremble at the apprehensions of. This was exemplified in me at this time in the most lively manner imaginable; for I, whose only affliction was that I seemed banished from human society, that I was alone, circumscribed by the boundless ocean, cut off from mankind, and condemned to what I call silent life; that I was as one whom Heaven thought not worthy to be numbered among the living, or to appear amongst the rest of His creatures; that to have seen one of my own species would have seemed to me a raising me from death to life, and the greatest blessing that Heaven itself, next to the supreme blessing of salvation, could bestow; I say, that I should now tremble at the very apprehensions of seeing a man and was ready to sink into the ground at but the shadow or silent appearance of a man having set his foot on the island!

Such is the uneven state of human life; and it afforded me a great many curious speculations afterward, when I had a little recovered my first surprise. I considered that this was the station of life the infinitely wise and good providence of God had determined for me; that as I could not foresee what the end of divine wisdom might be in all this, so I was not to dispute His sovereignty, who, as I was His creature, had an undoubted right by creation to govern and dispose of me absolutely as He thought fit; and who, as I was a creature who had offended Him, had likewise a judicial right to condemn me to what punishment He thought fit; and that it was my part to submit to bear His indignation, because I had sinned against Him. I then reflected that God, who was not only righteous, but omnipotent, as He had thought fit thus to punish and afflict me, so He was able to deliver me; that if He did not think fit to do it, it was my unquestioned duty to resign myself absolutely and entirely to His will; and on the other hand, it was my duty also to hope in Him, pray to Him, and quietly to attend the dictates and directions of His daily providence.

I Feel Encouraged

These thoughts took up many hours, days, nay, I may say weeks and months; and one particular effect of my cogitations on this occasion I cannot omit. One morning early, lying in my bed and filled with thoughts about my danger from the appearance of savages, I found it disturbed me very much; upon which those words of the Scripture came into my thoughts: "Call upon Me in the day of trouble: I will deliver thee, and thou shalt glorify Me." Upon this, rising cheerfully out of my bed, my heart was not only comforted, but I was guided and encouraged to pray earnestly to God for deliverance; when I had done praying, I took up my Bible, and opening it to read, the first words presented to me were, "Wait on the Lord: Be of good courage, and He shall strengthen thy heart; wait, I say, on the Lord." It is impossible to express the comfort this gave me, and in return I thankfully laid down the book and was no more sad, at least, not on that occasion.

In the middle of these cogitations, apprehensions, and reflections, it came into my thoughts one day that all this might be a mere chimera of my own, and that this foot might be the print of my own foot, when I came on shore from my boat. This cheered me up a little, too, and I began to persuade myself it was all a delusion; that it was nothing else but my own foot; and why might I not come that way from the boat, as well as I was going that way to the boat? Again I considered also that I could by no means tell for certain where I had trod and where I had not; and that if, at last, this was only the print of my own foot, I had played the part of those fools who try to make stories of specters and apparitions and then are themselves frightened at them more than anybody else.

Now I began to take courage and to peep abroad again, for I had not stirred out of my castle for three days and nights, so that I began to starve for provision; for I had little or nothing within doors but some barley-cakes and water. Then I knew that my goats needed to be milked, too, which usually was my evening diversion; and the poor creatures were in great pain and inconvenience for want of it; and, indeed, it almost spoiled some of them and almost dried up their milk.

Heartening myself, therefore, with the belief that this was nothing but the print of one of my own feet, and so I might be truly said to start at my own shadow, I began to go abroad again and went to my country house to milk my flock; but to see with what fear I went forward, how often I looked behind me, how I was ready, every now and then, to lay down my basket and run for my life, it would have made anyone have thought I was haunted with an evil

conscience, or that I had been lately most terribly frightened; and so, indeed, I had. However, as I went down thus two or three days and having seen nothing, I began to be a little bolder and to think there was really nothing in it but my own imagination; but I could not persuade myself fully of this till I should go down to the shore again and see this print of a foot, and measure it by my own, and see if there was any similitude or fitness, that I might be assured it was my own foot. But when I came to the place—first, it appeared evident to me that when I laid up my boat, I could not possibly have been on shore anywhere thereabouts; secondly, when I came to measure the mark with my own foot, I found my foot not so large by a great deal. Both these things filled my head with new fears and gave me the vapors again to the highest degree, so that I shook with cold like one in an ague; and I went home again, filled with the belief that some man or men had been on shore there; or, in short, that the island was inhabited, and I might be surprised before I was aware; and what course to take for my security I knew not.

I Contrive New Defenses

Oh, what ridiculous resolutions men take when possessed with fear! It deprives them of the use of those means that reason offers for their relief. The first thing I proposed to myself was to throw down my enclosures and turn all my tame cattle wild into the woods, that the enemy might not find them and then frequent the island in prospect of the same or the like booty; then the simple thing of digging up my two cornfields that they might not find such corn there and still be prompted to frequent the island; then to demolish my bower and tent, that they might not see any vestiges of habitation and be prompted to look further, in order to find out the persons inhabiting.

These were the subjects of the first night's cogitations, after I was come home again, while the apprehensions that had so overrun my mind were fresh upon me, and my head was full of vapors as above. Thus, fear of danger is ten thousand times more terrifying than danger itself, when apparent to the eyes; and we find the burden of anxiety greater, by much, than the evil that we are anxious about. But, which was worse than all this, I had not that relief in this trouble, from the resignation I used to practice, that I hoped to have. I looked, I thought, like Saul, who complained not only that the Philistines were upon him, but that God had forsaken him. For I did not now take due ways to compose my mind, by crying to God in my distress and resting upon His providence, as I had done before, for my defense and deliverance; which if I had done, I had at least been more cheerfully supported under this new surprise and perhaps carried through it with more resolution.

This confusion of my thoughts kept me waking all night; but in the morning I fell asleep; and having by the amusement of my mind been, as it were, tired and my spirits exhausted, I slept very soundly and awakened much better composed than I had ever been before. And now I began to think more clearly; and, upon the utmost debate with myself, I concluded that this island (which was so exceedingly pleasant, fruitful, and no farther from the mainland than I had seen) was not so entirely abandoned as I might imagine; that although there were no stated inhabitants who lived on the spot, yet that there might sometimes come boats from off the shore that, either with design, or perhaps never but when they were driven by crosswinds, might come to this place; that I had lived here fifteen years now and had not met with the least shadow or figure of any people yet; and that, if at any time they should be driven here, it was probable they went away again as soon as ever they could, seeing they had never thought fit to stay here upon any occasion to this time; that the most I could suggest any danger from was from any casual accidental landing of straggling people from the mainland, who, as it was likely, if they were driven here, were here against their wills; so they made no stay here, but went off again with all possible speed, seldom staying one night on shore, lest they should not have the help of the tides and daylight back again; and that, therefore, I had nothing to do but to consider some safe retreat, in case I should see any savages land upon the spot.

Now I began sorely to repent that I had dug my cave so large as to bring a door through again, which door, as I said, came out beyond where my fortification joined to the rock. Upon maturely considering this, therefore, I resolved to draw me a second fortification, in the same manner of a semicircle, at a distance from my wall, just where I had planted a double row of trees about twelve years before, of which I made mention. These trees having been planted so thick before, there wanted but few piles to be driven between them that they should be thicker and stronger and my wall would be soon finished. So that I had now a double wall; and my other wall was thickened with pieces of timber, old cables, and everything I could think of to make it strong, having in it seven little holes about as big as I might put my arm out at. In the inside of this, I thickened my wall to about ten feet thick, continually bringing earth out of my cave, laying it at the foot of the wall, and walking upon it; and through the seven holes I contrived to plant the muskets, of which I took notice that I got seven on shore out of the ship; these, I say, I planted like my cannon and fitted them into frames that held them like a carriage, so that I could fire all the seven guns in two minutes' time. This wall I was many a weary month in finishing, and yet I never thought myself safe till it was done.

When this was done, I stuck all the ground without my wall, for a great way in every direction, as full with stakes or sticks of the osierlike wood, which I found so apt to grow, as they could well stand; insomuch that I believe I might have set in nearly twenty thousand of them, leaving a pretty large space between them and my wall that I might have room to see an enemy and they might have no shelter from the young trees, if they attempted to approach my outer wall.

Thus, in two years' time, I had a thick grove; and in five or six years' time I had a wood before my dwelling grown so monstrous thick and strong that it was indeed perfectly impassable; and no man, of what kind soever, would ever imagine that there was anything beyond it, much less a habitation. As for the way that I proposed to myself to go in and out (for I left no avenue), it was by setting two ladders, one to a part of the rock that was low, and then broke in, and left room to place another ladder upon that; so when the two ladders were taken down, no man living could come down to me without harming himself; and if they had come down, they were still on the outside of my outer wall.

Thus I took all the measures human prudence could suggest for my own preservation; and it will be seen, at length, that they were not altogether without just reason; though I foresaw nothing at that time more than my mere fear suggested to me.

Further Precautions

While this was doing, I was not altogether careless of my other affairs; for I had a great concern upon me for my little herd of goats. They were not only a present supply to me upon every occasion and began to be sufficient for me without the expense of powder and shot, but also abated the fatigue of my hunting after the wild ones; and I was loath to lose the advantage of them and to have them all to nurse up over again.

For this purpose, after long consideration, I could think of but two ways to preserve them: One was to find another convenient place to dig a cave underground and to drive them into it every night; the other was to enclose two or three little bits of land, remote from one another and as much concealed as I could, where I might keep about half a dozen young goats in each place; so that if any disaster happened to the flock in general, I might be able to raise them again with little trouble and time. This, though it would require a good deal of time and labor, I thought was the most rational design.

Accordingly, I spent some time to find out the most remote parts of the island; and I pitched upon one that was as private indeed as my heart could wish: It was a little damp piece of ground in the middle of the hollow and thick woods, where, as is observed, I almost lost myself once before, endeavoring to come back that way from the eastern part of the island. Here I found a clear piece of land, nearly three acres, so surrounded with woods that it was almost an enclosure by nature; at least, it did not lack nearly so much labor to make it so as the other pieces of ground I had worked so hard at.

I immediately went to work with this piece of ground; and, in less than a month's time, I had so fenced it around that my flock, or herd, call it which you please, which was not so wild now as at first it might be supposed to be, was well enough secured in it. So, without any further delay, I removed ten she-goats and two he-goats to this place; and when they were there, I continued to perfect the fence, till I had made it as secure as the other; which, however, I did at more leisure, and it took me more time by a great deal.

All this labor I was at the expense of, purely from my apprehensions on the account of the print of a man's foot that I had seen; for, as yet, I had never seen any human creature come near the island; and I had now lived two years under this uneasiness, which, indeed, made my life much less comfortable than it was before, as may well be imagined by any who know what it is to live in the constant snare of the fear of man. And this I must observe, with grief, too, that the discomposure of my mind had too great impressions also upon the religious part of my thoughts; for the dread and terror of falling into the hands of savages and cannibals lay so upon my spirits that I seldom found myself in a due temper for application to my Maker; at least, not with the sedate calmness and resignation of soul that I was wont to do. I rather prayed to God as under great affliction and pressure of mind, surrounded with danger, and in expectation every night of being murdered and devoured before morning; and I must testify, from my experience, that a temper of peace, thankfulness, love, and affection is much the more proper frame for prayer than that of terror and discomposure; and that under the dread of mischief impending, a man is no more fit for a comforting performance of the duty of praying to God than he is for repentance on a sickbed; for these discomposures affect the mind, as the others do the body: and the discomposure of the mind must necessarily be as great a disability as that of the body, and much greater; praying to God being properly an act of the mind, not of the body.

But to go on: After I had thus secured one part of my little living stock, I went about the whole island, searching for another private place to make such another deposit; when, wandering more to the west point of the island than I had ever done yet, and looking out to sea, I thought I saw a boat upon the sea at a great distance. I had found a perspective glass or two in one of the seamen's chests, which I saved out of our ship, but I had it not about me; and this was so remote that I could not tell what to make of it, though I looked at it till my eyes were not able to hold to look any longer. Whether it was a boat or not, I do not know; but as I descended from the hill I could see no more of it, so I gave it up; only I resolved to go no more out without a perspective glass in my pocket.

When I was come down the hill to the end of the island, where, indeed, I had never been before, I was presently convinced that seeing the print of a man's foot was not such a strange thing on the island as I imagined; and but that it was a special providence that I was cast upon the side of the island where the savages never came, I should easily have known that nothing was more frequent than for the canoes from the mainland, when they happened to be a little too far out at sea, to shoot over to that side of the island for harbor. Likewise, as they often met and fought in their canoes, the victors, having taken any prisoners, would bring them over to this shore, where, according to their dreadful customs, being all cannibals, they would kill and eat them; of which more hereafter.

A Cannibal Orgy

When I was come down the hill to the shore, as I said above, being the southwest point of the island, I was perfectly confounded and amazed; nor is it possible for me to express the horror of my mind, at seeing the shore spread with skulls, hands, feet, and other bones of human bodies; and particularly, I observed a place where there had been a fire made and a circle dug in the earth, like a cockpit, where I supposed the savage wretches had sat down to the inhuman feastings upon the bodies of their fellow creatures.

I was so astonished with the sight of these things that I entertained no notions of any danger to myself from it for a long while; all my apprehensions were buried in the thoughts of such a pitch of inhuman, hellish brutality and the horror of the degeneracy of human nature, which, though I had heard of often, yet I never had so near a view of before. In short, I turned away my face from the horrid spectacle; my stomach grew sick, and I was just at the point of fainting, when nature discharged the disorder from my stomach; and having vomited with uncommon violence, I was a little relieved, but could

not bear to stay in the place a moment; so I got up the hill again with all the speed I could and walked on toward my own habitation.

When I came a little out of that part of the island, I stood still awhile, as amazed, and then, recovering myself, I looked up with the utmost affection of my soul and, with a flood of tears in my eyes, gave God thanks that He had cast my first lot in a part of the world where I was separated from such dreadful creatures as these; and that, though I had esteemed my present condition very miserable, had yet given me so many comforts in it that I had still more to give thanks for than to complain of; and this, above all, that I had, even in this miserable condition, been comforted with the knowledge of Himself and the hope of His blessing, which was a felicity more than sufficiently equivalent to all the misery that I had suffered or could suffer.

In this frame of thankfulness, I went home to my castle and began to be much easier now, as to the safety of my circumstances, than ever I was before. For I observed that these wretches never came to this island in search of what they could get; perhaps not seeking, not wanting, or not expecting, anything here; and having often, no doubt, been up in the covered, woody part of it, without finding anything to their purpose. I knew I had been here now almost eighteen years and never saw the least footsteps of human creature there before; and I might be eighteen years more as entirely concealed as I was now, if I did not disclose myself to them, which I had no manner of occasion to do; it being my only business to keep myself entirely concealed where I was, unless I found a better sort of creature than cannibals to make myself known to. Yet I entertained such an abhorrence of the savage wretches that I have been speaking of, and of the wretched inhuman custom of their devouring and eating one another up, that I continued pensive and sad and kept close within my own circle for almost two years after this. When I say my own circle, I mean by it my three plantations, namely, my castle, my countryseat (which I called my bower), and my enclosure in the woods. Nor did I look after this for any other use than as an enclosure for my goats; for the aversion that nature gave me to these hellish wretches was such that I was as fearful of seeing them as of seeing the devil himself, nor did I so much as go to look after my boat in all this time, but began rather to think of making me another; for I could not think of ever making any more attempts to bring the other boat around the island to me, lest I should meet with some of those creatures at sea; in which case, if I had happened to have fallen into their hands, I knew what would have been my lot.

Time, however, and the satisfaction I had that I was in no danger of being discovered by these people, began to wear off my uneasiness about them; and

I began to live just in the same composed manner as before, only with this difference, that I used more caution and kept my eyes more about me than I did before, lest I should happen to be seen by any of them; and particularly I was more cautious in firing my gun, lest any of them, being on the island, should happen to hear it; and it was, therefore, a very good providence to me that I had furnished myself with a tame breed of goats and that I had no need to hunt anymore about the woods or shoot at them; and if I did catch any of them after this, it was by traps and snares, as I had done before. For two years after this, I believe I never once fired off my gun, though I never went out without it; and, which was more, as I had saved three pistols out of the ship, I always carried them out with me, or at least two of them, sticking them in my goatskin belt. I likewise furbished up one of the great cutlasses that I had out of the ship and made me a belt to put it on also; so that I was now a most formidable fellow to look at when I went abroad, if you add to the former description of myself, the particular of two pistols and a great broadsword hanging at my side in a belt, but without a scabbard.

Chapter 13

A State of Siege

Things going on thus, as I have said, for some time, I seemed, excepting these cautions, to be reduced to my former calm, sedate way of living. All these things tended to show me, more and more, how far my condition was from being miserable, compared with some others; nay, with many other particulars of life that it might have pleased God to have made my lot. It put me upon reflecting how little repining there would be among mankind at any condition of life, if people would rather compare their condition with those that are worse, in order to be thankful, than be always comparing them with those that are better, to assist their murmurings and complainings.

Plans Against the Savages

As in my present condition there were not really many things that I wanted, so, indeed, I thought that the frights I had been in about these savage wretches, and the concern I had been in for my own preservation, had taken off the edge of my invention for my own conveniences; and I had dropped a good plan, which I had once bent my thoughts upon, and that was to try if I could not make some of my barley into malt and then try to brew myself some beer. This was really a whimsical thought, and I reproved myself often for the simplicity of it, for I presently saw there would be the lack of several things necessary to the making of my beer that it would be impossible for me to supply; as, first, casks to preserve it in, which was a thing that, as I have observed already, I could never compass; no, though I spent not many days, but weeks, nay, months, in attempting it, but to no purpose. In the next place, I had no hops to make it keep, no yeast to make it work, no copper kettle to make it boil; and yet had not all these things intervened—I mean the frights and terrors I was in about the savages—I had undertaken it and perhaps brought it to pass, too; for I seldom gave anything over without accomplishing it, when I once had determined to begin it. But my invention now ran quite another way: for, night and day, I could think of nothing but how I might destroy some of these monsters in their cruel, bloody entertainment and, if possible, save the victim they should bring here to destroy. It would take up a larger volume than this whole work is intended to be, to set down all the contrivances I hatched, or rather brooded upon, in my thoughts for the destroying of these creatures, or at least frightening them so as to prevent their coming here anymore. But all was abortive; nothing could be possible to take effect, unless I was to be there to do it myself. And what could one man do among them, when perhaps there might be twenty or thirty of them together with their darts, or their bows and arrows, with which they could shoot as true to a mark as I could with my gun?

Sometimes I thought of digging a hole under the place where they made their fire and putting in five or six pounds of gunpowder, which, when they kindled their fire, would consequently take fire and blow up all that was near it. But as, in the first place, I should be unwilling to waste so much powder upon them, my store being now within the quantity of one barrel, so neither could I be sure of its going off at any certain time, when it might surprise them; and, at best, that it would do little more than just blow the fire about their ears and frighten them, but not sufficient to make them forsake the place. So I laid it aside. I then proposed that I would place myself in ambush in some convenient place, with my three guns all double loaded, and in the middle of their bloody ceremony let fly at them, when I should be sure to kill or wound perhaps two or three at every shot; and then falling in upon them with my three pistols and my sword, I made no doubt but that, if there were twenty, I should kill them all. This fancy pleased my thoughts for some weeks, and I was so full of it that I often dreamed of it and, sometimes, that I was just going to let fly at them in my sleep. I went so far with it in my imagination that I employed myself several days to find out proper places to put myself in ambuscade, as I said, to watch for them, and I went frequently to the place itself, which was now grown more familiar to me; but while my mind was thus filled with thoughts of revenge and of a bloody putting of twenty or thirty of them to the sword, as I may call it, the horror I had at the place, and at the signals of the barbarous wretches devouring one another, abetted my malice.

Well, at length I found a place on the side of the hill where I was satisfied I might securely wait till I saw any of their boats coming; and might then, even before they would be ready to come on shore, convey myself unseen into some thickets of trees, in one of which there was a hollow large enough to conceal me entirely, and there I might sit and observe all their bloody doings and take my full aim at their heads, when they were so close together as that it would be next to impossible that I should miss my shot, or that I could fail of wounding three or four of them at the first shot. In this place, then, I resolved to fix my design; and accordingly I prepared two muskets and my ordinary fowling-piece. The two muskets I loaded with a brace of slugs each and four or five smaller bullets, about the size of pistol-bullets. The fowling-piece I loaded with nearly a handful of swan-shot of the largest size; I also loaded my pistols with about four bullets each; and in this posture, well provided with ammunition for a second and third charge, I prepared myself for my expedition.

After I had thus laid the scheme of my design, and in my imagination put it in practice, I continually made my tour every morning to the top of the hill, which was from my castle, as I called it, about three miles, or more, to see if I could observe any boats upon the sea, coming near the island or standing over toward it; but I began to tire of this hard duty, after I had for two or three months constantly kept my watch, but always came back without any discovery; there having not, in all that time, been the least appearance, not only on or near the shore, but on the whole ocean, as far as my eyes or glass could reach every way.

Ought I to Kill the Savages?

As long as I kept my daily tour to the hill to look out, so long also I kept up the vigor of my design, and my spirits seemed to be all the while in a suitable frame for so outrageous an execution as the killing of twenty or thirty naked savages, for an offense that I had not at all entered into a discussion of in my thoughts, any further than my passions were at first fired by the horror I conceived at the unnatural custom of the people of that country; who, it seems, had been suffered by Providence, in His wise disposition of the world, to have no other guide than that of their own abominable and vitiated passions; and, consequently, were left, and perhaps had been so for some ages, to do such horrid things and receive such dreadful customs, as nothing but nature, entirely abandoned by Heaven and actuated by some hellish degeneracy, could have resulted in such acts. But now, when, as I have said, I began to be weary of the fruitless excursion that I had made so long and so far every morning in vain, so my opinion of the action itself began to alter; and I began, with cooler and calmer thoughts, to consider what I was going to engage in; what authority or call I had to pretend to be judge and executioner of these men as criminals, whom Heaven had thought fit, for so many ages, to suffer, unpunished, to go on and to be, as it were, the executioners of His judgments, one upon another. Furthermore, how were these people offenders against me, and what right had I to engage in the quarrel of that blood which they shed promiscuously upon one another? I debated this very often with myself thus: "How do I know what God Himself judges in this particular case? It is certain these people do not commit this as a crime; it is not against their own consciences' reproving, or their light reproaching them; they do not know it to be an offense, and then commit it in defiance of divine justice, as we do in almost all the sins we commit. They think it no more a crime to kill a captive taken in war than we do to kill an ox; or to eat human flesh than we do to eat mutton."

When I considered this a little, it followed necessarily that I was certainly in the wrong in it; that these people were not murderers in the sense that I had before condemned them in my thoughts, any more than those Christians were murderers who often put to death the prisoners taken in battle; or more frequently, upon many occasions, put whole troops of men to the sword, without giving quarter, even when they threw down their arms and begged for mercy. In the next place, it occurred to me that while the usage they gave one another was thus brutish and inhuman, yet it was really nothing to me. These people had done me no injury; that if they attempted to kill me, or if I found it necessary, for my immediate preservation, to fall upon them, something might be said for it; but since I was yet out of their power, and they really had no knowledge of me and consequently no design upon me; therefore, it could not be just for me to fall upon them. In fact, were I to massacre them, this would justify the conduct of the Spaniards in all their barbarities practiced in America, where they destroyed millions of these people; who, while they were idolaters and barbarians and had several bloody and barbarous rites in their customs, such as sacrificing human bodies to their idols, were yet, as to the Spaniards, very innocent people; and that the rooting them out of the country is spoken of with the utmost abhorrence and detestation by even the Spaniards themselves, at this time, and by all other Christian nations in Europe, as a mere butchery, a bloody and unnatural piece of cruelty, unjustifiable either to God or man. As a result, the very name of a Spaniard is reckoned to be frightful and terrible to all people of humanity or of Christian compassion; thus the kingdom of Spain was particularly known for producing a race of men who were without principles of tenderness or pitying the miserable, both of which are desirable traits.

These considerations really put me to a pause and brought me to a kind of a full stop; and I began, little by little, to change my plans and to conclude I had taken wrong measures in my resolution to attack the savages; and that it was not my business to meddle with them, unless they first attacked me; and this it was my business, if possible, to prevent. But that if I were discovered and attacked by them, then I knew my duty. On the other hand, I argued with myself that this really was the way not to deliver myself, but entirely to ruin and destroy myself; for, unless I was sure to kill every one that not only should be on shore at that time, but that should ever come on shore afterward, if but one of them escaped to tell their country people what had happened, they would come over again by thousands to revenge the death of their fellows, and I should only bring upon myself a certain destruction, which, at present, I had no manner of occasion for. On the whole, I concluded that I ought neither in principle nor in policy, one way or other, to concern myself in this affair; that my business was, by all possible means, to conceal myself from them and not to leave the least sign for them to guess that there were any living creatures upon the island—I mean of human shape. Religion joined in with this prudential resolution; and I was convinced now, in many ways, that I was perfectly out of my duty when I was laying all my bloody schemes for the destruction of innocent creatures—I mean innocent as to me. As for the crimes they were guilty of toward one another, I had nothing to do with them;

these would be national punishments, to make a just retribution for national offenses, and to bring public judgment upon those who offend in a public manner, by such ways as best please God. This appeared so clear to me now that nothing was a greater satisfaction to me than that I had not been suffered to do a thing that I now saw so much reason to believe would have been no less a sin than that of willful murder, if I had committed it. I gave most humble thanks, on my knees, to God that He had thus delivered me from bloodguiltiness, beseeching Him to grant me the protection of His providence that I might not fall into the hands of the barbarians, or that I might not lay my hands upon them, unless I had a more clear call from Heaven to do it, in defense of my own life.

I Remove My Boat

In this disposition, I continued for nearly a year after this; and so far was I from desiring an occasion for falling upon these wretches that in all that time I never once went up the hill to see whether there were any of them in sight, or to know whether any of them had been on shore there or not, that I might not be tempted to renew any of my contrivances against them, or be provoked by any advantage that might present itself to fall upon them. Only this I did: I went and removed my boat, which I had on the other side of the island, and carried it down to the east end of the whole island, where I ran it into a little cove, which I found under some high rocks, and where I knew, by reason of the currents, the savages dared not, at least would not, come with their boats upon any account whatever. With my boat I carried away everything that I had left there belonging to her, though not necessary for the bare going there—namely, a mast and sail that I had made for her, and a thing like an anchor, but which indeed could not be called either anchor or grapnel; however, it was the best I could make of its kind: All these I removed, that there might not be the least shadow for discovery, or any appearance of any boat, or of any habitation upon the island.

Besides this, I kept myself, as I said, more retired than ever and seldom went from my cell, except upon my constant employment, that is, to milk my she-goats and manage my little flock in the wood, which, as it was quite on the other part of the island, was out of danger. For certain it is that these savage people who sometimes haunted this island never came with any thoughts of finding anyone here and consequently never wandered off from the coast, and I doubt not but they might have been several times on shore after my apprehensions of them had made me cautious, as well as before.

Indeed, I looked back with some horror upon the thoughts of what my condition would have been, if I had dropped upon them and been discovered before that; when, naked and unarmed except with one gun, and that loaded often only with small shot, I walked everywhere, peeping and peering about the island to see what I could get; what a surprise should I have been in if, when I discovered the print of a man's foot, I had instead of that seen fifteen or twenty savages and found them pursuing me, and by the swiftness of their running, no possibility of my escaping them! The thoughts of this sometimes sank my very soul within me and distressed my mind so much that I could not soon recover from it, to imagine what I should have done and how I should not only have been unable to resist them, but most likely should not have even had presence of mind enough to do what I ought to have done; much less what now, after so much consideration and preparation, I might be able to do. Indeed, after seriously thinking of these things, I would be very melancholy, and sometimes it would last a great while. But I resolved it all, at last, into thankfulness to that Providence which had delivered me from so many unseen dangers and had kept me from those mischiefs that I could have in no way been able to deliver myself from.

This brought back a subject that had often come into my thoughts in former times, when first I began to see the merciful dispositions of Heaven, in the dangers we run through in this life: how wonderfully we are delivered when we know nothing of it; how, when we are in a quandary (as we call it), a doubt or hesitation whether to go this way or that way, a secret hint shall direct us this way, when we intended to go that way. Nay, when sense, our own inclination, and perhaps business profession have called us to go the other way, yet a strange impression upon the mind, from we know not what springs and by we know not what power, shall overrule us to go this way—and it shall afterward appear that had we gone that way which we should have gone, and even to our imagination ought to have gone, we should have been ruined and lost. Upon these and many other reflections, I afterward made it a certain rule with me that whenever I found those secret hints or pressings of mind, to doing or not doing anything that presented, or going this way or that way, I never failed to obey the secret dictate; though I knew no other reason for it than that such a pressure, or such a hint, hung upon my mind. I could give many examples of the success of this conduct in the course of my life, but more especially in the latter part of my inhabiting this unhappy island; besides many occasions that it is very likely I might have taken notice of, if I had seen with the same eyes then that I see with now. But it is never too late to be wise; and I cannot but advise all considering men, whose lives are attended with such extraordinary incidents as mine, or even though not so extraordinary, not to slight such secret intimations of Providence, let them come from what invisible intelligence they will. That I shall not discuss and perhaps cannot account for; but certainly they are a proof of the converse of spirits and a secret communication between those embodied and those unembodied, and such a proof as can never be withstood; of which I shall have occasion to give some very remarkable instances in the remainder of my solitary residence in this dismal place.

I believe the reader of this will not think it strange if I confess that these anxieties, these constant dangers I lived in, and the concern that was now upon me, put an end to all invention and to all the contrivances that I had laid for my future accommodations and conveniences. I had the care of my safety more now upon my hands than that of my food. I cared not to drive a nail, or chop a stick of wood now, for fear the noise I should make should be heard; and much less would I fire a gun for the same reason. And, above all, I was intolerably uneasy at making any fire, lest the smoke, which is visible at a great distance in the day, should betray me. For this reason, I removed that part of my business which required fire, such as burning of pots and pipes, etc., into my new apartment in the woods; where, after I had been some time, I found, to my unspeakable consolation, a natural cave in the earth, which went in a vast way, and where, I dare say, no savage, had he been at the mouth of it, would be so hardy as to venture in; nor, indeed, would any man else, but one who, like me, wanted nothing so much as a safe retreat.

My Adventure in the Cave

The mouth of this hollow was at the bottom of a great rock, where, by mere accident (I would call it that, if I did not see abundant reason to ascribe all such things now to Providence), I was cutting down some thick branches of trees to make charcoal—and before I go on, I must observe the reason for my making this charcoal, which was thus: I was afraid of making a smoke about my habitation, as I said before, and yet I could not live there without baking my bread, cooking my meat, etc.; so I contrived to burn some wood here, as I had seen done in England, under turf, till it became chark, or dry coal; and then putting the fire out, I preserved the coal to carry home and perform the other services for which fire was needed, without danger of smoke. But this is by the by.

While I was cutting down some wood here, I perceived that, behind a very thick branch of low brushwood, or underwood, there was a kind of hollow place. I was curious to look in it; and getting with difficulty into the mouth of it, I found it was pretty large, that is to say, sufficient for me to stand upright in it and perhaps another with me; but I must confess to you that I made more haste out than I did in when, looking farther into the place, which was perfectly dark, I saw two broad shining eyes of some creature—whether devil or man I knew not—that twinkled like two stars; the dim light from the cave's mouth shining directly in and making the reflection. However, after some pause, I recovered myself and began to call myself a thousand fools and to think that he that was afraid to see the devil was not fit to live twenty years on an island all alone; and that I might well think there was nothing in this cave that was more frightful than myself. Upon this, plucking up my courage, I took up a firebrand, and in I rushed again, with the stick flaming in my hand. I had not gone three steps in before I was almost as much frightened as before; for I heard a very loud sigh, like that of a man in some pain, and it was followed by a broken noise, as of words half-expressed, and then a deep sigh again. I stepped back and was indeed struck with such a surprise that it put me into a cold sweat, and if I had had a hat on my head, I will not answer for it that my hair might not have lifted it off. But still plucking up my spirits as well as I could, and encouraging myself a little with considering that the power and presence of God was everywhere and was able to protect me, I stepped forward again, and by the light of the firebrand, holding it up a little over my head, I saw lying on the ground a monstrous, frightful old he-goat, just making his will, as we say, and gasping for life and dying indeed of mere old age. I stirred him a little to see if I could get him out, and he essayed to get up, but was not able to raise himself. I thought to myself he might as well remain there; for if he had frightened me, so he would certainly frighten any of the savages, if any one of them should be so foolhardy as to come in there while he had any life in him.

I had not yet recovered from my surprise, but had begun to look around me, when I found the cave was but very small, that is to say, it might be about twelve feet over, but in no manner of shape, neither round nor square, no hands having ever been employed in making it but those of mere nature. I observed also that there was a place at the farther side of it that went in farther, but was so low that it required me to creep upon my hands and knees to go into it, and where it went I knew not; so, having no candle, I gave it up for that time, but resolved to come again the next day provided with candles and a tinderbox, which I had made of the lock of one of the muskets, with some wildfire in the pan.

Accordingly, the next day I came provided with six large candles of my own making (for I made very good candles now of goats' tallow, but was hard set for candlewick, using sometimes rags or rope-yarn and sometimes the dried rind of a weed like nettles); and going into this low place I was obliged to creep upon all fours, as I have said, almost ten yards—which, by the way, I thought was adventure bold enough, considering that I knew not how far it might go, nor what was beyond it. When I had got through the strait, I found the roof rose higher up—I believe nearly twenty feet; but never was such a glorious sight seen in the island, I dare say, as it was to look around the sides and roof of this vault or cave. The wall reflected a hundred thousand lights to me from my two candles. What it was in the rock, whether diamonds, or any other precious stones, or gold—which I rather supposed it to be—I knew not. The place I was in was a most delightful cavity, or grotto, though perfectly dark; the floor was dry and level, and had a sort of a small loose gravel upon it, so that there was no nauseous or venomous creature to be seen; neither was there any damp or wet on the sides or roof. The only difficulty in it was the entrance—which, however, as it was a place of security and such a retreat as I wanted, I thought was a convenience—so that I really rejoiced at the discovery and resolved, without any delay, to bring some of those things that I was most anxious about to this place. Particularly, I resolved to bring here my magazine of powder and all my spare arms—namely, two fowling-pieces, for I had three in all, and three muskets, for of them I had eight in all; so I kept in my castle only five, which stood ready mounted like pieces of cannon on my outermost defense and were ready also to take out upon any expedition.

Upon this occasion of removing my ammunition, I happened to open the barrel of powder that I took up out of the sea, and which had been wet, and I found that the water had penetrated about three or four inches into the powder on every side, which, caking and growing hard, had preserved the inside like a kernel in a shell, so that I had nearly sixty pounds of very good powder in the center of the cask, and this was a very agreeable discovery to me at that time. I carried all away to that place, never keeping more than two or three pounds of powder with me in my castle, for fear of a surprise of any kind. I also carried there all the lead I had left for bullets.

A State of Siege

I fancied myself now like one of the ancient giants who were said to live in caves and holes in the rocks, where none could come at them; for I persuaded myself, while I was here, that if five hundred savages were to hunt me, they could never find me, or if they did, they would not venture to attack me here. The old goat whom I found expiring died in the mouth of the cave the next day after I made this discovery; and I found it much easier to dig a great hole there, and throw him in and cover him with earth, than to drag him out, so I interred him there, to prevent offense to my nose.

I was now in the twenty-third year of residence in this island and was so naturalized to the place and the manner of living that, could I but have enjoyed the certainty that no savages would come to the place to disturb me, I could have been resigned to spending the rest of my lifetime there, even to the last moment, till I had laid me down and died, like the old goat in the cave.

I had also come to enjoy some little diversions and amusements, which made the time pass more pleasantly with me, a great deal more than it did before. First, I had taught my Poll, as I noted before, to speak; and he did it so familiarly, and talked so articulately and plain, that it was very pleasant to me, and he lived with me no less than six-and-twenty years. How long he might have lived afterward I know not, though I know they have a notion in the Brazils that they live a hundred years. Perhaps some of my Polls may be alive there still, calling after poor Robinson Crusoe to this day. I wish no Englishman the ill luck to come there and hear them, but if he did he would certainly believe it was the devil. My dog was a pleasant and loving companion to me for no less than sixteen years of my time, and then he died of mere old age. As for my cats, they multiplied, as I have observed, to that degree that I was obliged to shoot several of them at first, to keep them from devouring me and all I had; but at length, when the old ones I brought with me were gone, and after some time continually driving them from me and letting them have no provision with me, they all ran wild into the woods, except two or three favorites, which I kept tame, and whose young, when they had any, I always drowned; and these were part of my family. Besides these I always kept two or three household kids about me, whom I taught to feed out of my hand; and I had two more parrots, which talked pretty well, and would all call "Robin Crusoe," but none like my first; nor, indeed, did I take the pains with any of them that I had done with him. I had also several tame seafowls, whose species I knew not, that I caught upon the shore and cut their wings; and the little stakes that I had planted before my castle wall having now grown up to a good thick grove, these fowls all lived among these low trees and bred there, which was very agreeable to me; so that, as I said above, I began to be very well contented with the life I led, if I could have been secured from the dread of the savages. But it was otherwise directed; and it may not be amiss for all people who shall meet with my story to make this just observation from it: that is, how frequently, in the course of our lives, the evil that in itself we seek most to shun and that, when we are fallen into, is the most dreadful to us, is oftentimes the very means or door of our deliverance, by which alone we can be raised again from the affliction we are fallen into. I could give many examples of this in the course of my unaccountable life, but in nothing was it more particularly remarkable than in the circumstances of my last years of solitary residence in this island.

Chapter 14

VISITORS

It was now the month of December, as I said before, in my three-and-twentieth year; and this, being the southern solstice (for winter I cannot call it), was the particular time of my harvest and required me to be pretty much abroad in the fields, when, going out pretty early in the morning, even before it was full daylight, I was surprised with seeing a light of some fire upon the shore at a distance from me of about two miles toward the end of the island where I had observed some savages had been, as before—and not on the other side, but, to my great affliction, it was on my side of the island!

I was indeed terribly surprised at the sight and stopped short within my grove, not daring to go out, lest I might be surprised; and yet I had no more peace within, from the apprehensions I had that if these savages, in rambling over the island, should find my corn standing or cut, or any of my works and improvements, they would immediately conclude that there were people in the place and would then never rest till they had found me out. In this extremity I went back directly to my castle and pulled up the ladder after me, having made all things without look as wild and natural as I could.

Then I prepared myself within, putting myself in a posture of defense; I loaded all my cannon, as I called them—that is to say, my muskets, which were mounted upon my new fortification, and all my pistols, and resolved to defend myself to the last gasp; not forgetting seriously to commend myself to divine protection and earnestly to pray to God to deliver me out of the hands of the barbarians. And in this posture I continued about two hours and began to be impatient for intelligence abroad, for I had no spies to send out. After sitting awhile longer and musing what I should do in this case, I was not able to bear sitting in ignorance any longer; so setting up my ladder to the side of the hill, where there was a flat place, as I observed before, and then pulling the ladder after me, I set it up again and mounted to the top of the hill; and pulling out my perspective glass, which I had taken on purpose, I laid me down flat on my belly on the ground and began to look for the place where I had seen them. I presently found there were no less than nine naked savages sitting around a small fire they had made—not to warm them, for they had no need of that, the weather being extremely hot—but, as I supposed, to dress some of their barbarous diet of human flesh that they had brought with them, whether alive or dead I could not know.

They had two canoes with them, which they had hauled up on the shore; and as it was then ebb of tide, they seemed to me to wait the return of the tide to go away again. It is not easy to imagine what confusion this sight put me into, especially seeing them come on *my* side of the island and so near me, too. But when I considered their coming must be always with the current of the incoming tide, I began afterward to relax my fears, being satisfied that I might always go abroad with safety at flood tide, if they were not on shore before; and having made this observation, I went abroad about my harvest work with more composure.

As I expected, so it proved; for, as soon as the tide made to the westward, I saw them all take boat and row (or paddle, as we call it) away. I also observed that for an hour or more before they went off they were dancing, and I could easily discern their postures and gestures through my glass. I could not but perceive, by my closest observation, that they were stark naked and had not the least covering upon them—but whether they were men or women, I could not distinguish.

As soon as I saw them shipped and gone, I took two guns upon my shoulders, two pistols in my girdle, and my great sword by my side, without a scabbard, and with all the speed I was able to make went away to the hill where I had discovered their first appearance; and as soon as I got there, which was in not less than two hours (for I could not go faster, being so loaded with arms as I was), I perceived there had been three more canoes of savages at that place; and, looking out farther, I saw they were all at sea together, heading out to the mainland. This was a dreadful sight to me, especially when, going down to the shore, I could see the marks of horror that the dismal work they had been about had left behind it: that is, the blood, the bones, and part of the flesh of human bodies eaten and devoured by those wretches with merriment and sport. I was so filled with indignation at the sight that I now began to premeditate the destruction of the next ones that I saw there, let them be whom or how many soever.

It seemed evident to me that the visits which they made to this island were not very frequent, for it was more than fifteen months before any more of them came on shore there again—that is to say, I neither saw them nor any footsteps or signs of them in all that time; for as to the rainy seasons, then they were sure not to come abroad, at least not so far. Yet all this while I lived uncomfortably, by reason of my constant fear that they might come upon me by surprise—from which I observe that the expectation of evil is worse than the evil itself, especially if there is no time in which to shake off that expectation or those apprehensions.

During all this time I was in a murdering mood and spent most of my hours, which should have been better employed, in contriving how to circumvent and fall upon them the very next time I should see them, especially if they should be divided, as they were the last time, into two parties; nor did I consider at all that if I killed one party—suppose ten or a dozen—I was still the next day, or week, or month, to kill another, and so another, even ad infinitum, till I should be, at length, no less a murderer than they were in being man-eaters, and perhaps much more so. I spent my days now in great perplexity and anxiety of mind, expecting that I should one day or another fall into the hands of these merciless creatures; and if I did at any time venture abroad, it was not without looking around me with the greatest care and caution imaginable. And now I found, to my great comfort, how happy it was that I had provided a tame flock or herd of goats; for I durst not upon any account fire my gun, especially near that side of the island where they usually came, lest I should alarm the savages; and if they had fled from me now, I was sure to have them come again with perhaps two or three hundred canoes with them in a few days, and then I knew what to expect. However, I wore out a year and three months more before I ever saw any more of these savages, and then I found them again, as I shall soon observe. It is true they might have been there once or twice, but either they made no stay, or at least

I did not hear them; but in the month of May, as nearly as I could calculate, and in my four-and-twentieth year on the island, I had a very strange encounter with them, of which more later.

Sounds of a Ship in Distress

The perturbation of my mind during this fifteen or sixteen months' interval was very great: I slept unquietly, dreamed always frightful dreams, and often started out of my sleep in the night. In the day, great troubles overwhelmed my mind; and in the night, I dreamed often of killing the savages and of the reasons why I might justify the doing of it. But I must waive all this for a while. It was in the middle of May, on the sixteenth day, I think, as well as my poor wooden calendar would reckon—for I marked all upon the post still—I say, it was on the sixteenth of May that it blew a very great storm of wind all day, with a great deal of lightning and thunder, and a very foul night it was after it. I knew not what was the particular occasion of it; but as I was reading in the Bible, and taken up with very serious thoughts about my present condition, I was surprised with the noise of a gun, as I thought, fired at sea. This was, to be sure, a surprise of a quite different nature from any I had met with before; for the notions this put into my thoughts were quite of another kind. I started up in the greatest haste imaginable; and, in a trice, clapped my ladder to the middle place of the rock and pulled it after me; and, mounting it the second time, I got to the top of the hill the very moment that a flash of fire bade me listen for a second gun, which, accordingly, in about half a minute, I heard. By the sound, I knew that it was from that part of the sea where I was driven out with the current in my boat. I immediately considered that this must be some ship in distress and that they had some comrade, or some other ship in company, and fired these for signals of distress and to obtain help. I had the presence of mind, at that minute, to think that though I could not help them, it might be they might help me; so I brought together all the dry wood I could get at hand, and making a good handsome pile, I set it on fire upon the hill. The wood was dry and blazed freely; and though the wind blew very hard, yet the flames burned fairly high, so that I was certain, if there was any such thing as a ship, they must needs see it—and no doubt they did: for as soon as my fire blazed up, I heard another gun, and after that several others, all from the same quarter. I plied my fire all night long, till daybreak; and when it was broad day, and the air cleared up, I saw something a great distance off at sea, full east of the island, whether a sail or a hull I could not distinguish—no, not with my glass; the distance was so great, and the weather still somewhat hazy also; at least, it was out at sea.

I looked frequently at it all that day and soon perceived that it did not move; so I presently concluded that it was a ship at anchor; and being eager, you may be sure, to be satisfied, I took my gun in hand and ran toward the south side of the island, to the rocks where I had formerly been carried away with the current. And getting up there, the weather by this time being perfectly clear, I could plainly see, to my great sorrow, the wreck of a ship, cast in the night upon those concealed rocks that I found when I was out in my boat. Which rocks, as they checked the violence of the stream and made a kind of counterstream or eddy, were the occasion of my recovering from the most desperate, hopeless condition that I had ever been in, in all my life. Thus, what is one man's safety is another man's destruction; for it seems that these men, whoever they were, being in uncharted waters and the rocks being wholly underwater, had been driven upon them in the night, the wind blowing hard at east and east-northeast. Had they seen the island, as I must necessarily suppose they did not, they must, as I thought, have endeavored to have saved themselves on shore by the help of their boat; but their firing off their guns for help, especially when they saw, as I imagined, my fire, filled me with many thoughts. First, I imagined that upon seeing my light they might have put themselves into their boat and endeavored to make it to the shore; but that the sea running very high, they might have been cast away. Or, I imagined that they might have lost their boat before, as might easily be the case—particularly by the breaking of the sea upon their ship, which many times obliged men to stave, or take in pieces, their boat and sometimes to throw it overboard with their own hands. Or perhaps, they may have had some other ship or ships in company, which, upon the signals of distress they made, had taken them up and carried them off. Or, it was even possible, I imagined, that they were all gone off to sea in their boat and, being hurried away by the current that I had been formerly in, were carried out into the great ocean, where there was nothing but misery and perishing; and that, perhaps, they might by this time think of starving and, later on, be so desperate as to eat one another.

Clearly, all these were but conjectures at best, so, in the condition I was in, I could do no more than look upon the misery of the poor men and pity them—which had still this good effect upon me: that it gave me more and more cause to give thanks to God, who had so happily and comfortably provided for me in my desolate condition; and that of two ships' companies, who were now cast away upon this part of the world, not one life should be spared but mine. I learned here again to observe that it is very rare that the providence of God casts us into any condition of life so low, or any misery so great, but we may see something or other to be thankful for and may see others in worse circumstances than our own. Such certainly was the case of these men, of whom I could not so much as see any reason to suppose any of them were saved; it seemed almost inconceivable that they had not all perished there, except for the possibility of their being taken up by another ship in company—but this was but mere possibility indeed, for I saw not the least signal or appearance of any such thing. I cannot explain, by any possible use of words, what a strange longing I felt in my soul upon this sight, breaking out sometimes thus: "Oh, that there had been but one or two, nay, or but one soul, saved out of this ship, to have escaped to me that I might but have had one companion, one fellow creature, to have spoken to me and to have conversed with!" In all the time of my solitary life, I never felt so earnest, so strong a desire after the society of my fellow creatures, or so deep a regret at the lack of it.

There are some secret moving springs in the affections, which, when they are set going by some object in view—or, though not in view, yet rendered present to the mind by the power of imagination—that motion carries out the soul, by its impetuosity, to such violent, eager embracings of the object that the absence of it is insupportable. Such were these earnest wishings that but one man had been saved. I believe I repeated the words, *Oh, that it had been but one!* a thousand times; and my desires were so moved by it that when I spoke the words my hands would clench together and my fingers would press the palms of my hands, so that if I had any soft thing in my hand, I would have crushed it involuntarily; and my teeth in my head would strike together and set against one another so strong that for some time I could not part them again. Let the naturalists explain these things, and the reason and manner of them. All I can say to them is—to describe my reactions, which were even surprising to me, when I realized them, though I knew not how they came to me—it was, doubtless, the effect of my ardent wishes and of strong desires that formed in my mind, realizing the comfort that the conversation of one of my fellow Christians would have been to me. But it was not to be; either their fate, or mine, or both, forbade it, for till the last year of my being on this island, I never knew whether any were saved out of that ship or not; and had only the affliction, some days after, to see the corpse of a drowned boy come on shore at the end of the island that was

closest to the shipwreck. He had no clothes on but a seaman's waistcoat, a pair of open-kneed linen drawers, and a blue linen shirt; but nothing to direct me so much as to guess what nation he was of. He had nothing in his pockets but two pieces of eight and a tobacco pipe—the last was to me of ten times more value than the first.

I Visit the Spanish Wreck

It was now calm, and I had a great mind to venture out in my boat to this wreck, not doubting but I might find something on board that would be useful to me. But that was really not the reason, so much as the possibility that there might yet be some living creature on board, whose life I might not only save, but might, by saving that life, comfort my own to the last degree; and this thought clung so to my heart that I could not be quiet night or day, but must venture out in my boat to board this wreck. Committing the rest to God's providence, I felt the impression to go was so strong that it could not be resisted, that it must come from some invisible direction, and that I could not live with myself should I fail to go.

Under the power of this impression, I hastened back to my castle, prepared everything for my voyage, took a quantity of bread, a great pot for fresh water, a compass to steer by, a bottle of rum (for I had still a great deal of that left), and a basket of raisins; and thus loading myself with everything necessary, I went down to my boat, got the water out of her, got her afloat, loaded all my cargo in her, and then went home again for more. My second cargo was a great bag full of rice; the umbrella to set up over my head for a shade; another large pot full of fresh water; and about two dozen small loaves, or barley cakes, more than before; with a bottle of goat's milk and a cheese: all which with great labor and sweat I brought to my boat. Then, praying to God to direct my voyage, I put out and, rowing or paddling the canoe along the shore, came at last to the farthest point of the island on the northeast side.

And now I was to launch out into the ocean, and either to venture or not to venture. I looked on the rapid currents that ran constantly on both sides of the island at a distance, and which were very terrible to me, from the remembrance of the hazard I had been in before, and my heart began to fail me; for I foresaw that if I was driven into either of those currents, I should be carried a great way out to sea and perhaps out of reach or sight of the island again; and that then, my boat being small, if any little gale of wind should rise, I should inevitably be lost.

These thoughts so oppressed my mind that I began to give up my enterprise; and having hauled my boat into a little creek on the shore, I stepped out and sat down upon a rising bit of ground, very pensive and anxious, alternating between fear and desire about my voyage. Then, even as I was musing, I could perceive that the tide had turned and the flood tide come, thus making my going impracticable for many hours. Upon this, presently it occurred to me that I should go up to the highest piece of ground I could find and observe, if I could, how the sets of the tide or currents lay, when the flood came in, that I might judge whether, if I was driven one way out, I might not expect to be driven another way home, with the same rapidity of the currents. This thought was no sooner in my head than I cast my eye upon a little hill, which sufficiently overlooked the sea both ways and from which I had a clear view of the currents, or sets of the tide, and which way I was to guide myself in my return. Here I found that as the current of ebb set out close by the south point of the island, so the current of the flood set in close by the shore of the north side; and that I had nothing to do but to keep to the north of the island in my return, and I should do well enough.

Salvage from the Wreck

Encouraged with this observation, I resolved, the next morning, to set out with the first of the tide. Thus, after reposing myself for the night in my canoe, under the great watch coat I mentioned, I launched out. I first made a little out to sea, full north, till I began to feel the benefit of the current, which set eastward, and which carried me at a great rate and yet did not so hurry me as the current on the south side had done before, so as to take from me all control of the boat; but having a strong steerage with my paddle, I went, at a great rate, directly for the wreck, and in less than two hours I came up to it. It was a dismal sight to look at: the ship, which by its building was Spanish, stuck fast, jammed between two rocks. All the stern and quarter of her were beaten to pieces by the sea; and as her forecastle, which stuck in the rocks, had run on with great violence, her mainmast and foremast were brought by the board, that is to say, broken off short; but her bowsprit was sound, and the head and bow appeared firm. When I came close to her, a dog appeared upon her, who, seeing me coming, yelped and cried; and, as soon as I called him, jumped into the sea to come to me. I took him into the boat, but found him almost dead with hunger and thirst. I gave him a cake of my bread, and he devoured it like a ravenous wolf that had been starving a fortnight in the snow; I then gave the poor creature some fresh water, with which, if I would have let him, he would have burst himself.

After this I went on board; but the first sight I met with was two men drowned in the cook room, or forecastle of the ship, with their arms fast about one another. I concluded, as is indeed probable, that when the ship struck, it being in a storm, the sea broke so high, and so continually over her, that the men were not able to bear it and were strangled with the constant rushing in of the water, as much as if they had been underwater. Besides the dog, there was nothing left in the ship that had life; nor any goods that I could see, but what were spoiled by the water. There were some casks of liquor, whether wine or brandy I knew not, which lay lower in the hold, and which, the water being ebbed out, I could see; but they were too big to meddle with. I saw several chests, which I believed belonged to some of the seamen; and I got two of them into the boat, without examining what was in them. Had the stern of the ship been intact and the forepart broken off, I am persuaded I might have found more, for, by what I found in these two chests, I had room to suppose the ship had a great deal of wealth on board; and, if I may guess from the course she steered, she must have been bound from Buenos Aires, or the Rio de la Plata, in the south part of America, beyond the Brazils, to Havanna, in the Gulf of Mexico, and so perhaps to Spain. She had, no doubt, a great treasure in her, but of no use, at that time, to anybody; but what became of the crew I then knew not.

I found, besides these chests, a little cask full of liquor, of about twenty gallons, which I got into my boat with much difficulty. There were several muskets in the cabin, and a great powder horn, with about four pounds of powder in it. As for the muskets, I had no occasion for them, so I left them, but took the powder horn. I took a fire shovel and tongs, which I wanted extremely, as also two little brass kettles, a copper pot to make chocolate in, and a gridiron; and with this cargo and the dog, I came away, the tide beginning to return again; and the same evening, about an hour within night, I reached the island again, weary and fatigued to the last degree.

I reposed that night in the boat; and in the morning I resolved to store what I had retrieved in my new cave and not carry it home to my castle. After refreshing myself, I got all my cargo on shore and began to examine the particulars. The cask of liquor I found to be a kind of rum, but not such as we had at the Brazils and, in a word, not at all good; but when I came to open the chests, I found several things of great use to me—for example, I found in one a fine case of bottles, of an extraordinary kind, and filled with cordial waters, fine and very good. The bottles held about three pints each and were tipped with silver. I found two pots of very good succades, or sweetmeats, so fastened also on the top that the saltwater had not hurt them; and two more of the same, which the water had spoiled. I found some very good shirts, which were very welcome to me; and about a dozen and a half of white linen handkerchiefs and colored neckcloths; the former were also very welcome, being

exceedingly refreshing to wipe my face on a hot day. Besides this, when I came to the till in the chest, I found there three great bags of pieces of eight, which held about eleven hundred pieces in all; and in one of them, wrapped up in a paper, six doubloons of gold and some small bars or wedges of gold; I suppose they might each weigh nearly a pound. In the other chest were some clothes, but of little value; by the circumstances, it must have belonged to the gunner's mate, though there was no powder in it, except two pounds of fine glazed powder, in three small flasks, kept, I suppose, for charging their fowling-pieces on occasion. On the whole, I got very little by this voyage that was of much value to me; for as to the money, I had no use for it; it was to me as the dirt under my feet—and I would have given it all for three or four pairs of English shoes and stockings, which were things I greatly wanted, but had had none on my feet for many years. I had, indeed, got two pair of shoes now, which I took off the feet of the two drowned men whom I saw in the wreck, and I found two pair more in one of the chests, which were very welcome to me; but they were not like our English shoes, either for ease or service, being rather what we call pumps than shoes. I found in this seaman's chest about fifty pieces of eight, in rials, but no gold: I suppose this belonged to a poorer man than the other, which seemed to belong to some officer. Well, be that as it may, I lugged this money home to my cave and laid it up, as I had done that before which I had brought from our own ship; but it was a great pity, as I said, that the other part of this ship had been wrecked, for I am satisfied I might have loaded my canoe several times over with money; which, if I had ever escaped to England, would have lain here safe enough till I might have come again and fetched it.

I Form New Projects

Having now brought all my things on shore and secured them, I went back to my boat and rowed or paddled her along the shore to her old harbor, where I laid her up, and made the best of my way to my old habitation, where I found everything safe and quiet. I began now to repose myself, live after my old fashion, and take care of my family affairs; and for a while I lived easy enough, only that I was more vigilant than I used to be, looked out oftener, and did not go abroad so much; and if, at any time, I did stir with any freedom, it was always to the east part of the island, where I was pretty well satisfied the savages never came, and where I could go without so many precautions, and such a load of arms and ammunition as I always carried with me if I went the other way.

I lived in this condition nearly two years more; but my unlucky head, which was always to let me know it was born to make my body miserable, was all these two years filled with projects and designs: how, if it were possible, I might get away from this island. Sometimes I was for making another voyage to the wreck, though my reason told me that there was nothing left there worth the hazard of my voyage; sometimes for a ramble one way, sometimes another. And I believe verily, if I had had the boat that I went from Sallee in, I should have ventured to sea, bound anywhere, I knew not where. I have been, in all my circumstances, a *memento* to those who are touched with the general plague of mankind, from which, for aught I know, one-half of their miseries flow; I mean that of not being satisfied with the station wherein God and nature hath placed them. For, not to look back upon my primitive condition and the excellent advice of my father, the opposition to which was, as I may call it, my *original sin*, my subsequent mistakes of the same kind had been the means of my coming into this miserable condition; for had that Providence, which so happily seated me at the Brazils as a planter, blessed me with more modest desires, I could have been contented to have gone on gradually, and I might have been by this time—I mean in the time of my being on this island—one of the most considerable planters in the Brazils. Nay, I am persuaded that by the improvements I had made in that little time I lived there, and the increase I should probably have made if I had remained, I might have been worth a hundred thousand moidores.[1] And what business had I to leave a settled fortune, a well-stocked plantation, improving and increasing, to accompany a supercargo to Guinea in order to fetch negroes, when patience and time would have so increased our stock at home that we could have bought them at our own door from those whose business it was to fetch them? And though it had cost us something more, yet the difference of that price was by no means worth saving at so great a hazard. But as this is ordinarily the fate of young heads, so reflection upon the folly of it is commonly the exercise of more years, or of the dear-bought experience of time. So it was with me now; and yet so deep had the mistake taken root in my mind that I could not be satisfied with what I had, but was continually poring upon the means and possibility of my escape from this place—and that I may, with the greater pleasure to the reader, bring on the remaining part of my story, it may not be improper to give some account of my first conceptions of this foolish scheme for my escape and how, and upon what foundation, I acted.

I am now to be supposed retired into my castle, after my late voyage to the wreck, my frigate laid up and secured underwater, as usual, and my condition

1. *Moidores,* gold coins of Portugal in circulation during the seventeenth and eighteenth centuries.

restored to what it was before: I had more wealth, indeed, than I had before, but was not at all the richer; for I had no more use for it than the Indians of Peru had before the Spaniards came there.

It was one of the nights in the rainy season in March, the four-and-twentieth year of my first setting foot in this island of solitude. I was lying in my bed or hammock, awake, very well in health, had no pain, no fever, no uneasiness of body, nor any uneasiness of mind more than ordinary, but could by no means close my eyes: that is, to sleep; no, not a wink all night long. It is impossible and needless to set down the innumerable crowd of thoughts that whirled through that great thoroughfare of the brain—the memory—in this night's time: I ran over the whole history of my life in miniature, or by abridgment, as I may call it, to my coming to this island, and also of that part of my life since I came to this island. In my reflections upon the state of my case since I came on shore on this island, I was comparing the happy posture of my affairs in the first years of my habitation here, with the life of anxiety, fear, and care, which I had lived in ever since I had seen the print of a foot in the sand; not that I did not believe the savages had frequented the island all the while, and that there might have been several hundreds of them at times on shore there; but since I had never known it, and was incapable of any apprehensions about it, my happiness had been unalloyed, though my danger was the same, and I was as happy in not knowing my danger as if I had never really been exposed to it. This furnished my thoughts with many very profitable reflections, and particularly this one: How infinitely good Providence is, which has provided, in its government of mankind, such narrow bounds to his sight and knowledge of things; and though he walks in the midst of so many thousand dangers, the sight of which, if discovered to him, would distract his mind and sink his spirits, he is kept serene and calm by having the events of things hidden from his eyes and knowing nothing of the dangers that surround him.

Terror of the Savages

After these thoughts had for some time entertained me, I came to reflect seriously upon the real danger I had been in for so many years on this very island, and how I had walked about in the greatest security and with all possible tranquility, even when perhaps nothing but the brow of a hill, a great tree, or the casual approach of night, had been between me and the worst kind of destruction, namely, that of falling into the hands of cannibals and savages, who would have seized me with the same view as I would have of a goat or a turtle and have thought it no more crime to kill and devour me than I did of a pigeon or a curlew. I would unjustly slander myself, if I should say I was not sincerely thankful to my great Preserver, to whose singular protection I acknowledged, with great humility, all these unknown deliverances were due, and without which I must inevitably have fallen into their merciless hands.

When these thoughts were over, my head was for some time taken up in considering the nature of these wretched creatures—I mean the savages—and how it came to pass in the world that the wise Governor of all things should give up any of His creatures to such inhumanity, nay, to something so much below even brutality itself, as to devour its own kind. But as this ended in some (at that time) fruitless speculations, it occurred to me to inquire what part of the world these wretches lived in? How far off the coast did they come from? What was the reason they ventured over so far from home? What kind of boats did they have? And why might I not order myself and my business so that I might be as able to go over there as they were to come to me?

I never so much as troubled myself to consider what I should do with myself when I went there, what would become of me if I fell into the hands of the savages, or how I should escape them if they attacked me; no, nor so much as how it was possible for me to reach the coast and not be attacked by some or other of them, without any possibility of delivering myself; and if I should not fall into their hands, what I should do for provision, or which way I should bend my course—none of these thoughts, I must say, came my way; but my mind was wholly bent upon the notion of my passing over in my boat to the mainland. I looked upon my present condition as the most miserable that could possibly be; that I was not able to throw myself into anything, but death, that could be called worse; and if I reached the shore of the mainland, I might perhaps meet with relief; or I might coast along, as I did on the African shore, till I came to some inhabited country, where I might find some relief. And, after all, perhaps I might fall in with some Christian ship that might take me in; and if the worse came to the worst, I could but die, which would put an end to all these miseries at once. Pray note, all this was the fruit of a disturbed mind, an impatient temper, made, as it were, desperate by the long continuance of my troubles and the disappointments I had met with in the wreck I had been on board of, and where I had been so near the obtaining what I so earnestly longed for: namely, somebody to speak to, and to learn some knowledge of the place where I was, and of the probable means of my deliverance. I say I was agitated wholly by these thoughts; all my calm of mind, in my resignation to Providence and waiting the issue of the dispositions of Heaven, seemed to be suspended; and I had, as it were, no power to turn my thoughts to anything but the project of a voyage to the mainland, which came upon me with such force and such an impetuosity of desire that it was not to be resisted.

When this had agitated my thoughts for two hours or more, with such violence that it set my very blood into a ferment, and my pulse beat as if I had been in a fever merely with the extraordinary fervor of my turbulent mind, nature, as if I had been fatigued and exhausted with the very thoughts of it, threw me into a sound sleep. One would have thought I should have dreamed of it, but I did not, nor of anything relating to it. But I dreamed that as I was going out in the morning as usual, from my castle, I saw upon the shore two canoes and eleven savages, coming to land, and that they brought with them another savage, whom they were going to kill, in order to eat him; when, suddenly, the savage that they were going to kill jumped away and ran for his life. Then I thought, in my sleep, that he came running into my little thick grove before my fortification, to hide himself; and that I, seeing him alone, and not perceiving that the others sought him that way, revealed myself to him, and smiling upon him, encouraged him, that he knelt down to me, praying that I would assist him, upon which I showed him my ladder, made him go up it, and carried him into my cave, and he became my servant; and that as soon as I had got this man, I said to myself, "Now I may certainly venture to the mainland, for this fellow will serve me as a pilot and will tell me what to do and where to go for provisions, and where not to go for fear of being devoured; what places to venture into, and what to escape." I waked with this thought and was under such inexpressible impressions of joy at the prospect of my escape in my dream that the disappointments which I felt upon coming to myself, and finding that it was no more than a dream, were equally inexpressible the other way and threw me into a deep dejection.

Upon this, however, I arrived at this conclusion: that my only way to successfully escape was, if possible, to get a savage into my possession; and, if possible, it should be one of their prisoners, whom they had condemned to be eaten and should bring here to kill. But these thoughts still were attended with this difficulty: that it was impossible to effect this without attacking a whole caravan of them and killing them all; and this was not only a very desperate attempt and might miscarry, but, on the other hand, I greatly questioned the lawfulness of it; and my heart trembled at the thought of shedding so much blood, though it be for my deliverance. I need not repeat the arguments that occurred to me against this, they being the same as mentioned before; but though I had other reasons to offer now—namely, that those men were enemies to my life and would devour me if they could; that it was self-preservation, in the highest degree, to deliver myself from this death of a life, and was acting in my own defense as much as if they were actually assaulting me, and the like—I say, though these things argued for it, yet the thought of shedding human blood for my deliverance was very terrible to me and such as I could by no means reconcile myself to for a great while. However, at last, after many secret disputes with myself, and after great perplexities about it (for all these arguments, one way and another, struggled in my head a long time), the eager determination to be delivered at length mastered all the rest; and I resolved, if possible, to get one of these savages into my hands, cost what it would. My next goal was to contrive how to do it, and this indeed was very difficult to resolve; but as I could pitch upon no probable means to accomplish it, I resolved to put myself upon the watch, to see them when they came on shore, and leave the rest to chance, taking such measures as the opportunity should present, be what it would be.

Chapter 15

FRIDAY

With these resolutions in mind, I set myself to scouting as often as possible, and indeed so often that I was heartily tired of it: for it was above a year and a half that I waited; and for the great part of that time went out to the west end and to the southwest corner of the island almost every day, to look for canoes, but none appeared. This was very discouraging and began to trouble me much, though I cannot say that it did in this case (as it had done some time before) wear off the edge of my desire to do the thing. But the longer it seemed to be delayed, the more eager I was for it. In a word, I was not at first so careful to shun the sight of these savages, and avoid being seen by them, as I was now eager to be upon them. Besides, I fancied myself able to manage one, nay, two or three savages, if I had them, so as to make them entirely slaves to me, to do whatever I should direct them, and to prevent their being able at any time to do me any harm. It was a great while that I pleased myself with this affair, but nothing happened; all my fancies and schemes came to nothing, for no savages came near me for a great while.

About a year and a half after I entertained these notions (and by long musing had, as it were, resolved them all into nothing, for want of an occasion to put them in execution), I was surprised early one morning by seeing no less than five canoes all on shore together on my side of the island, and the people who belonged to them all landed and out of my sight. The number of them broke my resolve, for seeing so many, and knowing that they always came four or six, or sometimes more, in a boat, I did not know what to think of it, or how to take measures for attacking twenty or thirty men single-handedly; so I lay still in my castle, perplexed and disturbed. However, I made all the same plans for an attack that I had formerly come up with and was ready for action, if opportunity presented itself.

Having waited a good while, listening to hear if they made any noise, at

length, being very impatient, I set my guns at the foot of my ladder and clambered up to the top of the hill, by my two stages, as usual; standing, however, so that my head did not appear above the hill, so that they could not perceive me by any means. Here I observed, by the help of my perspective glass, that they were no less than thirty in number; that they had a fire kindled, and that they had meat dressed. How they had cooked it, I knew not, nor what it was; but they were all dancing, in I know not how many barbarous gestures and figures, their own way, around the fire.

While I was thus looking on them, I perceived, by my perspective, two miserable wretches dragged from the boats, where, it seems, they were laid by and were now brought out for the slaughter. I perceived one of them immediately fall; being knocked down, I suppose, with a club, or wooden sword, for that was their way; and two or three others were at work immediately, . . . while the other victim was left standing by himself, till they should be ready for him. In that very moment, this poor wretch, seeing himself a little at liberty and unbound, nature inspired him with hopes of life, and he started away from them and ran with incredible swiftness along the sands, directly toward me; I mean, toward that part of the coast where my habitation was. I was dreadfully frightened, that I must acknowledge, when I perceived him run my way; and especially when, as I thought, I saw him pursued by the whole body; and now I expected that part of my dream was coming to pass and that he would certainly take shelter in my grove. But I could not depend, by any means, upon my dream that the other savages would not pursue him there and find him there. However, I kept my station, and my spirits began to recover when I found that there were not above three men that followed him; and still more was I encouraged when I found that he outstripped them exceedingly in running and gained ground on them; so that, if he could but hold it for half an hour, I saw that he would easily get away from them all.

Encounter with the Savages

There was between them and my castle, the creek, which I mentioned often in the first part of my story, where I landed my cargoes out of the ship; and this I saw plainly he must necessarily swim over, or the poor wretch would be taken there; but when the savage escaping came there, he made nothing of it, though the tide was then up: but, plunging in, swam through in about thirty strokes, or thereabouts, landed, and ran on with exceeding strength and swiftness. When the three pursuers came to the creek, I found that two of them could swim, but the third could not; and that, standing on the other side, he looked at the others, but went no farther, and soon after went softly back again—which, as it happened, was very well for him in the end. I observed that the two who swam were yet more than twice as long swimming over the creek than the fellow who fled from them.

I was deeply impressed, and indeed irresistibly, that now was the time to get me a servant and perhaps a companion or assistant; and that I was plainly called by Providence to save this poor creature's life. I immediately ran down the ladder with all possible speed, fetched my two guns—for they were both at the foot of the ladder, as I observed before—and getting up again with the same haste to the top of the hill, I crossed toward the sea; and having a favorite shortcut, ran down the hill, placing myself in the way between the pursuers and the pursued, halloing aloud to him that fled, who, looking back, was at first perhaps as much frightened at me as at them; but I beckoned with my hand to him to come back; and, in the meantime, I slowly advanced toward the two that followed; then rushing at once upon the foremost, I knocked

I was then obliged to shoot.

him down with the stock of my weapon. I was loath to fire, because I would not have the rest hear; though, at that distance, it would not have been easily heard, and being out of sight of the smoke, too, they would not have known what to make of it. Having knocked this fellow down, the other who pursued him stopped, as if he had been frightened, and I advanced toward him; but as I came nearer, I perceived presently he had a bow and arrow and was fitting it to shoot at me; so I was then obliged to shoot at him first, which I did, and killed him at the first shot.

The poor savage who fled had stopped, though he saw both his enemies fallen and killed, as he thought, yet was so frightened with the fire and noise of my gun that he stood stock-still, and neither came forward nor went backward, though he seemed rather more inclined still to fly than to come to me. I halloed again to him and made signs to come forward, which he easily understood. He came a little way and then stopped again, and then a little farther, and stopped again; and I could then perceive that he stood trembling, as if he had been taken prisoner, and just so he would be killed, as his two enemies were. I beckoned to him again to come to me and gave him all the signs of encouragement that I could think of; and he came nearer and nearer, kneeling down every ten or twelve steps, in token of acknowledgment for saving his life. I smiled at him, and looked pleasantly, and beckoned to him to come still nearer. At length, he came close to me; and then he knelt down again, kissed the ground, and laid his head upon the ground, and, taking me by the foot, set my foot upon his head; this, it seems, was in token of swearing to be my slave forever. I took him up, and made much of him, and encouraged him all I could.

But there was more work to do yet, for I perceived the savage whom I had knocked down was not killed, but merely stunned with the blow, and began to come to himself. So I pointed to him and showed him that the savage was not dead; upon this he spoke some words to me, and though I could not understand them, yet I thought they were most pleasant to hear: *For they were the first sound of a man's voice that I had heard, my own excepted, for about five-and-twenty years.* But there was no time for such reflections now. The savage who was knocked down recovered himself so far as to sit up on the ground, and I perceived that my savage began to be afraid; when I saw that, I aimed my other weapon at the man, as if I would shoot him. Upon this my savage, for so I called him now, made a motion to me to lend him my sword, which hung naked in a belt by my side, which I did. He no sooner had it but he ran to his enemy and at one blow cut off his head so cleverly, no executioner in Germany could have done it sooner or better, which I thought very strange for one who, I had reason to believe, had never seen a sword in his life before, except their own wooden swords. However, it seems, as I learned afterward, they make their wooden swords so sharp, so heavy, and the wood is so hard, that they will even cut off heads with them—aye, and arms, and that at one blow, too. When he had done this, he came laughing to me in sign of triumph and brought me the sword again, and with an abundance of gestures that I did not understand, laid it down, with the head of the savage that he had killed, just before me. But that which astonished him most was to know how I killed the other Indian so far off; so pointing to him, he made signs to me to let him go to him; and I bade him go, as best I could. When he came to him, he stood like one amazed, looking at him, turning him first on one side, then on the other; looked at the wound the bullet had made, which it seems was just in his breast, where it had made a hole, and no great quantity of blood had followed; but he had bled inwardly, for he was quite dead. He took up his bow and arrows and came back; so I turned to go away and beckoned him to follow me, making signs to him that more might come after them.

Upon this, he made signs to me that he should bury them with sand that they might not be seen by the rest, if they followed; and so I made signs to him again to do so. He fell to work; and in an instant he had scraped a hole in the sand with his hands, big enough to bury the first in, and then dragged him into it and covered him; and did so by the other also; I believe he had buried them both in a quarter of an hour. Then calling him away, I led him, not to my castle, but quite away to my cave, on the farther part of the island; so I did not let my dream come to pass in that part, that he came into my grove for shelter.

Here I gave him bread and a bunch of raisins to eat, and a draft of water, which I found he was indeed in great distress for because of his running; and having refreshed him, I made signs for him to go and lie down to sleep, showing him a place where I had laid some rice-straw and a blanket upon it, which I used to sleep upon myself sometimes; so the poor creature lay down and went to sleep.

He was a comely, handsome fellow, perfectly well made, with straight, strong limbs, not too large, tall and well shaped; and, as I reckon, about six-and-twenty years of age. He had a very good countenance, not a fierce and surly aspect, but seemed to have something very manly in his face; and yet he had all the sweetness and softness of a European in his countenance, too, especially when he smiled. His hair was long and black, not curled like wool; his forehead very high and large; and a great vivacity and sparkling sharpness in his eyes. The color of his skin was not quite black, but very tawny; and yet not an ugly, yellow, nauseous tawny, as the Brazilians and Virginians, and other natives of America are, but of a bright kind of a dun olive color that had in it something very agreeable, though not very easy to describe. His face was round and plump; his nose small, not flat like the negroes'; a very good mouth, thin lips, and his fine teeth well set and as white as ivory.

My Man Friday

After he had slumbered, rather than slept, about half an hour, he awoke again and came out of the cave to me; for I had been milking my goats, which I had in the enclosure just by; when he espied me, he came running to me, laying himself down again upon the ground, with all the possible signs of a humble, thankful disposition, making a great many antic gestures to show it. At last he laid his head flat upon the ground, close to my foot, and set my other foot upon his head, as he had done before; and after this, made all the signs to me of subjection, servitude, and submission imaginable, to let me know how he would serve so long as he lived. I understood him in many things and let him know I was very well pleased with him.

In a little while, I began to speak to him and teach him to speak to me; and, first of all, I let him know his name should be *Friday*, which was the day on which I saved his life. I called him so for the memory of it. I likewise taught him to say "Yes" and "No," and to know the meaning of them. I gave him some milk in an earthen pot, and I let him see me drink it before him and sop my bread in it; then I gave him a cake of bread to do the like, which he quickly complied with, and made signs that it tasted very good to him.

I stayed there with him all that night, but, as soon as it was day, I beckoned him to come with me and let him know I would give him some clothes; at which he seemed very glad, for he was stark naked.

As we went by the place where he had buried the two men, he pointed exactly to the place and showed me the marks that he had made to find them again, making signs to me that we should dig them up again and eat them. At this I appeared very angry, expressed my abhorrence of it, acted as if I would vomit at the thought of it, and beckoned him with my hand to come away, which he did immediately with great submission. I then led him up to the top of the hill, to see if his enemies were gone, and, pulling out my glass, I looked and saw plainly the place where they had been, but no appearance of them or their canoes; so it was plain that they were gone and had left their two comrades behind them, without any search after them.

But I was not content with this discovery, but having now more courage, and consequently more curiosity, I took my man Friday with me, giving him the sword in his hand, with the bow and arrows at his back, which I found he could use very dexterously, making him carry one gun for me, and I two for myself; and away we marched to the place where these creatures had been—for I had a mind now to gain some fuller intelligence of them. When I came to the place, my very blood ran cold in my veins and my heart sank within me at the horror of the spectacle: Indeed, it was a dreadful sight—at least, it was so to me, though Friday made nothing of it. The place was covered with human bones, the ground dyed with the blood, and great pieces of flesh left here and there, half-eaten, mangled, and scorched; and, in short, all the tokens of the triumphant feast they had been making there, after a victory over their enemies. I saw three skulls, five hands, and the bones of three or four legs and feet, and an abundance of other parts of the bodies; and Friday, by his signs, made me understand that they brought over four prisoners to feast upon; that three of them were eaten up, and that he, pointing to himself, was the fourth; that there had been a great battle between them and their next king, of whose subjects, it seems, he had been one, and that they had taken a great number of prisoners; all which were carried to several places by those who had taken them in the fight, in order to feast upon them, as was done here by these wretches upon those they brought here.

I caused Friday to gather all the skulls, bones, flesh, and whatever remained, and lay them together on a heap, making a great fire of it and burning them all to ashes. I found Friday still had a hankering for some of the flesh, a cannibal still by nature, but I expressed so much abhorrence at the very thought of it, and at the least appearance of it, that he dared not eat them—for I had, by some means, let him know that I would kill him if he tried it.

I Clothe Friday

When he had done this, we came back to our castle, and there I fell to work for my man Friday. First of all I gave him a pair of linen drawers, which I got out of the poor gunner's chest I mentioned, which I found in the wreck, and which, with a little alteration, fitted him very well. And then I made him a jerkin of goatskin, as well as my skill would allow (for I had now become a tolerably good tailor); and I gave him a cap that I made of hare's skin, very convenient and fashionable enough; and thus he was clothed, for the present, fairly well and was mighty well pleased to see himself almost as well clothed as his master. It is true, he went awkwardly in these clothes at first; wearing the drawers was very awkward to him, and the sleeves of the waistcoat galled his shoulders and the inside of his arms—but a little easing them where he complained they hurt him and getting used to them, at length he took to them very well.

The next day, after I came home to my hutch with him, I began to consider where I should lodge him; and, that I might do well for him, and yet be perfectly safe myself, I made a little tent for him in the vacant place between my two fortifications, in the inside of the last, and in the outside of the first. As there was a door or entrance there into my cave, I made a formal framed doorcase, and a door to it of boards, and set it up in the passage, a little within the entrance; and, causing the door to open from the inside, I barred it up in the night, taking in my ladders, too, so that Friday could no way come at me in the inside of my innermost wall, without making so much noise in getting over that it must needs awaken me. For my first wall had now a complete roof over it of long poles, covering all my tent, and leaning up to the side of the hill, which was again laid across with smaller sticks, instead of laths, and then thatched over a great thickness with rice-straw, which was strong, like reeds. And at the hole or place that was left to go in or out by the ladder, I had placed a kind of trapdoor, which, if someone had attempted to open it on the outside, it would not have opened at all, but would have fallen down and made a great noise. As to weapons, I took them all into my side every night. But I needed none of all this precaution, for never man had a more faithful, loving, sincere servant than Friday was to me: without passions, sullenness, or designs, perfectly obliged and engaged; his very affections were tied to me, like those of a child to a father; and I dare say he would have sacrificed his life for the saving of mine, upon any occasion whatsoever—the many testimonies he gave me of this put it beyond all doubt and soon convinced me that I needed no precautions for my safety on his account.

This frequently gave me occasion to observe, and that with wonder, that however it had pleased God in His providence, and in the government of the works of His hands, to take from so great a part of the world of His creatures the best uses to which their faculties and the powers of their souls are adapted, yet that He has bestowed upon them the same powers; the same reason; the same affections; the same sentiments of kindness and obligation;

the same passions and resentments of wrongs; the same sense of gratitude, sincerity, fidelity, and all the capacities of doing good and receiving good, that He has given to us; and that when He pleases to offer them occasions of exerting these, they are as ready, nay, more ready, to apply them to the right uses for which they were bestowed than we are. This made me very melancholy sometimes, in reflecting, as the several occasions presented, how mean a use we make of all these, even though we have these powers enlightened by the great lamp of instruction, the Spirit of God, and by the knowledge of His Word added to our understanding; and why it has pleased God to hide such saving knowledge from so many millions of souls who, if I might judge by this poor savage, would make a much better use of it than we did. From hence, I sometimes was led too far, to invade the sovereignty of Providence, and, as it were, arranging the justice of so arbitrary a disposition of things, that should hide that sight from some, and reveal it to others, and yet expect a like duty from both. However, I shut it up, and checked my thoughts with this conclusion: first, that we did not know by what light and law these should be condemned; but that as God was necessarily, and, by the nature of His being, infinitely holy and just, so it could not be but if these creatures were all sentenced to absence from Himself, it was on account of sinning against that light, which, as the Scripture says, was a law to themselves, and by such rules as their consciences would acknowledge to be just, though the foundation was not discovered to us; and, secondly, that still, as we are all clay in the hand of the Potter, no vessel could say to Him, "Why hast Thou formed me thus?"

Friday Taught and Trained

But to return to my companion: I was greatly delighted with him and made it my business to teach him everything that was proper to make him useful, handy, and helpful; but especially to make him speak and understand me when I spoke; and he was the aptest scholar that ever was; and particularly was so merry, so constantly diligent, and so pleased when he could but understand me, or make me understand him, that it was very pleasant to me to talk to him. And now my life began to be so easy that I began to say to myself that could I but have been safe from more savages, I cared not if I was never to remove from the place while I lived.

After I had been two or three days returned to my castle, I thought that, in order to bring Friday away from his horrid way of feeding and from the relish of a cannibal's stomach, I ought to let him taste other flesh; so I took him out with me one morning to the woods. I went, indeed, intending to kill a kid out of my own flock and bring it home and dress it; but as I was going, I saw a she-goat lying down in the shade and two young kids sitting by her. I caught hold of Friday.

"Hold," said I, making signs to him not to stir. "Stand still."

Immediately, I presented my piece and shot and killed one of the kids. The poor creature, who had, at a distance, indeed, seen me kill the savage, his enemy, but did not know nor could imagine how it was done, was sensibly surprised, trembled, shook, and looked so amazed that I thought he would have sunk down. He did not see the kid I shot at, or perceive I had killed it, but ripped up his waistcoat, to feel whether he was not wounded; and, as I found presently, thought I was resolved to kill him: for he came and knelt down to me and, embracing my knees, said a great many things I did not understand; but I could easily see the meaning was to pray me not to kill him.

I soon found a way to convince him that I would do him no harm; and taking him up by the hand, laughed at him, and pointing to the kid that I had killed, beckoned to him to run and fetch it, which he did; and while he was wondering and looking to see how the creature was killed, I loaded my

gun again. By and by I saw a great fowl, like a hawk, sitting upon a tree within shot; so, to let Friday understand a little what I would do, I called him to me again, pointed at the fowl, which was indeed a parrot, though I thought it had been a hawk; I say, pointing to the parrot, and to my gun, and to the ground under the parrot, and let him see I would make it fall, I made him understand that I would shoot and kill that bird. Accordingly, I fired and bade him look, and immediately he saw the parrot fall. He stood like one frightened again, notwithstanding all I had said to him; and I found he was the more amazed because he did not see me put anything into the gun, but thought that there must be some wonderful fund of death and destruction in that thing, able to kill man, beast, bird, or anything near or far off; and the astonishment this created in him was such as could not wear off for a long time; and, I believe, if I would have let him, he would have worshiped me and my gun. As for the gun itself, he would not so much as touch it for several days after; but he would speak to it and talk to it, as if it had answered him, when he was by himself; which, as I afterward learned of him, was to desire it not to kill him. Well, after his astonishment was a little over at this, I pointed to him to run and fetch the bird I had shot, which he did, but stayed some time; for the parrot, not being quite dead, had fluttered away a good distance from the place where she fell. However, he found her, took her up, and brought her to me; and as I had perceived his ignorance about the gun before, I took this advantage to charge the gun again and not to let him see me do it, that I might be ready for any other mark that might present; but nothing more offered at that time. I brought home the kid, and the same evening I took the skin off and cut it out as well as I could; and having a pot fit for that purpose, I boiled or stewed some of the flesh and made some very good broth. After I had begun to eat some, I gave some to my man, who seemed very glad of it and liked it very well; but that which was strangest to him was to see me eat salt[1] with it. He made a sign to me that the salt was not good to eat; and, putting a little into his own mouth, he seemed to nauseate at it and would spit and sputter at it, washing his mouth with fresh water after it. On the other hand, I took some meat into my mouth without salt, and I pretended to spit and sputter for want of salt, as fast as he had done at the salt, but it would not do—he never would care for salt with his meat, or in his broth; at least, not for a great while, and then but a very little.

Having thus fed him with boiled meat and broth, I was resolved to feast him the next day with roasting a piece of the kid. This I did by hanging it before the fire on a string, as I had seen many people do in England, setting

1. Evidently, he must have secured salt in one of the wrecks.

two poles up, one on each side of the fire, and one across the top, and tying the string to the cross-stick, letting the meat turn continually. This Friday admired very much; but when he came to taste the flesh, he took so many ways to tell me how well he liked it that I could not but understand him; and at last he told me, as well as he could, he would never eat man's flesh anymore, which I was very glad to hear.

The next day I set him to work at beating some corn out and sifting it in the manner I used to do, as I observed before; and he soon understood how to do it as well as I, especially after he had seen what the meaning of it was, and that it was to make bread of; for after that I let him see me make my bread and bake it, too; and in a little time Friday was able to do all the work for me, as well as I could do it myself.

I began now to consider that, having two mouths to feed instead of one, I must provide more ground for my harvest and plant a larger quantity of corn than I used to do; so I marked out a larger piece of land and began the fence in the same manner as before, in which Friday worked not only very willingly and very hard, but did it very cheerfully. I told him what it was for; that it was for corn to make more bread, because he was now with me, that I might have enough for him and myself, too. He appeared very aware of that aspect, and let me know that he thought I had much more labor upon me on his account than I had for myself; and that he would work the harder for me, if I would tell him what to do.

This was the pleasantest year of all the life I led in this place. Friday began to talk pretty well, and understand the names of almost everything I had occasion to call for, and of every place I had to send him to, and talk a great deal to me; so that, in short, I began now to have some use for my tongue again, which, indeed, I had very little occasion for before; that is to say, about speech. Besides the pleasure of talking to him, I had a singular satisfaction in the fellow himself: his simple, unfeigned honesty appeared to me more and more every day, and I began really to love the creature; and on his side I believe he loved me more than it was possible for him ever to love anything before.

I had a mind once to see if he had any hankering inclination to return to his own country again; and having taught him English so well that he could answer me almost any question, I asked him whether the nation that he belonged to ever conquered in battle. At which he smiled and said, "Yes, yes, we always fight the better"; that is, he meant, always get the better in a fight; and so we began the following discourse.

Conversation with Friday

Master: You always fight the better—how came you to be taken prisoner then, Friday?

Friday: My nation beat much, for all that.

Master: How beat? If your nation beat them, how came you to be taken?

Friday: They more many than my nation, in the place where me was; they take one, two, three, and me. My nation overbeat them in the yonder place, where me no was; here my nation take one, two, great thousand.

Master: But why did not your side recover you from the hands of your enemies, then?

Friday: They run, one, two, three, and me, and make me go in the canoe; my nation have no canoe that time.

Master: Well, Friday, and what does your nation do with the men they take? Do they carry them away and eat them, as these did?

Friday: Yes, my nation eat mans too: eat all up.

Master: Where do they carry them?

Friday: Go to other place, where they think.

Master: Do they come here?

Friday: Yes, yes, they come here; come other else place.

Master: Have you been here with them?

Friday: Yes, I been here (points to the northwest side of the island, which, it seems, was their side).

By this I understood that my man Friday had formerly been among the savages who used to come on shore on the farther part of the island, on the said man-eating occasions that he was not brought for: and, some time after, when I took the courage to lead him to that side, being the same I formerly mentioned, he immediately knew the place and told me he had been there once, when they ate up twenty men, two women, and one child. He could not say "twenty" in English, but he numbered them by laying so many stones in a row and pointing to me to count them.

I have shared this, because it introduces what follows: that after this discourse I had with him, I asked him how far it was from our island to the shore, and whether the canoes were not often lost. He told me there was no danger: no canoes were ever lost; but that after a little way out to sea, there was a current and wind, always one way in the morning, the other in the afternoon. This I understood to be no more than the sets of the tide, as going out or coming in; but I afterward understood it was occasioned by the great draft and reflux of the mighty river Oroonoko, in the mouth of which river, as I thought afterward, our island lay; and that this land which I perceived to the west and northwest was the great island Trinidad, on the north point of the mouth of the river. I asked Friday a thousand questions about the country, the inhabitants, the sea, the coast, and what nations were near; he told me all he knew, with the greatest openness imaginable. I asked him the names of the several nations of his sort of people, but could get no other name than Caribs: from which I easily understood that these were the Caribbees, which our maps place on the part of America that reaches from the mouth of the river Oroonoko to Guiana, and onward to St. Martha. He told me that up a great way beyond the moon (that was, beyond the setting of the moon, which must be west from their country) there dwelt white bearded men, like me, and pointed to my great whiskers, which I mentioned before; and that they had killed much mans—that was his word; by which I understood he meant the Spaniards, whose cruelties in America had been spread over the whole country and were remembered by all the nations, from father to son.

I inquired if he could tell me how I might come from this island and get among those white men; he told me, "Yes, yes, I might go in two canoe." I could not understand what he meant by "two canoe," till at last, with great difficulty, I found he meant it must be in a large, great boat, as big as two canoes. This part of Friday's discourse began to please me very well; and from this time on I entertained some hopes that, one time or other, I might find an opportunity to make my escape from this place, and that this poor savage might be a means to help me to do it.

Chapter 16

Friday Learns About God

During the long time that Friday had now been with me, and that he had begun to speak to me and understand me, I was not lacking in laying a foundation of religious knowledge in his mind; particularly I asked him one time who made him. The poor creature did not understand me at all, but thought I had asked him who his father was; so I took it by another handle and asked him who made the sea, the ground we walked on, and the hills and woods. He told me, "It was one Benamuckee that lived beyond all"; he could describe nothing of this great person, but that he was very old, "much older," he said, "than the sea or the land, than the moon or the stars." I asked him, then, if this old person had made all things, why did not all things worship him? He looked very grave and, with a perfect look of innocence, said, "All things said 'O!' to him." I asked him if the people who died in his country went away anywhere. He said, "Yes; they all went to Benamuckee." Then I asked him whether those they ate up went there, too. He said, "Yes."

From these things I began to instruct him in the knowledge of the true God. I told him that the great Maker of all things lived there, pointing up toward Heaven; that He governed the world by the same power and providence by which He made it; that He was omnipotent and could do everything for us, give everything to us, take everything from us; and thus, by degrees, I opened his eyes. He listened with great attention and received with pleasure the notion of Jesus Christ being sent to redeem us, and of the manner of making our prayers to God, and His being able to hear us, even into Heaven. He told me one day that if our God could hear us, up beyond the sun, He must needs be a greater God than their Benamuckee, who lived

but a little way off and yet could not hear till they went up to the great mountain where he dwelt to speak to him. I asked him if he ever went there to speak to him. He said, "No; they never went that were young men; none went there but the old men," whom he called their Oowokakee; that is, as I made him explain it to me, their religious leaders, or clergy; and that they went to say "O!" (so he called saying prayers) and then came back and told them what Benamuckee said. By this I observed that there is priestcraft even among the most blinded, ignorant pagans in the world; and the policy of making a secret of religion, in order to preserve the veneration of the people toward the clergy, is not only to be found in the Roman, but perhaps among all religions in the world, even among the most brutish and barbarous savages.

I endeavored to clear up this fraud to my man Friday, and told him that the pretense of their old men going up to the mountains to say "O!" to their god Benamuckee was a cheat; and their bringing word from there what he said was much more so; that if they met with any answer, or spoke with anyone there, it must be with an evil spirit; and then I entered into a long discourse with him about the devil, his origin, his rebellion against God, his enmity to man, the reason for it, his setting himself up in the dark parts of the world to be worshiped instead of God and as God, and the many stratagems he made use of to delude men to their ruin; how he had a secret access to our passions and to our affections and adapted his snares to our inclinations, so as to cause us to even be our own tempters and run upon our own destruction by our own choice.

An Inquiring Pupil

I found it was not as easy to imprint right notions in his mind about the devil as it was about the being of God. Nature assisted all my explanations to him, even the necessity of a great First Cause—an overruling, governing Power—a secret, directing Providence; and of the equity and justice of paying homage to Him that made us, and the like; but there appeared nothing of this kind in the notion of an evil spirit, of his origin, his being, his nature, and, above all, of his inclination to do evil and to draw us in to do so, too. The poor creature puzzled me once in such a manner, by a question so natural and innocent that I scarcely knew how to answer him. I had been talking a great deal to him of the power of God, His omnipotence, His aversion to sin, His being a consuming fire to the workers of iniquity; how, as He had made us all, He could destroy us and all the world in a moment. Friday listened with great seriousness to me all the while. After this, I had been telling him how the devil was God's enemy in the hearts of men and used all his malice and skill to defeat the good designs of Providence and to ruin the kingdom of Christ in the world, and the like.

"Well," said Friday, "but you say God is so strong, so great; is He not much strong, much might as the devil?"

"Yes, yes," said I. "Friday, God is stronger than the devil: God is above the devil, and therefore we pray to God to tread him down under our feet and to enable us to resist his temptations and quench his fiery darts."

"But," said he again, "if God much strong, much might as the devil, why God no kill the devil, so make him no more do wicked?"

I was strangely surprised at this question; and after all, though I was now an old man, yet I was but a young doctor, and ill qualified for a casuist, or a solver of difficulties; and at first I could not think what to say; so I pretended not to hear him and asked him what he said; but he was too eager for an answer to forget his question, so he repeated it again in the very same broken words as above.

By this time I had recovered myself a little, and I said, "God will at last punish him severely; he is reserved for the judgment, and he is to be cast into the bottomless pit, to dwell with everlasting fire."

This did not satisfy Friday; but he returned upon me, repeating my own words. "'*Reserve at last!*' me no understand; but why not kill the devil now; not kill great ago?"

"You may as well ask me," said I, "why God does not kill you or me, when we do wicked things here that offend Him. We are preserved to repent and be pardoned."

He mused awhile on this. "Well, well," said he mighty affectionately, "that well: So you, I, devil, all wicked, all preserve, repent, God pardon all."

Here I was run down by him to the last degree, and it was a testimony to me, how the mere notions of nature, though they will guide reasonable creatures to the knowledge of a God and of a worship or homage due to the supreme being of God, as the consequence of our nature, yet nothing but divine revelation can form the knowledge of Jesus Christ and of redemption purchased for us; of a Mediator of the new covenant and of an Intercessor at the footstool of God's throne; I say, nothing but a revelation from Heaven can form these in the soul; and that, therefore, the gospel of our Lord and Savior Jesus Christ, I mean the Word of God, and the Spirit of God, promised for the guide and sanctifier of His people, are the absolutely necessary Instructors of the souls of men in the saving knowledge of God and the means of salvation.

I therefore diverted the present discourse between me and my man, rising up hastily as upon some sudden occasion of going out; then sending him for something a good way off, I seriously prayed to God that He would enable me to instruct savingly this poor savage; assisting by His Spirit the heart of the poor ignorant creature to receive the light of the knowledge of God in Christ, reconciling him to Himself, and would guide me to speak so to him from the Word of God that his conscience might be convinced, his eyes opened, and his soul saved. When he came again to me, I entered into a long discourse with him upon the subject of the redemption of man by the Savior of the world and of the doctrine of the gospel preached from Heaven—that is, of repentance toward God and faith in our blessed Lord Jesus. I then explained to him as well as I could why our blessed Redeemer took not on Him the nature of angels, but the seed of Abraham; and how, for that reason, the fallen angels had no share in the redemption; that He came only to the lost sheep of the house of Israel, and the like.

I had, God knows, more sincerity than knowledge in all the methods I took for this poor creature's instruction, and must acknowledge, what I believe all that act upon the same principle will find, that, in laying things open to him, I really informed and instructed myself in many things that I either did not know, or had not fully considered before, but which occurred naturally to my mind upon searching into them, for the information of this poor savage. I had more affection in my inquiry after things upon this occasion than ever I felt before, so that, whether this poor wild wretch was the better for me or not, I had reason to be thankful that he came to me. My grief sat lighter upon me, my habitation grew comfortable to me beyond measure, and when I reflected that in this solitary life that I had been confined to, I had not only been moved to look up to Heaven myself and to seek the Hand that had brought me here, but was now to be made an instrument, under Providence, to save the life and, for aught I know, the soul of a poor savage and bring him to the true knowledge of religion and of the Christian doctrine, that he might know Christ Jesus, to know Whom is life eternal; I say, when I reflected upon all these things, a secret joy ran through every part of my soul, and I frequently rejoiced that I was brought to this place, which I had so often thought the most dreadful of all afflictions that could possibly have befallen me.

In this thankful frame I continued all the remainder of my time; and the conversation that employed the hours between Friday and me was such as made the three years that we lived there together perfectly and completely happy, if any such thing as complete happiness can be found in a sublunary state. This savage was now a good Christian, a much better one than I; though I have reason to hope, and bless God for it, that we were equally penitent, and comforted, restored penitents. We had here the Word of God to read, and no further off from His Spirit to instruct than if we had been in England. I always applied myself, in reading the Scriptures, to let him know, as well as I could, the meaning of what I read; and he again, by his serious inquiries and questionings, made me, as I said before, a much better scholar in scriptural knowledge than I should ever have been by my own mere private reading.

Another thing I cannot refrain from observing here also, from experience in this retired part of my life—namely, how infinite and inexpressible a blessing it is that the knowledge of God, and of the doctrine of salvation by Christ Jesus, is so plainly laid down in the Word of God, so easy to be received and understood that, as the bare reading of the Scripture made me capable of understanding enough of my duty to carry me directly on to the great work of sincere repentance for my sins, and of laying hold of a Savior for life and salvation, to a stated reformation in practice and obedience to all God's commands, and this without any teacher or instructor, I mean human; so the same plain instruction sufficiently served to the enlightening of this savage creature and bringing him to be such a Christian as I have known few to equal him in my life.

As to the disputes, wrangling, strife, and contention that have happened in the world about religion, whether niceties in doctrines or schemes of church government, they were all perfectly useless to us, and, for aught I can yet see, they have been to the rest of the world. We had the sure guide to Heaven, that is, the Word of God; and we had, blessed be God, comfortable views of the Spirit of God teaching and instructing us by His Word, leading us into all truth, and making us both willing and obedient to the instruction of His Word. And I cannot see the least use that the greatest knowledge of the disputed points of religion, which have made such confusions in the world, would have been to us, if we could have obtained it; but I must go on with the historical part of things and take every part in its order.

Friday's Nation

After Friday and I became more intimately acquainted, and he could understand almost all I said to him and speak fluently, though in broken English, to me, I acquainted him with my own story, or at least so much of it as related to my coming into this place; how I had lived there, and how long. I let him into the mystery—for such it was to him—of gunpowder and bullet and taught him how to shoot. I gave him a knife, with which he was wonderfully delighted; and I made him a belt, with a frog hanging to it, such as in England we wear hangers in; and in the frog, instead of a hanger, I gave him a hatchet, which was not only as good a weapon in some cases, but much more useful upon many occasions.

I described to him the countries of Europe, particularly England, which I came from; how we lived, how we worshiped God, how we behaved to one another, and how we traded in ships to all parts of the world. I gave him an account of the wreck that I had been on board of, and showed him, as nearly as I could, the place where she lay: but she was all beaten into pieces long before, and quite gone. I showed him the ruins of our boat, which we lost when we escaped, and which I could not stir with my whole strength then, but was now fallen almost all to pieces. Upon seeing this boat, Friday stood musing a great while and said nothing. I asked him what he was thinking about.

At last, he said, "Me see such boat come to place at my nation."

I did not understand him for a good while; but at last, when I had examined further into it, I understood by him that a boat, such as that had been, came on shore upon the country where he lived; as he explained it, it had been driven there by stress of weather. I presently imagined that some European ship must have been cast away upon their coast, and the boat might have gotten loose and drifted ashore; but I was so dull that I never once thought of men making their escape from a wreck to that shore, much less from where they might come, so I only inquired after the description of the boat.

Friday described the boat to me well enough, but helped me to better understand him when he added with some warmth, "We save the white mans from drown."

Then I presently asked if there were any white mans, as he called them, in the boat. "Yes," he said, "the boat full of white mans." I asked him how many. He told upon his fingers seventeen. I asked him then what became of them. He told me, "They live, they dwell at my nation."

This put new thoughts into my head, for I presently imagined that these might be the men belonging to the ship that was cast away in the sight of my island, as I now called it; and who, after the ship was struck on the rock and they saw her inevitably lost, had saved themselves in their boat and were landed upon that wild shore among the savages. Upon this I inquired of him more critically what had become of them. He assured me they lived there still; that they had been there about four years; that the savages left them alone and gave them victuals so they could live. I asked him how it came to pass that they did not kill them and eat them. He said, "No, they make brother with them"; that is, as I understood him, a truce; and then he added, "They no eat mans but when make the warfight"; that is to say, they never eat any men but such as come to fight with them and are taken in battle.

It was after this some considerable time that being upon the top of the hill, at the east side of the island, from which, as I have said, I had, on a clear day, discovered the mainland or continent of America, when Friday, the weather being very serene, looked very earnestly toward the mainland and, in a kind of surprise, fell to jumping and dancing and called out to me, for I was at some distance from him. I asked him what was the matter.

"Oh, joy!" said he. "Oh, glad! There see my country. There my nation!"

I observed that an extraordinary sense of pleasure appeared on his face, and his eyes sparkled, and his countenance discovered a strange eagerness, as if he had a mind to be in his own country again. This observation of mine put a great many thoughts into me, which made me, at first, not so easy about my new man Friday as I was before; and I had no doubt but that, if Friday could get back to his own nation again, he would not only forget all his religion, but all his obligation to me, and would be thankless enough to give his countrymen an account of me and come back, perhaps, with a hundred or two of them and make a feast upon me, at which he might be as merry as he used to be with those of his enemies when they were taken in war. But I wronged the poor, honest creature very much, for which I was very sorry afterward. However, as my suspicion increased and held me some weeks, I was a little more circumspect and not so familiar and kind to him as before, in which I was certainly in the wrong, too: the honest, grateful creature having no thought about it but what consisted with the best principles both as a religious Christian and as a grateful friend, as appeared afterward to my full satisfaction.

While my suspicion of him lasted, you may be sure I was every day pumping him, to see if he would discover any of the new thoughts that I suspected were in him; but I found everything he said was so honest and so innocent that I could find nothing to nourish my suspicion; and in spite of all my uneasiness, he made me at last entirely his own again; nor did he in the least perceive that I was uneasy, and therefore I could not suspect him of deceit.

Plans for Leaving the Island

One day, walking up the same hill, but the weather being hazy at sea, so that we could not see the continent, I called to him and said, "Friday, do not you wish yourself in your own country, your own nation?"

"Yes," he said, "I be much glad to be at my own nation."

"What would you do there?" said I. "Would you turn wild again, eat men's flesh again, and be a savage, as you were before?"

He looked full of concern, and shaking his head, he said, "No, no; Friday tell them to live good; tell them to pray God; tell them to eat corn bread, cattle flesh, milk; no eat man again."

"Why, then," said I to him, "they will kill you."

He looked grave at that, and then he said, "No, no; they no kill me, they willing love learn." He meant by this that they would be willing to learn. He added, they learned much of the "bearded mans" that came in the boat.

Then I asked him if he would go back to them. He smiled at that and told me he could not swim so far. I told him I would make a canoe for him. He told me he would go, if I would go with him.

"I go?" said I. "Why, they will eat me if I come there."

"No, no," said he. "Me make them no eat you; me make them much love you."

He meant he would tell them how I had killed his enemies and saved his life, and so he would make them love me. Then he told me, as well as he could, how kind they were to seventeen white men, or bearded men, as he called them, who came on shore in distress.

From this time, I confess, I had a mind to venture over, and see if I could possibly join with those bearded men, who, I had no doubt, were Spaniards or Portuguese; not doubting but, if I could, we might find some method to escape from there, being upon the continent and a good company together, better than I could from an island forty miles off the shore, alone, and without help. So, after some days, I took Friday to work again, by way of discourse, and told him I would give him a boat to go back to his own nation; and I, accordingly, carried him to my frigate, which lay on the other side of the island, and having cleared it of water (for I always kept it sunk in the water), I brought it out, showed it to him, and we both went into it. I found he was a most dexterous fellow at managing it and would make it go almost as swift and fast again as I could.

So when he was in, I said to him, "Well, now, Friday, shall we go to your nation?"

He looked very doubtful at my saying so; which it seems was because he thought the boat too small to go so far. I then told him I had a bigger one; so the next day I went to the place where the first boat lay that I had made, but which I could not get into the water. He said that was big enough; but then, as I had taken no care of it, and it had lain two- or three-and-twenty years there, the sun had so split and dried it that it was rotten. Friday told me that such a boat would do very well and would carry "much enough vittle, drink, bread"—that was his way of talking.

Upon the whole, I was by this time so fixed upon my design of going over with him to the continent that I told him we would go and make one as big as that, and he should go home in it. He answered not one word, but looked very grave and sad. I asked him what was the matter with him.

He asked me again, "Why you angry mad with Friday? What me done?"

I asked him what he meant. I told him I was not angry with him at all.

"No angry!" said he, repeating the words several times. "Why send Friday home away to my nation?"

"Why," said I, "Friday, did not you say you wished you were there?"

"Yes, yes," said he. "Wish we both there; no wish Friday there, no master there." In a word, he would not think of going there without me.

"I go there, Friday?" said I. "What shall I do there?"

He turned very quickly upon me at this. "You do great deal much good," said he. "You teach wild mans be good, sober, tame mans; you tell them know God, pray God, and live new life."

"Alas, Friday!" said I. "Thou knowest not what thou sayest. I am but an ignorant man myself."

"Yes, yes," said he, "you teachee me good, you teachee them good."

"No, no, Friday," said I, "you shall go without me. Leave me here to live by myself, as I did before."

He looked confused again at that word; and running to one of the hatchets that he used to wear, he took it up hastily and gave it to me.

"What must I do with this?" said I to him.

"You take kill Friday," said he.

"What must I kill you for?" said I again.

He returned very quickly: "What you send Friday away for? Take kill Friday, no send Friday away."

This he spoke so earnestly that I saw tears stand in his eyes. In a word, I so plainly discovered the utmost affection in him to me, and a firm resolution in him, that I told him then, and often after, that I would never send him away from me, if he was willing to stay with me.

A New Canoe Made

Upon the whole, as I found by all his discourse a settled affection for me and that nothing could part him from me, so I found all the foundation of his desire to go to his own country was laid in his ardent affection to the people and his hopes of my doing them good—a thing that, as I had no notion of myself, so I had not the least thought, or intention, or desire of undertaking it. But still I found a strong inclination to my attempting an escape, founded on the supposition gathered from the former discourse that there were seventeen bearded men there. Therefore, without any more delay, I went to work with Friday to find out a great tree proper to fell and make a large *periagua* to undertake the voyage. There were trees enough in the island to have built a little fleet, not of *periaguas*, but even of good large vessels; but the main thing I looked at was to get one so near the water that we might launch it when it was made, to avoid the mistake I committed at first. At last, Friday pitched upon a tree; for I found he knew much better than I what kind of wood was fittest for it; nor can I tell, to this day, what wood to call the tree we cut down, except that it was very like the tree we call fustic, or between that and the Nicaragua wood, for it was much of the same color and smell. Friday was for burning the hollow or cavity of this tree out, to make it into a boat, but I showed him how rather to cut it with tools; which, after

I had showed him how to use them, he did very handily. In about a month's hard labor, we finished it and made it very handsome; especially when, with our axes, which I showed him how to handle, we cut and hewed the outside into the true shape of a boat. After this, however, it cost us nearly a fortnight's time to get her along, as it were, inch by inch upon great rollers into the water; but when she was in, she would have carried twenty men with great ease.

When she was in the water, though she was so big, it amazed me to see with what dexterity and how swiftly my man Friday could manage her, turn her, and paddle her along. So I asked him if we might venture over in her. "Yes," he said, "we venture over in her very well, though great blow wind." However, I had a further design that he knew nothing of, and that was to make a mast and a sail and to fit her with an anchor and cable. As to a mast, that was easy enough to get; so I pitched upon a straight young cedar tree, which I found near the place, and of which there were a great plenty on the island, and I set Friday to work to cut it down and gave him directions how to shape and order it. But as to the sail, that was my particular care. I knew I had old sails, or rather pieces of old sails, enough; but as I had had them now six-and-twenty years by me and had not been very careful to preserve them, not imagining that I should ever have this kind of use for them, I did not doubt but they were all rotten; and, indeed, most of them were so. However, I found two pieces that appeared pretty good, and with these I went to work; and with a great deal of pains, and awkward, tedious stitching, you may be sure, for want of needles, I at length made a three-cornered, ugly thing, like what we call in England a shoulder-of-mutton sail, to go with a boom at bottom, and a little short sprit at the top, such as usually our ships' longboats sail with, and such as I best knew how to manage, because it was such a one as I used in the boat in which I made my escape from Barbary, as related in the first part of my story.

I was nearly two months performing this last work, that is, rigging and fitting my mast and sails; for I finished them very complete, making a small stay, and a sail or foresail to it, to assist if we should turn to windward; and, even more important, I fixed a rudder to the stern of her to steer with. And though I was but a bungling shipwright, yet as I knew the usefulness and even the necessity of such a thing, I applied myself with so much pains to do it that at last I brought it to pass; though, considering the many dull contrivances I had for it that failed, I think it cost me almost as much labor as making the boat.

After all this was done, I had my man Friday to teach as to what belonged to the navigation of my boat; for, though he knew very well how to paddle the canoe, he knew nothing of what belonged to a sail and a rudder, and was the most amazed when he saw me work the boat to and fro in the sea by the rudder, and how the sail jibbed and filled this way or that way as the course we sailed changed; I say, when he saw this, he stood like one astonished and amazed. However, with a little use, I made all these things familiar to him, and he became an expert sailor, except that as to the compass—I could make him understand very little of that. On the other hand, as there was very little cloudy weather and seldom or never any fogs in those parts, there was the less occasion for the compass, seeing the stars were always to be seen by night and the shore by day, except in the rainy seasons, and then nobody cared to stir abroad either by land or sea.

I was now entered on the seven-and-twentieth year of my captivity in this place; though the three last years that I had this creature with me ought rather to be left out of the account, my habitation being quite of another kind than in all the rest of my time. I kept the anniversary of my landing here with the same thankfulness to God for His mercies as at first; and if I had such cause of acknowledgment at first, I had much more so now, having such additional testimonies of the care of Providence over me and the great hopes I had of being effectually and speedily delivered; for I had a strong conviction that my deliverance was at hand and that I should not be another year in this place. However, I went on with my husbandry: digging, planting, and fencing, as usual. I gathered and cured my grapes and did every necessary thing as before.

The rainy season was in the meantime upon me, when I kept more within doors than at other times. I had stowed our new vessel as secure as we could, bringing her up into the creek, where, as I said in the beginning, I landed my rafts from the ship; and hauling her up to the shore at high-water mark, I made my man Friday dig a little dock, just big enough to hold her, and just deep enough to give her water enough to float in; and then, when the tide was out, we made a strong dam across the end of it, to keep the water out; and so she lay dry as to the tide from the sea; and to keep the rain off, we laid on a great many boughs of trees, so thick that she was as well thatched as a house; and thus we waited for the months of November and December, in which I designed to make my adventure.

Chapter 17

NEW SUBJECTS

When the settled season began to come in, and the thought of my design returned with the fair weather, I began preparing daily for the voyage. And the first thing I did was to lay by a certain quantity of provisions, being the stores for our voyage; and intended, in a week or a fortnight's time, to open the dock and launch out our boat. I was busy one morning upon something of this kind, when I called to Friday and bid him go to the seashore and see if he could find a turtle, or tortoise, a thing that we generally got once a week, for the sake of the eggs, as well as the flesh. Friday had not been gone long when he came running back and flew over my outer wall, or fence, like one that felt not the ground or the steps he set his feet on; and before I had time to speak to him, he cried out to me, "O master! O master! O sorrow! O bad!"

"What's the matter, Friday?" said I.

"Oh! Yonder there," said he. "One, two, three canoes; one, two, three!"

By this way of speaking, I concluded there were six; but on inquiry I found there were but three.

"Well, Friday," said I, "do not be frightened."

So I heartened him up as well as I could. However, I saw the poor fellow was most terribly scared, for he was convinced beyond a doubt that they had come back to look for him and would cut him into pieces and eat him; and the poor fellow trembled so that I scarcely knew what to do with him. I comforted him as well as I could and told him I was in as much danger as he and that they would eat me as well as him.

"But," said I, "Friday, we must resolve to fight them. Can you fight, Friday?"

"Me shoot," said he, "but there come many great number."

"No matter for that," said I again. "Our guns will frighten them that we do not kill."

So I asked him whether, if I resolved to defend him, he would defend me and stand by me and do just as I bid him. He said, "Me die, when you bid die, Master." So I went and fetched a good dram of rum and let him know—for I had been so good a husband of my rum—that I had a great deal left. When he had drunk it, I made him take the two fowling-pieces, which we always carried, and load them with large swan-shot as big as small pistol-bullets. Then I took four muskets and loaded them with two slugs and five small bullets each; and my two pistols I loaded with a brace of bullets each. I hung my great sword, as usual, naked by my side and gave Friday his hatchet.

When I had thus prepared myself, I took my perspective glass and went up to the side of the hill, to see what I could discover; and I found quickly by my glass that there were one-and-twenty savages, three prisoners, and three canoes; and that their whole business seemed to be the triumphant banquet upon these three human bodies: a barbarous feast indeed, but nothing more than, as I had observed, was usual with them. I observed also that they landed not where they had when Friday made his escape, but nearer to my creek, where the shore was low and where a thick wood came close almost down to the sea. This, with the abhorrence of the inhuman errand these wretches came about, filled me with such indignation that I came down again to Friday and told him I was resolved to go down to them and kill them all, and I asked him if he would stand by me. He had now got over his fright, and his spirits being a little raised with the dram I had given him, he was very cheerful and told me, as before, he would die when I bid die.

Attack on the Savages

In this fit of fury, I took first and divided the arms that I had charged, as before, between us; I gave Friday one pistol to stick in his girdle and three guns upon his shoulder, and I took one pistol and the other three myself; and in this posture, we marched out. I took a small bottle of rum in my pocket and gave Friday a large bag with more powder and bullets; and as to orders, I charged him to keep close behind me and not to stir, or shoot, or do anything till I bid him, and in the meantime, he was not to speak a word. In this posture, I circled to my right nearly a mile, as well to get over the creek as to get into the wood, so that I might come within shot of them before I should be discovered, which I had seen by my glass it was easy to do.

While I was making this march, my former thoughts returning, I began to abate my resolution—I do not mean that I entertained any fear of their number, for, as they were naked, unarmed wretches, it is certain I was superior to them—nay, though I had been alone. But it occurred to me, what call, what occasion, much less what necessity, I was in to go and dip my hands in blood, to attack people who had neither done nor intended me any wrong?—who, as to me, were innocent and whose barbarous customs were their own disaster, being in them a token, indeed, of God's having left them, with the other nations of that part of the world, to such stupidity and to such inhuman courses, but did not call me to take upon myself to be a judge of their actions, much less an executioner of His justice—that whenever He thought fit He would take the cause into His own hands and by national vengeance punish them for national crimes; but that, in the meantime, it was none of my business—that it was true Friday might justify it, because he was a declared enemy and in a state of war with those very particular people, and it was lawful for him to attack them; but I could not say the same with regard to myself. These things were so warmly pressed upon my thoughts all the way as I went that I resolved I would only go and place myself near them so that I might observe their barbarous feast and that I would act then as God should direct; and that unless something offered that was more a call to me than yet I knew of, I would not meddle with them.

With this resolution I entered the wood, and with all possible wariness and silence, Friday following close at my heels, I marched till I came to the skirt of the wood on the side that was next to them, only that one corner of the wood lay between me and them. Here I called softly to Friday, and showing him a great tree that was just at the corner of the wood, I bade him go to the tree and bring me word if he could see there plainly what they were doing. He did so, and came immediately back to me and told me they might be plainly viewed there—that they were all about their fire eating the flesh of one of their prisoners, and that another lay bound upon the sand a little way from them, whom he said they would kill next; and this fired the very soul within me. He told me it was not one of their nation, but one of the bearded men whom he had told me of, that came to their country in the boat. I was filled with horror at the very naming of the white bearded man; and going to the tree, I saw plainly by my glass a white man, who lay upon the beach of the sea with his hands and his feet tied with flags, or things like rushes, and that he was a European and had clothes on.

There was another tree and a little thicket beyond it, about fifty yards nearer to the place where I was, which, by going a little way about, I saw I might come at undiscovered, and that then I should be within half a shot of them; so I withheld my passion, though I was indeed enraged to the highest degree; and going back about twenty paces, I got behind some bushes, which held all the way till I came to the other tree, and then came to a little rising ground, which gave me a full view of them at the distance of about eighty yards.

I had now not a moment to lose, for nineteen of the dreadful wretches sat on the ground, all closely huddled together, and had just sent the other two to butcher the poor Christian and bring him . . . to their fire, and they were stooping down to untie the bands at his feet. I turned to Friday.

"Now, Friday," said I, "do as I bid thee."

Friday said he would.

"Then, Friday," said I, "do exactly as you see me do; fail in nothing."

So I set down one of the muskets and the fowling-piece upon the ground, and Friday did the like by his, and with the other musket I took my aim at the savages, bidding him do the like; then asking him if he was ready, he said yes.

"Then fire at them," said I; and at the same moment I fired also.

Friday took his aim so much better than I that on the side he shot, he killed two of them and wounded three more; and on my side I killed one and wounded two. They were, you may be sure, in a dreadful consternation; and all of them that were not hurt jumped upon their feet, but did not immediately know which way to run, or which way to look, for they knew not from what direction their destruction came. Friday kept his eyes close upon me that, as I had bid him, he might observe what I did; so, as soon as the first

shot was made, I threw down the piece and took up the fowling-piece, and Friday did the like; he saw me cock and present; he did the same again.

"Are you ready, Friday?" said I.

"Yes," said he.

"Let fly, then," said I, "in the name of God!"

With that I fired again among the amazed wretches, and so did Friday. As our pieces were now loaded with what I call swan-shot, or small pistol-bullets, we found only two dropped; but so many were wounded that they ran about yelling and screaming like mad creatures, all bloody, and most of them miserably wounded; three more fell quickly after, though not quite dead.

"Now, Friday," said I, laying down the discharged pieces and taking up the musket that was yet loaded, "follow me," which he did with a great deal of courage.

I rushed out of the wood and showed myself and Friday close at my foot. As soon as I perceived they saw me, I shouted as loud as I could and bade Friday do so, too, and running as fast as I could—which by the way was not

I made directly toward the poor victim.

very fast, being loaded with arms as I was—I made directly toward the poor victim, who was, as I said, lying upon the beach, between the place where they sat and the sea. The two butchers who were just going to kill him had left him at the surprise of our first fire and fled in a terrible fright to the seaside, where they jumped into a canoe; three more of the rest headed the same way. I turned to Friday and bade him step forward and fire at them; he understood me immediately, and running about forty yards nearer them, he shot at them; and I thought he killed them all, for I saw them all fall of a heap into the boat, though I saw two of them up again quickly; however, he killed two of them and wounded the third so that he lay down in the bottom of the boat as if he had been dead.

A Spaniard Rescued

While my man Friday fired at them, I pulled out my knife and cut the flags that bound the poor victim; and loosing his hands and feet, I lifted him up and asked him, in the Portuguese tongue, what he was. He answered in Latin, "*Christianus*," but was so weak and faint that he could scarcely stand or speak. I took my bottle out of my pocket and gave it to him, making signs that he should drink, which he did; and I gave him a piece of bread, which he ate. Then I asked him what countryman he was, and he said "*Espagnole*"; and being a little recovered, let me know, by all the signs he could possibly make, how much he was in my debt for his deliverance.

"*Seignior*," said I with as much Spanish as I could make up, "we will talk afterward, but we must fight now; if you have any strength left, take this pistol and sword and lay about you."

He took them very thankfully; and no sooner had he the arms in his hands than, as if they had put new vigor into him, he flew upon his murderers like a fury and had cut two of them into pieces in an instant. The truth is, as the whole was a surprise to them, so the poor creatures were so much frightened with the noise of our weapons that they fell down for mere amazement and fear and had no more power to attempt their own escape than their flesh had to resist our shot: and that was the case of those five that Friday shot at in the boat; for as three of them fell with the hurt they received, so the other two fell with the fright.

I kept my piece in my hand still without firing, being willing to keep my charge ready, because I had given the Spaniard my pistol and sword; so I called to Friday and bade him run up to the tree from which we first fired and fetch the arms which lay there that had been discharged, which he did with great swiftness; and then giving him my musket, I sat down myself to load all the rest again. While I was loading them, there happened a fierce engagement between the Spaniard and one of the savages, who made at him with one of their great wooden swords, the same weapon that was to have killed him before, had I not prevented it. The Spaniard, who was as bold and brave as could be imagined, though weak, had fought this Indian a good while and had cut two great wounds on his head; but the savage being a stout, lusty fellow, closing in with him, had thrown him down, being faint, and was wringing my sword out of his hand, when the Spaniard, though undermost, wisely quitted the sword, drew the pistol from his girdle, shot the savage through the body, and killed him on the spot, before I, who was running to help him, could come near him.

Friday, being now left to his liberty, pursued the flying wretches, with no

weapon in his hand but his hatchet; and with that he dispatched those three who, as I said before, were wounded at first, and fallen, and all the rest he could come up with; and the Spaniard coming to me for a gun, I gave him one of the fowling-pieces, with which he pursued two of the savages and wounded them both; but as he was not able to run, they both got away from him into the wood, where Friday pursued them and killed one of them, but the other was too nimble for him; and though he was wounded, yet had plunged into the sea and swam with all his might off to those two who were left in the canoe. Those three in the canoe, with one wounded—we knew not whether he died or not—were all that escaped our hands, of one-and-twenty. The account of the whole is as follows: Three killed at our first shot from the tree; two killed at the next shot; two killed by Friday in the boat; two killed by Friday, of those at first wounded; one killed by Friday in the wood; three killed by the Spaniard; four killed, being found dropped here and there, of the wounds, or killed by Friday in his chase of them; four escaped in the boat, whereof one wounded, if not dead—twenty-one in all.

Those that were in the canoe worked hard to get out of gunshot, and though Friday took two or three shots at them, I did not find that he hit any of them. Friday would fain have had me take one of their canoes and pursue them; and, indeed, I was very anxious about their escape, lest, carrying the news home to their people, they should come back perhaps with two or three hundred of the canoes and devour us by mere numbers; so I consented to pursue them by sea, and running to one of their canoes, I jumped in and bade Friday follow me; but when I was in the canoe, I was surprised to find another poor creature lying there, bound hand and foot, as the Spaniard was, for the slaughter, and almost dead with fear, not knowing what was the matter; for he had not been able to look up over the side of the boat. He was tied so hard neck and heels, and had been tied so long, that he had really little life in him.

Friday and His Father

I immediately cut the twisted flags or rushes, which they had bound him with, and would have helped him up; but he could not stand or speak, but groaned most piteously, believing, it seems, still, that he was only unbound in order to be killed. When Friday came to him, I bade him speak to him and tell him of his deliverance; and pulling out my bottle, I made him give the poor wretch a dram; which, with the news of his being delivered, revived him, and he sat up in the boat. But when Friday came to hear him speak and look in his face, it would have moved anyone to tears to have seen how Friday kissed him, embraced him, hugged him, cried, laughed, halloed, jumped about, danced, sang; then cried again, wrung his hands, beat his own face and head; and then sang and jumped about again like a distracted creature. It was a good while before I could make him speak to me, or tell me what was the matter; but when he came to himself a little, he told me that it was his father.

It is not easy for me to express how it moved me to see what ecstasy and filial affection had been expressed in this poor savage at the sight of his father and of his being delivered from death; nor, indeed, can I describe half the extravagances of his affection after this; for he went into the boat and out of the boat a great many times. When he went into it, he would sit down by him, bare his chest, and hold his father's head close to him half an hour together, to reassure him; then he took his arms and ankles, which were numbed and stiff with the binding, and chafed and rubbed them with his hands; and I, perceiving what the case was, gave him some rum out of my bottle to rub them with, which did them a great deal of good.

This action put an end to our pursuit of the canoe with the other savages, who were now almost out of sight; and it was happy for us that we did not, for it blew so hard within two hours after, and before they could have reached even a quarter of their way across, and continued blowing so hard all night, and that from the northwest, which was against them, that I could not even imagine that their boat could have made it, or that they could ever have reached their own coast.

But to return to Friday: He was so busy about his father that I could not find in my heart to take him away for some time; but after I thought he could leave him a little, I called him to me, and he came jumping and laughing and pleased to the highest extreme. Then I asked him if he had given his father any bread. He shook his head and said, "None; ugly dog eat all up self." I then gave him a cake of bread, out of a little pouch I carried on purpose; I also gave him a dram for himself; but he would not taste it, but carried it to his father. I had in my pocket also two or three bunches of raisins, so I gave him a handful of them for his father. He had no sooner given his father these raisins, but I saw him come out of the boat and run away as if he had been bewitched, for he was the swiftest fellow on his feet that ever I saw. He ran at such a rate that he was out of sight, as it were, in an instant; and though I called and halloed out, too, after him, it was all one—away he went, and in a quarter of an hour I saw him come back again, though not so fast as he went. As he came nearer, I found his pace slacken, because he had something in his hand. When he came up to me, I found he had gone clear home for an earthen jug, or pot, to bring his father some fresh water and that he had got two more cakes or loaves of bread. The bread he gave me, but the water he carried to his father; however, as I was very thirsty, too, I took a little sip of it. This water revived his father more than all the rum or spirits I had given him, for he was just fainting with thirst.

When his father had drunk, I called to Friday to ask if there was any water left; he said yes, and I bade him give it to the poor Spaniard, who was in as much want of it as his father; and I sent one of the cakes that Friday brought to the Spaniard, too, who was indeed very weak and was reposing himself upon a green place under the shade of a tree; and whose limbs were also very stiff and very much swelled by the rude bindings he had been tied with. When I saw that upon Friday's coming to him with the water, he sat up and drank and took the bread and began to eat, I went to him and gave him a handful of raisins. He looked up in my face with all the tokens of gratitude and thankfulness that could possibly appear in a face, but was so weak—having overexerted himself in the fight—that he could not stand up on his feet; he tried to do it two or three times, but was really not able, his ankles were so swelled and so painful to him. So I bade him sit still and caused Friday to rub his ankles and bathe them with rum, as he had done his father's.

After the Fight

I observed the poor affectionate creature, every two minutes, or perhaps less, all the while he was there, turn his head about, to see if his father was in the same place and posture where he left him sitting; and at last he found he was not to be seen; at which he started up and, without speaking a word, flew with such swiftness to him that one could scarcely perceive his feet to touch the ground as he went; but when he got there, he only found his father had laid himself down to ease his limbs, so Friday came back to me presently. I then spoke to the Spaniard to let Friday help him up, if he could, and lead him to the boat, and then he should bring him to our dwelling, where I would take care of him. But Friday, a strong young fellow, lifted the Spaniard upon his back and carried him away to the boat, and there set him down softly upon the side or gunwale of the canoe, with his feet in the inside of it; then he lifted him quite in and set him close to his father. Presently, stepping out again, he launched the boat off and paddled it along the shore faster than I could walk, though the wind blew pretty hard, too. So he brought them both safely into our creek and, leaving them in the boat, ran away to fetch the other canoe. As he passed me, I spoke to him and asked him where he went. He told me, "Go fetch more boat"; so away he went like the wind, for surely never man nor horse ran like him; and he had the other canoe in the creek almost as soon as I got to it by land; so he wafted me over and then went to help our new guests out of the boat, which he did; but they were neither of them able to walk, so that poor Friday knew not what to do.

To remedy this, I did some thinking; then, calling to Friday to bid them sit down on the bank while he came to me, I soon made a kind of handbarrow to lay them on, and Friday and I carried them both up together.

But when we got them to the outside of our wall, or fortification, we were at a worse loss than before, for it was impossible to get them over, and I was resolved not to break it down; so I set to work again, and Friday and I, in about two hours' time, made a very handsome tent covered with old sails and above that with boughs of trees, being in the space outside our outward fence, and between that and the grove of young wood that I had planted. Here we made them two beds of such things as I had, that is, of good rice-straw, with blankets laid upon it, to lie on, and another to cover them, on each bed.

My island was now peopled, and I thought myself very rich in subjects; and it was a merry reflection, which I frequently made, how like a king I looked. First of all, the whole country was my own property, so that I had an undoubted right of dominion. Secondly, my people were perfectly subjected: I was absolute lord and lawgiver; they all owed their lives to me and were ready to lay down their lives, if there had been occasion for it, for me. It was remarkable, too, I had but three subjects, and they were of different religions: my man Friday was a Protestant, his father was a pagan and a cannibal, and the Spaniard was a papist. However, I allowed liberty of conscience throughout my dominions—but this is by the way.

As soon as I had secured my two weak, rescued prisoners and given them shelter and a place to rest them upon, I began to think of making some provision for them; and the first thing I did, I ordered Friday to take a yearling goat, betwixt a kid and a goat, out of my particular flock, to be killed. I cut off the hinder quarter, and chopping it into small pieces, I set Friday to work on boiling and stewing and made them a very good dish, I assure you, of flesh and broth, having put some barley and rice also into the broth; and as I cooked it outdoors, for I made no fire within my inner wall, so I carried it all into the new tent, and having set a table there for them, I sat down and ate my own dinner also with them and, as well as I could, cheered them and encouraged them. Friday was my interpreter, especially to his father and, indeed, to the Spaniard, too; for the Spaniard spoke the language of the savages pretty well.

After we had dined, or rather supped, I ordered Friday to take one of the canoes and go and fetch our muskets and other firearms, which, for want of time, we had left upon the place of battle. The next day, I ordered him to go and bury the dead bodies of the savages, which lay open to the sun and would presently be offensive. I also ordered him to bury the horrid remains of their barbarous feast, which I could not think of doing myself—nay, I could not bear to see them, if I went that way—all of which he punctually performed and effaced the very appearance of the savages being there; so that when I went again, I could scarcely know where it was, other than by the corner of the wood pointing to the place.

I then began to enter into a little conversation with my two new subjects; and, first, I set Friday to inquire of his father what he thought of the escape of the savages in that canoe, and whether we might expect a return of them, with a power too great for us to resist. His first opinion was that the savages in the boat never could live out the storm which blew that night they went off, but must of necessity be drowned, or driven south to those other shores, where they were as sure to be devoured as they were to be drowned if they were cast away. As to what they would do if they came safe on shore, he said he knew not; but it was his opinion that they were so dreadfully frightened with the manner of their being attacked, the noise, and the fire, that he believed they would tell the people they were all killed by thunder and lightning, not by the hand of man; and that the two which appeared, namely, Friday and I, were two heavenly spirits, or furies, come down to destroy them, and not men with weapons. This he said he knew, because he heard them all cry out so, in their language, one to another; for it was impossible for them to conceive that a man could dart fire, and speak thunder, and kill at a distance, without lifting up the hand, as was done. And this old savage was in the right; for, as I understood since, by other hands, the savages never attempted to go over to the island afterward: They were so terrified with the accounts given by those four men (for it seems they *did* escape the sea) that they believed whoever went to that enchanted island would be destroyed with fire from the gods. This, however, I knew not; and therefore was under continual apprehension for a good while and kept always upon my guard, I and all my army; for, as there now were four of us, I would have ventured upon a hundred of them, fairly in the open field, at any time.

A Discourse with the Spaniard

In a little while, however, no more canoes appearing, the fear of their coming wore off; and I began to take my former thoughts of a voyage to the mainland into consideration; being likewise assured, by Friday's father, that I might depend upon good usage from their nation, on his account, if I would go. But my thoughts were a little suspended when I had a serious discourse with the Spaniard, and when I understood that there were sixteen more of his countrymen and Portuguese, who, having been cast away and made their escape to that side, lived there at peace, indeed, with the savages, but were very sore put for necessaries and, indeed, for life. I asked him all the particulars of their voyage and found they were a Spanish ship bound from the Rio de la Plata to Havanna, being directed to leave their loading there, which was chiefly hides and silver, and to bring back what European goods they could meet with there; that they had five Portuguese seamen on board, whom they took out of another wreck; that five of their own men were drowned, when first the ship was lost, and that these escaped through infinite danger and hazards and arrived, almost starved, on the cannibal coast, where they expected to have been devoured every moment. He told me they had some arms with them, but they were perfectly useless, for that they had neither powder nor ball, the washing of the sea having spoiled all their powder, but a little that they used at their first landing, to provide themselves some food.

I asked him what he thought would become of them there, and if they had planned to make an escape. He said they had many consultations about it; but having neither vessel, nor tools to build one, nor provisions of any kind, their councils always ended in tears and despair. I asked him how he thought they would receive a proposal from me, which might tend toward an escape; and whether, if they were all here, it might not be done. I told him with freedom, I feared mostly their treachery and ill-usage of me, if I put my life in their hands—for gratitude was no inherent virtue in the nature of man, nor did men always square their dealings by the obligations they had received, so much as they did by the advantages they expected. I told him it would be very hard that I should be the instrument of their deliverance and that they should afterward make me their prisoner in New Spain, where an Englishman was certain to be made a sacrifice, what necessity or what accident soever brought him there; and that I had rather be delivered up to the savages, and be devoured alive, than fall into the merciless claws of the priests and be carried into the Inquisition. I added that, otherwise, I was persuaded, if they were all here, we might, with so many hands, build a bark large enough to carry us all away, either to the Brazils southward, or to the islands or Spanish coast northward; but that if, in requital, they should, when I had put weapons into their hands, carry me by force among their own people, I might be ill-used for my kindness to them and make my case worse than it was before.

He answered with a great deal of candor and ingenuousness that their condition was so miserable, and that they were so aware of it, that he believed they would abhor the thought of using any man unkindly that should contribute to their deliverance; and that, if I pleased, he would go to them, with the old man, and discourse with them about it and return again, and bring me their answer; that he would make conditions with them upon their solemn oath: that they should be absolutely under my direction, as their commander and captain; and they should swear upon the Holy Sacrament and Gospel to be true to me and go to such Christian country as I should agree to, and no other; and to be directed wholly and absolutely by my orders, till they were landed safely in such country as I intended; and that he would bring a contract from them, under their hands, for that purpose. Then he told me he would first swear to me himself, that he would never stir from me as long as he lived, till I gave him orders; and that he would take my side to the last drop of his blood, if there should happen the least breach of faith among his countrymen. He told me they were all of them very civil, honest men, and they were under the greatest distress imaginable, having neither weapons nor clothes, nor any food, but at the mercy and discretion of the savages, having given up all hope of ever returning to their own country; and that he was sure, if I would undertake their relief, they would live and die by me.

Upon these assurances, I resolved to venture to rescue them, if possible, and to send the old savage and this Spaniard over to them to negotiate. But when we had got all things in readiness to go, the Spaniard himself made an objection that had so much prudence in it on one hand, and so much sincerity on the other hand, that I could not but be well satisfied in it—and, by his advice, put off the deliverance of his comrades for at least half a year. The case was thus: He had been with us now about a month, during which time I had let him see in what manner I had provided, with the assistance of Providence, for my support; and he evidently saw what stock of corn and rice I had laid up; which, though it was more than sufficient for myself, yet it was not sufficient, without good husbandry, for my family, now it was increased to four—but much less would it be sufficient if his countrymen, who were, as he said, sixteen, still alive, should come over. And least of all would it be sufficient to victual our vessel, if we should build one, for a voyage to any of the Christian colonies of America. So he told me he thought it would be more advisable to let him and the other two dig and cultivate some more land, as much as I could spare seed to sow, and that we should wait another harvest, so that we might have a supply of corn for his countrymen, when they should come; for want might be a temptation to them to disagree, or not to think themselves delivered, otherwise than out of one difficulty into another.

"You know," said he, "the children of Israel, though they rejoiced at first for their being delivered out of Egypt, yet rebelled even against God Himself, that delivered them, when they came to want bread in the wilderness."

We Prepare for Escape

His caution was so seasonable, and his advice so good, that I could not but be very well pleased with his proposal, as well as I was satisfied with his fidelity; so we fell to digging, all four of us, as well as the wooden tools we were furnished with permitted; and in about a month's time, by the end of which it was seedtime, we had got as much land cured and trimmed up as we sowed two-and-twenty bushels of barley on, and sixteen jars of rice, which was, in short, all the seed we had to spare; indeed, we left ourselves barely sufficient for our own food for the six months that we had to expect our crop; that is to say, reckoning from the time we set our seed aside for sowing; for it is not to be supposed it is six months in the ground in that country.

Having now society enough, and our number being sufficient to put us out of fear of the savages, if they had come, unless their number had been very great, we went freely all over the island, whenever we found occasion; and as we had our escape or deliverance ever in our thoughts, it was impossible, at least for me, to have the means of it out of mine. For this purpose, I marked out several trees that I thought fit for our work, and I set Friday and his father to cut them down; and then I caused the Spaniard, to whom I imparted my thoughts on that affair, to oversee and direct their work. I showed them with what indefatigable pains I had hewed a large tree into single planks, and I caused them to do the like, till they had made about a dozen large planks of good oak, nearly two feet broad, thirty-five feet long, and from two inches to four inches thick; what prodigious labor it took up, anyone may imagine.

At the same time, I contrived to increase my little stock of tame goats as much as I could; and for this purpose I made Friday and the Spaniard go out one day, and myself with Friday the next day (for we took our turns), and by this means we got about twenty young kids to breed up with the rest; for whenever we shot the dam, we saved the kids and added them to our flock.

But above all, the season for curing the grapes coming on, I caused such a prodigious quantity to be hung up in the sun, that I believe, had we been at Alicant, Spain, where the raisins of the sun are cured, we could have filled sixty or eighty barrels; and with our bread, these formed a great part of our food—and very good living, too, I assure you, for they are exceedingly nourishing.

It was now harvest, and our crop in good order; it was not the most plentiful increase I had seen in the island; however, it was enough to answer our end: for, from two-and-twenty bushels of barley, we brought in and thrashed out above two hundred twenty bushels; and the like in proportion for the rice, which was store enough for our food to the next harvest, though all the sixteen Spaniards had been on shore with me; or, if we had been ready for a voyage, it would very plentifully have victualed our ship to have carried us to any part of the world, that is to say, America. When we had thus housed and secured our magazine of corn, we fell to work to make more wickerwork, namely, great baskets, in which we kept it; and the Spaniard was very handy and dexterous at this part and often asked me why I did not make some things for defense of this kind of work; but I saw no need of it.

And now, having a full supply of food for all the guests expected, I gave the Spaniard leave to go over to the mainland to see what he could do with those he had left behind him there. I gave him a strict charge not to bring any man with him who would not first swear, in the presence of himself and the old savage, that he would no way injure, fight with, or attack the person he should find on the island who was so kind as to send for them in order to effect their deliverance; but that they would stand by him and defend him against all such attempts, and wherever they went, would be entirely under and subjected to his command; and that this should be put in writing and signed with their hands. How they were to have done this, when I knew they had neither pen nor ink—that, indeed, was a question that we never asked. Under these instructions, the Spaniard and the old savage, the father of Friday, went away in one of the canoes that they might be said to have come in, or rather were brought in, when they came as prisoners to be devoured by the savages. I gave each of them a musket, with a firelock on it, and about eight charges of powder and ball, instructing them to be very good husbands of both and not to use either of them but upon urgent occasion.

Chapter 18
MUTINEERS

This was a cheerful work, being the first measures used by me, in view of my deliverance, for now eight-and-twenty years and some days. I gave them provisions of bread, and of dried grapes, sufficient for themselves for many days, and sufficient for all the Spaniards for about eight days' time; and wishing them a good voyage, I saw them go, agreeing with them about a signal they should hang out at their return, by which I should know them again, when they came back, at a distance, before they came on shore. They went away, with a fair gale, on the day the moon was at full, by my account in the month of October; but as for an exact reckoning of days, after I had once lost it, I could never recover it again; nor had I kept even the number of years so punctually as to be sure I was right; though, as it proved, when I afterward examined my account, I found I had kept a true reckoning of years.

A Ship in Sight

It was no less than eight days I had waited for them, when a strange and unforeseen accident intervened, of which the like has not, perhaps, been heard of in history. I was fast asleep in my hutch one morning, when my man Friday came running in to me and called aloud, "Master, Master, they are come, they are come!"

I jumped up, and regardless of danger, I went out as soon as I could get my clothes on, through my little grove, which, by the way, was by this time grown to be a very thick wood; I say, regardless of danger, I went without my arms, which was not my custom to do. I was surprised when, turning my eyes to the sea, I presently saw a boat at about a league and a half distant, standing in for the shore, with a shoulder-of-mutton sail, as they call it, and the wind blowing pretty fair to bring them in; also I observed, presently, that they did not come from that side which the shore lay on, but from the southernmost end of the island. Upon seeing this, I called Friday in and bade him lie close, for these

were not the people we looked for, and we might not know yet whether they were friends or enemies.

Next, I went in to fetch my perspective glass, to see what I could make of them; and, having taken the ladder out, I climbed up to the top of the hill, as I used to do when I was apprehensive of anything, to take my view plainer, without being discovered. I had scarcely set my foot upon the hill, when my eye plainly discovered a ship lying at an anchor, about two leagues and a half distance from me, south-southeast, but not above a league and a half from the shore. By my observation, it appeared plainly to be an English ship, and the boat appeared to be an English longboat.

I cannot express the confusion I was in, though the joy of seeing a ship, and one that I had reason to believe was manned by my own countrymen and consequently friends, was such as I cannot describe; but yet I had some secret doubts about me—I cannot tell where they came from—bidding me keep up my guard. In the first place, it occurred to me to consider what business an English ship could have in that part of the world, since it was not the way to or from any part of the world where the English had any traffic; and I knew there had been no storms to drive them in here in distress; and that if they were really English, it was most probable that they were here on no good design; and that I had better continue as I was rather than fall into the hands of thieves and murderers.

Let no man despise the secret hints and notices of danger that sometimes are given him when he may think there is no possibility of its being real. That such hints and notices are given us, I believe few that have made any observations of things can deny; that they are certain discoveries of an invisible world and a converse of spirits, we cannot doubt; and if the tendency of them seems to be to warn us of danger, why should we not suppose they are from some friendly agent (whether supreme, or inferior and subordinate, is not the question) and that they are given for our good?

Arrivals from the Ship

The present question abundantly confirms me in the justice of this reasoning; for had I not been made cautious by this secret admonition, come from where it will, I had been undone inevitably and in a far worse condition than before, as you will see presently. I had not kept myself long in this posture till I saw the boat draw near the shore, as if they looked for a creek to thrust in at, for the convenience of landing; however, as they did not come quite far enough, they did not see the little inlet where I formerly landed my rafts, but ran their boat on shore upon the beach, at about half a mile from me; which was very happy for me; for otherwise they would have landed just at my door, as I may say, and would soon have beaten me out of my castle and perhaps have plundered me of all I had. When they were on shore, I was fully satisfied they were Englishmen, at least most of them; one or two I thought were Dutch, but it did not prove so; there were in all eleven men, whereof three of them I found were unarmed, and, as I thought, bound; and when the first four or five of them had jumped onto shore, they took those three out of the boat, as prisoners. One of the three I could perceive using the most passionate gestures of entreaty, affliction, and despair, even to a kind of extravagance; the other two, I could perceive, lifted up their hands sometimes and appeared concerned, indeed, but not to such a degree as the first. I was perfectly confounded at the sight and knew not what the meaning of it should be.

Friday called out to me in English as well as he could, "O master, you see English mans eat prisoner as well as savage mans."

"Why, Friday," said I, "do you think they are going to eat them, then?"

"Yes," said Friday, "they will eat them."

"No, no," said I. "Friday, I am afraid they will murder them, indeed; but you may be sure they will not eat them."

All this while, I had no thought of what the matter really was, but stood trembling with the horror of the sight, expecting every moment that the three prisoners should be killed; nay, once I saw one of the villains lift up his arm with a great cutlass, as the seamen call it, or sword, to strike one of the poor men; and I expected to see him fall every moment; at which all the blood in my body seemed to run chill in my veins. I heartily wished now for my Spaniard and the savage that was gone with him, or that I had any way to have come undiscovered within shot of them that I might have secured the three men, for I saw no firearms among them; but it fell out another way. After I had observed the outrageous usage of the three men by the insolent seamen, I observed the fellows run scattering about the land, as if they wanted to see the country. I observed also that the three other men had liberty to go where they pleased; but they sat down all three upon the ground, very pensive, and looked like men in despair. This put me in mind of the first time when I came on shore and began to look about me; how I gave myself over for lost; how wildly I looked around me; what dreadful apprehensions I had; and how I lodged in the tree all night, for fear of being devoured by wild beasts. As I knew nothing, that night, of the supply I was to receive by the providential drifting of the ship nearer the land by the storms and tide, by which I have since been so long nourished and supported; so these three poor desolate men knew nothing how certain of deliverance and supply they were, how near it was to them, and how effectually and truly they were in a condition of safety, at the same time they thought themselves lost and their case desperate. So little do we see before us in the world, and so much reason have we to depend cheerfully upon the great Maker of the world, that He does not leave His creatures so absolutely destitute, but that, in the worst circumstances, they have always something to be thankful for, and sometimes are nearer their deliverance than they imagine; nay, are even brought to their deliverance by the means by which they seem to be brought to their destruction.

It was just at high tide when these people came on shore; and while they rambled about to see what kind of a place they were in, they carelessly stayed till the tide was spent, and the water had ebbed away considerably, leaving their boat aground. They had left two men in the boat, who, as I found afterward, having drunk a little too much brandy, fell asleep; however, one of them waking a little sooner than the other, and finding the boat too fast aground for him to stir it, halloed out for the rest, who were straggling about; upon which they all soon came to the boat; but it was past all their strength to launch her, the boat being very heavy and the shore on that side being a soft oozy sand, almost like a quicksand. In this condition, like true seamen, who are, perhaps, the least likely of mankind given to forethought, they gave it up, and away they strolled about the country again; and I heard one of them say aloud to another, calling from the boat, "Why, let her alone, Jack, can't you? She'll float next tide"; by which I was fully confirmed in my main inquiry: *Of what country were they?*

All this while, I kept myself close, not once daring to stir out of my castle, any farther than to my place of observation near the top of the hill; and very glad I was to think how well it was fortified. I knew it was no less than ten hours before the boat could float again, and by that time it would be dark, and I might be at more liberty to see their motions and to hear their discourse, if they had any. In the meantime, I fitted myself up for a battle, as before, though with more caution, knowing that I had to do with another kind of enemy than I had at first. I ordered Friday also, whom I had made an excellent marksman with his gun, to load himself with arms. I took myself two fowling-pieces, and I gave him three muskets. My figure, indeed, was very fierce; I had my formidable goatskin coat on, with the great cap I have mentioned, a naked sword, two pistols in my belt, and a gun upon each shoulder.

It was my design, as I said above, not to have made any attempt till it was dark; but about two o'clock, being the heat of the day, I found, in short, they were all gone straggling into the woods and, as I thought, were all laid down to sleep. The three poor distressed men, too anxious for their condition to get any sleep, had, however, sat down under the shelter of a great tree at about a quarter of a mile from me and, as I thought, out of sight of any of the rest. Upon this I resolved to reveal myself to them and learn something of their condition; immediately I marched as above, my man Friday at a good distance behind me, as formidable for his arms as I, but not making quite such a specterlike figure as I did.

I came as near them undiscovered as I could, and then, before any of them saw me, I called aloud to them in Spanish: "What are ye, gentlemen?"

They started up at the noise, but were ten times more confounded when they saw me and the uncouth figure that I made. They made no answer at all, but I thought I perceived them just going to fly from me, when I spoke to them in English.

"Gentlemen," said I, "do not be surprised at me; perhaps you may have a friend near, when you did not expect it."

"He must be sent directly from Heaven, then," said one of them very gravely to me and pulling off his hat at the same time, "for our condition is past the help of man."

"All help is from Heaven, sir," said I, "but can you put a stranger in the way to help you? For you seem to be in some great distress. I saw you when you landed; and when you seemed to make application to the brutes that came with you, I saw one of them lift up his sword to kill you."

The poor man, with tears running down his face and trembling, looked like one astonished and returned, "Am I talking to God or man? Is it a real man or an angel?"

"Be in no fear about that, sir," said I. "If God had sent an angel to relieve you, he would have come better clothed and armed after another manner than you see me in. Pray lay aside your fears; I am a man, an Englishman, and disposed to assist you. You see I have one servant only; we have arms and ammunition. Tell us freely, can we serve you? What is your case?"

"Our case, sir," said he, "is too long to tell you, while our murderers are so near us; but, in short, sir, I was commander of that ship; my men have mutinied against me; they have been barely prevailed on not to murder me and, at last, have set me on shore in this desolate place, with these two men with me—one my mate, the other a passenger—where we expected to perish, believing the place to be uninhabited, and know not yet what to think of it."

"Where are these brutes, your enemies?" said I. "Do you know where they are gone?"

"There they lie, sir," said he, pointing to a thicket of trees. "My heart trembles for fear they have seen us and heard you speak; if they have, they will certainly murder us all."

"Have they any firearms?" said I.

He answered, "They had only two pieces, one of which they left in the boat."

"Well, then," said I, "leave the rest to me. I see they are all asleep; it is an easy thing to kill them all; or shall we rather take them prisoners?"

He told me there were two desperate villains among them that it was scarcely safe to show any mercy to; but if they were secured, he believed all the rest would return to their duty. I asked him which they were.

He told me he could not at that distance distinguish them, but he would obey my orders in anything I would direct.

"Well," said I, "let us retreat out of their view or hearing, lest they awaken, and we will resolve further."

So they willingly went back with me, till the woods covered us from them.

The Captain's Proposal

"Look you, sir," said I, "if I venture upon your deliverance, are you willing to make two conditions with me?"

He anticipated my proposals by telling me that both he and the ship, if recovered, should be wholly directed and commanded by me in everything; and if the ship was not recovered, he would live and die with me in what part of the world soever I would send him; and the two other men said the same.

"Well," said I, "my conditions are but two: first, that while you stay on this island with me, you will not pretend to any authority here; and if I put arms in your hands, you will, upon all occasions, give them up to me and do no prejudice to me or mine upon this island, and in the meantime be governed by my orders; secondly, that if the ship is or may be recovered, you will carry me and my man to England passage free."

He gave me all the assurance that the invention and faith of a man could devise that he would comply with these most reasonable demands, and besides would owe his life to me and acknowledge it upon all occasions as long as he lived.

"Well, then," said I, "here are three muskets for you, with powder and ball. Tell me next what you think is proper to be done."

He showed all the testimony of his gratitude that he was able, but offered to be wholly guided by me. I told him I thought it was hard venturing anything; but the best method I could think of was to fire on them at once as they lay, and if any were not killed at the first volley and offered to submit, we might save them and so put it wholly upon God's providence to direct the shot. He said, very gravely, that he was loath to kill them, if he could help it; but that those two were incorrigible villains and had been the authors of all the mutiny in the ship, and if they escaped, we should be undone still, for they would go on board and bring the whole ship's company and destroy us all.

"Well, then," said I, "necessity legitimates my advice, for it is the only way to save our lives."

However, seeing him still cautious of shedding blood, I told him they should go themselves and manage as they found convenient.

In the middle of this discourse, we heard some of them awaken, and soon after we saw two of them on their feet. I asked him if either of them were the men who he had said were the heads of the mutiny. He said no.

"Well, then," said I, "you may let them escape; and Providence seems to have awakened them on purpose to save themselves. Now, if the rest escape you, it is your fault."

Animated with this, he took the musket I had given him in his hand and a pistol in his belt, and his two comrades with him, with each man a piece in his hand; the two men who were with him going first made some noise, at which one of the seamen, who was awake, turned about and, seeing them coming, cried out to the rest; but it was too late for them, for the moment he cried out they fired—I mean the two men, the captain wisely reserving his own piece. They had so well aimed their shot at the men they knew that one of them was killed on the spot, and the other was very much wounded; but not being dead, he started up on his feet and called eagerly for help to the other. But the captain, stepping to him, told him it was too late to cry for help, and he should call upon God to forgive his villainy. With that word the captain knocked him down with the stock of his musket, so that he never

spoke more. There were three more in the company, and one of them was slightly wounded. By this time I was come; and when they saw their danger, and that it was in vain to resist, they begged for mercy. The captain told them he would spare their lives if they would give him an assurance of their abhorrence of the treachery they had been guilty of, and would swear to be faithful to him in recovering the ship, and afterward in carrying her back to Jamaica, from which they came. They gave him all the protestations of their sincerity that could be desired; and he was willing to believe them and spare their lives, which I was not against, only I obliged him to keep them bound hand and foot while they were upon the island.

While this was doing, I sent Friday with the captain's mate to the boat, with orders to secure her and bring away the oars and sails, which they did. By and by, the three straggling men who were (happily for them) parted from the rest came back upon hearing the guns fired; and seeing the captain, who before was their prisoner, now their conqueror, they submitted to be bound also; and so our victory was complete.

I Show the Captain My Castle

It now remained that the captain and I should inquire into one another's circumstances. I began first and told him my whole history, which he heard with an attention even to amazement—and particularly at the wonderful manner of my being furnished with provisions and ammunition; and, indeed, as my story is a whole collection of wonders, it affected him deeply. But when he reflected after this upon himself, and how I seemed to have been preserved there on purpose to save his life, the tears ran down his face, and he could not speak a word more. After this communication was at an end, I took him and his two men into my apartments, leading them in just where I came out, that is, at the top of the house, where I refreshed him with such provision as I had and showed them all the contrivances I had made during my long, long inhabiting that place.

All I showed them, all I said to them, was perfectly amazing; but above all, the captain admired my fortification, and how perfectly I had concealed my retreat with a grove of trees, which, having been now planted nearly twenty years, and the trees growing much faster than in England, was become a little wood, so thick that it was impassable in any part of it but at that one side where I had reserved my little winding passage into it. I told him this was my castle and my residence, but that I had a seat in the country, as most princes have, where I could retreat upon occasion, and I would show him that, too, another time; but at present our business was to consider how to recover the ship. He agreed with me as to that, but told me he was perfectly at a loss what measures to take, for that there were still six-and-twenty hands on board, who, having entered into a cursed conspiracy, by which they had all forfeited their lives to the law, would be hardened in it now by desperation and would carry it on, knowing that if they were subdued they should be brought to the gallows as soon as they came to England, or to any of the English colonies, and that, therefore, there would be no attacking them with so small a number as we were.

I mused for some time upon what he had said and found it was a very rational conclusion and that therefore something had to be resolved on very speedily, as well to draw the men on board into some snare for their surprise, as to prevent their landing upon us and destroying us. Upon this, it presently occurred to me that in a little while the ship's crew, wondering what was become of their comrades and of the boat, would certainly come on shore in their other boat to look for them, and that then, perhaps, they might come armed and be too strong for us; this he allowed to be likely. Upon this, I told him the first thing we had to do was to stave the boat, which lay upon the beach, so that they might not carry her off; and taking everything out of her, leave her so far useless as not to be fit to use. Accordingly, we went on board and took the arms that were left on board out of her and whatever else we found there—which was a bottle of brandy and another of rum, a few biscuit-cakes, a horn of powder, and a great lump of sugar in a piece of canvas (the sugar was five or six pounds); all which was very welcome to me, especially the brandy and sugar, of which I had none left for many years.

When we had carried all these things on shore (the oars, mast, sail, and rudder of the boat were carried away before), we knocked a great hole in her bottom, so that if they had come strong enough to master us, yet they could not carry off the boat. Indeed, it was not much in my thoughts that we could be able to recover the ship; but my view was that if they went away without the boat, I did not much question being able to make her again fit to carry us to the Leeward Islands and call upon our friends the Spaniards in my way, for I still had them in my thoughts.

Another Boat Lands

While we were thus preparing our designs and had first, by main strength, heaved the boat upon the beach, so high that the tide would not float her off at high-water mark, then broken a hole in her bottom too big to be quickly stopped, and were sat down musing what we should do, we heard the ship fire a gun and make a waft with her ancient as a signal for the boat to come on board. But no boat stirred; and they fired several times, making other signals for the boat. At last, when all their signals and firing proved fruitless, and they found the boat did not stir, we saw them, by the help of my glasses, hoist another boat out and row toward the shore; and we found, as they approached, that there were no less than ten men in her and that they had firearms with them.

As the ship lay almost two leagues from the shore, we had a full view of them as they came and a plain sight even of their faces; because the tide having set them a little to the east of the other boat, they rowed up under shore, to come to the same place where the other had landed and where the boat lay. By this means, I say, we had a full view of them, and the captain knew the persons and characters of all the men in the boat, of whom, he said, there were three very honest fellows, who, he was sure, were led into this conspiracy by the rest, being overpowered and frightened; but that as for the boatswain, who it seems was the chief officer among them, and all the rest, they were as dangerous as any of the ship's crew and were no doubt made desperate in their new enterprise; and terribly apprehensive he was that they would be too powerful for us. I smiled at him and told him that men in our circumstances were past the consideration of fear; that seeing almost every condition that could be was better than that which we were supposed to be in, we ought to expect that the consequence, whether death or life, would be sure to be a deliverance. I asked him what he thought of the circumstances of my life and whether a deliverance were not worth venturing for.

"And where, sir," said I, "is your belief in my being preserved here on purpose to save your life, which elevated you a little while ago? For my part, there seems to be but one thing amiss in all the prospect of it."

"What is that?" said he.

"Why," said I, "it is that you say there are three or four honest fellows among them, which should be spared. Had they been all of the wicked part of the crew, I should have thought God's providence had singled them out to deliver them into your hands; for depend upon it, every man that comes ashore is our own and shall die or live as they behave to us."

As I spoke this with a raised voice and cheerful countenance, I found it greatly encouraged him; so we set vigorously to our business.

We had, upon the first appearance of the boat coming from the ship, considered separating our prisoners, and we had, indeed, secured them effectually. Two of them, of whom the captain was less assured than ordinary, I sent with Friday and one of the three delivered men to my cave, where they were remote enough, and out of danger of being heard or discovered, or of finding their way out of the woods, if they could have delivered themselves; here they left them bound, but gave them provisions and promised them, if they continued there quietly, to give them their liberty in a day or two; but that if they attempted their escape, they should be put to death without mercy. They promised faithfully to bear their confinement with patience and were very thankful that they had such good usage as to have provisions and a light left them—for Friday gave them candles (such as we made ourselves) for their comfort; and they did not know but that he stood sentinel over them at the entrance.

The other prisoners had better usage; two of them were kept pinioned, indeed, because the captain was not free to trust them; but the other two were taken into my service, upon the captain's recommendation and upon their solemnly engaging to live and die with us. So with them and the three honest men, we were seven men, well armed; and I made no doubt we should be able to deal well enough with the ten that were coming, considering that the captain had said there were three or four honest men among them also. As soon as they got to the place where their other boat lay, they ran their boat into the beach and came all on shore, hauling the boat up after them, which I was glad to see, for I was afraid they would rather have left the boat at an anchor some distance from the shore, with some hands in her, to guard her, and so we should not be able to seize the boat. Being on shore, the first thing they did was to run to their other boat; and it was easy to see they were under a great surprise to find her stripped of all that was in her and a great hole in her bottom. After they had mused awhile upon this, they set up two or three great shouts, halloing with all their might, to try if they could make their companions hear; but all was to no purpose; then they came all close in a ring and fired a volley of their small arms, which, indeed, we heard, and the echoes made the woods ring, but it was all one: Those in the cave, we were sure, could not hear, and those in our keeping, though they heard it well enough, yet dared give no answer to them. They were so astonished at this that, as they told us afterward, they resolved to go all on board again to their ship and let them know that the men were all murdered and the long-boat staved. Accordingly, they immediately launched their boat again and got all of them on board.

The captain was terribly amazed, and even confounded, at this, believing they would go on board the ship again and set sail, giving their comrades over for lost, and so he should still lose the ship, which he was in hopes we should have recovered; but he was quickly as much frightened the other way.

They had not been long put off with the boat, when we perceived them all coming on shore again; but with this new measure in their conduct, which it seems they consulted together upon, namely, to leave three men in the boat, and the rest to go on shore and go up into the country to look for their fellows. This was a great disappointment to us, for now we were at a loss what to do, as our seizing those seven men on shore would be no advantage to us if we let the boat escape; because they would row away to the ship, and then the rest of them would be sure to weigh and set sail, and so our chance to recover the ship would be lost. However, we had no remedy but to wait and see what the issue of things might present. The seven men came on shore, and the three who remained in the boat put her off to a good distance from the shore and came to an anchor to wait for them; so that it was impossible for us to come at them in the boat. Those that came on shore kept close together, marching toward the top of the little hill under which my habitation lay; and we could see them plainly, though they could not perceive us. We should have been very glad if they would have come nearer to us, so that we might have fired at them, or that they would have gone farther off, so that we might come abroad. But when they were come to the brow of the hill where they could see a great way into the valleys and woods, which lay toward the northeast part and where the island lay lowest, they shouted and halloed till they were weary. Not caring, it seems, to venture far from the shore, nor far from one another, they sat down together, under a tree, to consider of it. Had they thought fit to have gone to sleep there, as the other party of them had done, they had done the job for us; but they were too full of apprehensions of danger to venture to go to sleep, though they could not tell what the danger was they had to fear.

The captain made a very just proposal to me upon this consultation of theirs, namely, that perhaps they would all fire a volley again, to endeavor to make their fellows hear, and that we should all sally upon them just at the juncture when their pieces were all discharged, and they would certainly yield, and we should have them without bloodshed. I liked this proposal, provided it was done while we were near enough to come up to them before they could load their pieces again. But this event did not happen; and we lay still a long time, very irresolute what course to take. At length, I told them there would be nothing done, in my opinion, till night; and then if they did not return to the boat, perhaps we might find a way to get between them and the shore and so might use some stratagem with them in the boat to get them on shore. We waited a great while, though very impatient for their removing, and were very uneasy, when, after long consultation, we saw them all start up and march down toward the sea. It seems they had such dreadful apprehensions of the danger of the place that they resolved to go on board the ship again, give their companions over for lost, and so go on with their intended voyage with the ship.

The Mutineers Surprised

As soon as I perceived them go toward the shore, I imagined it to be as it really was, that they had given over their search and were for going back again; and the captain, as soon as I told him my thoughts, was ready to sink at the apprehensions of it. But I presently thought of a stratagem to fetch them back again and which answered my end to a tittle. I ordered Friday and the captain's mate to go over the little creek westward, toward the place where the savages came on shore when Friday was rescued, and as soon as they came to a little rising ground, at about half a mile distant, I bade them hallo out as loud as they could and wait till they found the seamen heard them; that as soon as they heard the seamen answer them, they should return it again; and, then keeping out of sight, take a round, always answering when the others halloed, to draw them as far into the island and among the woods, as possible, and then wheel about again to me by such ways as I directed.

They were just going into the boat when Friday and the mate halloed; and they presently heard them and, answering, ran along the shore westward, toward the voices they heard, when they were presently stopped by the creek, where, the water being up, they could not get over; and they called for the boat to come up and set them over, as, indeed, I expected. When they had set themselves over, I observed that the boat being gone up a good way into the creek, and, as it were, in a harbor within the land, they took one of the three men out of her, to go along with them, and left only two in the boat, having fastened her to the stump of a little tree on the shore. This was what I wished for; and immediately leaving Friday and the captain's mate to their business, I took the rest with me, and crossing the creek out of their sight, we surprised the two men before they were aware; one of them lying on the shore, and the other being in the boat. The fellow on shore was between sleeping and waking, and as he started to get up, the captain, who was foremost, ran in upon him and knocked him down; then he called out to him in the boat to yield, or he was a dead man. There needed very few arguments to persuade a single man to yield when he saw five men upon him and his comrade knocked down. Besides, this was, it seems, one of the three who were not so hearty in the mutiny as the rest of the crew; and, therefore, he was easily persuaded not only to yield, but afterward to join very sincerely with us. In the meantime, Friday and the captain's mate so well managed their business with the rest that they drew them, by halloing and answering, from one hill to another, and from one wood to another, till they not only heartily tired them, but left them where they could not reach back to the boat before it was dark; and, indeed, they were heartily tired themselves also, by the time they came back to us.

We had nothing now to do but to watch for them in the dark and to fall upon them, so as to make sure work with them. It was several hours after Friday came back to me before they came back to their boat; and we could hear the foremost of them, long before they came quite up, calling to those behind to come along; and could also hear them answer and complain how lame and tired they were, and that they were not able to come any faster: which was very welcome news to us. At length they came up to the boat; but it was impossible to express their confusion when they found their boat fast aground in the creek, the tide ebbed out, and their two men gone. We could hear them call to one another in the most lamentable manner, telling one another they were got into an enchanted island; that either there were inhabitants on it, and they should all be murdered, or else there were devils and spirits on it, and they should be all carried away and devoured. They halloed again and called their two comrades by their names a great many times, but no answer. After some time, we could see them, by the little light there was, running about, wringing their hands like men in despair; and sometimes they would go and sit down in the boat to rest themselves, then come ashore again and walk about again, and so the same thing over again. My men would fain have had me give them leave to fall upon them at once in the dark; but I was willing to take them at some advantage, so to spare them and kill as few of them as I could; and especially I was unwilling to hazard the killing of any of our men, knowing the others were very well armed. I resolved to wait, to see if they did not separate; and therefore, to make sure of them, I drew my ambuscade nearer and ordered Friday and the captain to creep upon their hands and feet, as close to the ground as they could, that they might not be discovered, and get as near them as they possibly could before they offered to fire.

Surrender at Discretion

They had not been long in that posture when the boatswain, who was the principal ringleader of the mutiny, and had now shown himself the most dejected and dispirited of all the rest, came walking toward them with two more of the crew; the captain was so eager at having the principal rogue so much in his power that he could hardly have patience to let him come so near as to be sure of him, for they only heard his talking before; but when they came nearer, the captain and Friday, starting up on their feet, let fly at them. The boatswain was killed upon the spot; the next man was shot in the body and fell just by him, though he did not die till an hour or two after; and the third ran for it. At the noise of the fire, I immediately advanced with my whole army, which was now eight men: namely, myself, generalissimo; Friday, my lieutenant-general; the captain and his two men, and the three prisoners of war whom we had trusted with arms. We came upon them, indeed, in the dark, so that they could not see our number; and I made the man they had left in the boat, and who was now one of us, call them by name, to try if I could bring them to a parley and so perhaps reduce them to terms; which fell out just as we desired; for, indeed, it was easy to think, as their condition then was, they would be very willing to capitulate.

So he called out as loud as he could to one of them, "Tom Smith! Tom Smith!"

Tom Smith answered immediately, "Who's that? Robinson?" for it seems he knew the voice.

The other answered, "Aye, aye; for God's sake, Tom Smith, throw down your arms and yield, or you are all dead men this moment."

"Who must we yield to? Where are they?" said Smith again.

"Here they are," said he. "Here's our captain and fifty men with him, who have been hunting you these two hours; the boatswain is killed, Will Frye is wounded, and I am a prisoner; and if you do not yield, you are all lost."

"Will they give us quarter then?" said Tom Smith. "If so, we will yield."

"I'll go and ask, if you promise to yield," said Robinson.

So he asked the captain, and the captain himself then called out, "You, Smith, you know my voice; if you lay down your arms immediately and submit, you shall have your lives, all but Will Atkins."

Upon this, Will Atkins cried out, "For God's sake, Captain, give me quarter; what have I done? They have all been as bad as I"—which, by the way, was not true; for it seems this Will Atkins was the first man that laid hold of the captain, when they first mutinied, and used him barbarously, in tying his hands and in speaking harshly to him.

However, the captain told him he must lay down his arms at discretion and trust to the governor's mercy; by which he meant me, for they all called me "Governor." In a word, they all laid down their arms and begged for their lives; and I sent the man that had parleyed with them, and two more, who bound them all. Then my great army of fifty men, which, with those three, were in all but eight, came up and seized them and their boat; only I kept myself and one more out of sight, for reasons of state.

Our next work was to repair the boat and think of seizing the ship; and as for the captain, now he had leisure to parley with them, he expostulated with them upon the villainy of their treatment of him, and upon the further wickedness of their plans, and how certainly it must bring them to misery and distress in the end, and perhaps to the gallows. They all appeared very penitent and begged hard for their lives. As for that, he told them they were none of them his prisoners, but the commander of the island's; that they mistakenly thought they had set him on shore in a barren, uninhabited island; but it had pleased God so to direct them that it was inhabited and that the governor was an Englishman; that he might hang them all there, if he pleased—but as he had given them all quarter, he supposed he would send them to England to be dealt with there as justice required, except Atkins, whom he was commanded by the governor to advise to prepare for death, for that he would be hanged in the morning.

Though this was all a fiction of his own, yet it had its desired effect: Atkins fell upon his knees to beg the captain to intercede with the governor for his life; and all the rest begged of him, for God's sake, that they might not be sent to England.

It now occurred to me that the time of our deliverance was come and that it would be a most easy thing to persuade these fellows to be hearty in getting possession of the ship; so I retired in the dark from them that they might not see what kind of a governor they had and called the captain to me.

When I called, as at a good distance, one of the men was ordered to speak again, and he said to the captain, "Captain, the commander calls for you," and presently the captain replied, "Tell his excellency, I am just coming."

This more perfectly amazed them, and they all believed that the commander was just by, with his fifty men. Upon the captain coming to me, I told him my project for seizing the ship, which he liked wonderfully well and resolved to put it in execution the next morning. But in order to execute it with more art and to be secure of success, I told him we must divide the prisoners, and that he should go and take Atkins and two more of the worst of them and send them pinioned to the cave where the others lay. This was committed to Friday and the two men who came on shore with the captain. They conveyed them to the cave as to a prison: and it was, indeed, a dismal place, especially to men in their condition. The others I ordered to my bower, as I called it, of which I have given a full description; and as it was fenced in, and they were pinioned, the place was secure enough, considering they were upon their best behavior.

To these in the morning I sent the captain, who was to enter into a parley with them; in a word, to try them and tell me whether he thought they might be trusted or not to go on board and surprise the ship. He talked to them of the injury done him, of the condition they were brought to, and that though the governor had given them quarter for their lives as to the present action, yet that if they were sent to England, they would be all hanged in chains; but that if they would join in such an attempt as to recover the ship, he would have the governor's engagement for their pardon.

Anyone may guess how readily such a proposal would be accepted by men in their position. They fell down on their knees to the captain and promised, with the deepest fervor, that they would be faithful to him to the last drop and that they should owe their lives to him and would go with him all over the world; that they would own him for a father to them as long as they lived.

"Well," said the captain, "I must go and tell the governor what you say, and see what I can do to bring him to consent to it."

So he brought me an account of the temper he found them in, and that he verily believed they would be faithful. However, that we might be very secure, I told him he should go back again and choose out five of them and tell them that they might see that he did not lack men, that he would take out those five to be his assistants, and that the governor would keep the other two and the three that were sent prisoners to the castle (my cave), as hostages for the fidelity of those five; and that if they proved unfaithful in the execution, the five hostages should be hanged in chains alive on the shore. This looked severe and convinced them that the governor was in earnest; however, they had no way left them but to accept it; and it was now the business of the prisoners, as much as of the captain, to persuade the other five to do their duty.

Our strength was now thus ordered for the expedition: first, the captain, his mate, and passenger; second, the two prisoners of the first gang, to whom, having their character from the captain, I had given their liberty and trusted them with arms; third, the other two whom I had kept till now in my bower pinioned, but, upon the captain's motion, had now released; fourth, these five released at last: so that they were twelve in all, besides five we kept prisoners in the cave for hostages.

I asked the captain if he was willing to venture with these hands on board the ship; for as for me and my man Friday, I did not think it was proper for us to stir, having seven men left behind; and it was employment enough for us to keep them asunder and supply them with victuals. As to the five in the cave, I resolved to keep them fast, but Friday went in twice a day to them, to supply them with necessaries; and I made the other two carry provisions to a certain distance, where Friday was to take it from there.

When I showed myself to the two hostages, it was with the captain, who told them I was the person the governor had ordered to look after them; and that it was the governor's pleasure that they should not stir anywhere but by my direction; that if they did, they would be fetched into the castle and be laid in irons: so that as we never suffered them to see me as governor, I now appeared as another person and spoke of the governor, the garrison, the castle, and the like, upon all occasions.

The Attack on the Ship

The captain now had no difficulty before him, but to furnish his two boats, stop the breach of one, and man them. He made his passenger captain of one, with four other men; and himself, his mate, and five more went in the other; and they contrived their business very well, for they came up to the ship about midnight. As soon as they came within call of the ship, he made Robinson hail them and tell them they had brought off the men and the boat, but that it was a long time before they had found them, and the like, holding them in a chat till they came to the ship's side; when the captain and the mate, entering first with their arms, immediately knocked down the second mate and carpenter with the butt end of their muskets, being very faithfully seconded by their men; they secured all the rest that were upon the main and quarterdecks and began to fasten the hatches to keep them down that were below; when the other boat and their men, entering at the fore-chains, secured the forecastle of the ship and the scuttle that went down into the cook-room, making three men they found their prisoners.

When this was done, and all safe upon deck, the captain ordered the mate, with three men, to break into the roundhouse, where the new rebel captain lay, who, having taken the alarm, had got up and with two men and a boy had got firearms in their hands. When the mate, with a crowbar, split open the door, the new captain and his men fired boldly among them and wounded the mate with a musket-ball, which broke his arm, and wounded two more of the men, but killed nobody. The mate, calling for help, rushed, however, into the roundhouse, wounded as he was, and, with his pistol, shot the new captain through the head, . . . so that he never spoke a word more; upon which the rest yielded, and the ship was taken effectually, without any more lives lost.

Chapter 19

Leaving the Island

As soon as the ship was thus secured, the captain ordered seven guns to be fired, which was the signal agreed upon with me to give me notice of his success, which, you may be sure, I was very glad to hear, having sat watching upon the shore for it till nearly two o'clock in the morning. Having thus heard the signal plainly, I laid me down; and it having been a day of great fatigue to me, I slept very soundly, till I was something surprised with the noise of a gun; and presently starting up, I heard a man calling me by the name of "Governor! Governor!" and presently I knew the captain's voice; when climbing up to the top of the hill, there he stood, and, pointing to the ship, he embraced me in his arms.

"My dear friend and deliverer," said he, "there's your ship; for she is all yours, and so are we, and all that belongs to her."

I cast my eyes to the ship, and there she rode, within little more than half a mile of the shore; for they had weighed her anchor as soon as they were masters of her and, the weather being fair, had brought her to an anchor just against the mouth of the little creek; and, the tide being up, the captain had brought the pinnace in near the place where I first landed my rafts and so landed just at my door. I was at first ready to sink down with the surprise, for I saw my deliverance, indeed, visibly put into my hands, all things easy, and a large ship just ready to carry me away wherever I pleased to go.

At first, for some time, I was not able to answer one word; but as he had taken me in his arms, I held fast by him, or I should have fallen to the ground. He perceived the surprise and immediately pulled a bottle out of his pocket and gave me a dram of cordial, which he had brought on purpose for me. After I had drunk it, I sat down upon the ground; and though it brought me to myself, yet it was a good while before I could speak a word to him. All this while, the poor man was in as great an ecstasy as I, only not under any surprise as I was; and he said a thousand kind and gentle things to me, to compose and bring me to myself, but such was the flood of joy in my breast that it put all my spirits into confusion; at last I broke into tears. In a little while after, I recovered my speech; then I took my turn and embraced him as my deliverer, and we rejoiced together. I told him I looked upon him as a man sent from Heaven to deliver me and that the whole transaction seemed to be a chain of wonders; that such things as these were the testimonies we had of a secret hand of Providence governing the world and an evidence that the eye of an Infinite Power could search into the remotest corner of the world and send help to the miserable whenever He pleased. I forgot not to lift up my heart in thankfulness to Heaven; and what heart could forbear to bless Him, Who had not only in a miraculous manner provided for one in such a wilderness and in such a desolate condition, but from Whom every deliverance must always be acknowledged to proceed.

When we had talked awhile, the captain told me he had brought me some little refreshments, such as the ship afforded and such as the wretches that had been so long his masters had not plundered him of. Upon this, he called aloud to the boat and bade his men bring the things ashore that were for the governor; and, indeed, it was a present as if I had been one that was not to be carried away along with them, but as if I had been to dwell upon the island still, and they were to go without me. First, he had brought me a case of bottles full of excellent cordial waters, six large bottles of Madeira wine (the bottles held two quarts each), two pounds of excellent good tobacco, twelve good pieces of the ship's beef, and six pieces of pork, with a bag of peas, and about a hundredweight of biscuit; he also brought me a box of sugar, a box of flour, a bag full of lemons, and two bottles of lime juice, and an abundance of other things. But besides these, and what was a thousand times more useful, he brought me six new clean shirts, six very good neckcloths, two pair of gloves, one pair of shoes, a hat, and one pair of stockings, and a very good suit of clothes of his own, which had been worn but very little: In a word, he clothed me from head to foot. It was a very kind and agreeable present, as anyone may imagine, to one in my circumstances; but never was anything in the world of that kind so unpleasant, awkward, and uneasy as it was to me to wear such clothes at their first putting on.

After these ceremonies were past, and after all his good things were brought into my little apartment, we began to consult what was to be done with the prisoners we had; for it was worth considering whether we might venture to take them away with us or no, especially two of them, whom he knew to be incorrigible and refractory to the last degree; and the captain said he knew they were such rogues that there was no obliging them, and if he did carry them away, it must be in irons, as malefactors, to be delivered over to justice at the first English colony he could come at; and I found that the captain himself was very anxious about it. Upon this, I told him that, if he desired it, I would undertake to bring the two men he spoke of to make it their own request that he should leave them upon the island.

"I should be very glad of that," said the captain, "with all my heart."

"Well," said I, "I will send for them and talk with them for you."

So I caused Friday and the two hostages, for they were now discharged, their comrades having performed their promise; I say, I caused them to go to the cave and bring up the five men, pinioned as they were, to the bower and keep them there till I came. After some time, I came there dressed in my new habit; and now I was called governor again. Being all met and the captain with me, I caused the men to be brought before me, and I told them I had got a full account of their villainous behavior to the captain, and how they had run away with the ship and were preparing to commit further robberies, but that Providence had ensnared them in their own ways and that they were fallen into the pit that they had dug for others. I let them know that by my direction the ship had been seized; that she lay now in the road[1]; and they might see by and by that their new captain had received the reward of his villainy. For they might see him hanging at the yardarm. That, as for them, I wanted to know what they had to say why I should not execute them as pirates, taken in the act, for by my commission they could not doubt but I had authority to do so.

One of them answered in the name of the rest: that they had nothing to say but this, that when they were taken, the captain promised them their lives, and they humbly implored my mercy. But I told them I knew not what mercy to show them; for as for myself I had resolved to quit the island with all my men and had taken passage with the captain to go to England; and as for the captain, he could not carry them to England other than as prisoners in irons, to be tried for mutiny and running away with the ship; the consequence of which, they must needs know, would be the gallows; so that I could not tell what was the best for them, unless they had a mind to take their fate on the island. If they desired that, I did not care. As I had liberty to leave it, I had some inclination to give them their lives, if they thought they could shift on shore. They seemed very thankful for it, and said they would much rather venture to stay there than be carried to England to be hanged. So I left it at that.

1. *Road,* main shipping lane or channel.

The Fate of the New Captain

However, the captain seemed to make some difficulty of it, as if he dared not leave them there. Upon this I seemed a little angry with the captain and told him that they were my prisoners, not his; and that seeing I had offered them so much favor, I would be as good as my word; and that if he did not think fit to consent to it, I would set them at liberty, as I found them; and if he did not like it, he might take them again if he could catch them. Upon this they appeared very thankful, and I accordingly set them at liberty and bade them retire into the woods, to the place from which they had come, and I would leave them some firearms, some ammunition, and some directions on how they

should live very well, if they thought fit. Upon this I prepared to go on board the ship, but told the captain I would stay that night to prepare my things and desired him to go on board in the meantime, and keep order there, and send the boat on shore the next day for me; ordering him, in the meantime, to cause the new captain, who was killed, to be hanged at the yardarm, that these men might see him.

When the captain was gone, I had the men brought up to me in my apartment and entered seriously into discourse with them of their circumstances. I told them I thought they had made a right choice; but if the captain had carried them away, they would certainly be hanged. I showed them the new captain hanging at the yardarm of the ship and told them they had nothing less to expect.

When they had all declared their willingness to stay, I told them I would let them into the story of my living there and put them into the way of making it easy for them. Accordingly, I gave them the whole history of the place and of my coming to it; I showed them my fortifications, the way I made my bread, planted my corn, cured my grapes—in a word, all that was necessary to make them comfortable. I told them the story also of the sixteen Spaniards who were to be expected, for whom I left a letter, and made them promise to treat them in common with themselves.

I left them my firearms, namely, five muskets, three fowling-pieces, and three swords. I had a little more than a barrel and a half of powder left; for after the first year or two, I used but little and wasted none. I gave them a description of the way I managed the goats, and directions to milk and fatten them and to make both butter and cheese. In a word, I gave them every part of my story and told them I should prevail with the captain to leave them two barrels of gunpowder more and some garden seeds, which I told them I would have been very glad of. Also, I gave them the bag of peas that the captain had brought me to eat and bade them be sure to sow and increase them.

Having done all this, I left the next day and went on board the ship. We prepared immediately to sail, but did not weigh that night. The next morning early, two of the five men came swimming to the ship's side and made the most lamentable complaint of the other three, begged to be taken into the ship for God's sake, for they should be murdered, and begged the captain to take them on board, though he hanged them immediately. Upon this, the captain pretended to have no power without me; but after some difficulty, and after their solemn promises of reformation, they were taken on board and were, some time after, soundly whipped and pickled,[2] after which they proved very honest and quiet fellows.

Some time after this, I went with the boat on shore, the tide being up, with the things promised to the men; to which the captain, at my intercession, caused their chests and clothes to be added, which they took and were very thankful for. I also encouraged them by telling them that if it lay in my way to send any vessel to take them in, I would not forget them.

When I took leave of this island, I carried on board, for relics, the great goatskin cap I had made, my umbrella, and one of my parrots; also I forgot not to take the money I formerly mentioned, which had lain by me so long useless that it was grown rusty or tarnished and could hardly pass for silver till it had been a little rubbed and handled, and also the money I found in the wreck of the Spanish ship. And thus I left the island, the 19th of December, as I found by the ship's account, in the year 1686, after I had been upon it eight-and-twenty years, two months, and nineteen days; being delivered from the second captivity the same day of the month that I first made my escape in the longboat from among the Moors of Sallee. In this vessel, after a long voyage, I arrived in England the 11th of June, in the year 1687, having been five-and-thirty years absent.

In England Again

When I came to England, I was a perfect stranger to all the world, as if I had never been known there. My benefactor and faithful steward, whom I had left my money in trust with, was alive, but had had great misfortunes in the world; was become a widow the second time, and was very low in the world. I made her easy as to what she owed me, assuring her I would give her no trouble; but, on the contrary, in gratitude for her former care and faithfulness to me, I relieved her as my little stock would afford; which at that time would, indeed, allow me to do but little for her. But I assured her I would never forget her former kindness to me; nor did I forget her when I had sufficient to help her, as shall be observed in its place. I went down afterward into Yorkshire; but my father was dead, and my mother and all the family extinct, except that I found two sisters and two of the children of one of my brothers; and as I had been long ago given over for dead, there had been no provision made for me; so that in a word, I found nothing to relieve or assist me; and what little money I had would not do much for me as to settling in the world.

I met with one piece of gratitude, indeed, which I did not expect; and this

---

2. *Pickled,* rubbing salt and vinegar on back wounds after whipping, both to heighten the punishment and to prevent infection.

was that the master of the ship, whom I had so happily delivered, and by the same means saved the ship and cargo, gave a very handsome account to the owners of the manner how I had saved the lives of the men and the ship, and they invited me to meet them and some other merchants concerned, and altogether made me a very handsome compliment upon the subject and a present of almost two hundred pounds sterling.

But after making several reflections upon the circumstances of my life and how little these funds would go toward settling me in the world, I resolved to go to Lisbon and see if I might not come by some information of the state of my plantation in the Brazils and of what was become of my partner, who, I had reason to suppose, had some years now given me over for dead. With this view I took shipping for Lisbon, where I arrived in April following, my man Friday accompanying me in all these ramblings and proving a most faithful servant upon all occasions. When I came to Lisbon, I found, by inquiry and to my particular satisfaction, my old friend, the captain of the ship that first took me up at sea off the shore of Africa. He was now grown old and had left the sea, having put his son, who was far from a young man, into his ship and who still used the Brazil trade. The old man did not know me; and indeed, I hardly knew him. But I soon brought myself to his remembrance when I told him who I was.

The Old Captain's Accounts

After some passionate expressions of the old acquaintance between us, I inquired, you may be sure, after my plantation and my partner. The old man told me he had not been in the Brazils for about nine years; but that he could assure me that when he came away my partner was living; but the trustees, whom I had joined with him to take cognizance of my part, were both dead; that, however, he believed that I would have a very good account of the improvement of the plantation; for that, upon the general belief of my being cast away and drowned, my trustees had given in the account of the produce of my part of the plantation to the procurator-fiscal, who had appropriated it, in case I never came to claim it: one-third to the king, and two-thirds to the monastery of St. Augustine, to be expended for the benefit of the poor and for the conversion of the Indians to the Catholic faith; but that, if I appeared, or anyone for me, to claim the inheritance, it would be restored. Only the improvement, or annual production, being distributed to charitable uses, could not be restored, but he assured me that the steward of the king's revenue from lands, and the providore, or steward of the monastery, had taken great care all along that the incumbent, that is to say, my partner, gave every year a faithful account of the produce, of which they had received duly my moiety. I asked him if he knew to what height of improvement he had brought the plantation, and whether he thought it might be worth looking after; or whether, on my going there, I should meet with any obstruction to my possessing my just right in the moiety. He told me he could not tell exactly to what degree the plantation was improved; but this he knew, that my partner was grown exceedingly rich upon enjoying but one-half of it; and that to the best of his remembrance, he had heard that the king's third of my part, which was, it seems, granted away to some other monastery or religious house, amounted to above two hundred moidores a year: that as to my being restored to a quiet possession of it, there was no question to be made of that, my partner being alive to witness my title and my name being also enrolled in the register of the country. Also, he told me that the survivors of my two trustees were very fair, honest people, and very wealthy; and he believed I would not only have their assistance for putting me in possession, but would find a very considerable sum of money in their hands for my account, being the produce of the farm while their father held the trust and before it was given up, as above; which, as he remembered, was for about twelve years.

I showed myself a little concerned and uneasy at this account and inquired of the old captain how it came to pass that the trustees should thus dispose of my effects, when he knew that I had made my will and had made him, the Portuguese captain, my universal heir, etc.

He told me that was true; but that as there was no proof of my being dead, he could not act as executor until some certain account should come of my death; and that besides, he was not willing to intermeddle with a thing so remote; that it was true he had registered my will and put in his claim; and could he have given any account of my being dead or alive, he would have acted by procuration and taken possession of the *ingenio*, and have given his son, who was now in the Brazils, orders to do it.

"But," said the old man, "I have one piece of news to tell you, which perhaps may not be so acceptable to you as the rest; and that is, believing you were lost, and all the world believing so also, your partner and trustees did offer to account with me, in your name, for the first six or eight years' profits, which I received. There being at that time great disbursements for increasing the works, building an *ingenio*, and buying slaves, it did not amount to nearly so much as afterward it produced; however, I shall give you a true account of what I have received in all, and how I have disposed of it."

After a few days' further conference with this old friend, he brought me an account of the first six years' income of my plantation, signed by my partner and the merchant-trustees, being always delivered in goods, that is, tobacco in rolls, and sugar in chests, besides rum, molasses, etc., which is the consequence of a sugar work; and I found by this account that every year the income considerably increased; but, as above, the disbursements being large, the sum at first was small. However, the old man let me see that he was debtor to me for four hundred and seventy moidores of gold, besides sixty chests of sugar, and fifteen double rolls of tobacco, which were lost in his ship; he having been shipwrecked coming home to Lisbon about eleven years after my leaving the place. The good man then began to complain of his misfortunes and how he had been obliged to make use of my money to recover his losses and buy him a share in a new ship.

"However, my old friend," said he, "you shall not want a supply in your necessity; and as soon as my son returns, you shall be fully satisfied."

Upon this he pulled out an old pouch and gave me one hundred and sixty Portuguese moidores in gold; and giving me the writings of his title to the ship, which his son was gone to the Brazils in, of which he was quarter-part owner and his son another, he put them both in my hands for security of the rest.

I was too much moved with the honesty and kindness of the poor man to be able to bear this; and remembering what he had done for me, how he had taken me up at sea, and how generously he had used me on all occasions, and particularly how sincere a friend he was now to me, I could hardly refrain from weeping at what he had said to me; therefore, first, I asked him if his circumstances admitted him to spare so much money at that time, and if it would not straiten him? He told me he could not say but it might straiten him a little; however, it was my money, and I might need it more than he.

Everything the good man said was full of affection, and I could hardly refrain from tears while he spoke; in short, I took one hundred of the moidores and called for a pen and ink to give him a receipt for them; then I returned him the rest and told him if ever I had possession of the plantation I would return the other to him also (as, indeed, I afterward did); and that as to the bill of sale of his part in his son's ship, I would not take it by any means; but that if I wanted the money, I found he was honest enough to pay me; and if I did not, but came to receive what he gave me reason to expect, I would never have a penny more from him.

Wealth

When this was past, the old man began to ask me if he should put me into a method to make my claim to my plantation. I told him I thought to go over to it myself. He said I might do so if I pleased; but that, if I did not, there were ways enough to secure my right and immediately to appropriate the profits to my use. As there were ships in the river of Lisbon just ready to go away to Brazil, he made me enter my name in a public register, with his affidavit, affirming, upon oath, that I was alive and that I was the same person who took up the land for planting the said plantation at first. This being regularly attested by a notary and a procuration affixed, he directed me to send it, with a letter of his writing, to a merchant of his acquaintance at the place; and then proposed my staying with him till an account came of the return.

Never was anything more honorable than the proceedings upon this procuration; for in less than seven months I received a large packet from the survivors of my trustees, the merchants for whose account I went to sea, in which were the following particular letters and papers enclosed.

First, there was the account-current of the produce of my farm or plantation, from the year when their father had balanced with my old Portuguese captain, being for six years; the balance appeared to be 1,174 moidores in my favor.

Secondly, there was the account of four years more, while they kept the effects in their hands, before the government claimed the administration, as being the effects of a person not to be found, which they called civil death; and the balance of this, the value of the plantation increasing, amounted to 19,446 crusadoes, being about 3,240 moidores.

Thirdly, there was the Prior of St. Augustine's account, who had received the profits for above fourteen years; but not being able to account for what was disposed of by the hospital, very honestly declared he had 872 moidores not distributed, which he acknowledged to my account. As to the king's part, that refunded nothing.

There was also a letter of my partner's, congratulating me very affectionately upon my being alive, giving me an account of how the estate was improved and what it produced a year; with the particulars of the number of squares or acres that it contained, how planted, and how many slaves there were upon it. And making two-and-twenty crosses for blessings, told me he had said so many Ave Marias to thank the Blessed Virgin that I was alive and urged me to come over and take possession of my own; and, in the meantime, to give him orders to whom he should deliver my effects, if I did not come myself. He concluded with a hearty tender of his friendship and that of his family; and sent me, as a present, seven fine leopards' skins, which he had, it seems, received from Africa, by some other ship that he had sent there, and which, it seems, had made a better voyage than I. He sent me also five chests of excellent sweetmeats and a hundred pieces of gold uncoined, not quite so large as moidores. By the same fleet, my two merchant-trustees shipped me one thousand two hundred chests of sugar, eight hundred rolls of tobacco, and the rest of the whole account in gold.

I might well say now, indeed, that the latter end of Job was better than the beginning. It is impossible to express the flutterings of my very heart when I looked over these letters, and especially when I found all my wealth about me; as the Brazil ships come all in fleets, the same ships that brought my letters brought my goods: and the effects were safe on the river before the letters came to my hand. In a word, I turned pale and grew ill; and, had not the old man run and fetched me a cordial, I believe the sudden surprise of joy had overset nature, and I had died upon the spot. After that, I continued very ill and was so some hours, till a physician being sent for, and something of the real cause of my illness being known, he ordered me to let blood; after which I had relief and grew well. But I verily believe, if I had not been eased by the vent given in that manner to the spirits, I should have died.

I was now master, all of a sudden, of above fifty thousand pounds sterling in money and had an estate, as I might well call it, in the Brazils, of above a thousand pounds a year, as sure as an estate of lands in England: and, in a word, I was in a condition that I scarcely knew how to understand or how to compose myself for the enjoyment of. The first thing I did was to recompense my original benefactor, my good old captain, who had been first charitable to me in my distress, kind to me in the beginning, and honest to me at the end. I showed him all that was sent to me; I told him that, next to the providence of Heaven, which disposes all things, it was owing to him; and that it now behooved me to reward him, which I would do a hundredfold. I first returned to him the hundred moidores I had received of him; then I sent for a notary and caused him to draw up a general release or discharge from the four hundred and seventy moidores, which he had acknowledged he owed me, in the fullest and firmest manner possible. After which, I caused a procuration to be drawn, empowering him to be the receiver of the annual profits of my plantation; and appointing my partner to account him and make the returns, by the usual fleets, to him in my name; and by a clause in the end, made a grant of one hundred moidores a year to him during his life, out of the effects, and fifty moidores a year to his son after him, for his life: and thus I requited my old man.

I had now to consider which way to steer my course next and what to do with the estate that Providence had thus put into my hands; and indeed, I had more care upon my head now than I had in my silent state of life in the island, where I wanted nothing but what I had and had nothing but what I wanted; whereas I had now a great charge upon me, and my business was how to secure it. I had not a cave now to hide my money in, or a place where it might lie without lock or key, till it grew moldy and tarnished before anybody would meddle with it; on the contrary, I knew not where to put it, or whom to trust with it. My old patron, the captain, indeed, was honest, and that was the only refuge I had. In the next place, my interest in the Brazils seemed to summon me there; but now I could not tell how to think of going there till I had settled my affairs and left my effects in some safe hands behind me. At first I thought of my old friend the widow, who I knew was honest and would be just to me; but then she was in years, and but poor, and, for aught I knew, might be in debt; so that, in a word, I had no way but to go back to England myself and take my effects with me.

It was some months, however, before I resolved upon this; and therefore, as I had rewarded the old captain fully, and to his satisfaction, who had been my former benefactor, so I began to think of my poor widow, whose husband had been my first benefactor, and she, while it was in her power, my faithful steward and instructor. So, the first thing I did, I got a merchant in Lisbon to write to his correspondent in London, not only to pay a bill, but to go find her out and carry her, in money, a hundred pounds from me, and to talk with her and comfort her in her poverty by telling her she should, if I lived, have a further supply. At the same time, I sent my two sisters in the country a hundred pounds each, they being, though not in want, yet not in very good circumstances; one having been married and left a widow; and the other having a husband not so kind to her as he should be. But, among all my relations or acquaintances, I could not yet pitch upon one to whom I dared to commit the gross of my stock that I might go away to the Brazils and leave things safe behind me; and this greatly perplexed me.

I had once a mind to have gone to the Brazils and have settled myself there, for I was, as it were, naturalized to the place; but I had some little scruple in my mind about religion, which insensibly drew me back, of which I shall say more presently. However, it was not religion that kept me from going there for the present; and as I had made no scruple of being openly of the religion of the country all the while I was among them, so neither did I yet; only that, now and then, having of late thought more of it than formerly, when I began to think of living and dying among them, I began to regret my having professed myself a papist and thought it might not be the best religion to die with.

But, as I have said, this was not the main thing that kept me from going to the Brazils, but that really I did not know with whom to leave my effects behind me; so I resolved at last to go to England with them, where, if I arrived, I concluded I should make some acquaintance, or find some relations, who would be faithful to me; and, accordingly, I prepared to go to England with all my wealth.

Preparations for Departure

In order to prepare things for my going home, I first (the Brazil fleet being just going away) resolved to give answers suitable to the just and faithful account of things I had from there; and, first, to the Prior of St. Augustine, I wrote a letter full of thanks for his just dealings and the offer of the 872 moidores that were undisposed of, which I desired might be given, 500 to the monastery, and 372 to the poor, as the Prior should direct; desiring the good padre's prayers for me, and the like. I wrote next a letter of thanks to my two trustees, with all the acknowledgment that so much justice and honesty called for; as for sending them any present, they were far above having any occasion of it. Lastly, I wrote to my partner, acknowledging his industry in improving the plantation and his integrity in increasing the stock of the works; giving him instructions for his future government of my part, according to the powers I had left with my old patron, to whom I desired him to send whatever became due to me, till he should hear from me more particularly; assuring him that it was my intention not only to come to him, but to settle myself there for the remainder of my life. To this I added a very handsome present of some Italian silks for his wife and two daughters, for such the captain's son informed me he had; with two pieces of fine English broadcloth, the best I could get in Lisbon, five pieces of black baize, and some Flanders lace of good value.

Having thus settled my affairs, sold my cargo, and turned all my effects into good bills of exchange, my next difficulty was which way to going to England: I had been accustomed enough to the sea, and yet I had a strange aversion to go to England by sea at that time; and though I could give no reason for it, yet the difficulty increased upon me so much that though I had once shipped my baggage in order to go, yet I altered my mind, and that not once, but two or three times.

It is true I had been very unfortunate by sea, and that might be one of the reasons; but let no man slight the strong impulses of his own thoughts in cases of such moment: two of the ships that I had singled out to go in—I mean, more particularly singled out than any other—having put my things on board one of them, and in the other having agreed with the captain; I say two of these ships miscarried; namely, one was taken by the Algerines, and the other was cast away on the Start, near Torbay, and all the people drowned, except three; so that in either of those vessels I had been made miserable, in which most, it was hard to say.

Having been thus harassed in my thoughts, my old pilot, to whom I communicated everything, pressed me earnestly not to go by sea, but either to go by land to the Groyne and cross over the Bay of Biscay to Rochelle, from which city it was but an easy and safe journey by land to Paris, and so to Calais and Dover; or to go up to Madrid, and so all the way by land through France. In a word, I was so prepossessed against my going by sea at all, except from Calais to Dover, that I resolved to travel all the way by land; which, as I was not in haste and did not mind the extra expense, was by much the pleasanter way: and to make it more so, my old captain brought an English gentleman, the son of a merchant in Lisbon, who was willing to travel with me; after which we picked up two more English merchants also, and two young Portuguese gentlemen, the last going to Paris only; so that in all, there were six of us, and five servants; the two merchants and the two Portuguese contenting themselves with one servant between two, to save the charge; and as for me, I got an English sailor to travel with me as a servant, besides my man Friday, who was too much a stranger to be capable of supplying the place of a servant upon the road.

In this manner, I set out from Lisbon; and our company being very well mounted and armed, we made a little troop, whereof they did me the honor to call me "Captain," as well because I was the oldest man as because I had two servants and, indeed, was the originator of the whole journey.

As I have troubled you with none of my sea journals, so I shall trouble you now with none of my land journals; but some adventures that happened to us in this tedious and difficult journey I must not omit.

Chapter 20
WOLVES

When we came to Madrid, being all of us strangers to Spain, we were willing to stay some time to see the court of Spain and what was worth observing; but it being the latter part of the summer, we hastened away and set out from Madrid about the middle of October. When we came to the edge of Navarre, we were alarmed, at several towns on the way, with an account that so much snow was fallen on the French side of the mountains that several travelers were obliged to come back to Pamplona after having attempted at extreme hazard to get through.

When we came to Pamplona itself, we found it so indeed; and to me, who had been always used to a hot climate and to countries where I could scarcely bear any clothes on, the cold was insufferable; nor, indeed, was it more painful than it was surprising to come but ten days before out of Old Castile, where the weather was not only warm but very hot, and immediately to feel a wind from the Pyrenean Mountains so very keen, so severely cold, as to be intolerable and to threaten benumbing and perishing of our fingers and toes.

Poor Friday was really frightened when he saw the mountains all covered with snow and felt cold weather, which he had never seen or felt before in his life. To make matters worse, after we came to Pamplona, it continued snowing with so much violence, and so long, that the people said winter was come before its time; and the roads, which had been difficult before, were now quite impassable; in a word, the snow lay in some places too thick for us to travel, and being not hard frozen, as is the case in the northern countries, there was no going on without being in danger of being buried alive every step. We stayed no less than twenty days at Pamplona, when (seeing the winter coming on and no likelihood of its being better, for it was the severest winter all over Europe that had been known in many years) I proposed that we should go away to Fontarabia, and there take shipping for Bordeaux, which was a very little voyage. But, while I was considering this, there came in four French gentlemen, who, having been stopped on the French side of the passes, as we were on the Spanish, had found out a guide, who, traversing the country near the head of Languedoc, had brought them over the mountains by such ways that they were not much incommoded with the snow; for where they met with snow in any quantity, they said it was frozen hard enough to bear them and their horses. We sent for this guide, who told us he would undertake to lead us the same way, with no hazard from the snow, provided we were armed sufficiently to protect ourselves from wild beasts; for, he said, in these great snows, frequently wolves would show themselves at the foot of the mountains, being made ravenous for want of food, the ground being covered with snow. We told him we were well enough prepared for such creatures as they were, if he would ensure us from a kind of two-legged wolves, which, we were told, we were in most danger from, especially on the French side of the mountains. He satisfied us that there was no danger of that kind in the way that we were to go; so we readily agreed to follow him, as did also twelve other gentlemen, with their servants, some French, some Spanish, who, as I said, had attempted to go and were obliged to come back again.

Accordingly, we set out from Pamplona with our guide on the 15th of November; and, indeed, I was surprised when, instead of going forward, he came directly back with us on the same road that we came on from Madrid, about twenty miles; when, having passed two rivers and come into the plain country, we found ourselves in a warm climate again, where the country was pleasant, and no snow to be seen. However, on a sudden turning to his left, he approached the mountains another way; and though it is true the hills and precipices looked dreadful, yet he made so many turns, so many meanders, and led us by such winding ways, that we unknowingly passed the crest of the mountains without being much encumbered with the snow; and suddenly, he showed us the pleasant and fruitful providences of Languedoc and Gascony, all green and flourishing, though, indeed, they were at a great distance, and we had some rough way to pass still.

We were a little uneasy, however, when we found it snowed one whole day and a night so fast that we could not travel; but he bid us be at ease; we should soon be past it all. We found, indeed, that we began to descend every day and to come more north than before; and so, depending upon our guide, we went on.

It was about two hours before night, when, our guide being somewhat ahead of us and not just in sight, out rushed three monstrous wolves and

after them a bear, from a hollow way adjoining to a thick wood. Two of the wolves flew upon the guide, and had he been far ahead of us, he would have been devoured before we could have helped him; one of them fastened upon his horse, and the other attacked the man with such violence that he had not time or presence of mind enough to draw his pistol, but halloed and cried out to us most lustily. My man Friday being next to me, I bade him ride up and see what was the matter. As soon as Friday came in sight of the man, he halloed out as loud as the other, "O master! O master!" but like a bold fellow, rode directly up to the man and, with his pistol, shot in the head the wolf that attacked him.

It was happy for the poor man that it was my man Friday; for, having been used to such creatures in his country, he had no fear of him, but went close up to him and shot him; whereas, any other of us would have fired at a farther distance and have perhaps either missed the wolf or risked shooting the man.

But it was enough to have terrified a bolder man than I; and, indeed, it alarmed all our company, when, with the noise of Friday's pistol, we heard on both sides the most dismal howling of wolves; and the noise, redoubled by the echo of the mountains, was to us as if there had been a prodigious number of them; and perhaps there were not such a few as that we had no cause of apprehension. However, as Friday had killed this wolf, the other that had fastened upon the horse left him immediately and fled, without doing the horse any damage, having luckily fastened upon his head, where the bosses of the bridle had stuck in his teeth. But the man was most hurt; for the raging creature had bitten him twice, once in the arm, and the other time a little above his knee; he was just, as it were, tumbling down by the disorder of his horse when Friday came up and shot the wolf.

Friday and the Bear

Not surprisingly, at the noise of Friday's pistol we all mended our pace and rode up as fast as the way, which was very difficult, would give us leave, to see what was the matter. As soon as we came clear of the trees, which blinded us before, we saw plainly what had been the case, and how Friday had disengaged the poor guide, though we did not presently discern what kind of a creature it was he had killed.

But never was a fight managed so hardily, and in such a surprising manner, as that which followed between Friday and the bear, which gave us all, though at first we were surprised and afraid for him, the greatest diversion imaginable. As the bear is a heavy, clumsy creature and does not gallop as the wolf does, which is swift and light, so he has two particular qualities, which generally are the rule of his actions; first, as to men, who are not his proper prey (he does not usually attempt them, except they first attack him, unless he be excessively hungry, which it is probable might now be the case, the ground being covered with snow), if you do not meddle with him, he will not meddle with you; but then you must take care to be very civil to him and give him the road, for he is a very nice gentleman; he will not go a step out of his way for a prince; nay, if you are really afraid, your best way is to look another way and keep going on; for sometimes if you stop, and stand still, and look steadfastly at him, he takes it for an affront; but if you throw or toss anything at him, and it hits him, though it were but a bit of stick as big as your finger, he takes it for an affront and sets all other business aside to pursue his revenge and will have satisfaction in point of honor—that is his first quality. The next is that if he be once affronted, he will never leave you, night or day, till he has had his revenge, but follow at a good round rate till he overtakes you.

My man Friday had delivered our guide, and when we came up to him, he was helping him off from his horse, for the man was both hurt and frightened, and indeed the last more than the first, when on a sudden we espied the bear coming out of the wood, and a vast, monstrous one it was, the biggest by far that ever I saw. We were all a little surprised when we saw him; but when Friday saw him, it was easy to see joy and courage in the fellow's countenance.

"Oh, oh, oh!" said Friday three times, pointing to him. "O master! You give me te leave, me shakee te hand with him; me makee you good laugh."

I was surprised to see the fellow so pleased. "You fool," said I, "he will eat you up."

"Eatee me up! Eatee me up!" said Friday twice over again. "Me eatee him up; me makee you good laugh; you all stay here, me show you good laugh."

So down he sat; he got his boots off in a moment and put on a pair of pumps (as we call the flat shoes they wear, and which he had in his pocket); then he gave my other servant his horse, and with his gun away he flew, swift as the wind.

The bear walked softly on and offered to meddle with nobody, till Friday, coming pretty near, called to him as if the bear could understand him.

"Hark ye, hark ye," said Friday, "me speakee with you."

We followed at a distance, for now being come down to the Gascony side of the mountains, we had entered a vast, great forest, where the country was plain and pretty open, though it had many trees in it scattered here and there. Friday, who had, as we say, the heels of the bear, came up with him quickly and took up a great stone and threw it at him, hitting him just on the head; but did him no more harm than if he had thrown it against a wall. But it answered Friday's end, for the rogue was so void of fear that he did it purely to make the bear follow him and show us some laugh, as he called it. As soon as the bear felt the stone and saw him, he turned about and came after him, taking very long strides and shuffling on at a strange rate, so as would have put a horse to a middling gallop. Away ran Friday, and he took his course as if he ran toward us for help; so we all resolved to fire at once upon the bear and deliver my man; though I was angry at him heartily for bringing the bear back upon us, when he was going about his own business another way; and especially I was angry that he had turned the bear upon us and then run away.

I called out to him. "You dog!" said I. "Is this your way of making us laugh? Come away, and take your horse, that we may shoot the creature."

He heard me and cried out, "No shoot, no shoot. Stand still, and get much laugh."

As the nimble creature ran two feet for the beast's one, he turned on a sudden on one side of us, and seeing a great oak tree fit for his purpose, he beckoned us to follow. Doubling his pace, he got nimbly up the tree, laying his gun down upon the ground at about five or six yards from the bottom of the tree. The bear soon came to the tree, and we followed at a distance; the first thing he did, he stopped at the gun, smelled it, but let it lie, and up he scrambled into the tree, climbing like a cat, though so monstrous heavy. I was amazed at the folly, as I thought it, of my man and could not for my life see anything to laugh at yet, till seeing the bear get up the tree, we all rode near to him.

When we came to the tree, there was Friday out at the small end of a large limb of the tree, and the bear about halfway to him. As soon as the bear got out to that part where the limb of the tree was weaker—"Ha!" said he to us. "Now you see me teachee the bear dance." He began jumping and shaking the bough, at which the bear began to totter, but stood still, and began to look behind him to see how he should get back; then, indeed, we did laugh heartily.

But Friday had not done with him by a great deal; when seeing him stand still, he called out to him again, as if he had supposed the bear could speak English, "What, you no come farther? Pray you come farther."

So he left jumping and shaking the bough, and the bear, just as if he had understood what he said, did come a little farther. Then he began jumping again, and the bear stopped again. We thought now was a good time to knock him on the head and called to Friday to stand still, and we would shoot the bear; but he cried out earnestly, "Oh pray! Oh pray! No shoot—me shoot by and then"; he would have said by and by.

However, to shorten the story, Friday danced so much, and the bear stood so ticklish, that we had laughing enough indeed, but still could not imagine what the fellow would do. At first we thought he depended upon shaking the bear off; but we found the bear was too cunning for that, too, for he would not go out far enough to be thrown down, but clung fast with his great broad claws and feet, so that we could not imagine what would be the end of it, and what the jest would be at last. But Friday put us out of doubt quickly.

Seeing that the bear clung fast to the bough and would not be persuaded to come any farther, Friday said, "Well, well, you no come farther, me go. You no come to me, me come to you."

Upon this he went out to the smaller end of the bough where it would bend with his weight and gently let himself down by it, sliding down the bough till he came near enough to jump down on his feet; and away he ran to his gun, took it up, and stood still.

"Well," said I to him, "Friday, what will you do now? Why don't you shoot him?"

"No shoot," said Friday. "No yet; me shoot now, me no kill; me stay, give you one more laugh."

And, indeed, so he did, as you will see presently; for when the bear saw his enemy gone, he came back from the bough where he stood, but did it very cautiously, looking behind him every step and coming backward till he got into the body of the tree; then, with the same hinder end foremost, he came down the tree, grasping it with his claws and moving one foot at a time very leisurely. At this juncture, and just before he could set his hind feet upon the ground, Friday stepped up close to him, clapped the muzzle of his piece into his ear, and shot him dead as a stone. Then the rogue turned about to see if we did not laugh; and when he saw we were pleased, by our looks, he began to laugh very loud.

"So we kill bear in my country," said Friday.

"So you kill them?" said I. "Why, you have no guns."

"No," said he, "no gun, but shoot great much long arrow."

This was a good diversion to us, but we were still in a wild place and our guide very much hurt, and what to do we hardly knew; the howling of wolves ran much in my head; and, indeed, except the noise I once heard on the shore of Africa, of which I have said something already, I never heard anything that filled me with so much horror.

Attacked by Wolves

These things, and the approach of night, called us off, or else, as Friday would have had us, we should certainly have taken the skin of this monstrous creature off, which was worth saving; but we had nearly three leagues to go, and our guide hastened us; so we left the bear and went forward on our journey.

The ground was still covered with snow, though not so deep and dangerous as on the mountains; and the ravenous creatures, as we heard afterward, were come down into the forest and plain country, pressed by hunger to seek for food, and had done a great deal of mischief in the villages, where they surprised the country people, killing a great many of their sheep and horses, and some people, too. We had one dangerous place to pass, and our guide told us, if there were more wolves in the country, we should find them there. This was a small plain surrounded with woods on every side, and a long narrow defile, or lane, that we were to pass to get through the wood, and then we should come to the village where we were to lodge. It was within half an hour of sunset when we entered the wood, and a little after sunset when we came into the plain: We met with nothing in the first wood, except that in a little plain within the wood that was not above two furlongs over, we saw five great wolves cross the road, full speed, one after another, as if they had been in chase of some prey and had it in view; they took no notice of us and were gone out of sight in a few moments. Upon this, our guide, who, by the way, was but a fainthearted fellow, bid us keep in a ready posture, for he believed there were more wolves coming. We kept our arms ready and our eyes about us; but we saw no more wolves till we came through that wood, which was nearly half a league, and entered the plain.

As soon as we came into the plain, we had occasion enough to look about us: The first object we met with was a dead horse; that is to say, a poor horse that the wolves had killed and at least a dozen of them at work, we could not say eating him, but picking his bones rather; for they had eaten up all the flesh before. We did not think fit to disturb them at their feast, neither did they take much notice of us. Friday would have let fly at them, but I would not suffer him by any means; for I found we were likely to have more business upon our hands than we were aware of. We had not gone half over the plain when we began to hear the wolves howl in the wood on our left in a frightful manner, and presently after we saw about a hundred coming on directly toward us, all in a body, and most of them in a line, as regularly as an army drawn up by experienced officers. I scarcely knew in what manner to receive them, but found to draw ourselves in a close line was the only way, so we formed in a moment. That we might not have too much interval, I ordered that only every other man should fire, and that the others, who had not fired, should stand ready to give them a second volley immediately, if they continued to advance upon us; and then those who had fired at first, should not pretend to load their fusils again, but stand ready, every one with a pistol, for we were armed with a fusil and a pair of pistols, each man; so we were, by this method, able to fire six volleys, half of us at a time. However, at present we had no necessity; for upon firing the first volley, the enemy made a full stop, being terrified as well with the noise as with the fire. Four of them being shot in the head, dropped; several others were wounded and went bleeding off, as we could see by the snow. I found they stopped, but did not immediately retreat; whereupon, remembering that I had been told that the fiercest creatures were terrified at the voice of a man, I caused all the company to hallo as loud as we could; and I found the notion not altogether mistaken; for upon our shout they began to retire and turn about. I then ordered a second volley to be fired in their rear, which put them to a gallop, and away they went to the woods. This gave us leisure to charge our pieces again; and that we might lose no time, we kept going; but we had but little more than loaded our fusils and put ourselves in readiness when we heard a terrible noise in the same wood on our left, only that it was farther onward, the same way we were to go.

The night was coming on, and the light began to be dusky, which made it worse on our side; but the noise increasing, we could easily perceive that it was the howling and yelling of those hellish creatures; and, suddenly, we perceived three troops of wolves, one on our left, one behind us, and one in our front, so that we seemed to be surrounded with them. However, as they did not fall upon us, we kept on our way, as fast as we could make our horses go, which, the way being very rough, was only a good hard trot. In this manner, we came in view of the entrance of a wood, through which we were to pass, at the farther side of the plain; but we were greatly surprised when, coming nearer the lane or pass, we saw a confused number of wolves standing just at the entrance. All of a sudden, at another opening of the wood, we heard the noise of a gun, and looking that way, out rushed a horse, with a saddle and a bridle on him, flying like the wind, and sixteen or seventeen wolves after him full speed. Indeed, the horse had the advantage of them; but as we supposed that he could not hold it at that rate, we doubted not but they would get up with him at last—and no question but they did.

But here we had a most horrible sight; for, riding up to the entrance where the horse came out, we found the carcasses of another horse and of two men, devoured by the ravenous creatures; and one of the men was no doubt the same whom we heard fire the gun, for there lay a gun just by him fired off; but as to the man, his head and the upper part of his body were eaten up. This filled us with horror, and we knew not what course to take; but the creatures resolved us soon, for they gathered about us presently, in hopes of prey; and I verily believe there were three hundred of them. It happened, very much to our advantage, that at the entrance into the wood, but a little way from it, there lay some large timber trees, which had been cut down the summer before and I suppose lay there for carriage. I drew my little troop in among those trees, and placing ourselves in a line behind one long tree, I advised them all to alight and, keeping that tree before us for a breastwork, to stand in a triangle, or three fronts, enclosing our horses in the center. We did so, and it was well we did; for never was a more furious charge than the creatures made upon us in this place. They came on us with a growling kind of noise and mounted the piece of timber, which, as I said, was our breastwork, as if they were only rushing upon their prey; and this fury of theirs, it seems, was principally occasioned by their seeing our horses behind us, which was the prey they aimed at. I ordered our men to fire as before, every other man, and they took their aim so sure that indeed they killed several of the wolves at the first volley; but there was a necessity to keep a continual firing, for they came on like devils, those behind pushing on those before.

When we had fired a second volley of our fusils, we thought they stopped a little, and I hoped they would have gone off, but it was but a moment, for others came forward again; so we fired two volleys of our pistols; and I believe in these four firings we had killed seventeen or eighteen of them and lamed twice as many, yet they came on again. I was loath to spend our last shot too hastily; so I called my servant—not my man Friday, for he was better employed, for, with the greatest dexterity imaginable, he had charged my fusil and his own while we were engaged—but, as I said, I called my other man, and giving him a horn of powder, I bade him lay a train all along the piece of timber, and let it be a large train. He did so, and had but just time to get away, when the wolves came up to it, and some got upon it, when

I, snapping an uncharged pistol close to the powder, set it on fire; those that were upon the timber were scorched with it, and six or seven of them fell, or rather jumped in among us with the force and fright of the fire. We dispatched these in an instant, and the rest were so frightened with the light, which the night—for it was now very near dark—made more terrible, that they drew back a little; upon which I ordered our last pistols to be fired off in one volley, and after that we gave a shout. Upon this the wolves turned tail, and we sallied immediately upon nearly twenty lame ones that we found struggling on the ground and fell to cutting them with our swords, which answered our expectation, for the crying and howling they made was better understood by their fellows; so that they all fled and left us.

We had, first and last, killed about threescore of them, and had it been daylight we had killed many more. The field of battle being thus cleared, we made forward again, for we had still nearly a league to go. We heard the ravenous creatures howl and yell in the woods as we went several times, and sometimes we fancied we saw some of them; but the snow dazzling our eyes, we were not certain. So in about an hour more we came to the town where we were to lodge, which we found in a terrible fright and all in arms; for it seems that the night before, the wolves and some bears had broken into the village and put them in such terror that they were obliged to keep guard night and day, but especially in the night, to preserve their cattle, and indeed their people.

The next morning our guide was so ill, and his limbs swelled so much with the festering of his two wounds, that he could go no farther; so we were obliged to take a new guide here and go to Toulouse, where we found a warm climate, a fruitful, pleasant country, and no snow, no wolves, nor anything like them. When we told our story at Toulouse, they told us it was nothing but what was ordinary in the great forest at the foot of the mountains, especially when the snow lay on the ground; but they inquired much what kind of a guide we had got, who would venture to bring us that way in such a severe season, and told us it was surprising we were not all devoured. When we told them how we placed ourselves and the horses in the middle, they blamed us exceedingly and told us it was fifty to one but we had been all destroyed, for it was the sight of the horses that made the wolves so furious, seeing their prey; and that at other times they are really afraid of a gun; but being excessively hungry, and raging on that account, the eagerness to come at the horses had made them senseless of danger; and that if we had not by the continued fire and at last, by the stratagem of the train of powder, mastered them, it had been great odds but that we had been torn to pieces. Whereas, had we been content to have sat still on horseback and fired as horsemen, they would not have taken the horses so much for their own, when men were on their backs, as otherwise; and, withal, they told us that at last, if we had stood all together and left our horses, they would have been so eager to have devoured them that we might have come off safely, especially having our firearms in our hands and being so many in number. For my part, I was never so sensible of danger in my life; for, seeing above three hundred devils come roaring and open-mouthed to devour us, and having nothing to shelter us or retreat to, I gave myself over for lost; and, as it was, I believe I shall never care to cross those mountains again; I think I would much rather go a thousand leagues by sea, though I was sure to meet with a storm once a week.

I have nothing uncommon to take notice of in my passage through France—nothing but what other travelers have given an account of with much more advantage than I can. I traveled from Toulouse to Paris, and without any considerable stay came to Calais, and landed safely at Dover the 14th of January, after having a severe cold season to travel in.

I was now come to the center of my travels and had in a little time all my newly discovered estate safely about me, the bills of exchange that I brought with me having been very currently paid.

My principal guide and privy counselor was my good old widow, who, in gratitude for the money I had sent her, thought no pains too much nor care too great to employ for me; and I trusted her so entirely with everything that I was perfectly at ease as to the security of my effects; and, indeed, I was very happy from the beginning, and now to the end, in the unspotted integrity of this good gentlewoman.

And now, having resolved to dispose of my plantation in the Brazils, I wrote to my old friend at Lisbon, who having offered it to the two merchants, the survivors of my trustees, who lived in the Brazils, they accepted the offer and remitted thirty-three thousand pieces of eight to a correspondent of theirs at Lisbon to pay for it.

In return, I signed the instrument of sale in the form that they sent from Lisbon and sent it to my old man, who sent me the bills of exchange for thirty-two thousand eight hundred pieces of eight for the estate, reserving the payment of one hundred moidores a year to him (the old man) during his life, and fifty moidores afterward to his son for his life, which I had promised them and which the plantation was to make good as a rent charge. And thus I have given the first part of a life of fortune and adventure—a life of Providence's checkerwork and of a variety that the world will seldom be able to show the like of—beginning foolishly, but closing much more happily than any part of it ever gave me leave so much as to hope for.

Seeking Fresh Adventures

Anyone would think that in this state of complicated good fortune, I was past running any more hazards; and so, indeed, I had been, if other circumstances had concurred; but I was inured to a wandering life, had no family, nor many relations; nor however rich, had I contracted much acquaintance; and though I had sold my estate in the Brazils, yet I could not keep that country out of my head and had a great mind to be upon the wing again; especially I could not resist the strong inclination I had to see my island and to know if the poor Spaniards were also living there. My true friend, the widow, earnestly dissuaded me from it and so far prevailed with me that for almost seven years she prevented my running abroad, during which time I took my two nephews, the children of one of my brothers, into my care; the eldest, having something of his own, I bred up as a gentleman and gave him a settlement of some addition to his estate after my decease. The other I placed with the captain of a ship, and after five years, finding him a sensible, bold, enterprising young fellow, I put him into a good ship and sent him to sea; and this young fellow afterward drew me in, as old as I was, to further adventures myself.

In the meantime, I in part settled myself here; for, first of all, I married, and that not either to my disadvantage or dissatisfaction, and had three children, two sons and one daughter; but my wife, dying, and my nephew coming home with good success from a voyage to Spain, my inclination to go abroad and his importunity prevailed, and he engaged me to go in his ship as a private trader to the East Indies; this was in the year 1694.

In this voyage I visited my new colony in the island; saw my successors the Spaniards; had the whole story of their lives and of the villains I left there; how at first they insulted the poor Spaniards; how they afterward agreed, disagreed, united, separated, and how at last the Spaniards were obliged to use violence with them; how they were subjected to the Spaniards; how honestly the Spaniards used them; a history, if it were entered into, as full of variety and wonderful accidents as my own part, particularly as to their battles with the Caribbees, who landed several times upon the island, and as to the improvements they made upon the island itself—and how five of them made an attempt upon the mainland and brought away eleven men and five women prisoners, by which, at my coming, I found about twenty young children on the island.

Here I stayed about twenty days, left them supplies of all necessary things, and particularly of arms, powder, shot, clothes, tools, and two workmen, whom I brought from England with me, namely, a carpenter and a smith.

Besides this, I divided the lands into parts with them, reserved to myself the property of the whole, but gave them such parts respectively as they agreed on; and having settled all things with them and engaged them not to leave the place, I left them there.

From there I touched at the Brazils, from which I sent a bark, which I brought there, with more people to the island; and in it, besides other supplies, I sent seven women, being such as I found proper for service or for wives to such as would take them. As to the Englishmen, I promised to send them some women from England, with a good cargo of necessaries, if they would apply themselves to planting—which I afterward could not perform. The fellows proved very honest and diligent after they were mastered and had their properties set apart for them. I sent them, also, from the Brazils, five cows, three of them being big with calf, some sheep, and some hogs, which when I came again were considerably increased.

But all these things, with an account of how three hundred Caribbees came and invaded them and ruined their plantations, and how they fought with that whole number twice and were at first defeated and one of them killed; but, at last, a storm destroying their enemies' canoes, they starved or destroyed almost all the rest, and renewed and recovered the possession of their plantations, and still lived upon the island—all these things, with some very surprising incidents in some new adventures of my own, for ten years more, I shall give a further account of in the second part of my history.[1]

END OF PART I

1. Part two, *The Farther Adventures of Robinson Crusoe,* will be released in 1998.

Afterword

Discussion with Professor Wheeler

(For Formal School, Home School, and Book Club Discussions)

First of all, permit me to define my perception of the role of the teacher. I believe that the ideal teaching relationship involves the teacher and the student, both looking in the same direction, and both with a sense of wonder. A teacher is *not* an important person dishing out rote learning to an unimportant person. I furthermore do not believe that a Ph.D. automatically brings with it omniscience, despite the way some of us act. In discussions, I tell my students beforehand that my opinions and conclusions are no more valid than theirs, for each of us sees reality from a different perspective.

Now that my role is clear, let's continue. The purpose of the discussion section of the series is to encourage debate, to dig deeper into the books than would be true without this section, and to spawn other questions that may build on the ones I begin with here. If you take advantage of this section, you will be gaining just as good an understanding of the book as you would were you actually sitting in one of my classroom circles.

As you read the story, record your thoughts and reactions each day in a journal. Also, an unabridged dictionary is almost essential in completely understanding this book. If your vocabulary is to grow, something else is needed *besides* the dictionary: vocabulary cards. Take a stack of 3x5 cards, and write the words you don't know on one side and their definitions on the other, with each word used in a sentence. Every time you stumble on words you are unsure of—and I found quite a number myself!—make a card for it. Continually go over these cards; and keep all, except those you never miss, in a card file. You will be amazed at how fast your vocabulary will grow!

Questions to Deepen Your Understanding

Chapter 1. My Father's Advice and My Obstinacy

1. The parental counsel was to remain near home in safe, fairly predictable grooves, rather than venture out into the great unknown and deliberately seek danger. Do young people today graciously accept such counsel and follow it? Should they? Why or why not?

   What about this divinely instilled restlessness within each of us that causes us to empathize with the mariner in Tennyson's epic "Ulysses"?

   I cannot rest from travel; I will drink
   Life to the lees. All times I have enjoyed
   Greatly, have suffered greatly, both with those
   That have loved me, and alone; on shore, and when
   Through scudding drifts the rainy Hyades
   Vext the dim sea. I am become a name;
   For always roaming with a hungry heart
   Much have I seen and known—cities of men,
   And manners, climates, councils, governments,
   Myself not least, but honored of them all
   And drunk delight of battle with my peers,
   Far on the ringing plains of windy Troy.
   I am a part of all that I have met;
   Yet all experience is an arch wherethrough
   Gleams that untraveled world, whose margin fades
   For ever and for ever when I move.
   How dull it is to pause, to make an end,
   To rust unburnished, not to shine in use!
   As though to breathe were life! Life piled on life
   Were all too little, and of one to me
   Little remains; but every hour is saved
   From that eternal silence, something more,
   A bringer of new things; and vile it were
   For some three suns to store and hoard myself,
   And this grey spirit yearning in desire

To follow knowledge like a sinking star,
Beyond the utmost bound of human thought.
. . . There lies the port; the vessel puffs her sail:
There gloom the dark, broad seas. My mariners,
Souls that have toiled, and wrought, and thought with me—
That ever with a frolic welcome took
The thunder and the sunshine, and opposed
Free hearts, free foreheads—you and I are old;
Old age hath yet his honor and his toil.
Death closes all; but something ere the end,
Some work of noble note, may yet be done,
Not unbecoming men that strove with gods.
The lights begin to twinkle from the rocks;
The long day wanes; the slow moon climbs; the deep
Moans round with many voices. Come, my friends,
'Tis not too late to seek a newer world.
Push off, and sitting well in order smite
The sounding furrows; for my purpose holds
To sail beyond the sunset, and the baths
Of all the western stars, until I die.
It may be that the gulfs will wash us down;
It may be we shall touch the Happy Isles,
And see the great Achilles, whom we knew.
Though much is taken, much abides; and though
We are not now that strength which in old days
Moved earth and heaven, that which we are, we are:
One equal temper of heroic hearts,
Made weak by time and fate, but strong in will
To strive, to seek, to find, and not to yield.

Alfred, Lord Tennyson (1809–1892)

What is there that calls us to leave safety and to dare the unknown? To go "where angels fear to tread"? Why is it that we are happiest in our most unsettled times—in the dream process rather than in the fulfilled dream? How much of what we consider "progress" has resulted from dreams like those of Robinson Crusoe and Ulysses, who took life-risking chances? What does all this mean to us today?

2. Are the decisions we make under extreme stress likely to be the ones we stick with? In other words, if forced to make a decision by someone else, what is likely to be our response once that external force is removed? What should that tell us both on the receiving and "dishing-out" ends?

3. Defoe believed that God expresses Himself through the elements, especially storms. Do you believe God still does so today? If yes, how should we respond? What are the dangers in taking such atmospheric disasters too literally? In other words, how can we incorporate God into unfolding atmospheric-induced events without unduly boxing Him in or accounting for our own lack of good judgment or failure to take wise precautions?

4. How often do we do foolish things or refuse to make the right decisions simply because we are afraid of what people might say if we appear less than perfect? What does that kind of behavior reveal about us? How should we handle it?

Chapter 2. Escape from the Moors

5. If you compare Defoe's life given in the introduction with Crusoe's life, you'll see that both men, when confronted by a crucial, life-changing decision, invariably ended up choosing the worst possible option (in terms of the effects on them). Is such self-destructive decision-making common to us today, or was it only a problem with Defoe? If it is still true today, what does that say about us as a species?

Chapter 3. Shipwreck

6. Crusoe, just like the apostle Paul, continues in his self-destructive ways. Why is it that even when we *know* something will hurt us and those we love, we often end up doing them anyway? Does the mind, after all, not control the body? What can be done to counter such self-destructive tendencies?

7. This question is an extension of question 1 above, as it is further developed in this chapter. What is there about life that leaves us unsatisfied—even with success? Why are so many of us not content to sit quietly by and mind the store, rather than leaving it behind and rushing into an

uncertain future? How much of this itch to keep moving is God's doing? How much of it is our own? What effect does being married have on it? Having children?

Chapter 4. The Calm Between Storms

8. On the island, Crusoe finds gold in the partly sunken ship. How does he react to it? What is the significance of the experience to us (or what *ought* to be the significance)?

   What does all this mean in terms of the real, enduring values in life? Do the priorities we live by tend to be egocentric or selfless? Discuss.

9. What is the significance of the storm holding off until Crusoe had practically denuded the ship? Is this evidence of a force Defoe calls "Providence"? What lessons may we learn from it?

Chapter 5. First Year on the Island

10. To maintain his sanity, Crusoe keeps busy. Each day, he works hard to construct living and storage quarters. Of what value is that daily work to him? To us today? Even if we are extremely wealthy, should we work anyway? Why? What role does work have in terms of God's will for us? His expectations of us?

11. Even though Crusoe, at this stage of the book, attaches little spiritual application to the keeping of Sabbath-day, he attempts to observe it anyway. Why do you think he does so? What role does Sabbath-day play in our lives today? What role should it play?

Chapter 6. Beginning the Diary

12. Crusoe starts a journal soon after landing on the island. What lessons or truths does he learn as a result of keeping it? What would have been lost had he not kept one? Why should we keep one? What will be lost if we fail to keep one?

Chapter 7. Earthquake, Storm, and God

13. Crusoe does not surrender to God until he is virtually at death's door. Why is it so difficult for us to recognize our need for God during good times? What is it about suffering that makes us more receptive to Him?

What is it that finally causes Crusoe to throw himself on God's mercy? What about us today? Is the story similar for us?

Chapter 8. The Other Side of the Island

14. I could not help but think as I read this chapter that if we ever experienced a complete breakdown—through some disaster—of our industrialized way of life, most of us wouldn't have the slightest idea of how to survive on our own. In such a life-or-death struggle, this book—especially the sections describing how Crusoe has to build a life out of very little—would be extremely helpful in terms of a guide. Is this perhaps a real danger for us today: that we have virtually forgotten how to use our hands—to exercise simple survival skills? Why or why not?

Chapter 9. Farming and Inventing Operations

15. Mere survival is not enough: The amenities of civilization include much more than staying alive. Defoe explores these in this chapter. Interestingly, since there is no market for his produce, Crusoe finds it to be a waste of time and energy to plant more than he can use personally. In our days of overproduction and overconsumption, what ought to be the significance of this to us?

Chapter 10. A Canoe to Escape In

16. We have already discussed "value" in an earlier chapter. In this chapter, Crusoe moves deeper into the significance of "value" as he discovers that gold and diamonds are worthless to him; the only things worth having are what he needs to survive. And for those things, he is supremely grateful to his God. In everything, good as well as bad, he finds reason for giving thanks. What lessons can we learn in this book about gratitude—about continually giving thanks to God? Note this quotation from the chapter: "All our discontents about what we want appear to me to spring from a lack of thankfulness for what we have."

Chapter 11. Pots, Wickerware, and Goats

17. Ever since his conversion experience, Crusoe has been studying the Bible daily. What effect has the daily reading had on him and on his attitudes? What effects would such a program have on us?

Chapter 12. Footprint in the Sand

18. *Cannibalism*—we recoil in horror at the very word. What are the lessons about life and death we can learn here?

Chapter 13. A State of Siege

19. At the very time we are the most despondent, and it appears as if our dreams are dead, God may be planning something wonderful for us, opening a door to a new life. This is what happens to Crusoe. What can this mean to us with our disappointments and slammed doors?

Chapter 14. Visitors

20. Note how uncertain life was in the eighteenth century—much more so than it is for us today. Daily living was uncertain enough when one stayed at home; but when traveling, one faced the possibility of death at any moment. Does knowing this fact about life in the 1700s change your view of the type of man Crusoe was? If yes, in what way? Be specific.

Chapter 15. Friday

21. Crusoe was not content with merely having a slave or servant: He (and Defoe) felt that everyone has a soul worth saving. How does Crusoe go about trying to save Friday's?

Chapter 16. Friday Learns About God

22. What enables Crusoe to break through to Friday with the message of salvation? What lessons can we learn from this in terms of our own ministering to the needs of others (both within our culture and outside of it)?

Chapter 17. New Subjects

23. We say women have intuition and men do not. Is that true? There is much in this book about intuition, insights that have no basis in fact. Defoe obviously felt that we avoid such impressions at our own peril—that God uses such messages deliberately. The Bible is full of stories about people receiving important messages from God, through visions and dreams, or in other ways.

Do you think God speaks to us in the same way He did centuries ago? Discuss.

Chapter 18. Mutineers

24. Years ago, life on a ship was nightmarish because the captain had total control. If the crew members mutinied—no matter how evil the captain—and were caught, the penalty was death.

    How is a sailor's life different today? How is it the same? Are there ways it can or should be improved?

Chapter 19. Leaving the Island

25. Some people think that gratitude is a lost art today. Compare Defoe's view of gratitude (as discussed in the introduction) with Crusoe's. How are they different? How are they the same? Note how, to Defoe, gratitude is one of life's highest virtues.

    What lessons can we learn here about ourselves? How important is it that we show gratitude daily?

    Discuss the significance of the following quote in terms of our own daily walks: "Where I wanted nothing but what I had, and had nothing but what I wanted."

Chapter 20. Wolves

26. Wolves are an integral part of our folklore and even our daily language. Like any other animal—human beings included—a wolf is one creature during ordinary times and quite another when it is starving. This differentiation needs to be taken into consideration when discussing this chapter.

Coda

Reactions, responses, and suggestions are very important to us. Also, if a particular book—especially an older one—has been loved by you or your family, and you would like to see us incorporate it into this series, drop us a line, with details you know about its earliest publisher, printing date, and so on, and send it to

Joe Wheeler, Ph.D.
c/o Focus on the Family
Colorado Springs, CO 80920

About the Editor

Joseph Leininger Wheeler's earliest memories have to do with books and stories—more specifically, of listening to his mother read aloud both in public and to him at home. Wheeler recalls that, as soon as he was able to read, he followed his mother around the house, relentlessly reading his storybooks to her.

Shortly after Wheeler turned eight, his parents moved from California to Latin America as missionaries. From the third through the tenth grade, he was home-schooled by his mother. Of those years, he says today, "I was incredibly lucky and blessed. My mother, a trained teacher and elocutionist, was a voracious reader of books worth reading and had memorized thousands of pages of readings, poetry, and stories. All of that she poured into me. Wherever we went, she encouraged me to devour entire libraries."

At 16, Wheeler returned to California to complete his high school years at Monterey Bay Academy near Santa Cruz. Because of his inherited love of the printed word, Wheeler majored in history at Pacific Union College in the Napa Valley, completing both bachelor's and master's degrees there. After completing a master's in English at California State University in Sacramento, Wheeler attended Vanderbilt University, where he obtained a Ph.D. in English.

Today, after 34 years of teaching at the adult education, college, high school, and junior high levels, Wheeler is Professor Emeritus at Columbia Union College in Takoma Park, Maryland. The world's foremost authority on frontier writer Zane Grey, Wheeler is also the founder and executive director of Zane Grey's West Society and Senior Fellow for Cultural Studies at the Center for the New West in Denver, Colorado. He is editor/compiler of the popular *Christmas in My Heart* series (Review & Herald; Doubleday, Dell, Bantam); editor/compiler of the story anthologies *Dad in My Heart* and *Mom in My Heart* (Tyndale House); and editor/compiler of the *Great Stories Remembered* and Classic Collection series for Focus on the Family. Along the way, Wheeler has established nine libraries in schools and colleges, as well as building up his own collection (as large as some college libraries).

Joe Wheeler and his wife, Connie, are the parents of two grown children, Greg and Michelle, and now make their home in Conifer, Colorado.